#3

BATTLE STATION PRIME

THE QUEST FOR THE ENCHANTED SWORD

AN UNOFFICIAL GRAPHIC NOVEL FOR MINECRAFTERS

D0150298

CARA J. STEVENS

ILLUSTRATED BY SAM NEEDHAM

SKY PONY PRESS
NEW YORK

WITHDRAWN

Copyright © 2020 by Hollan Publishing, Inc.

Minecraft® is a registered trademark of Notch Development AB.

The Minecraft game is copyright © Mojang AB.

Sky Pony Press books may be purchased in bulk at special discounts for sales promotion, corporate gifts, fund-raising, or educational purposes. Special editions can also be created to specifications. For details, contact the Special Sales Department,Sky Pony Press, 307 West 36th Street, 11th Floor, New York, NY 10018 or info@ skyhorsepublishing.com.

Sky Pony® is a registered trademark of Skyhorse Publishing, Inc.®, a Delaware corporation.

Minecraft® is a registered trademark of Notch Development AB.
The Minecraft game is copyright © Mojang AB.

Visit our website at www.skyponypress.com.

10 9 8 7 6 5 4 3 2 1

Library of Congress Cataloging-in- Publication Data is available on file.

Cover design by Brian Peterson
Cover and interior art by Sam Needham

Print ISBN: 978-1-5107-4725-8
Ebook ISBN: 978-1-5107-4736-4

Printed in the United States of America

#3

BATTLE STATION PRIME

THE QUEST FOR THE ENCHANTED SWORD

MEET THE

PELL: A boy with a talent for getting lost and for making the best of every situation.

LOGAN: Pell's best friend, who is an expert hacker and redstone programmer.

MADDY: Logan's very smart little sister, who has a talent for enchanting objects.

UNCLE COLIN: Pell's uncle, who is an excellent politician and leader.

CHARACTERS

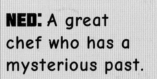

MR. JAMES: The leader of Battle Station Prime.

NED: A great chef who has a mysterious past.

BEN FROST: A programmer who has a talent for inventing clever solutions.

CLOUD, ZOE, AND BROOKLYN: Residents of Battle Station Prime.

INTRODUCTION

A world at peace stays at peace unless acted upon by an outside force. And a world at war stays at war until something happens that's big enough to change the balance of power.

Most people at Battle Station Prime believe that the story of the Prime Knight and the Enchanted Sword is just a fairy tale. But for the kids hearing it for the first time, the story seems just logical enough that it could be true.

Our story resumes at Battle Station Prime, the headquarters of all battle stations, where Pell, Logan, and Maddy have finally been accepted into the community by Brooklyn, Zoe, and Cloud. They have all become part of the local army, fighting waves of armed skeletons sent by an unknown leader. With Cloud's home city destroyed, Brooklyn's mom being held captive in a secret jail, and the battle station under constant attack, the kids resolve to do more than stay and fight the skeleton invasions. They decide in secret to set out on their own on a quest to find the enchanted sword, save their world from the endless attacks, and finally begin rebuilding the outposts of Battle Station Prime.

CHAPTER 1

INVASION

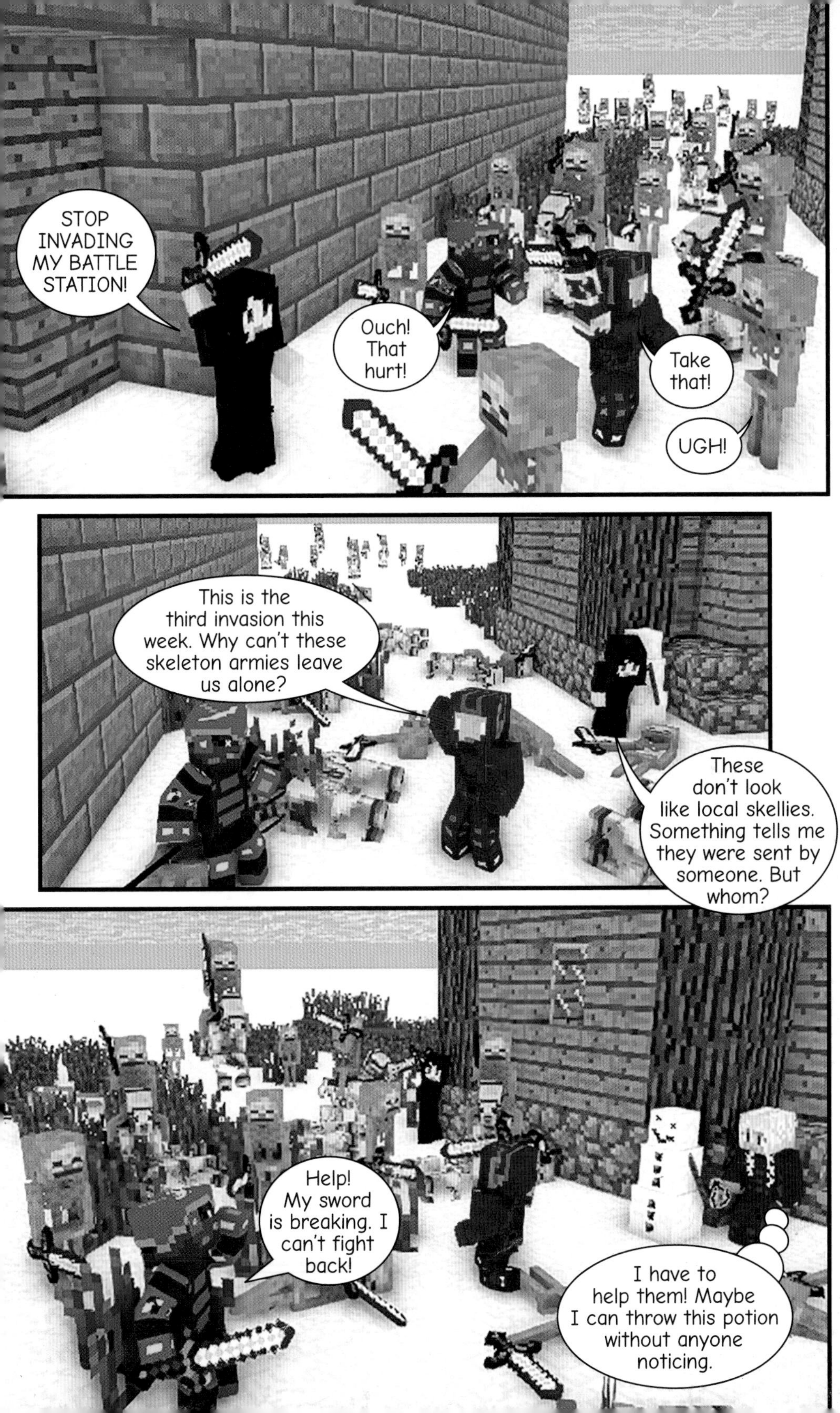
STOP INVADING MY BATTLE STATION!
Ouch! That hurt!
Take that!
UGH!
This is the third invasion this week. Why can't these skeleton armies leave us alone?
These don't look like local skellies. Something tells me they were sent by someone. But whom?
Help! My sword is breaking. I can't fight back!
I have to help them! Maybe I can throw this potion without anyone noticing.

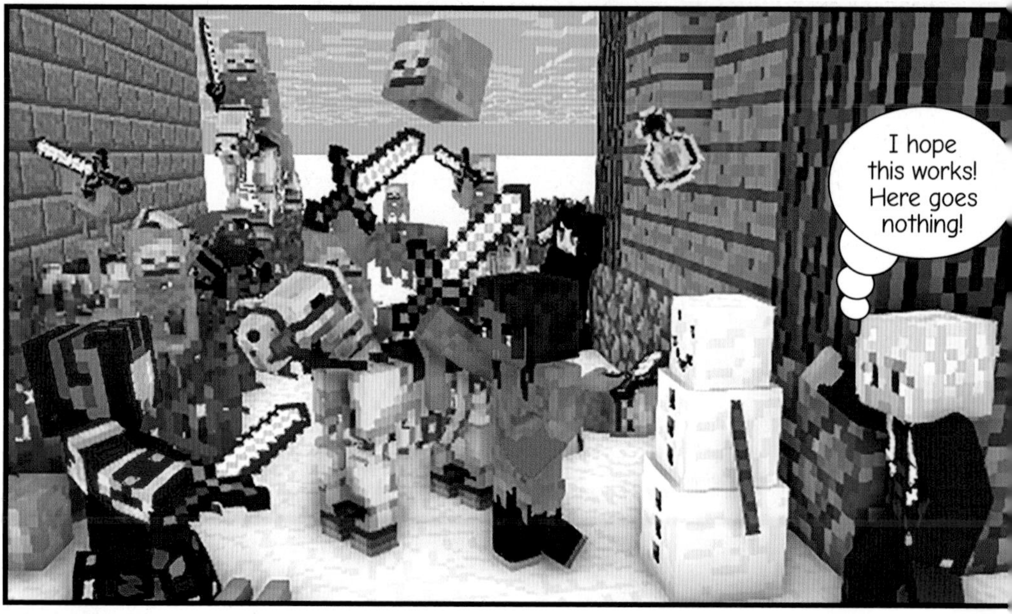
I hope this works! Here goes nothing!

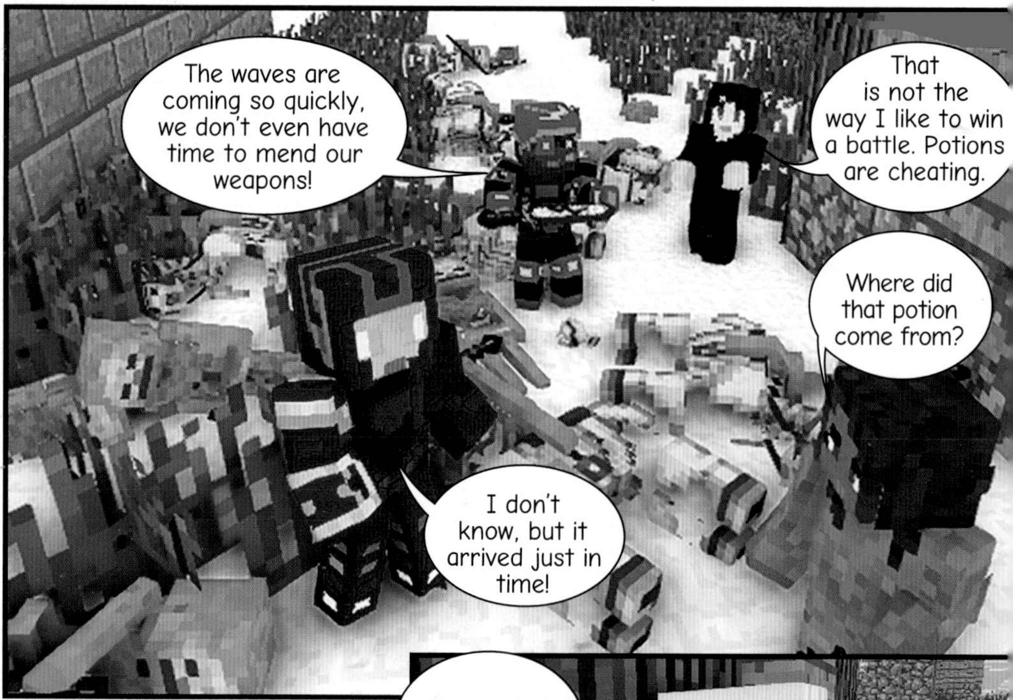
The waves are coming so quickly, we don't even have time to mend our weapons!
That is not the way I like to win a battle. Potions are cheating.
Where did that potion come from?
I don't know, but it arrived just in time!

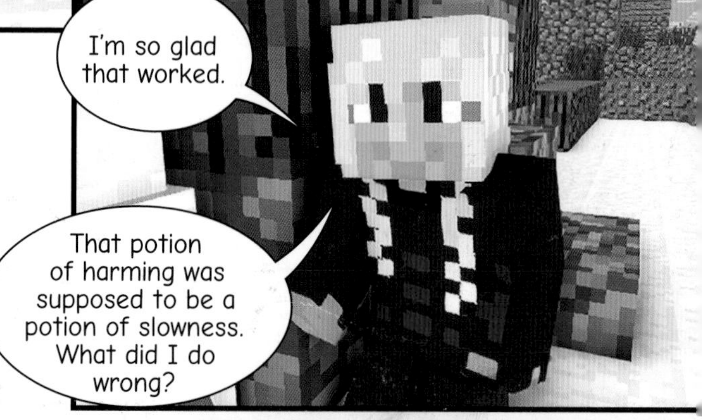
I'm so glad that worked.
That potion of harming was supposed to be a potion of slowness. What did I do wrong?

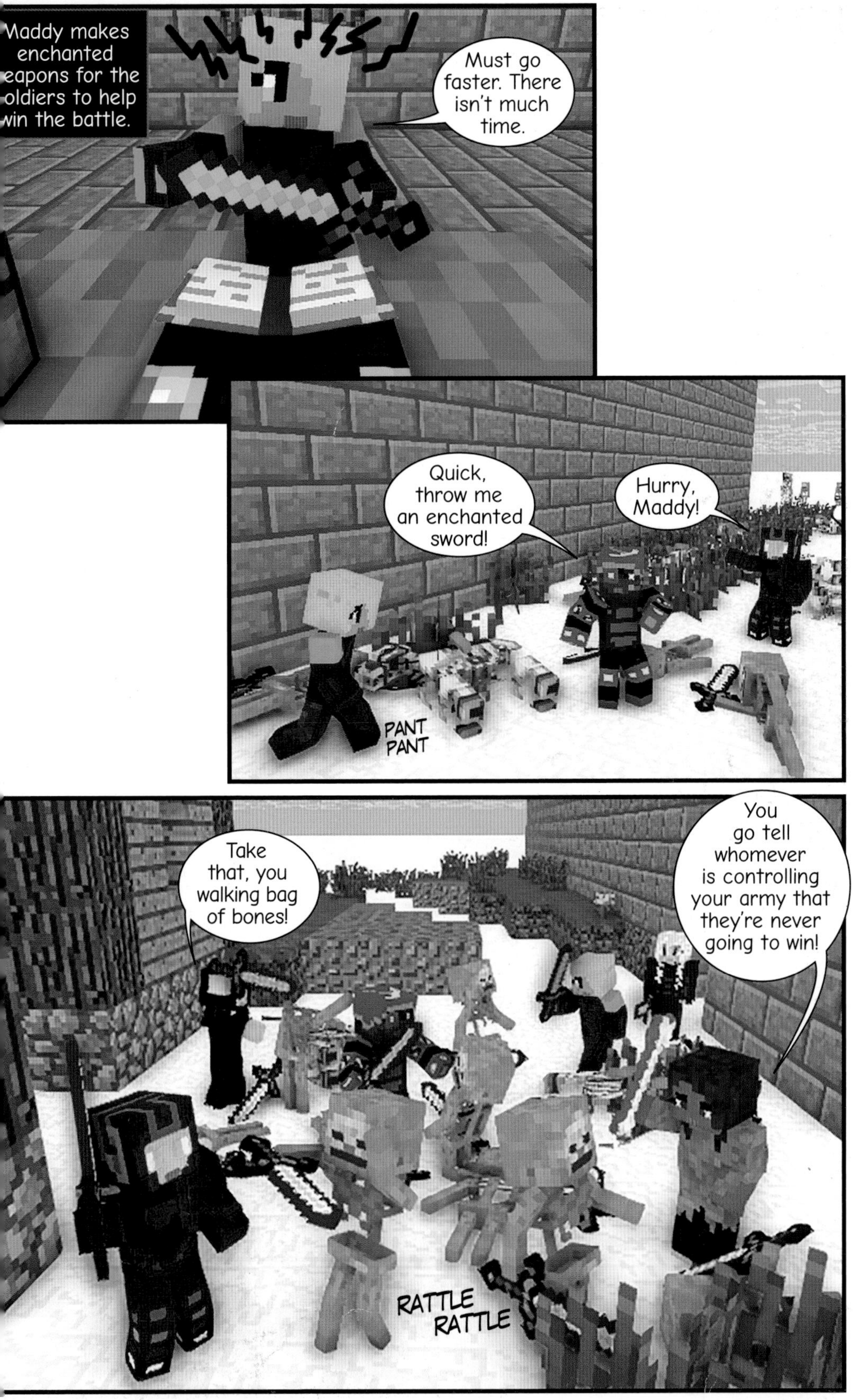

Maddy makes enchanted eapons for the oldiers to help win the battle.
Must go faster. There isn't much time.
Quick, throw me an enchanted sword!
Hurry, Maddy!
PANT PANT
Take that, you walking bag of bones!
You go tell whomever is controlling your army that they're never going to win!
RATTLE RATTLE

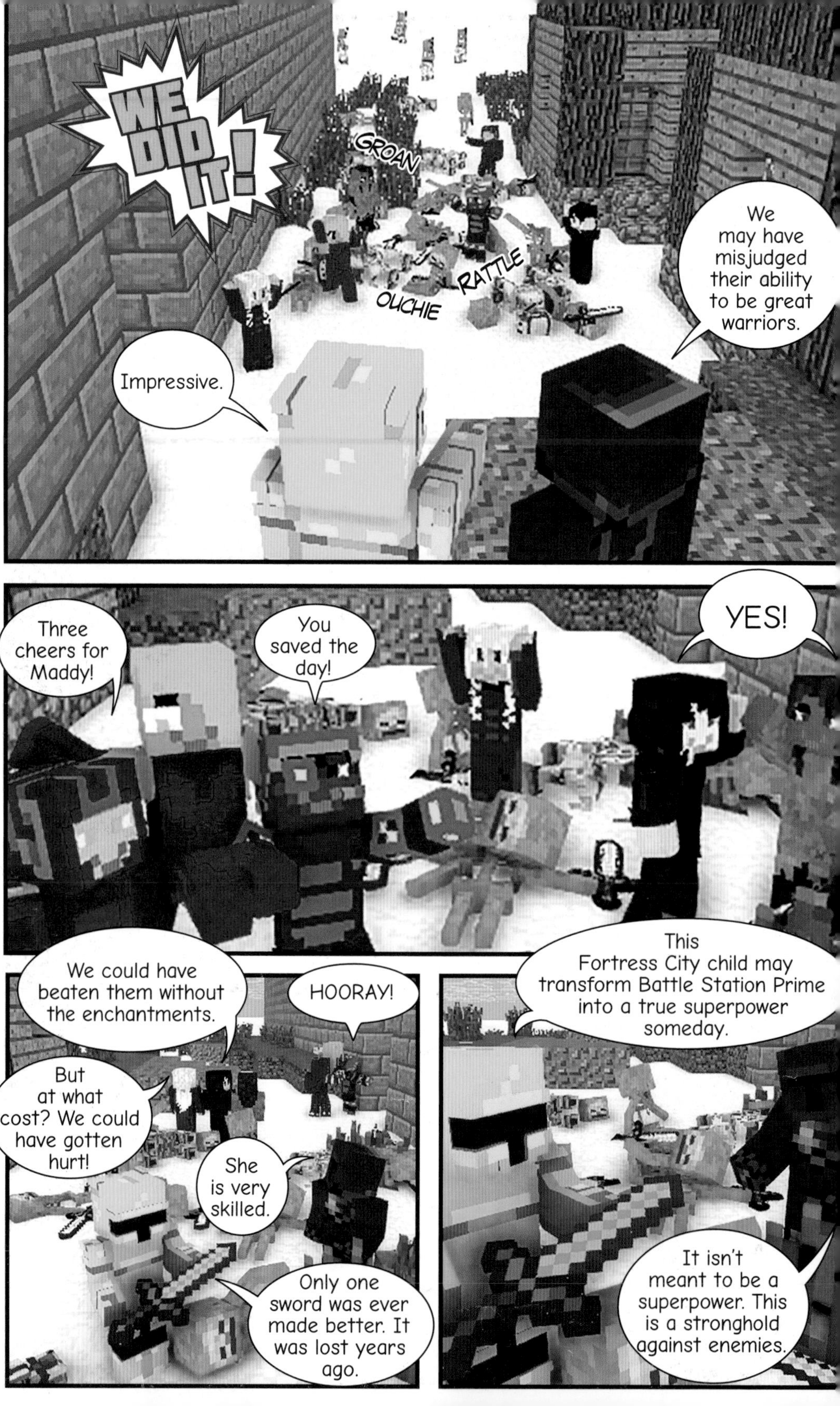
WE DID IT!
GROAN
RATTLE
OUCHIE
Impressive.
We may have misjudged their ability to be great warriors.
Three cheers for Maddy!
You saved the day!
YES!
We could have beaten them without the enchantments.
HOORAY!
But at what cost? We could have gotten hurt!
She is very skilled.
Only one sword was ever made better. It was lost years ago.
This Fortress City child may transform Battle Station Prime into a true superpower someday.
It isn't meant to be a superpower. This is a stronghold against enemies.

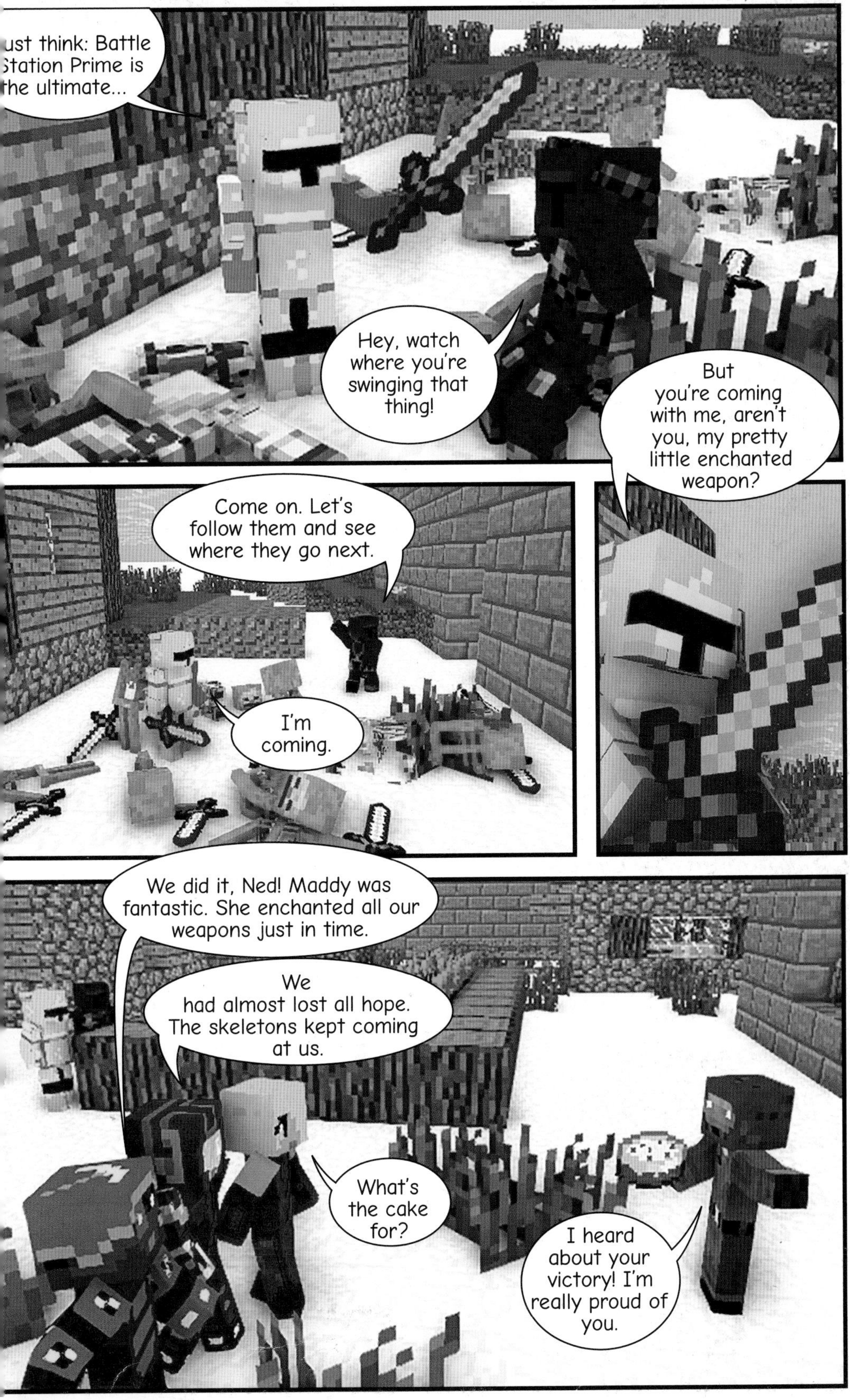
ust think: Battle Station Prime is the ultimate...
Hey, watch where you're swinging that thing!
But you're coming with me, aren't you, my pretty little enchanted weapon?
Come on. Let's follow them and see where they go next.
I'm coming.
We did it, Ned! Maddy was fantastic. She enchanted all our weapons just in time.
We had almost lost all hope. The skeletons kept coming at us.
What's the cake for?
I heard about your victory! I'm really proud of you.

I still don't understand what we're fighting for. We keep fighting against enemies just to survive, but who is sending them? And why?
We don't need to question why, soldier. We just need to FIGHT! We will definitely win if we keep getting beautiful weapons like this one.
Enchanting is an impressive skill, but anyone can learn it if they have the time. Like, say, if they weren't spending all their time fighting off invasions.
So if it's not the little enchanting one, which one of them do you think is the secret weapon? The one who has the power to change everything?
The one with the blue helmet seems skilled. But the one with the gray helmet seems so quiet, it could be him.... We will have to keep a close eye on them and see what they do.

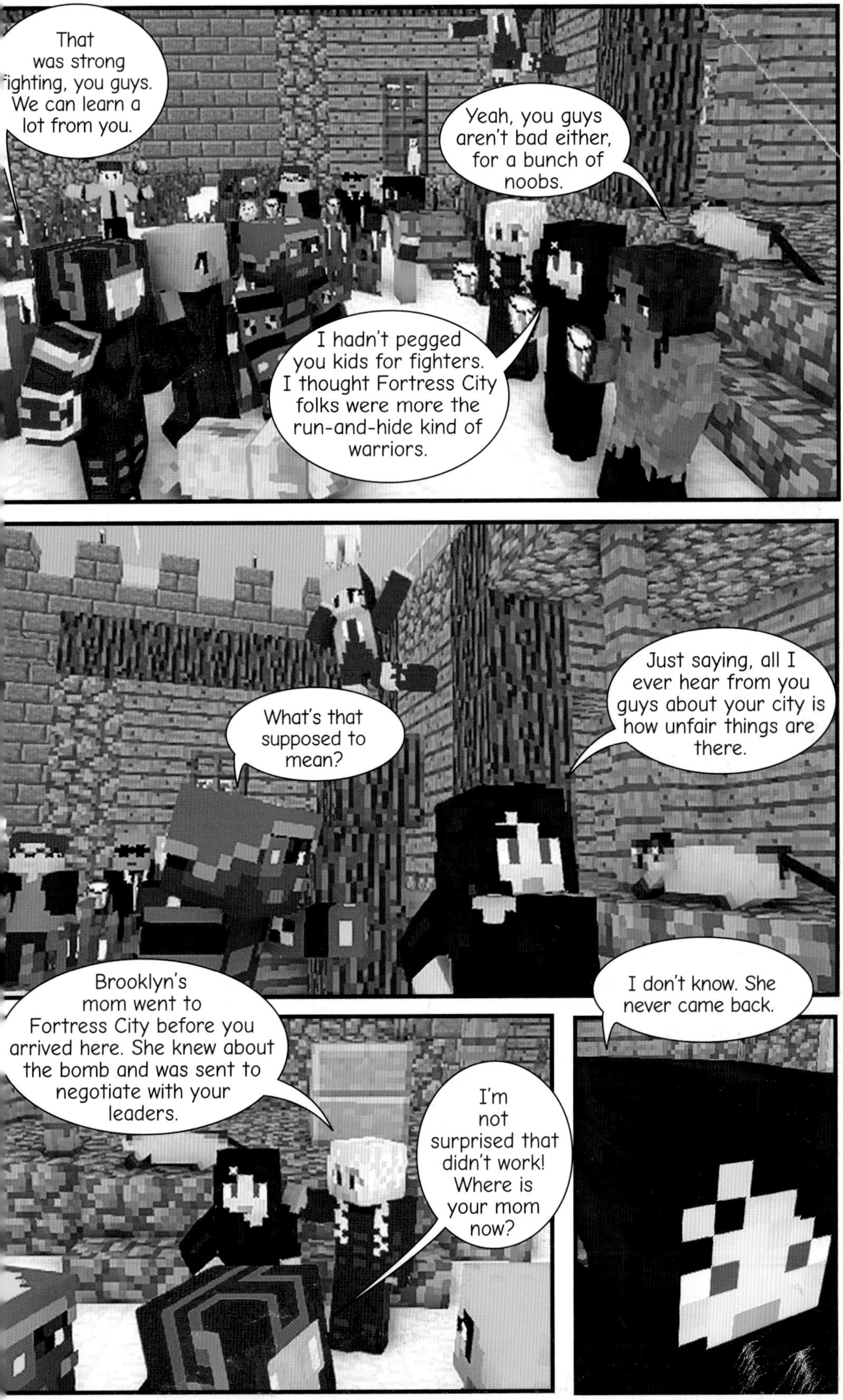
That was strong fighting, you guys. We can learn a lot from you.
Yeah, you guys aren't bad either, for a bunch of noobs.
I hadn't pegged you kids for fighters. I thought Fortress City folks were more the run-and-hide kind of warriors.
What's that supposed to mean?
Just saying, all I ever hear from you guys about your city is how unfair things are there.
Brooklyn's mom went to Fortress City before you arrived here. She knew about the bomb and was sent to negotiate with your leaders.
I'm not surprised that didn't work! Where is your mom now?
I don't know. She never came back.

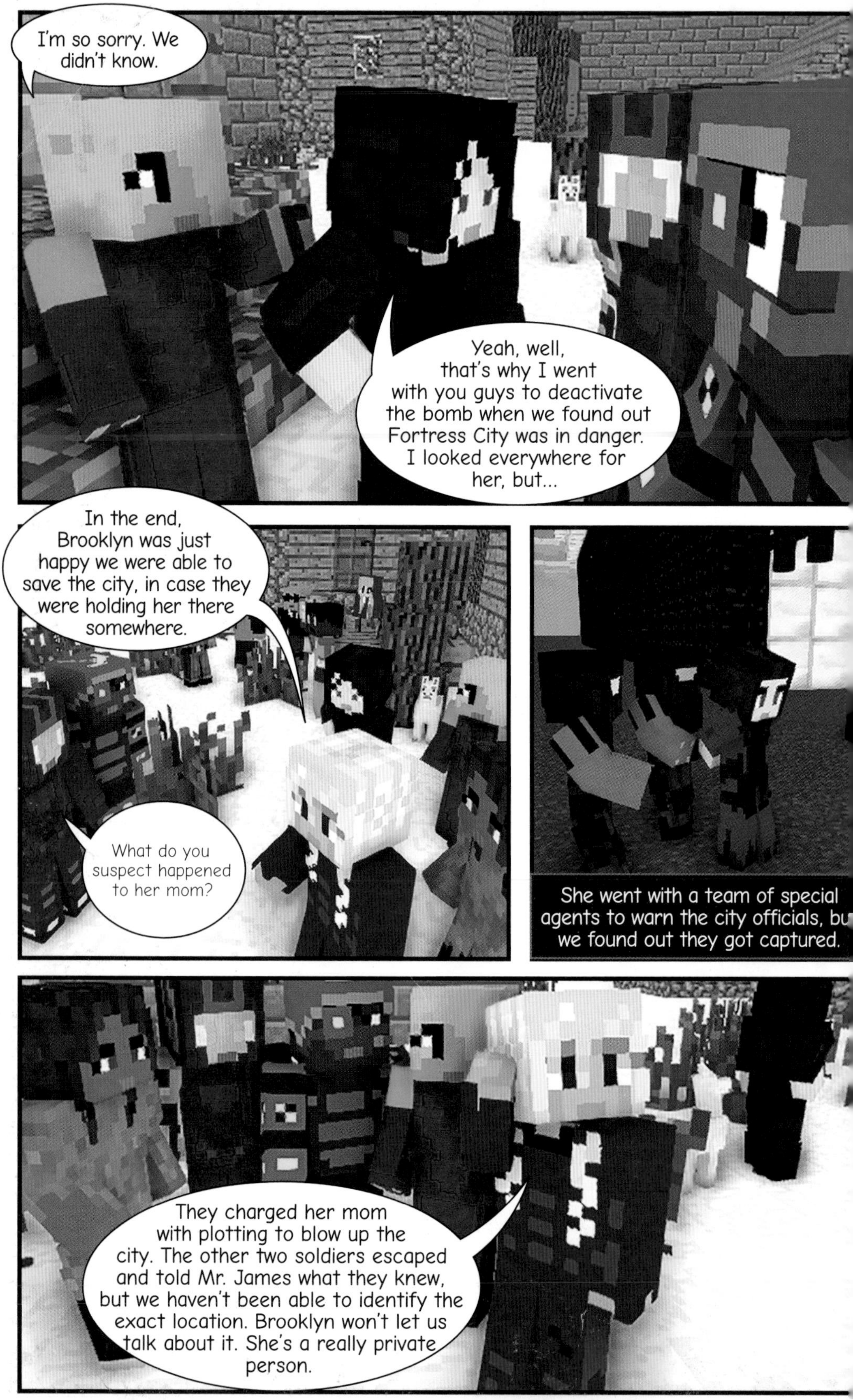
I'm so sorry. We didn't know.
Yeah, well, that's why I went with you guys to deactivate the bomb when we found out Fortress City was in danger. I looked everywhere for her, but...
In the end, Brooklyn was just happy we were able to save the city, in case they were holding her there somewhere.
What do you suspect happened to her mom?
She went with a team of special agents to warn the city officials, but we found out they got captured.
They charged her mom with plotting to blow up the city. The other two soldiers escaped and told Mr. James what they knew, but we haven't been able to identify the exact location. Brooklyn won't let us talk about it. She's a really private person.

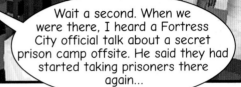

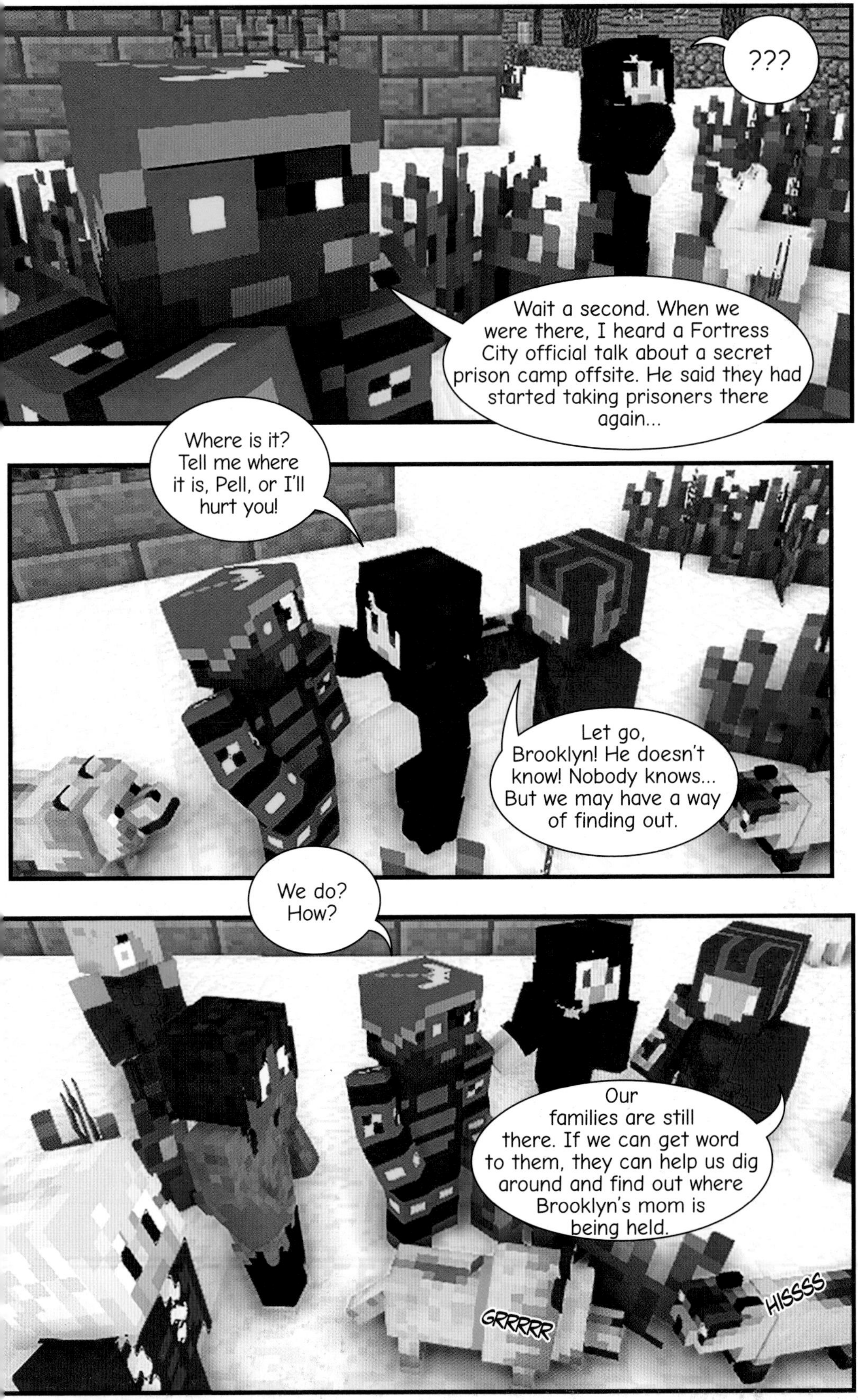

???

Wait a second. When we were there, I heard a Fortress City official talk about a secret prison camp offsite. He said they had started taking prisoners there again...

Where is it? Tell me where it is, Pell, or I'll hurt you!

Let go, Brooklyn! He doesn't know! Nobody knows... But we may have a way of finding out.

We do? How?

Our families are still there. If we can get word to them, they can help us dig around and find out where Brooklyn's mom is being held.

GRRRRR

HISSSS

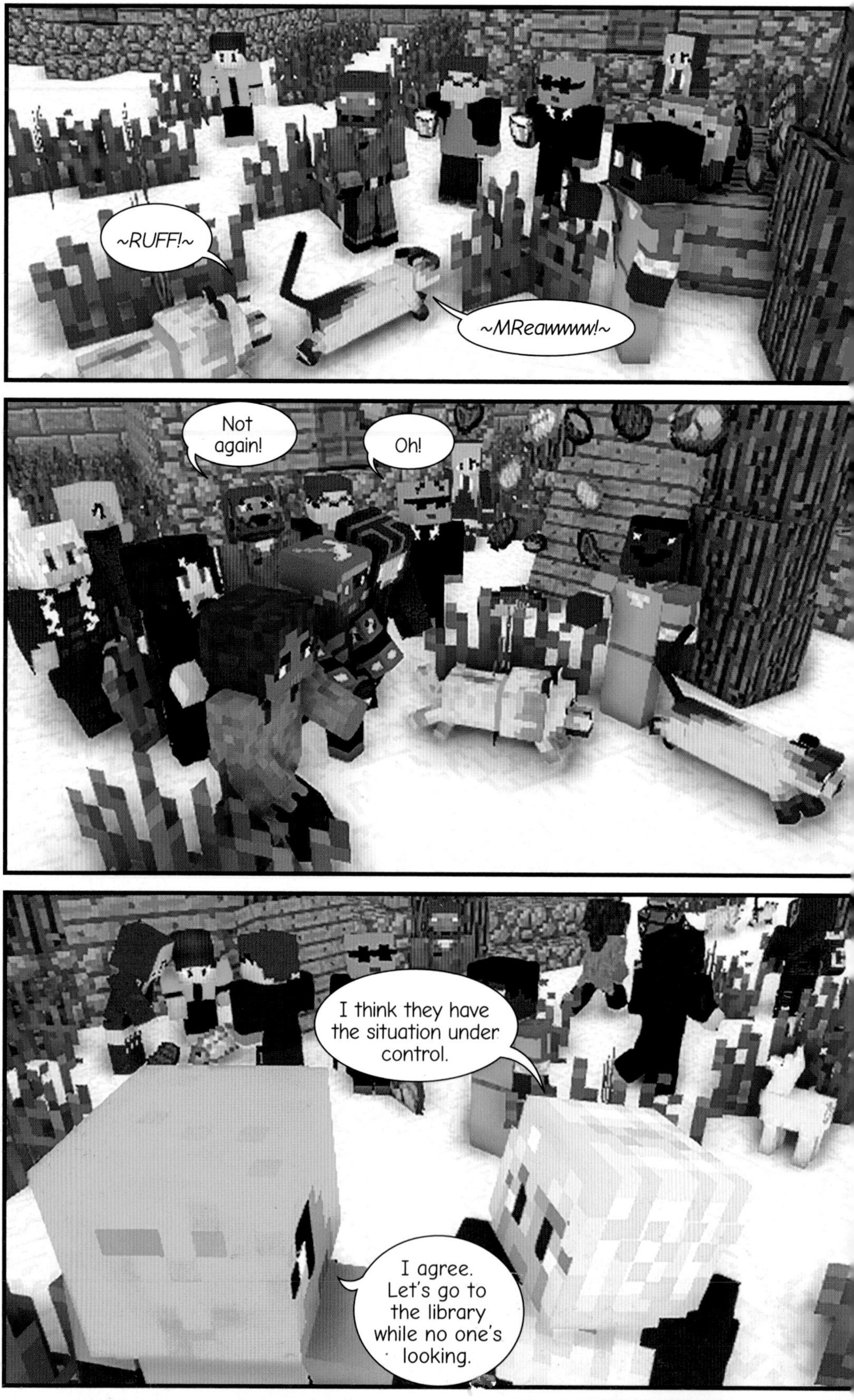
~RUFF!~
~MReawwww!~
Not again!
Oh!
I think they have the situation under control.
I agree. Let's go to the library while no one's looking.

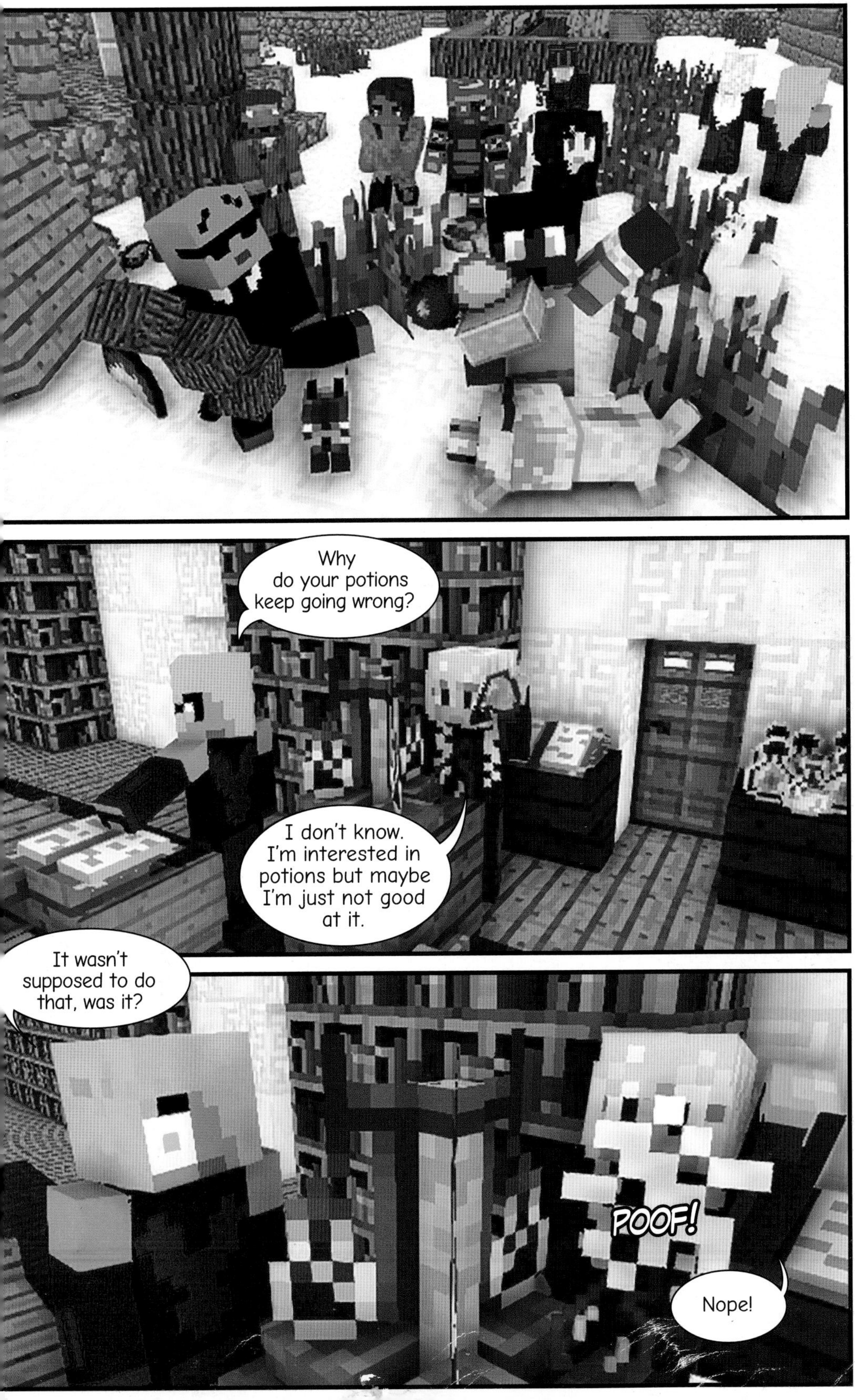
Why do your potions keep going wrong?
I don't know. I'm interested in potions but maybe I'm just not good at it.
It wasn't supposed to do that, was it?
POOF!
Nope!

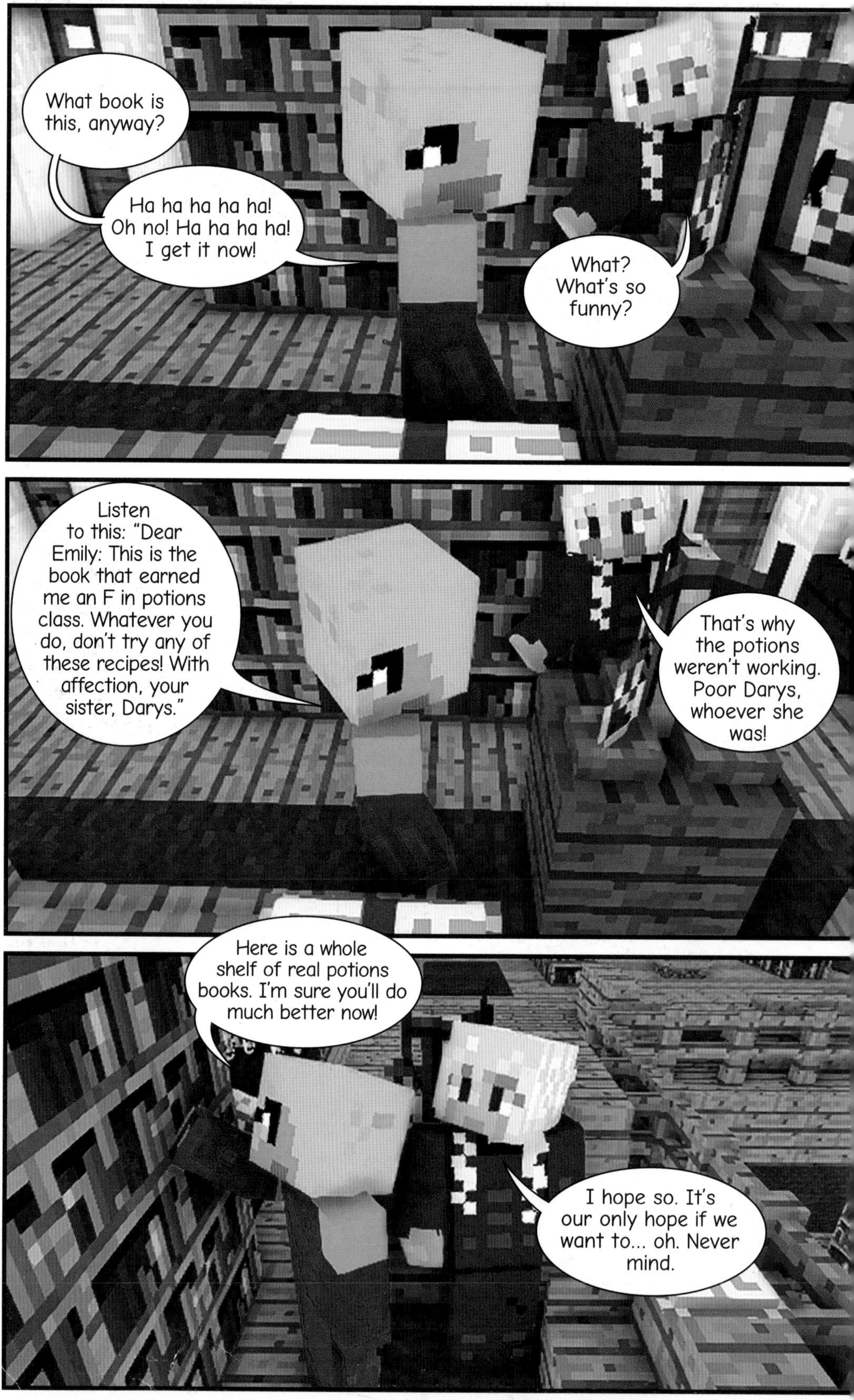
What book is this, anyway?
Ha ha ha ha ha! Oh no! Ha ha ha ha! I get it now!
What? What's so funny?
Listen to this: "Dear Emily: This is the book that earned me an F in potions class. Whatever you do, don't try any of these recipes! With affection, your sister, Darys."
That's why the potions weren't working. Poor Darys, whoever she was!
Here is a whole shelf of real potions books. I'm sure you'll do much better now!
I hope so. It's our only hope if we want to... oh. Never mind.

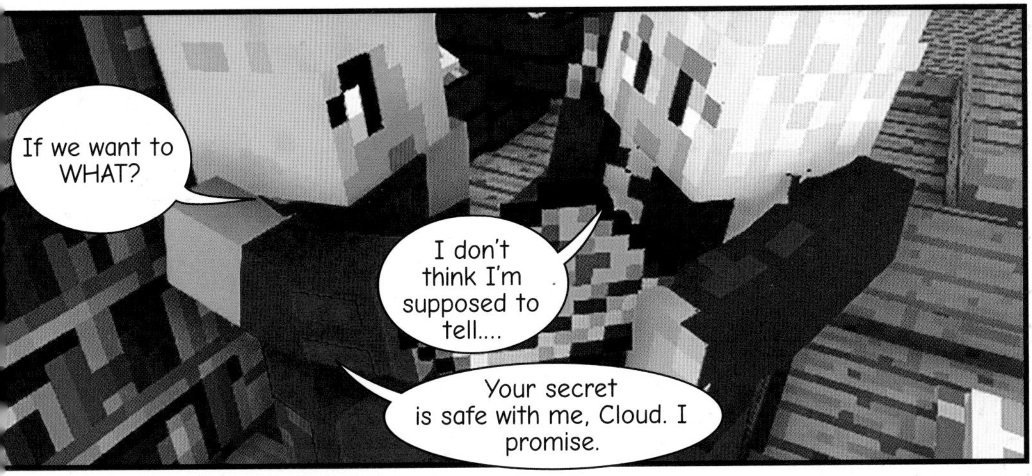
If we want to WHAT?
I don't think I'm supposed to tell....
Your secret is safe with me, Cloud. I promise.

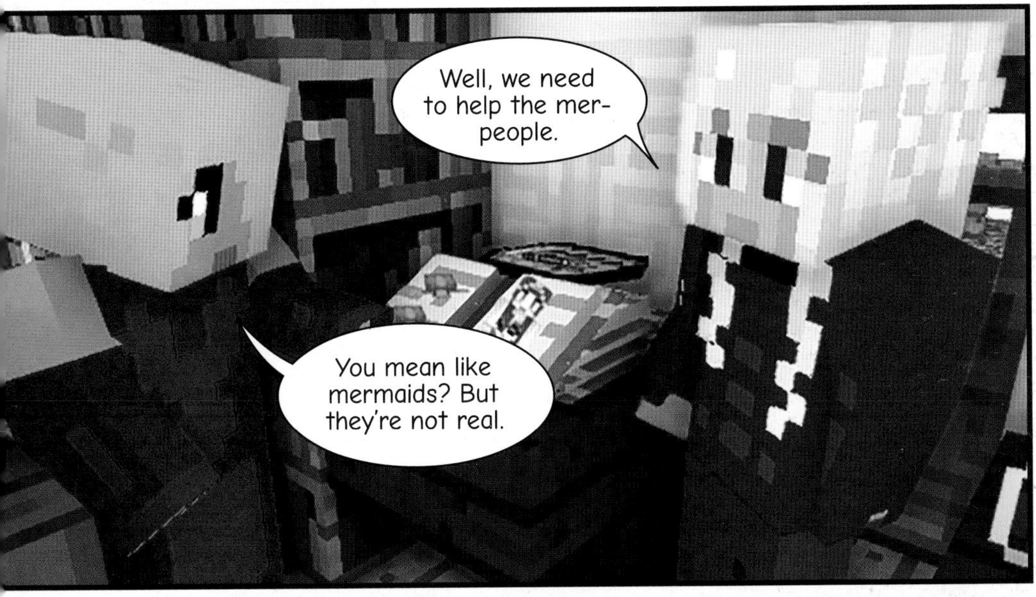
Well, we need to help the mer-people.
You mean like mermaids? But they're not real.

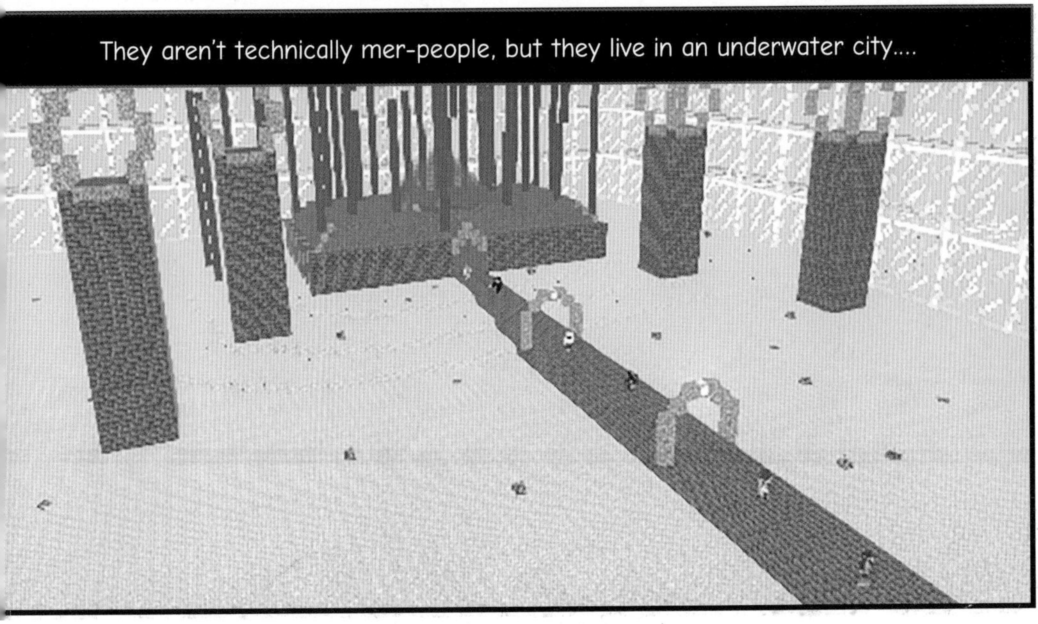
They aren't technically mer-people, but they live in an underwater city....

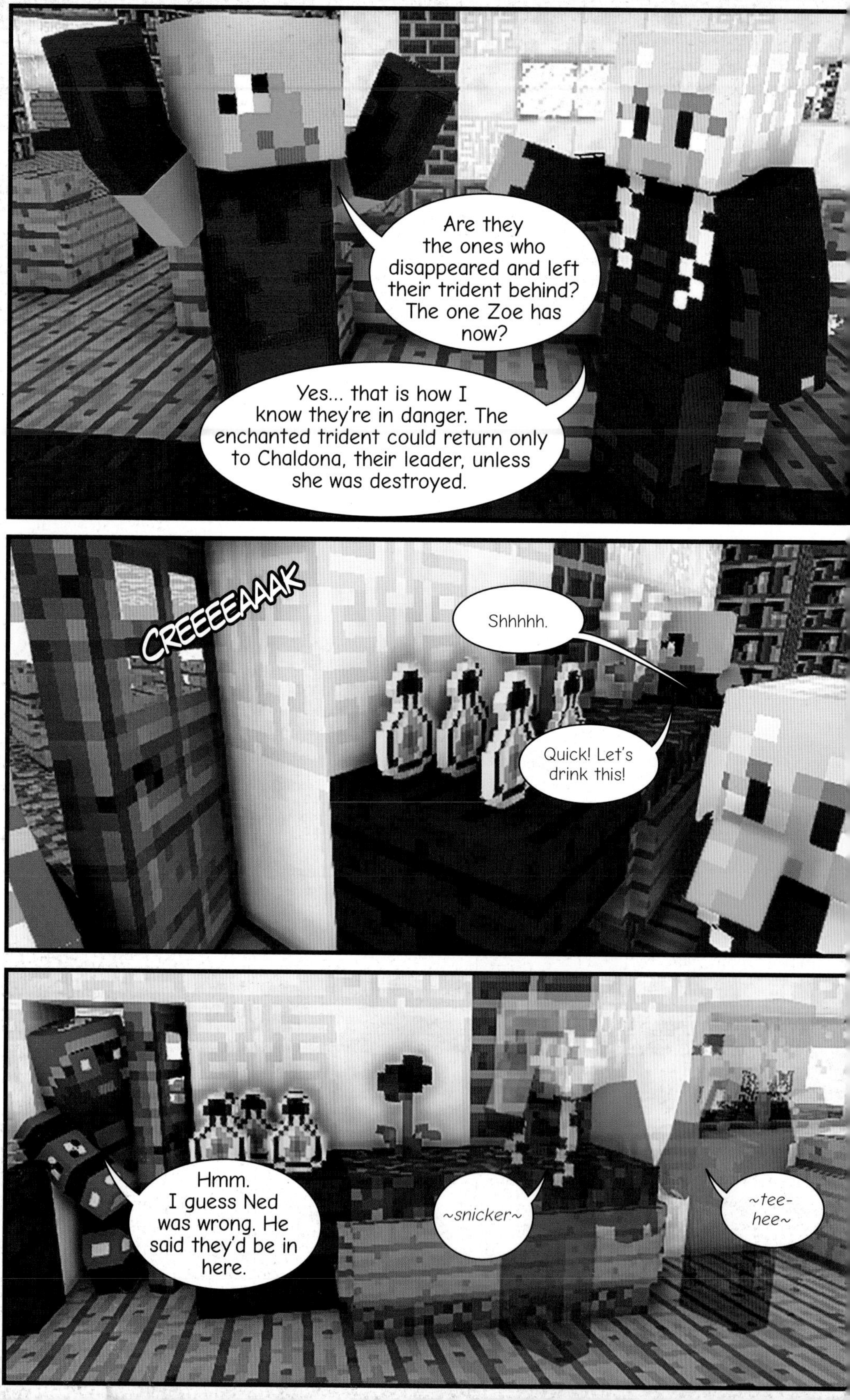
Are they the ones who disappeared and left their trident behind? The one Zoe has now?
Yes... that is how I know they're in danger. The enchanted trident could return only to Chaldona, their leader, unless she was destroyed.
CREEEEAAAK
Shhhhh.
Quick! Let's drink this!
Hmm. I guess Ned was wrong. He said they'd be in here.
~snicker~
~tee-hee~

CHAPTER 2

CHALLENGE
DAY

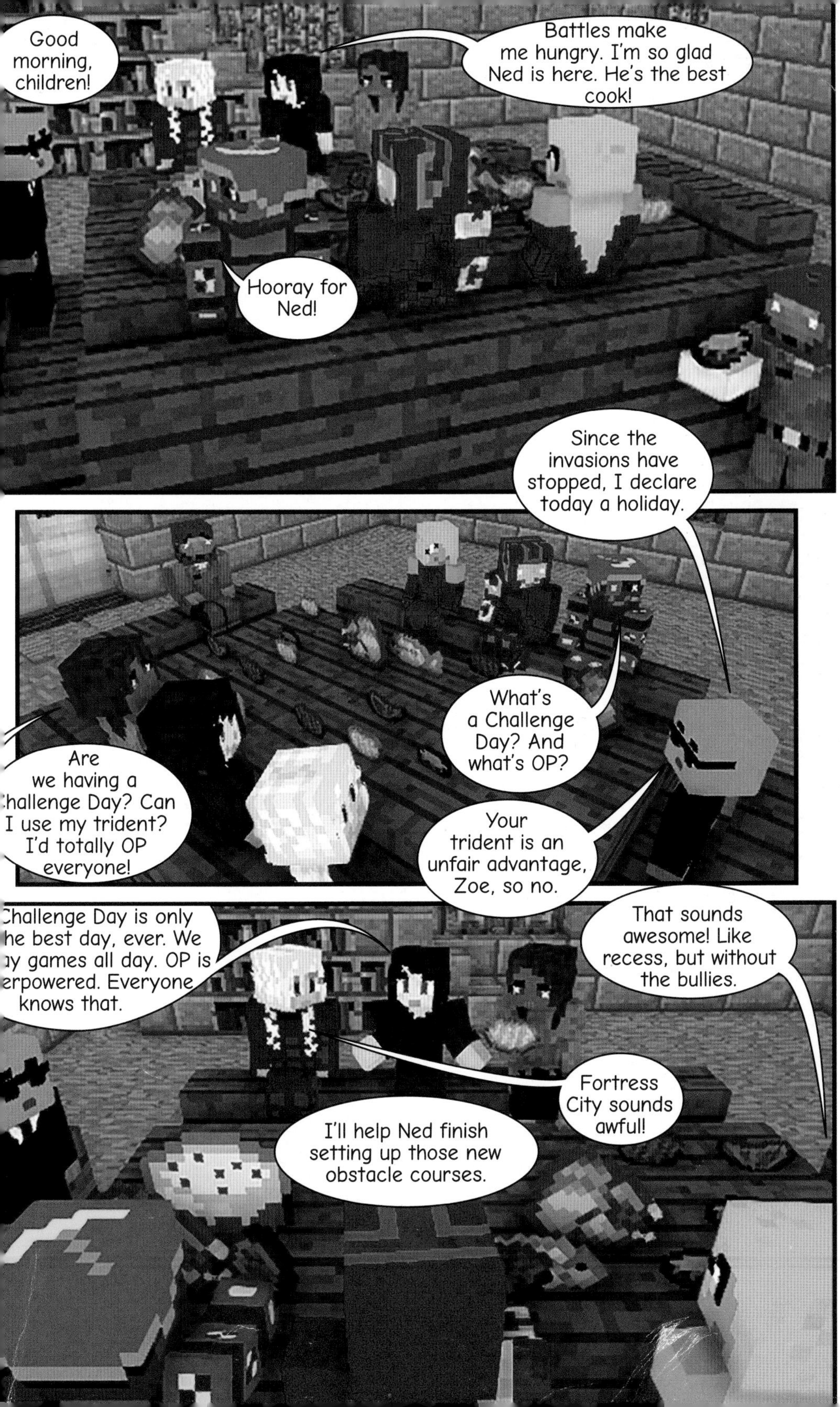
Good morning, children!
Battles make me hungry. I'm so glad Ned is here. He's the best cook!
Hooray for Ned!
Since the invasions have stopped, I declare today a holiday.
Are we having a
hallenge Day? Can I use my trident? I'd totally OP everyone!
What's a Challenge Day? And what's OP?
Your trident is an unfair advantage, Zoe, so no.
hallenge Day is only
he best day, ever. We
y games all day. OP is
erpowered. Everyone
knows that.
That sounds awesome! Like recess, but without the bullies.
Fortress City sounds awful!
I'll help Ned finish setting up those new obstacle courses.

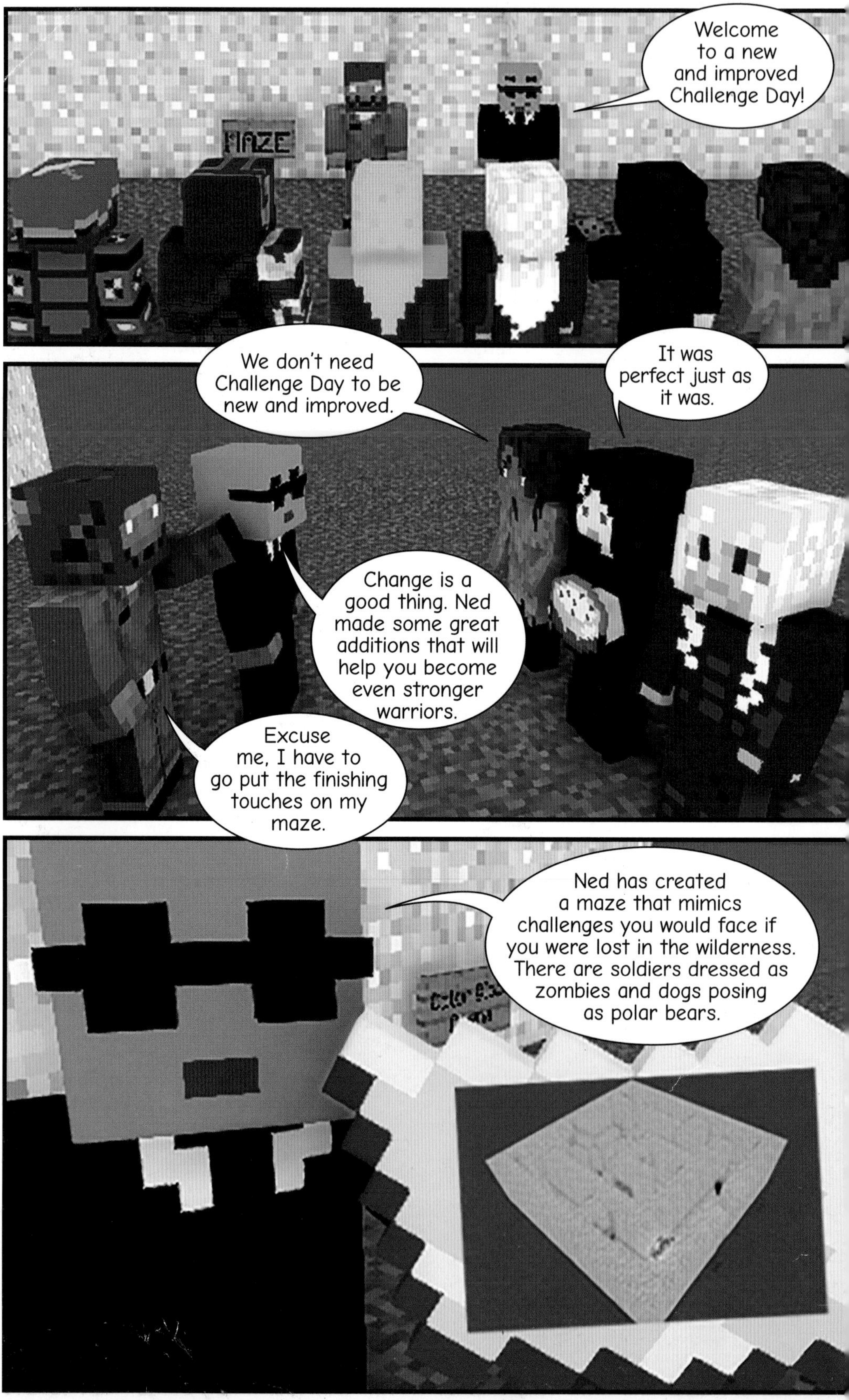
Welcome to a new and improved Challenge Day!
We don't need Challenge Day to be new and improved.
It was perfect just as it was.
Change is a good thing. Ned made some great additions that will help you become even stronger warriors.
Excuse me, I have to go put the finishing touches on my maze.
Ned has created a maze that mimics challenges you would face if you were lost in the wilderness. There are soldiers dressed as zombies and dogs posing as polar bears.

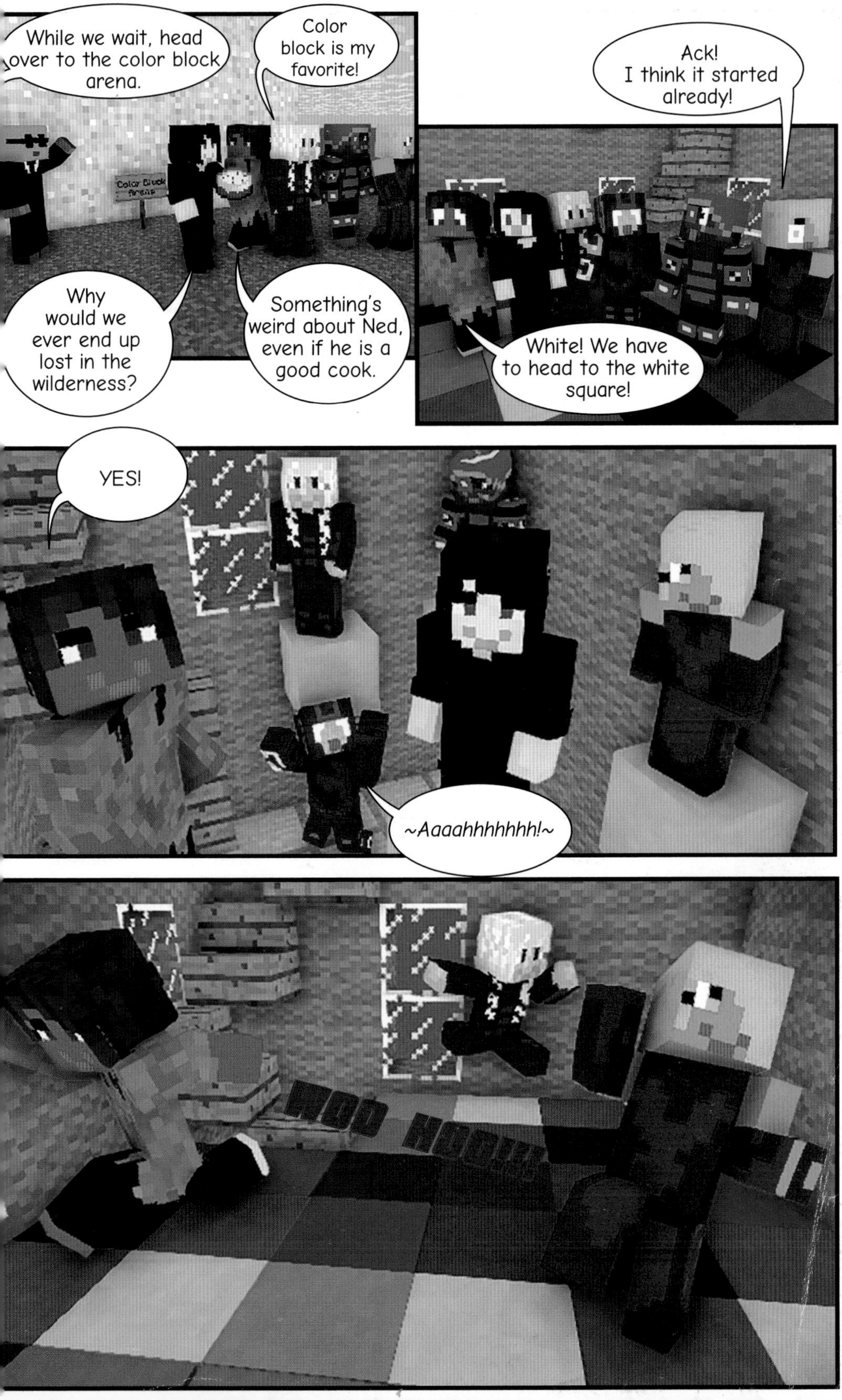
While we wait, head over to the color block arena.
Color block is my favorite!
Why would we ever end up lost in the wilderness?
Something's weird about Ned, even if he is a good cook.
Ack! I think it started already!
White! We have to head to the white square!
YES!
~Aaaahhhhhhh!~

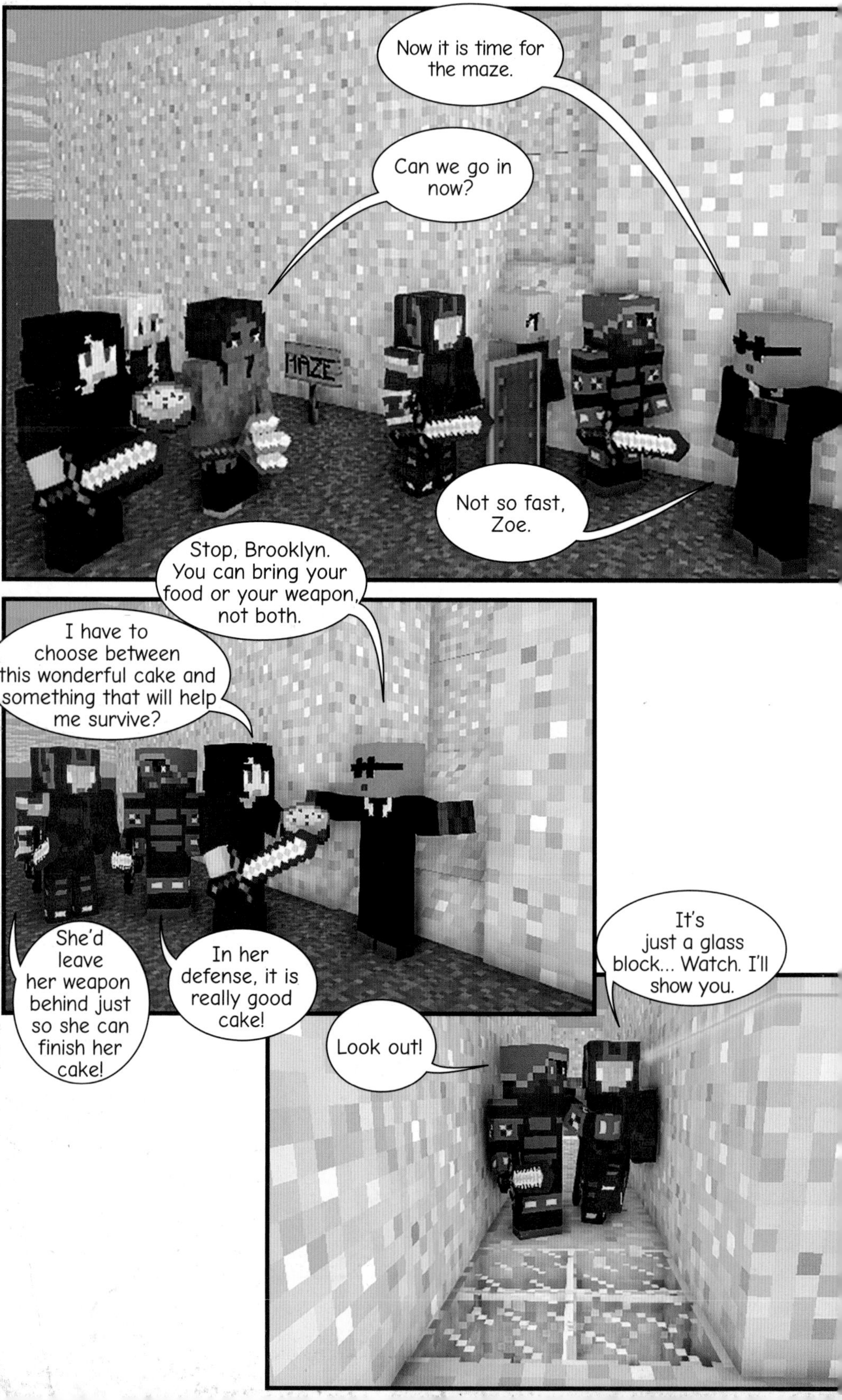
Now it is time for the maze.
Can we go in now?
MAZE
Not so fast, Zoe.
Stop, Brooklyn. You can bring your food or your weapon, not both.
I have to choose between this wonderful cake and something that will help me survive?
She'd leave her weapon behind just so she can finish her cake!
In her defense, it is really good cake!
It's just a glass block... Watch. I'll show you.
Look out!

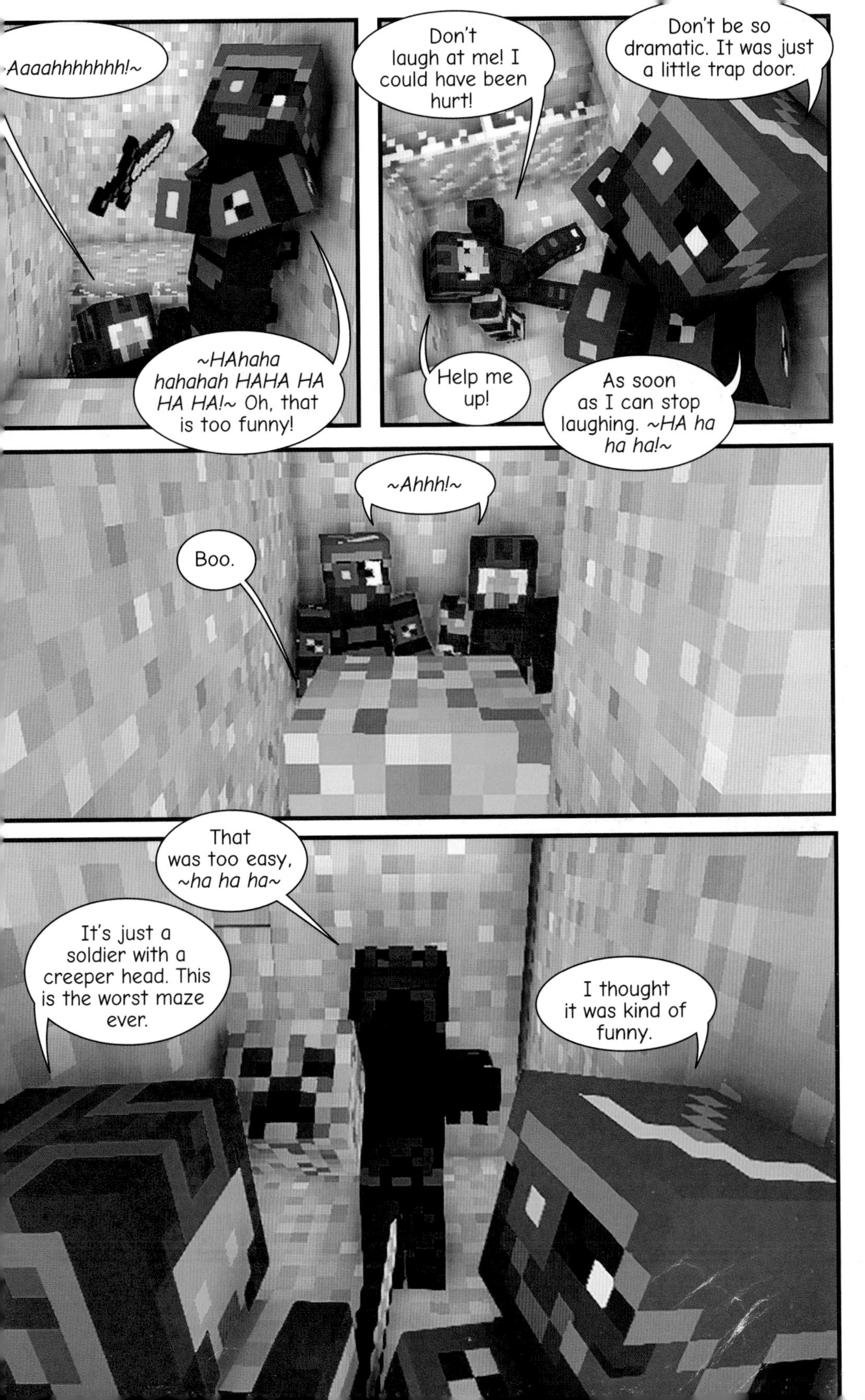

Aaaahhhhhhh!~
~HAhaha hahahah HAHA HA HA HA!~ Oh, that is too funny!
Don't laugh at me! I could have been hurt!
Don't be so dramatic. It was just a little trap door.
Help me up!
As soon as I can stop laughing. ~HA ha ha ha!~
~Ahhh!~
Boo.
That was too easy, ~ha ha ha~
It's just a soldier with a creeper head. This is the worst maze ever.
I thought it was kind of funny.

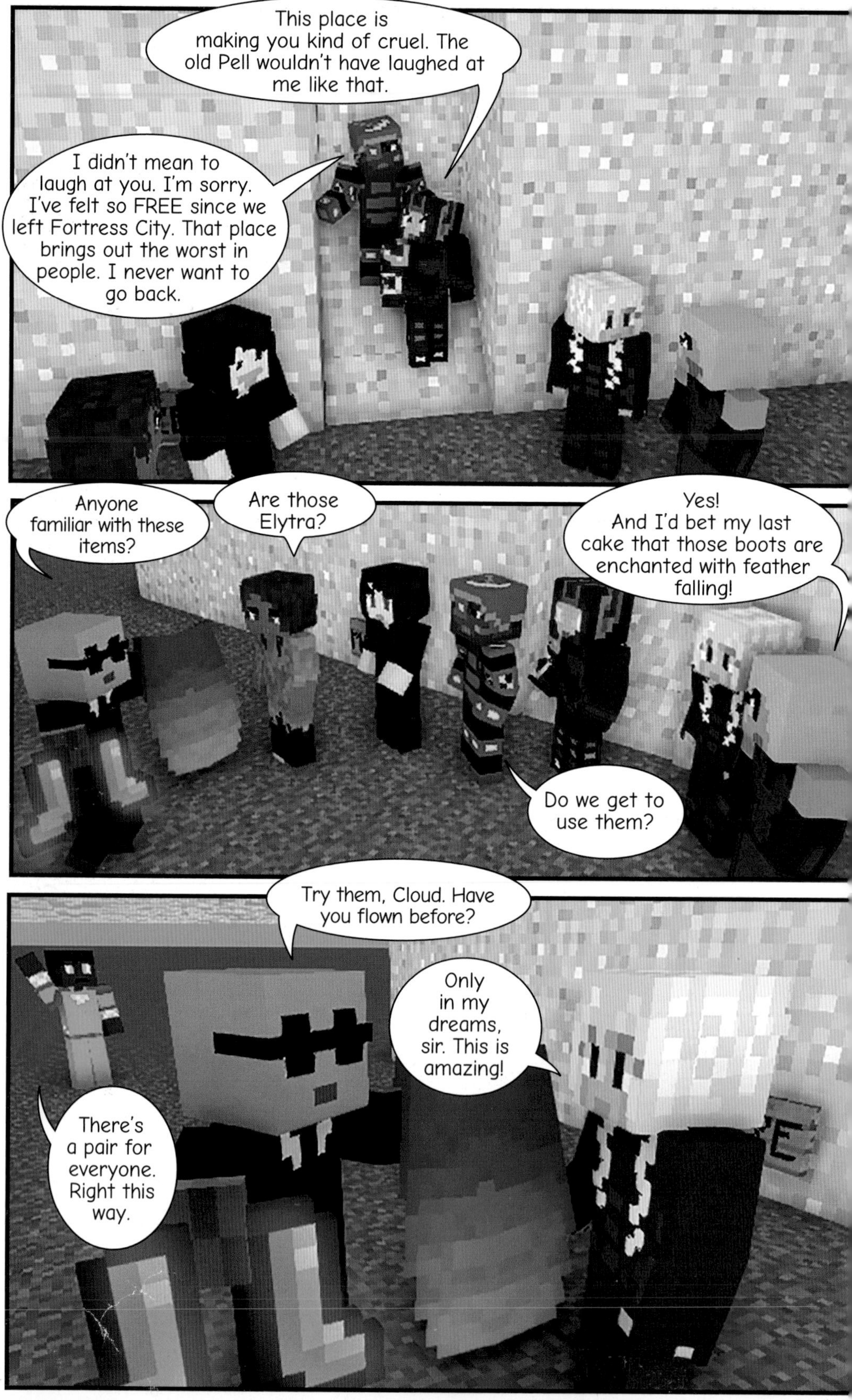
This place is making you kind of cruel. The old Pell wouldn't have laughed at me like that.
I didn't mean to laugh at you. I'm sorry. I've felt so FREE since we left Fortress City. That place brings out the worst in people. I never want to go back.
Anyone familiar with these items?
Are those Elytra?
Yes! And I'd bet my last cake that those boots are enchanted with feather falling!
Do we get to use them?
Try them, Cloud. Have you flown before?
Only in my dreams, sir. This is amazing!
There's a pair for everyone. Right this way.

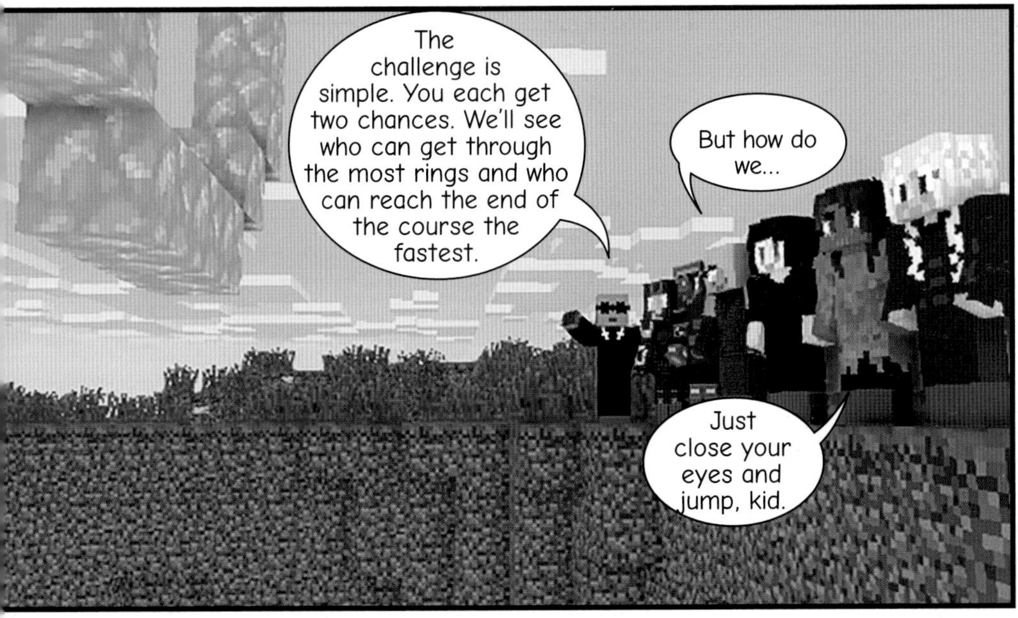
The challenge is simple. You each get two chances. We'll see who can get through the most rings and who can reach the end of the course the fastest.
But how do we...
Just close your eyes and jump, kid.

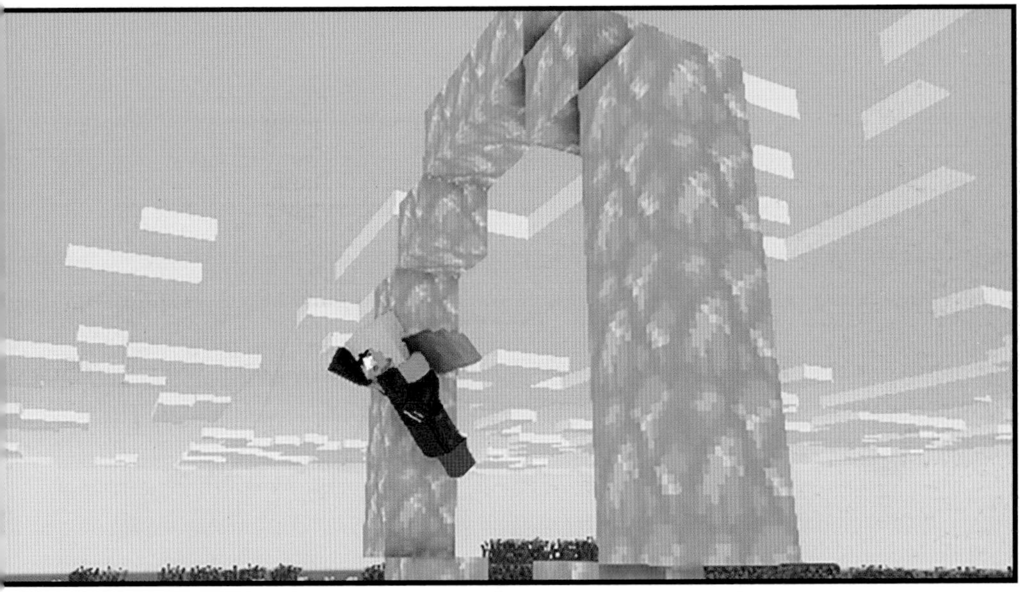

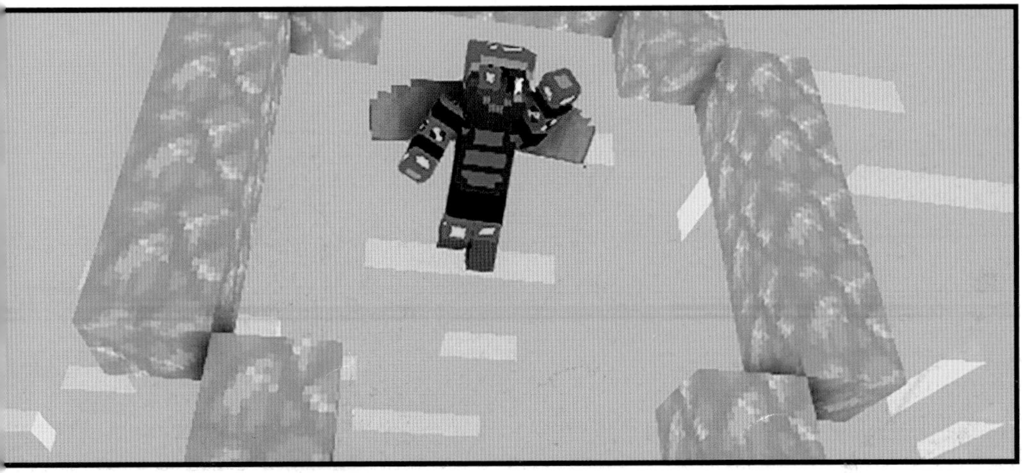

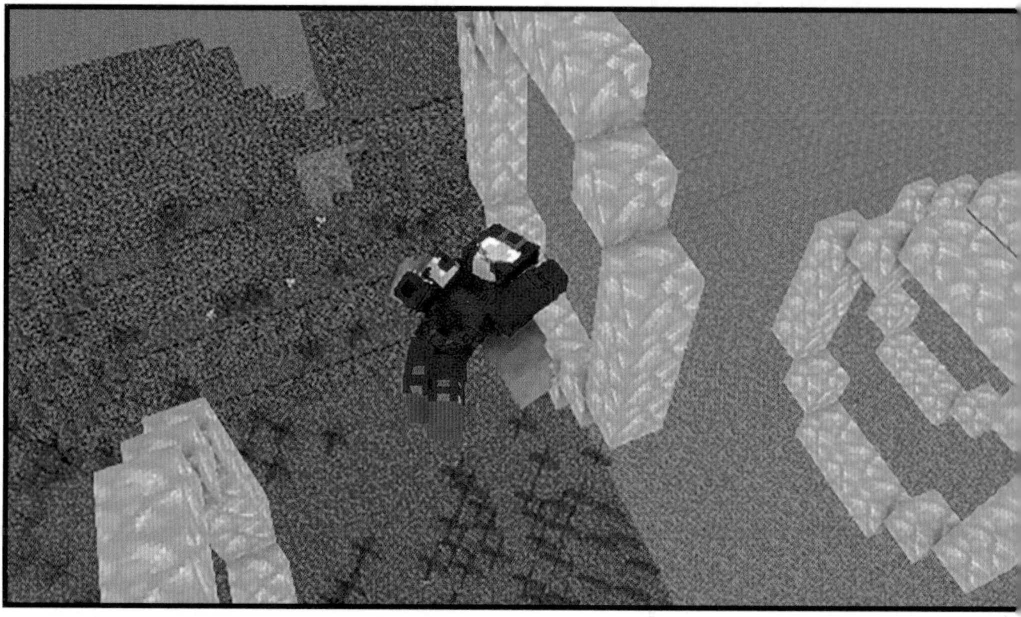
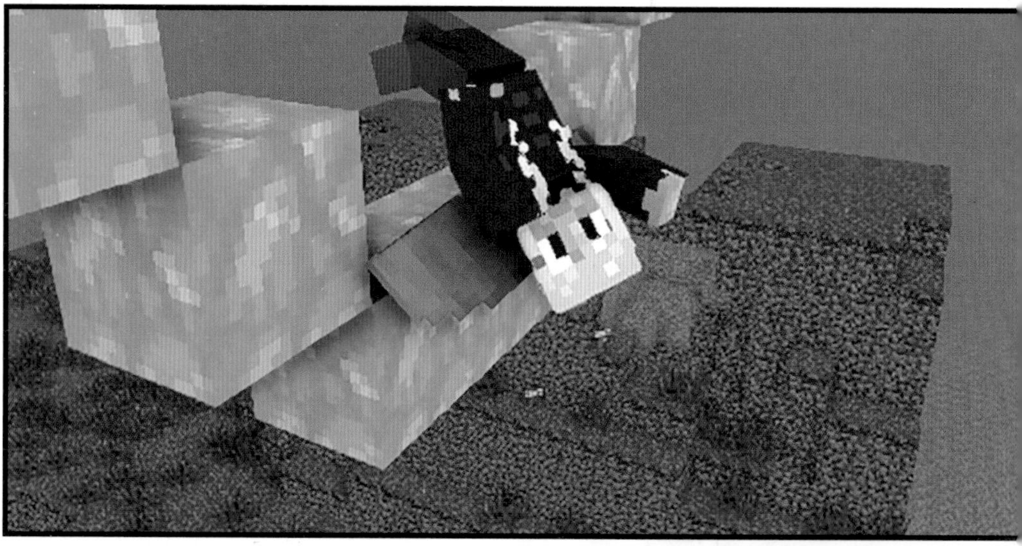
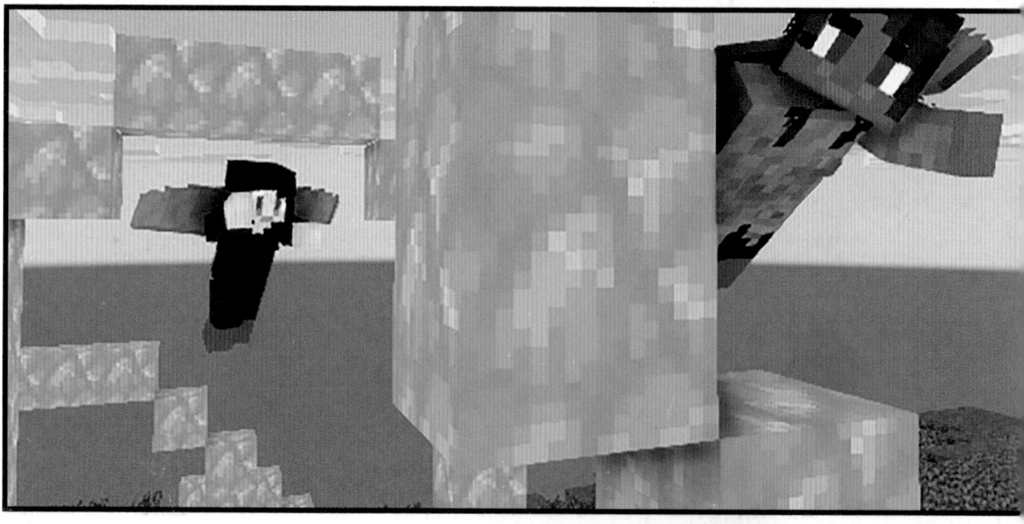

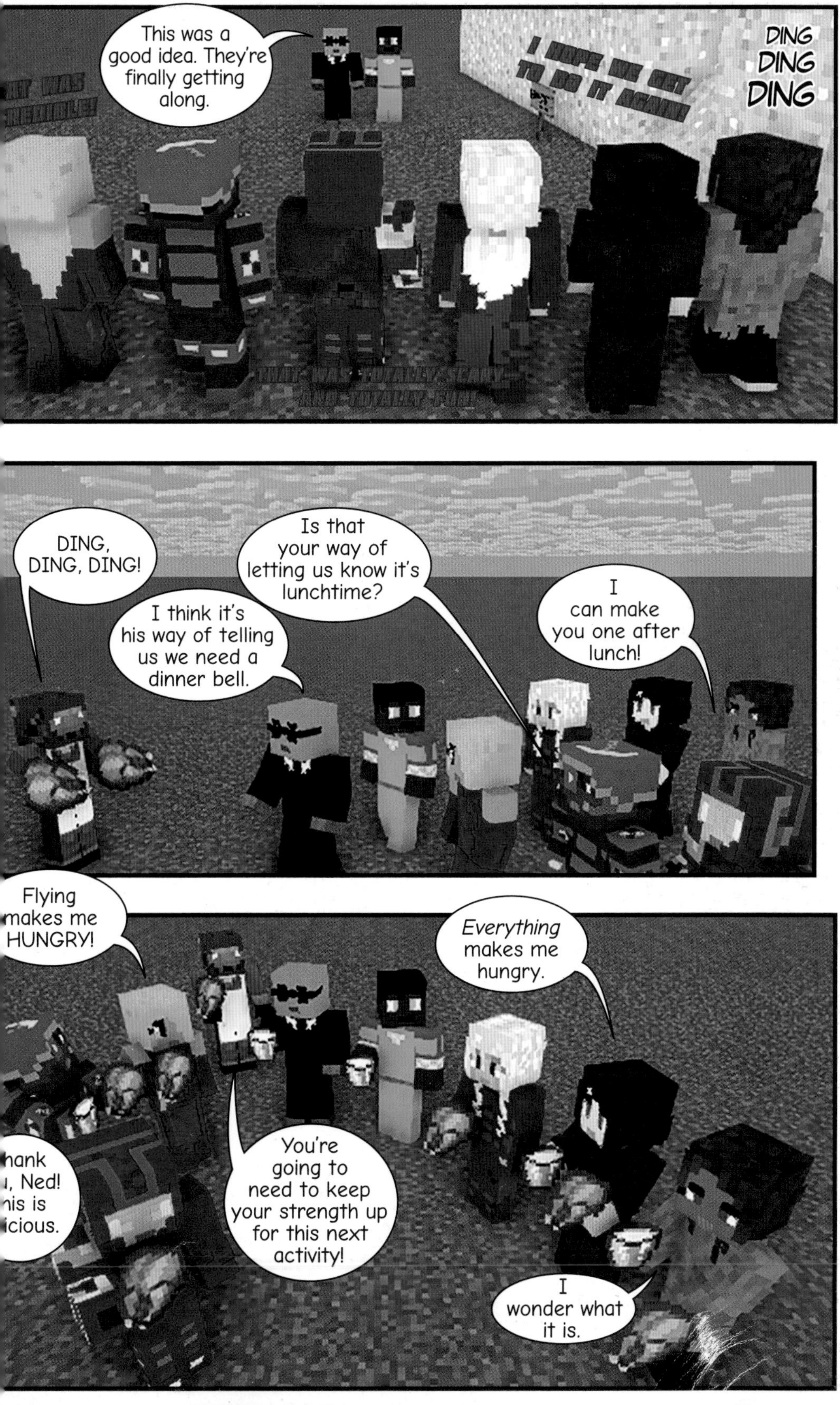

This was a good idea. They're finally getting along.
I HOPE WE GET TO DO IT AGAIN!
DING DING DING
THAT WAS TOTALLY SCARY AND TOTALLY FUN!
DING, DING, DING!
Is that your way of letting us know it's lunchtime?
I think it's his way of telling us we need a dinner bell.
I can make you one after lunch!
Flying makes me HUNGRY!
Everything makes me hungry.
hank , Ned! his is icious.
You're going to need to keep your strength up for this next activity!
I wonder what it is.

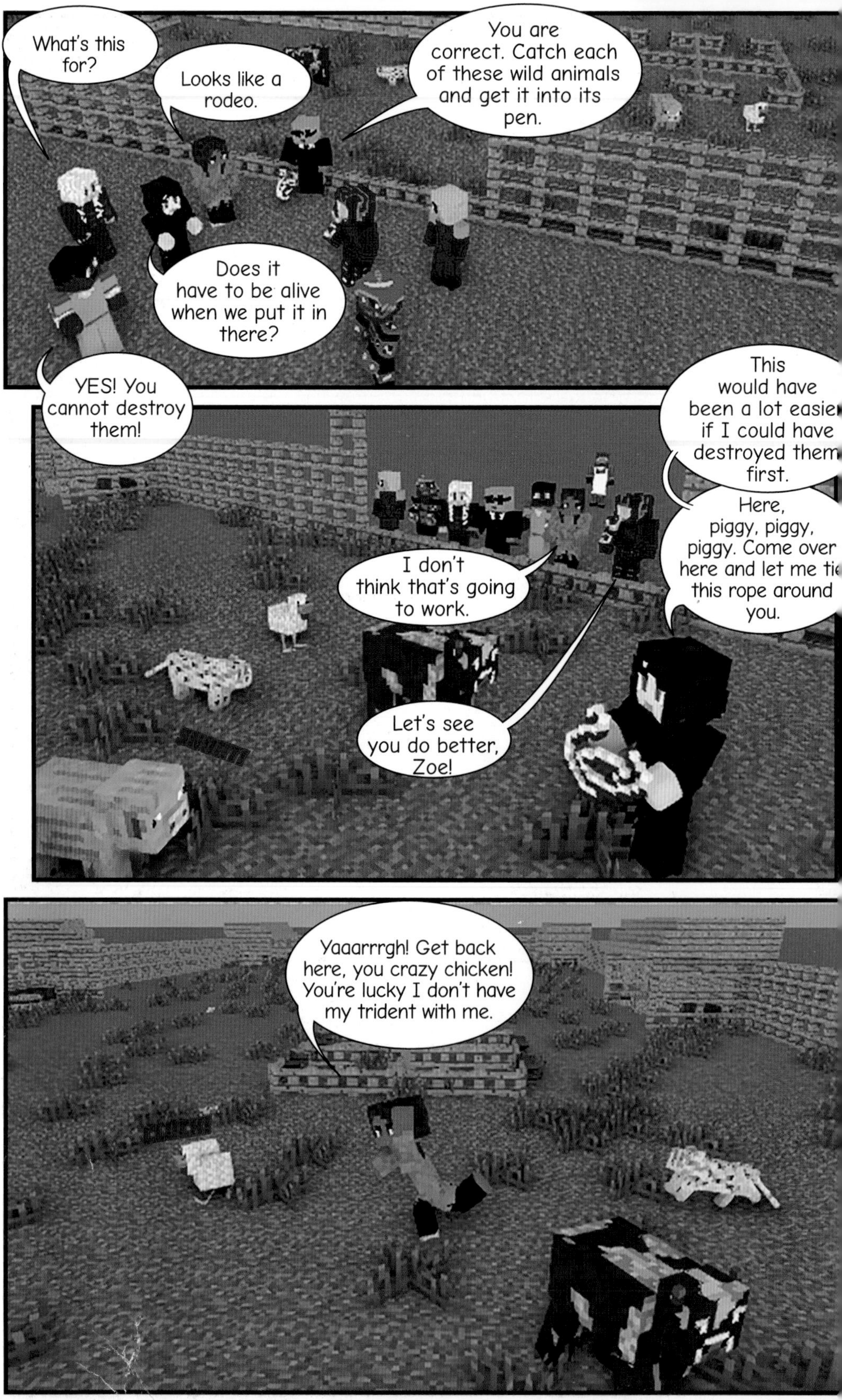
What's this for?
Looks like a rodeo.
You are correct. Catch each of these wild animals and get it into its pen.
Does it have to be alive when we put it in there?
YES! You cannot destroy them!
This would have been a lot easie if I could have destroyed them first.
Here, piggy, piggy, piggy. Come over here and let me ti this rope around you.
I don't think that's going to work.
Let's see you do better, Zoe!
Yaaarrrgh! Get back here, you crazy chicken! You're lucky I don't have my trident with me.

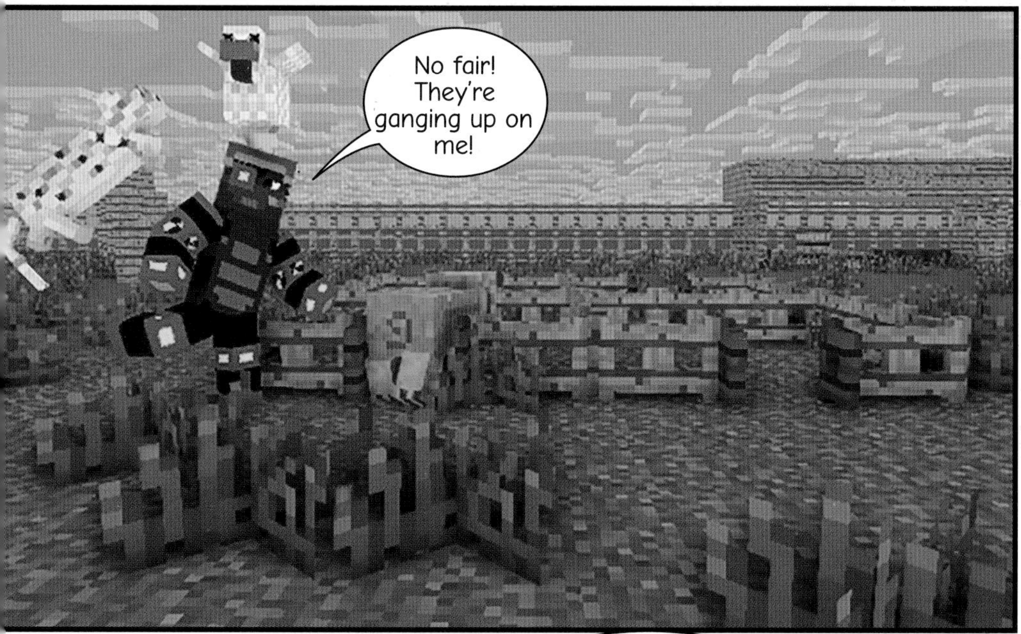
No fair! They're ganging up on me!

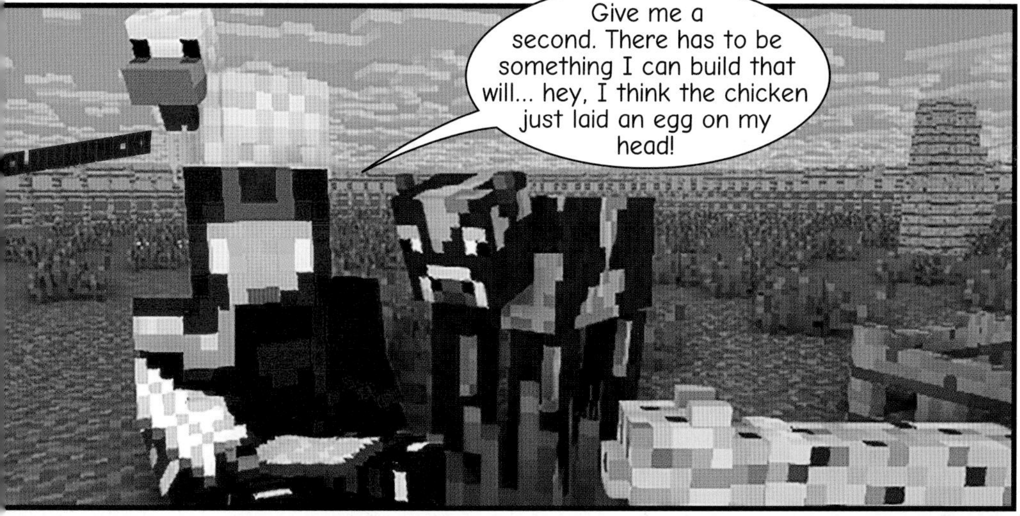
Give me a second. There has to be something I can build that will... hey, I think the chicken just laid an egg on my head!

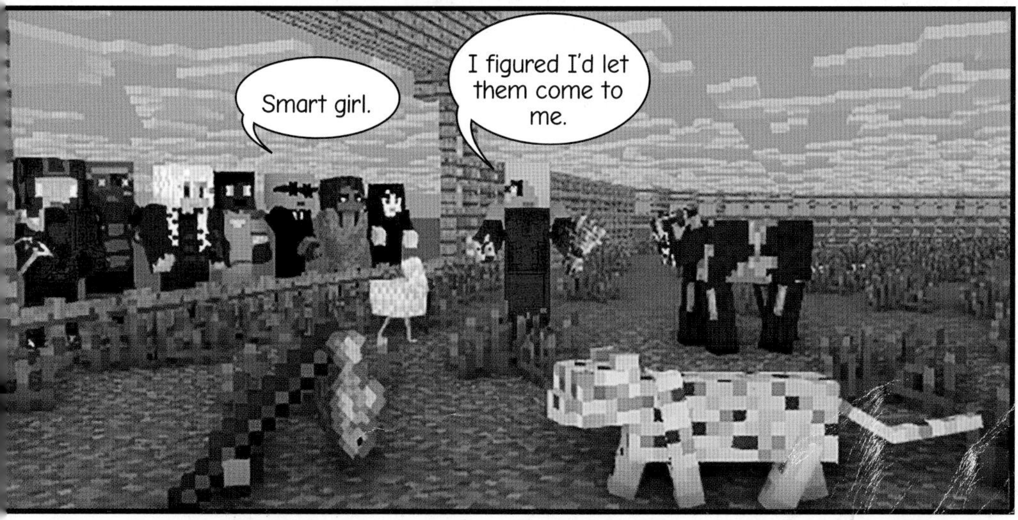
Smart girl.
I figured I'd let them come to me.

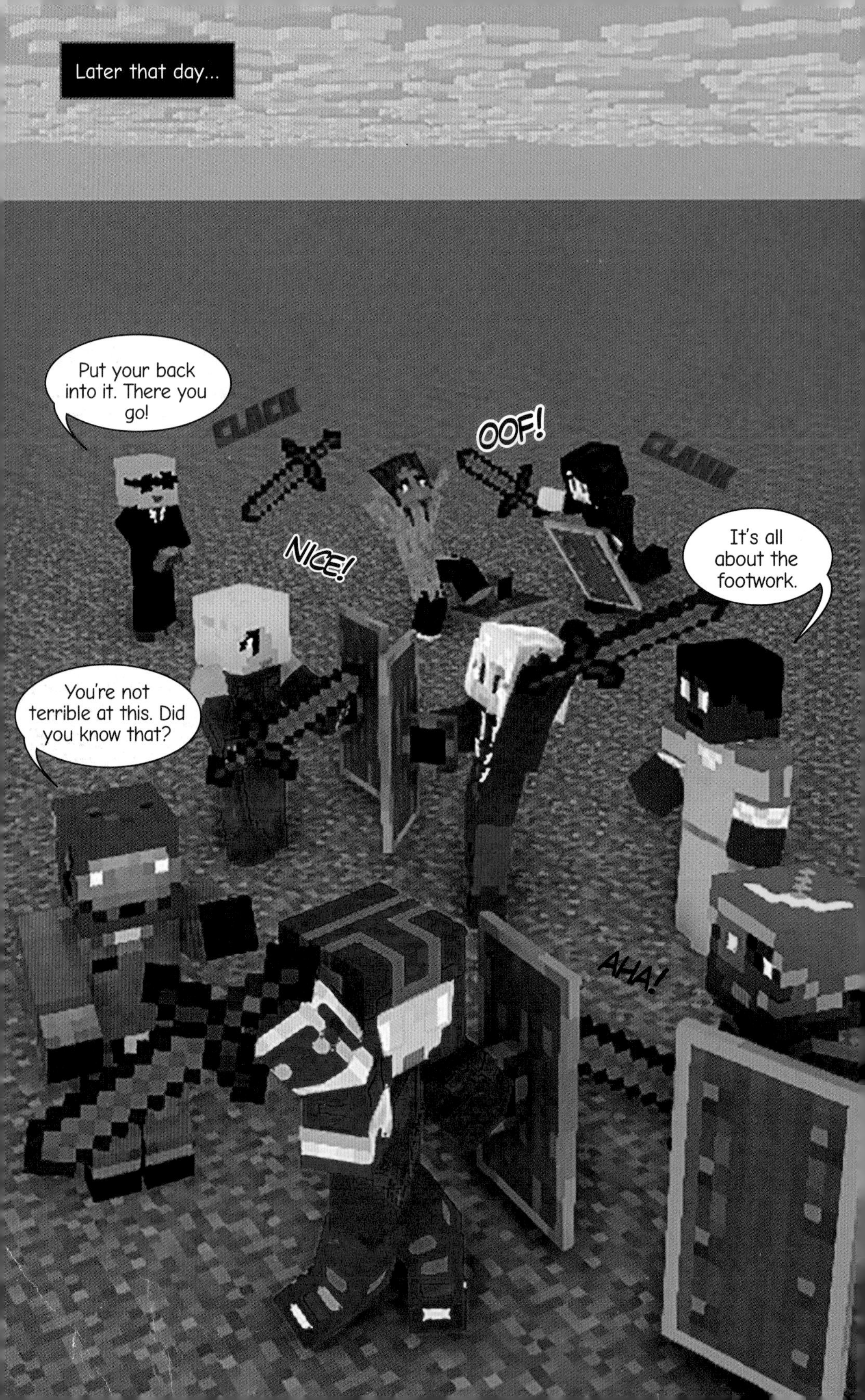
Later that day...
Put your back into it. There you go!
CLACK
OOF!
CLANK
NICE!
It's all about the footwork.
You're not terrible at this. Did you know that?
AHA!

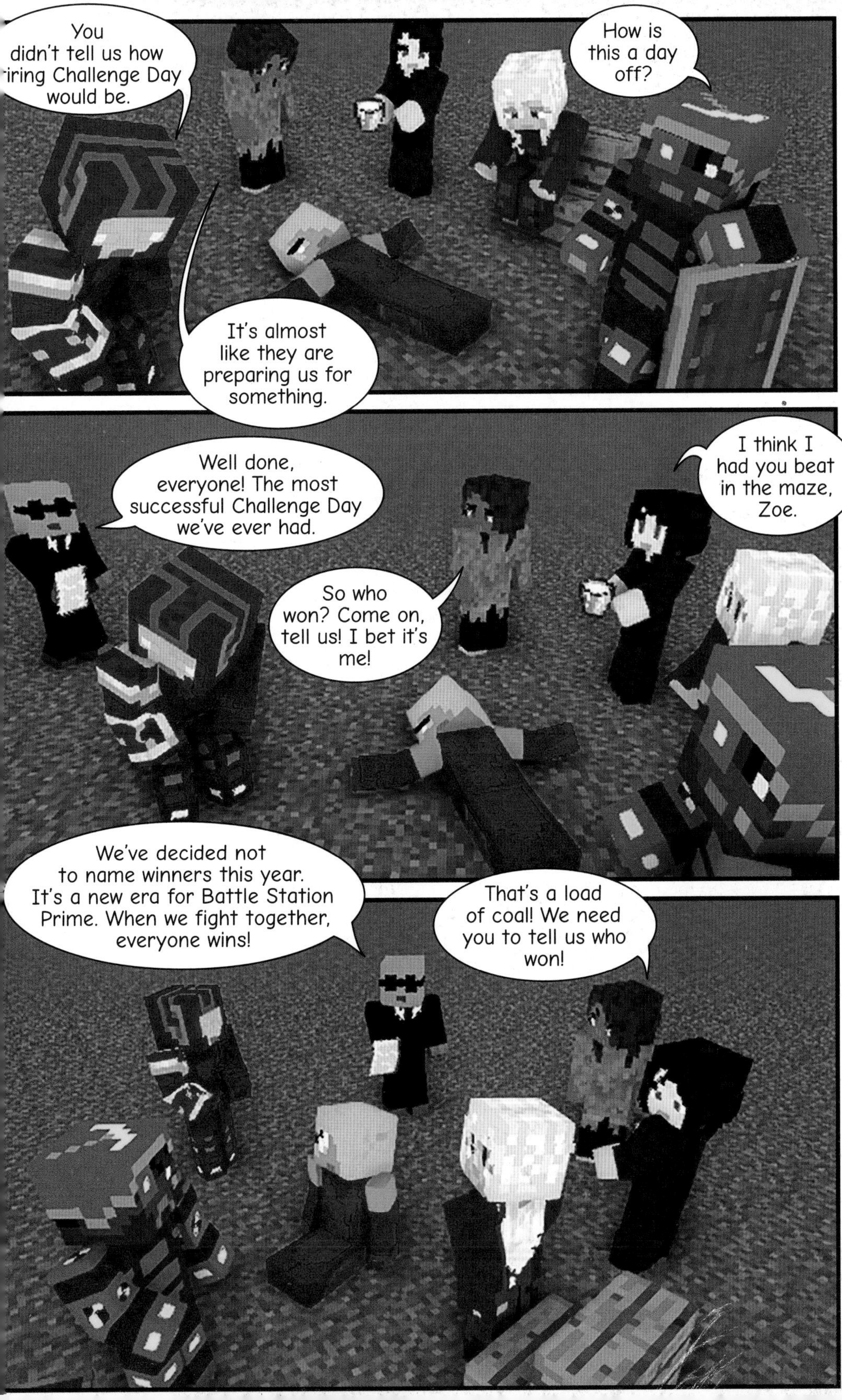
You didn't tell us how iring Challenge Day would be.
How is this a day off?
It's almost like they are preparing us for something.
Well done, everyone! The most successful Challenge Day we've ever had.
I think I had you beat in the maze, Zoe.
So who won? Come on, tell us! I bet it's me!
We've decided not to name winners this year. It's a new era for Battle Station Prime. When we fight together, everyone wins!
That's a load of coal! We need you to tell us who won!

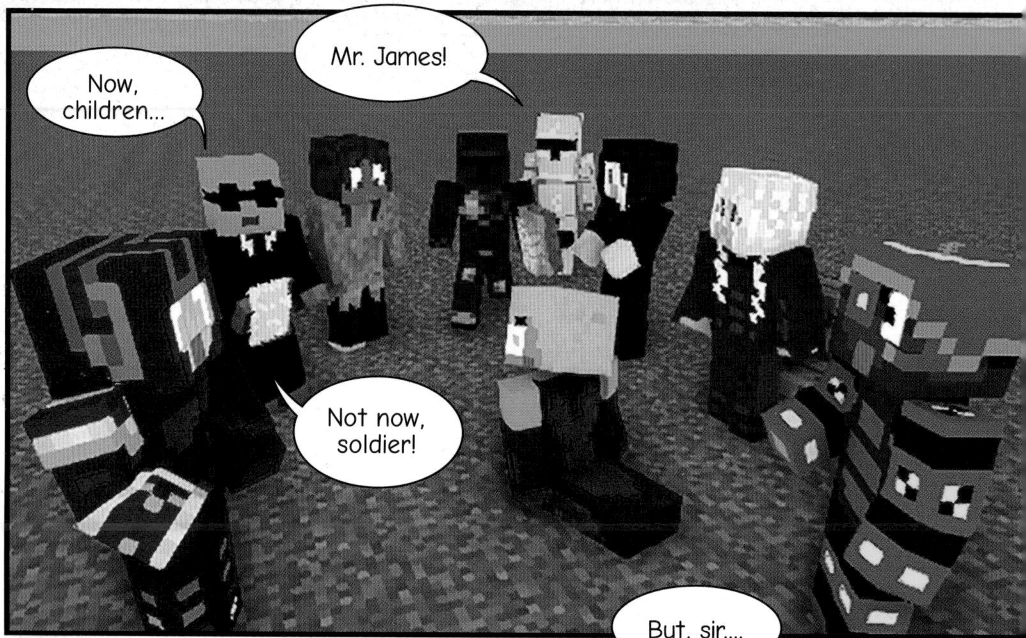
Now, children...
Mr. James!
Not now, soldier!

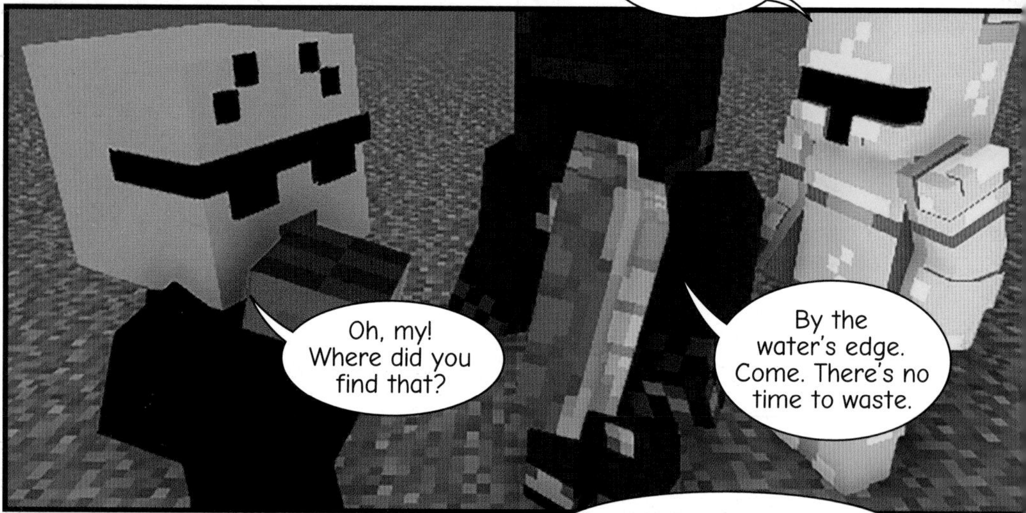
But, sir....
Oh, my! Where did you find that?
By the water's edge. Come. There's no time to waste.

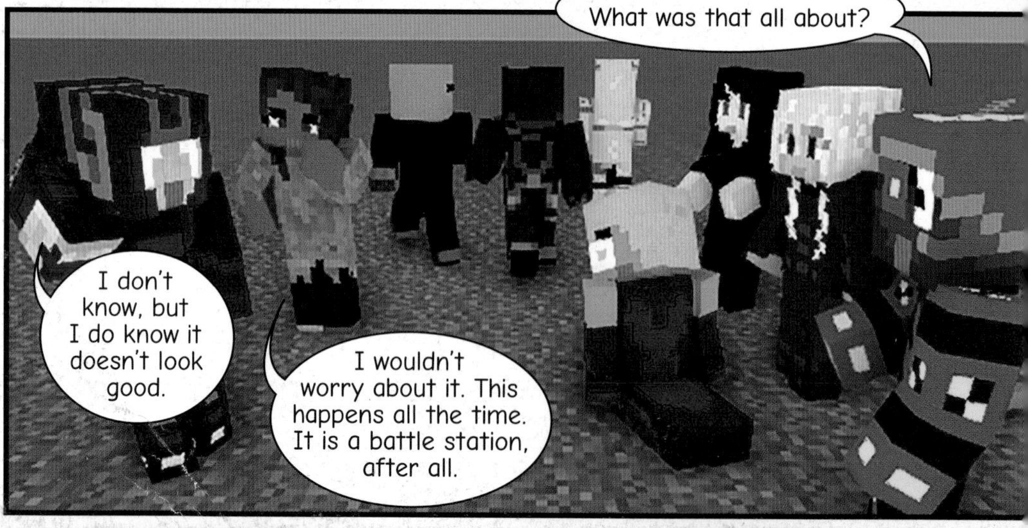
What was that all about?
I don't know, but I do know it doesn't look good.
I wouldn't worry about it. This happens all the time. It is a battle station, after all.

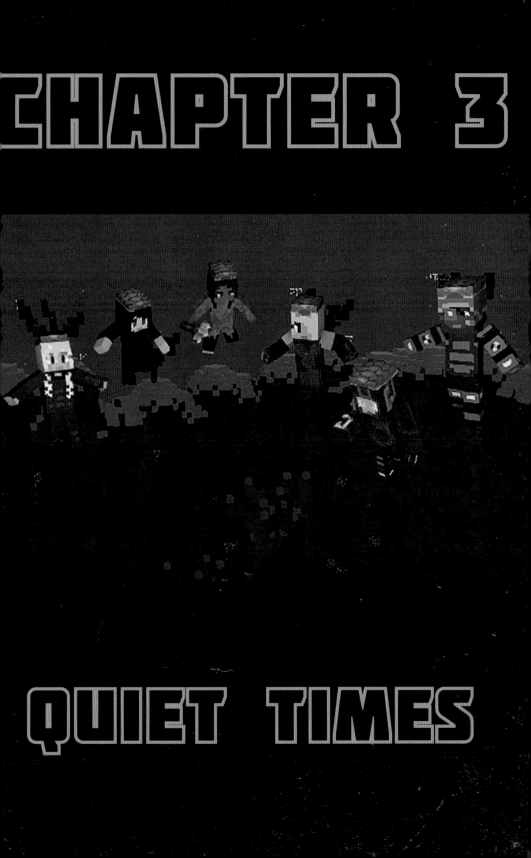

CHAPTER 3

QUIET TIMES

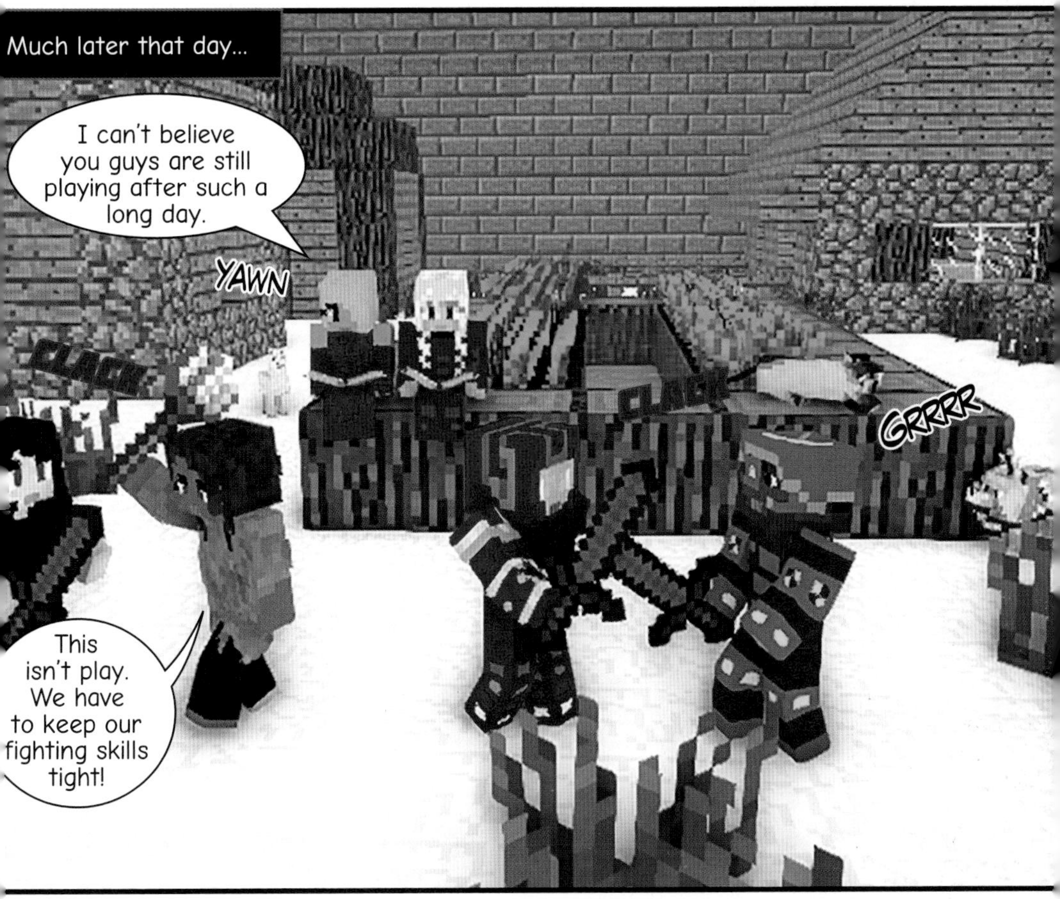
Much later that day...
I can't believe you guys are still playing after such a long day.
YAWN
CLACK
CLACK
GRRRR
This isn't play. We have to keep our fighting skills tight!

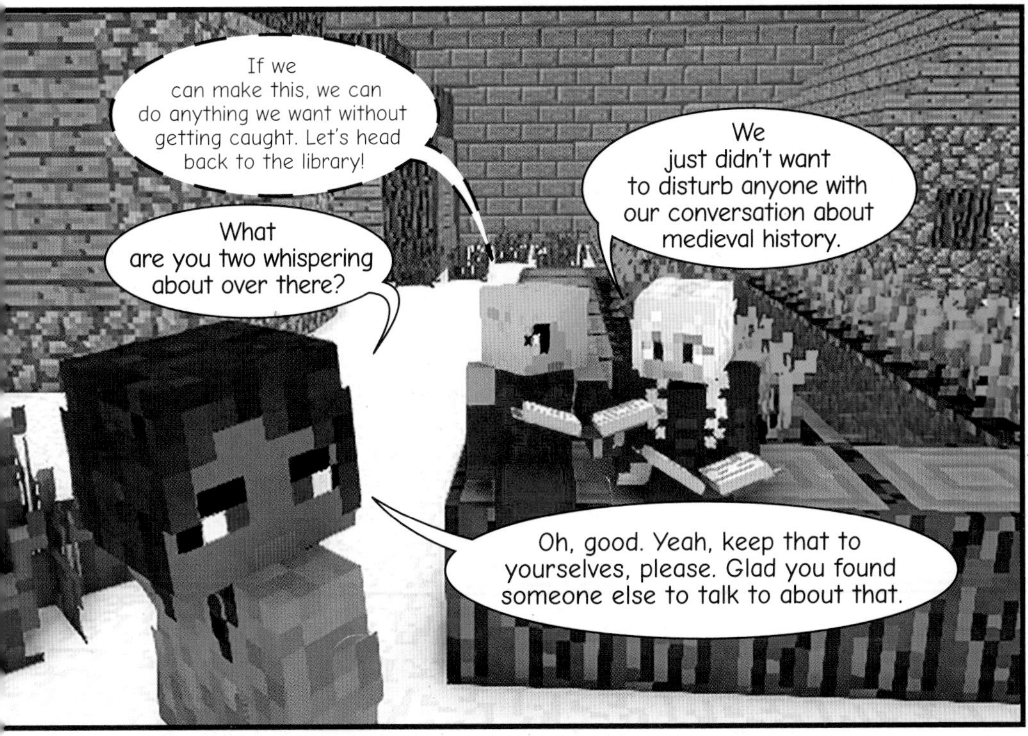
If we can make this, we can do anything we want without getting caught. Let's head back to the library!
What are you two whispering about over there?
We just didn't want to disturb anyone with our conversation about medieval history.
Oh, good. Yeah, keep that to yourselves, please. Glad you found someone else to talk to about that.

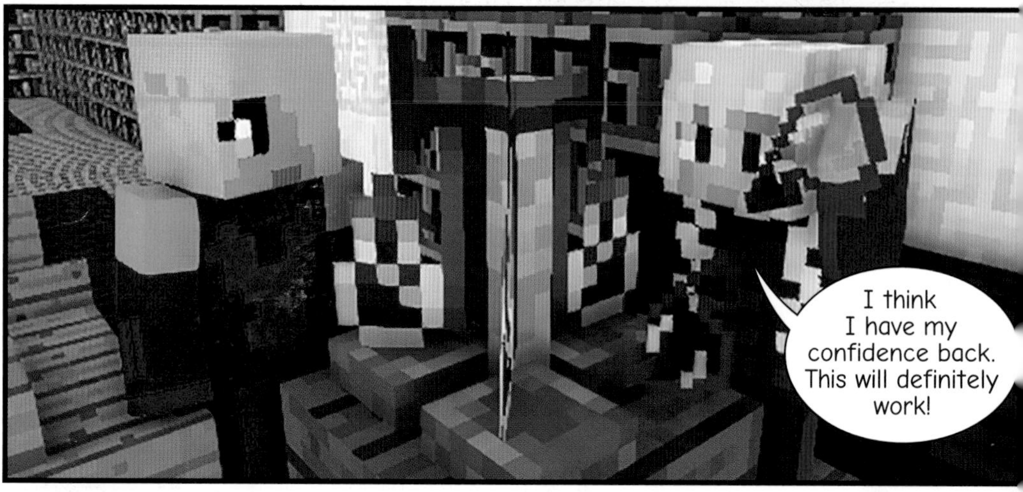
I think I have my confidence back. This will definitely work!

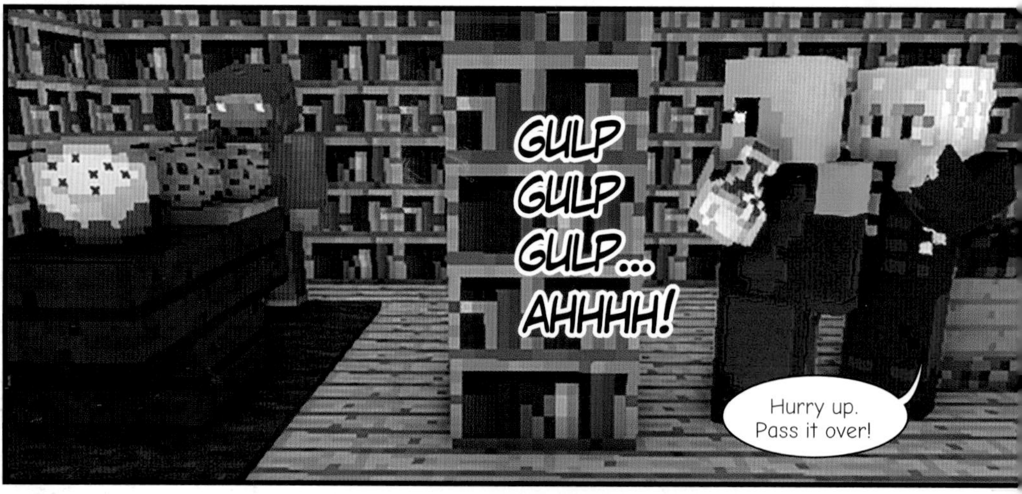
GULP
GULP
GULP...
AHHHH!
Hurry up. Pass it over!

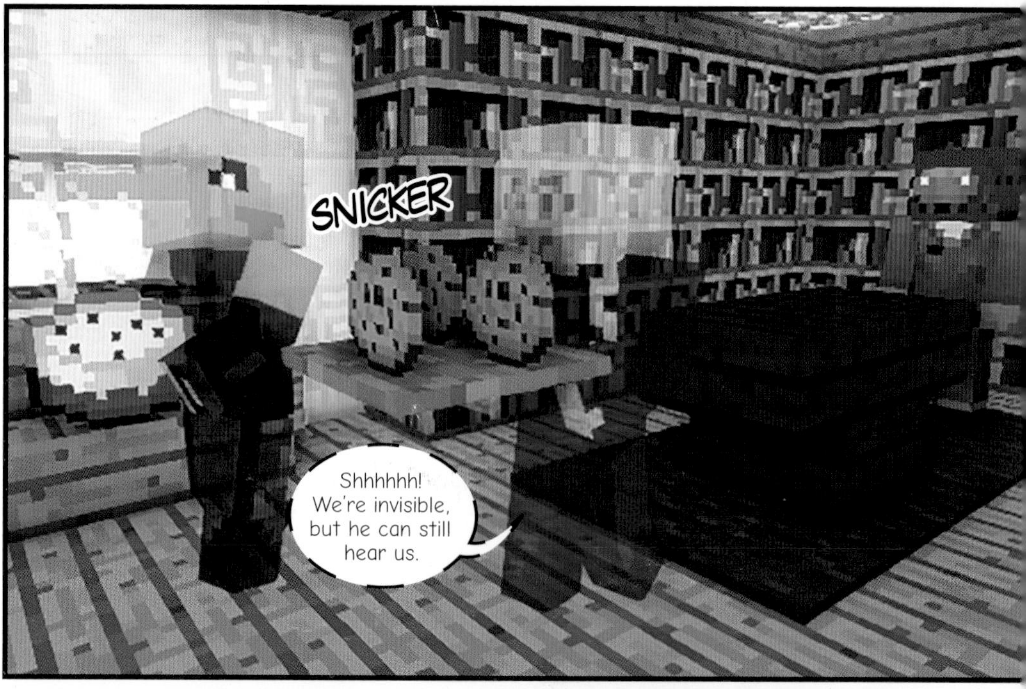
SNICKER
Shhhhhh! We're invisible, but he can still hear us.

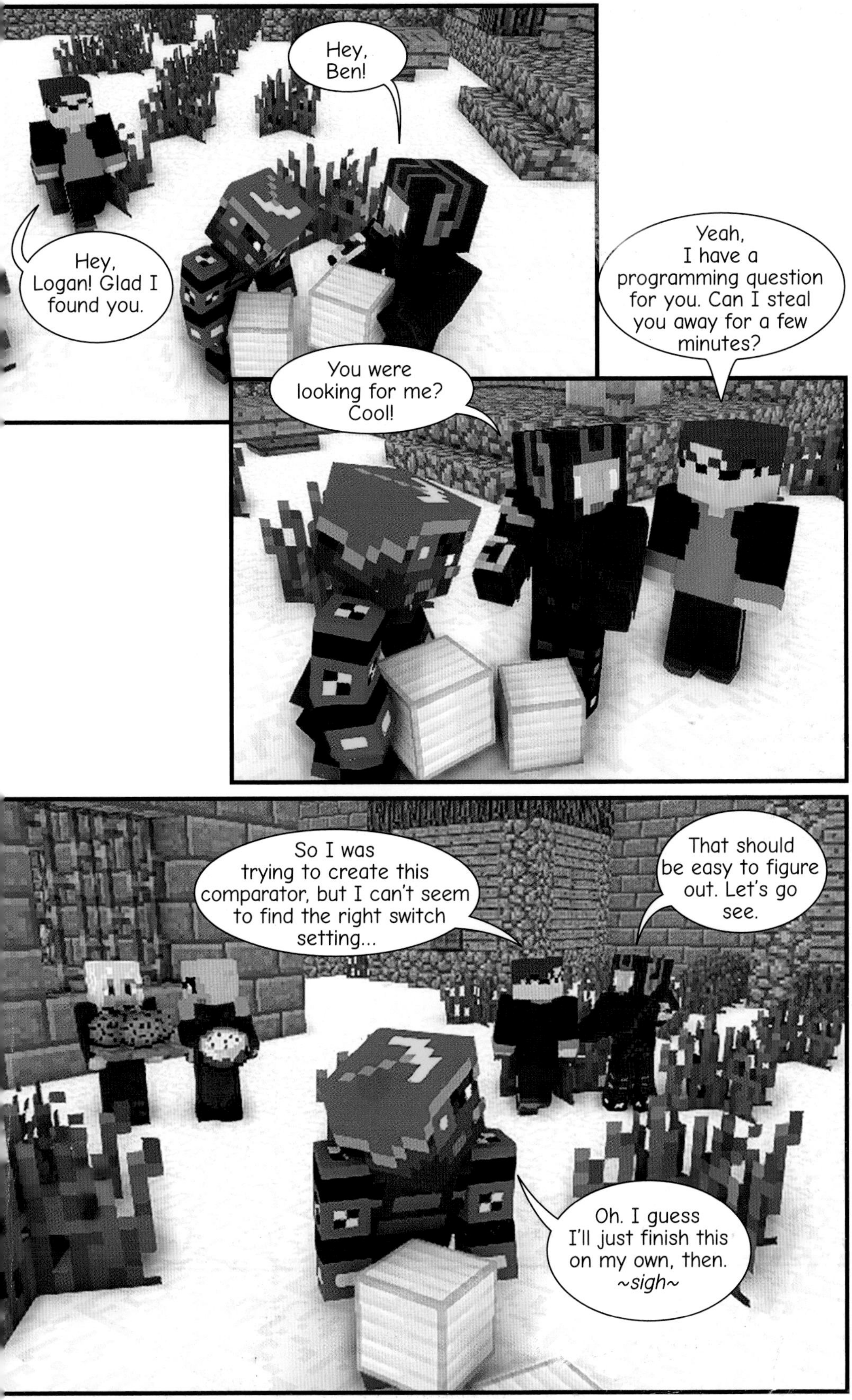
Hey, Ben!
Hey, Logan! Glad I found you.
You were looking for me? Cool!
Yeah, I have a programming question for you. Can I steal you away for a few minutes?
So I was trying to create this comparator, but I can't seem to find the right switch setting...
That should be easy to figure out. Let's go see.
Oh. I guess I'll just finish this on my own, then. *~sigh~*

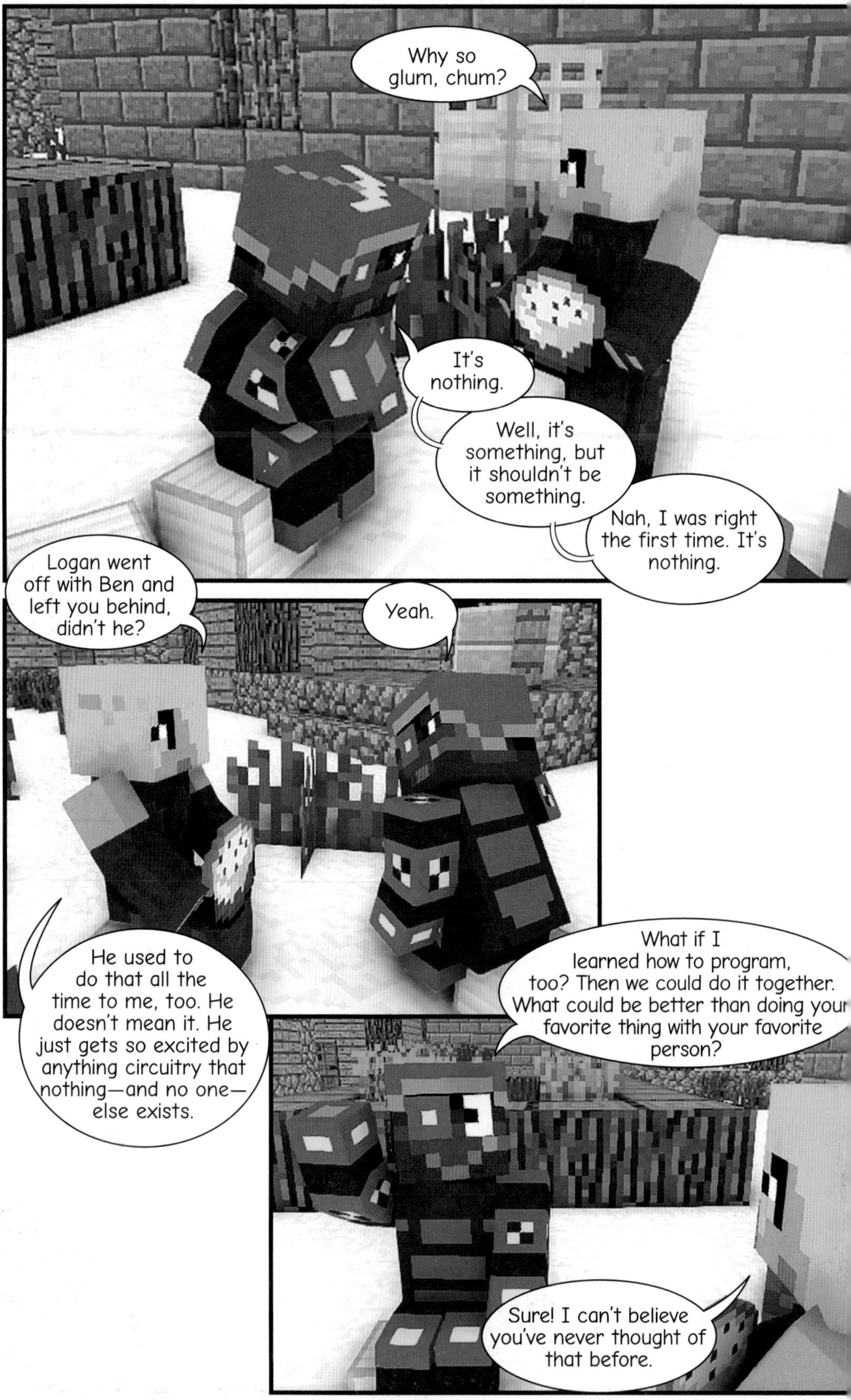
Why so glum, chum?
It's nothing.
Well, it's something, but it shouldn't be something.
Nah, I was right the first time. It's nothing.
Logan went off with Ben and left you behind, didn't he?
Yeah.
He used to do that all the time to me, too. He doesn't mean it. He just gets so excited by anything circuitry that nothing—and no one—else exists.
What if I learned how to program, too? Then we could do it together. What could be better than doing your favorite thing with your favorite person?
Sure! I can't believe you've never thought of that before.

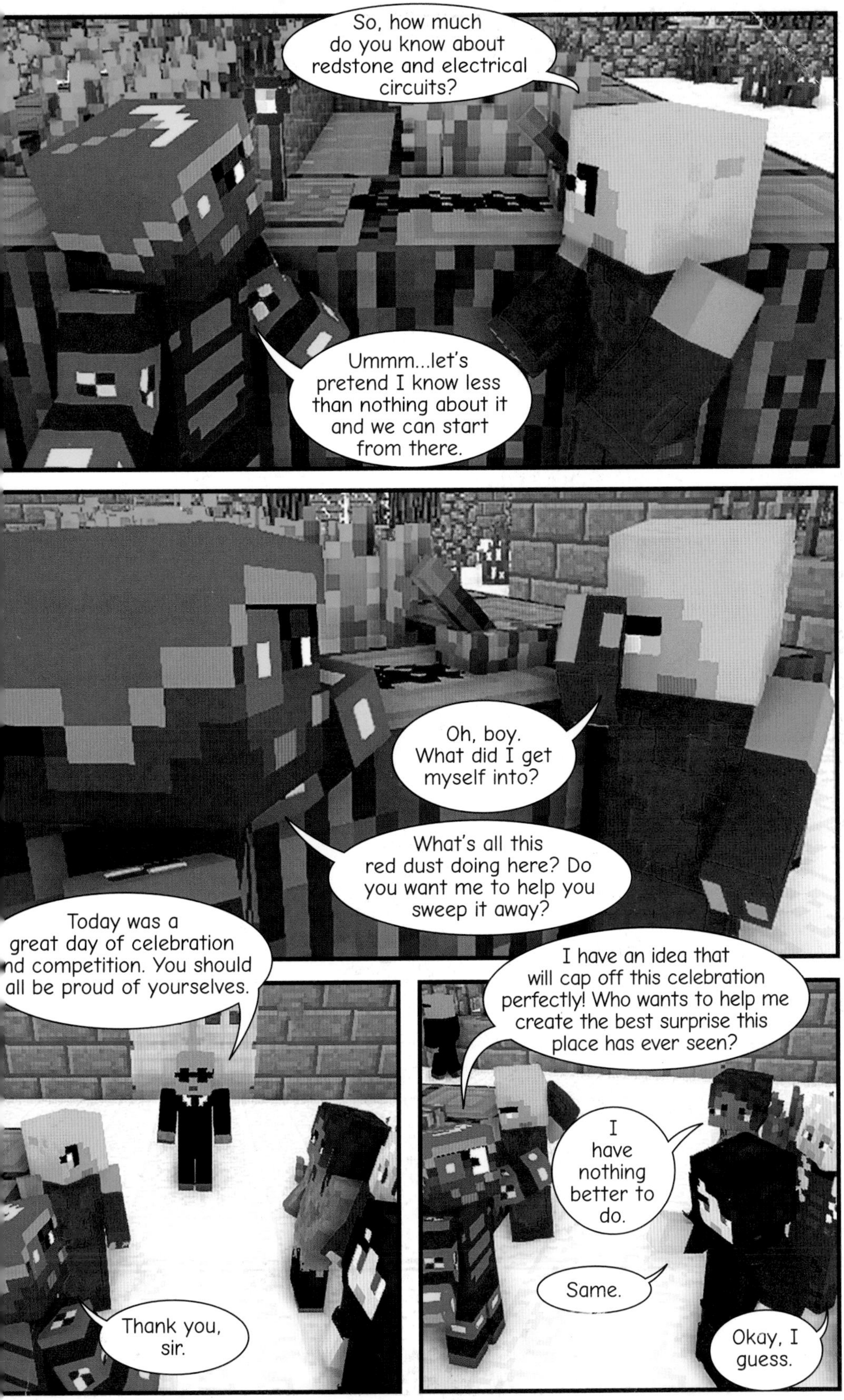
So, how much do you know about redstone and electrical circuits?
Ummm...let's pretend I know less than nothing about it and we can start from there.
Oh, boy. What did I get myself into?
What's all this red dust doing here? Do you want me to help you sweep it away?
Today was a great day of celebration nd competition. You should all be proud of yourselves.
Thank you, sir.
I have an idea that will cap off this celebration perfectly! Who wants to help me create the best surprise this place has ever seen?
I have nothing better to do.
Same.
Okay, I guess.

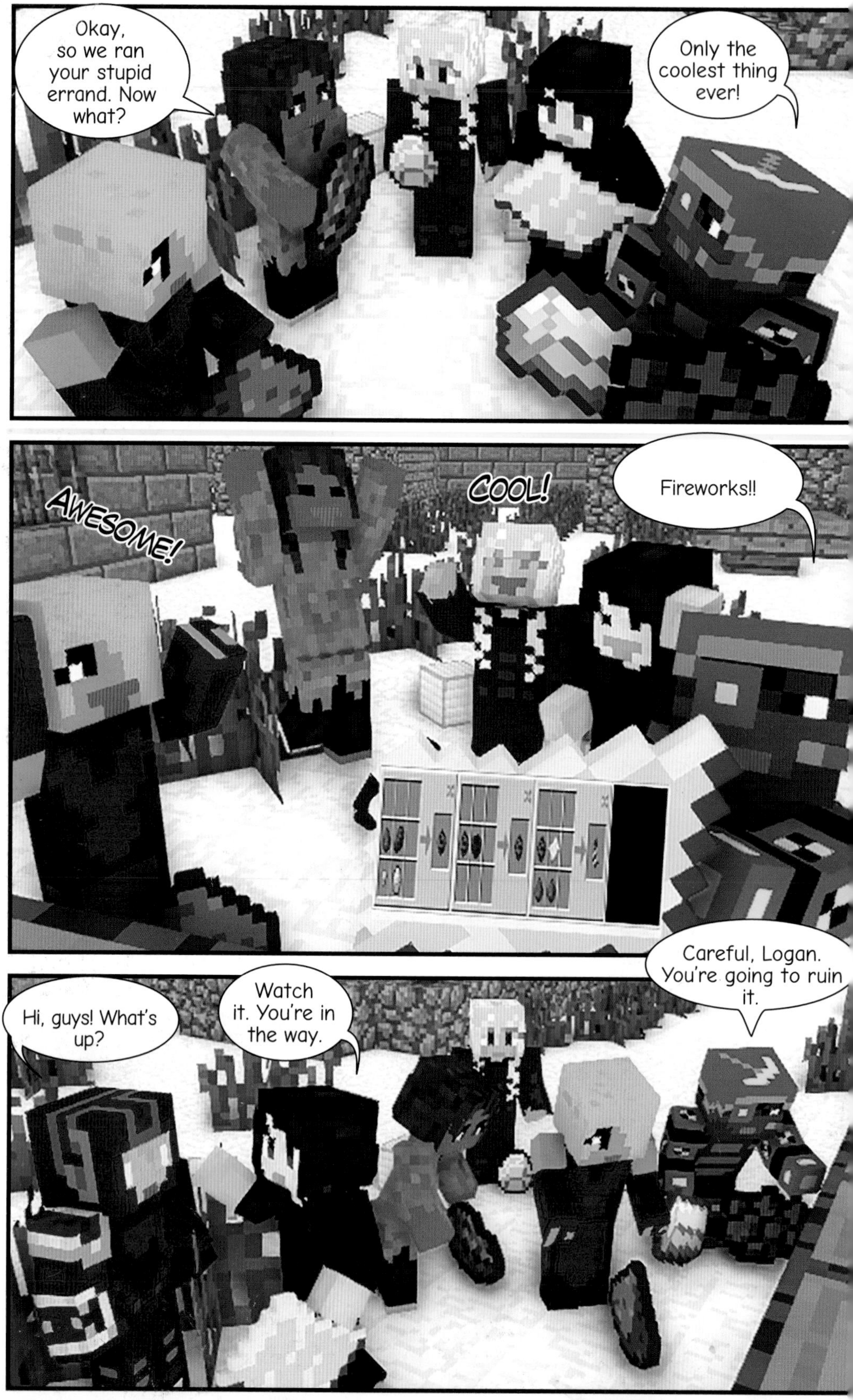

Okay, so we ran your stupid errand. Now what?
Only the coolest thing ever!
AWESOME!
COOL!
Fireworks!!
Hi, guys! What's up?
Watch it. You're in the way.
Careful, Logan. You're going to ruin it.

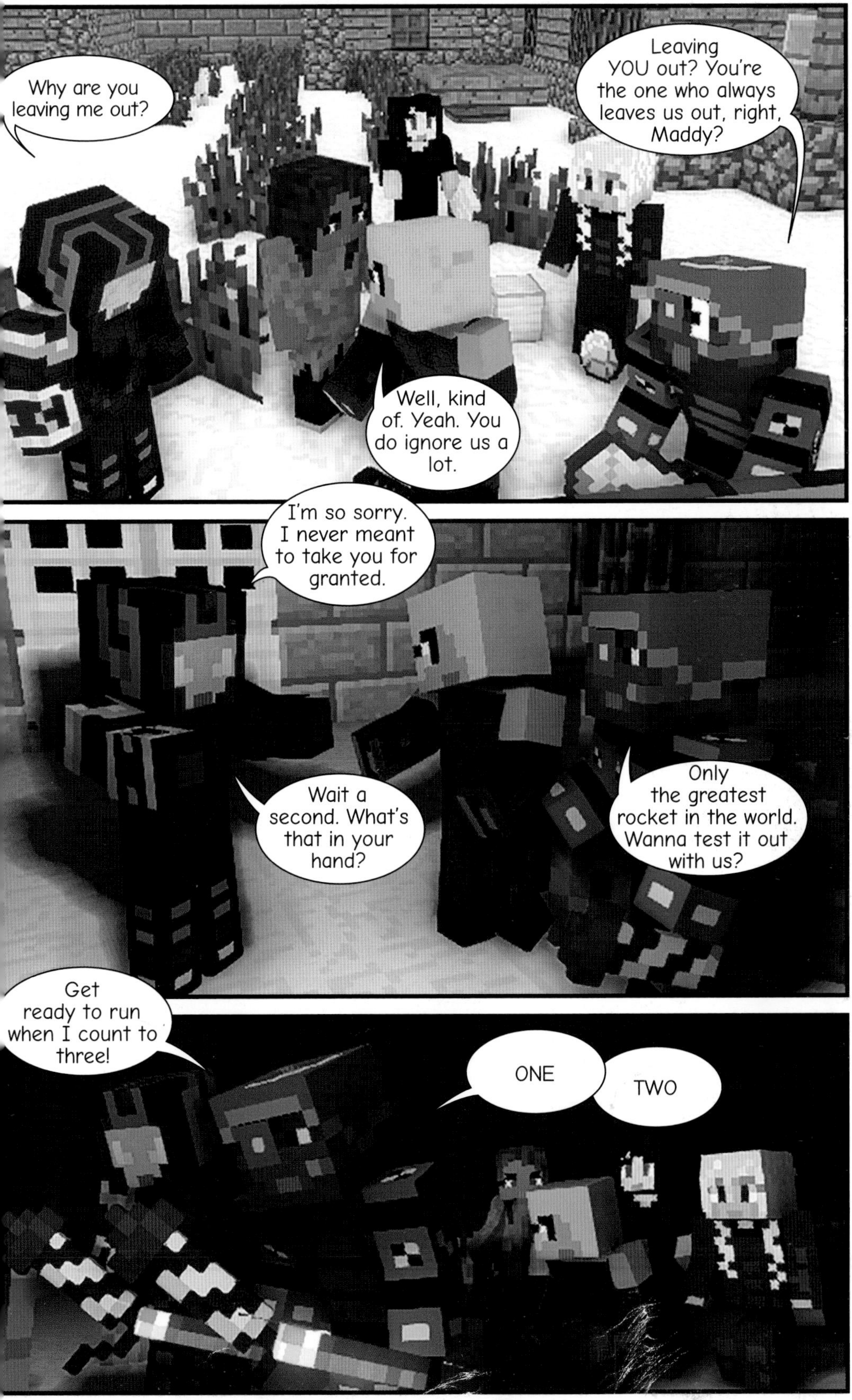
Why are you leaving me out?
Leaving YOU out? You're the one who always leaves us out, right, Maddy?
Well, kind of. Yeah. You do ignore us a lot.
I'm so sorry. I never meant to take you for granted.
Wait a second. What's that in your hand?
Only the greatest rocket in the world. Wanna test it out with us?
Get ready to run when I count to three!
ONE
TWO

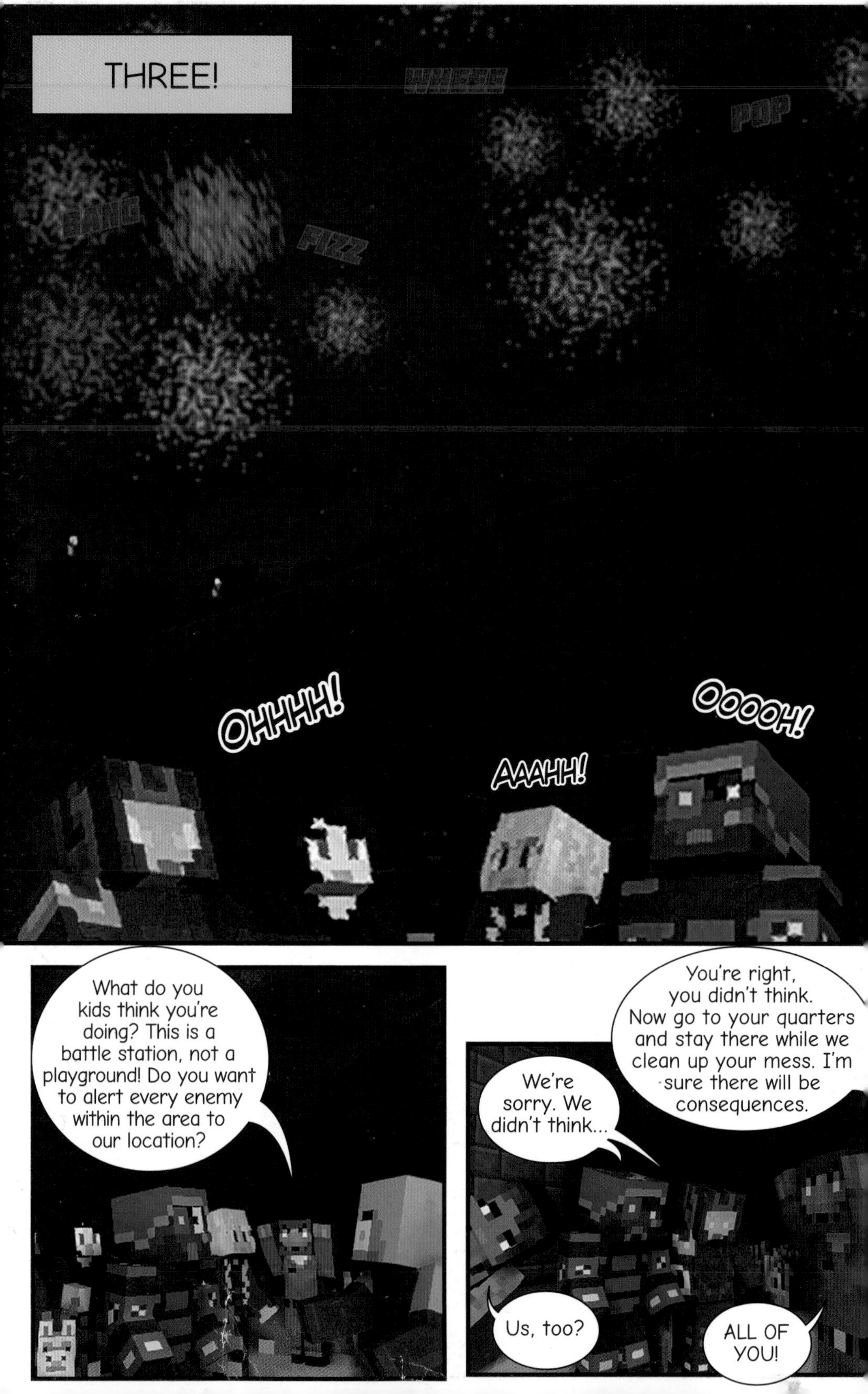
THREE!
POP
BANG
FIZZ
OHHHH!
AAAHH!
OOOOH!
What do you kids think you're doing? This is a battle station, not a playground! Do you want to alert every enemy within the area to our location?
We're sorry. We didn't think...
You're right, you didn't think. Now go to your quarters and stay there while we clean up your mess. I'm sure there will be consequences.
Us, too?
ALL OF YOU!

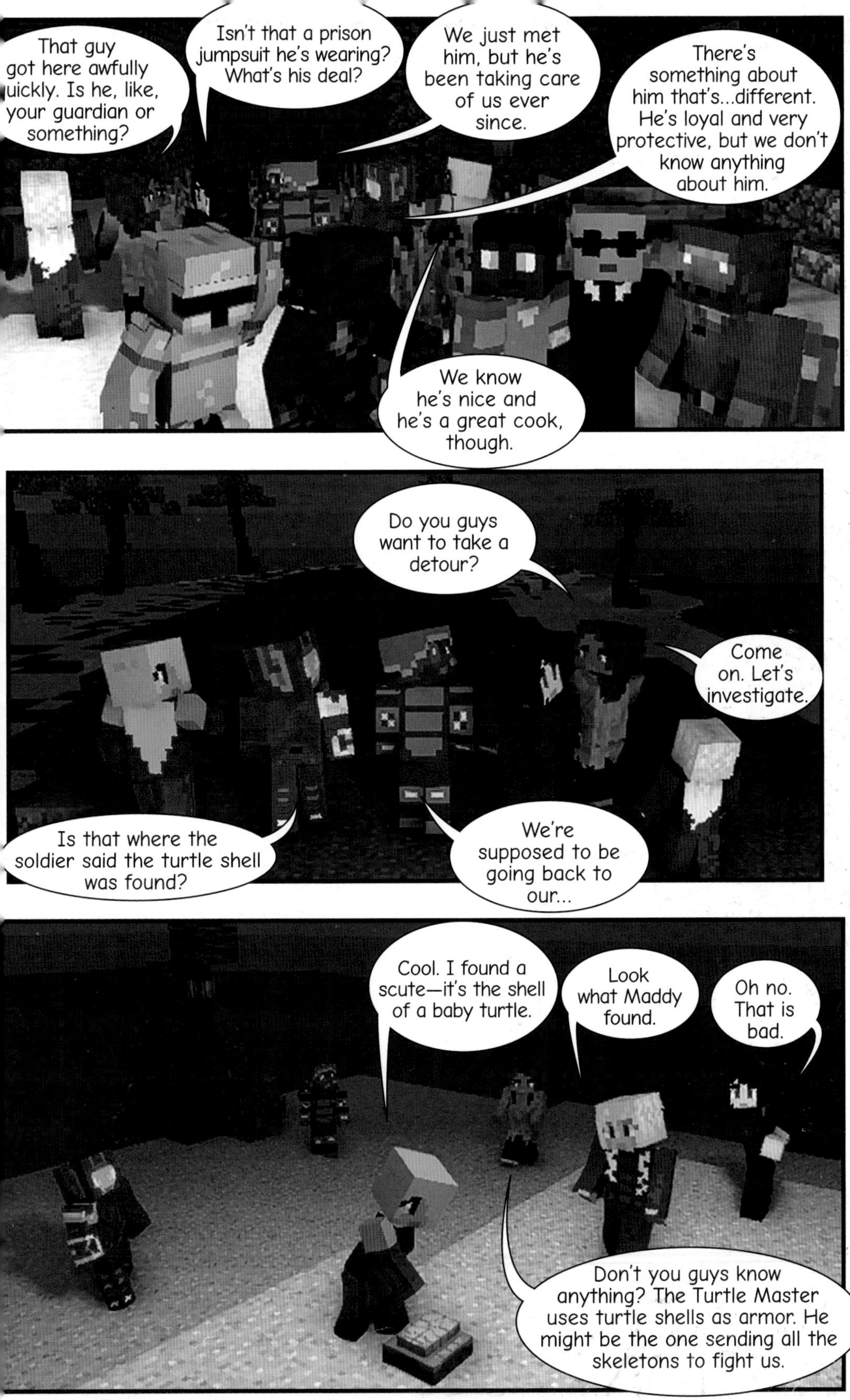

That guy got here awfully uickly. Is he, like, your guardian or something?
Isn't that a prison jumpsuit he's wearing? What's his deal?
We just met him, but he's been taking care of us ever since.
There's something about him that's...different. He's loyal and very protective, but we don't know anything about him.
We know he's nice and he's a great cook, though.
Do you guys want to take a detour?
Come on. Let's investigate.
Is that where the soldier said the turtle shell was found?
We're supposed to be going back to our...
Cool. I found a scute—it's the shell of a baby turtle.
Look what Maddy found.
Oh no. That is bad.
Don't you guys know anything? The Turtle Master uses turtle shells as armor. He might be the one sending all the skeletons to fight us.

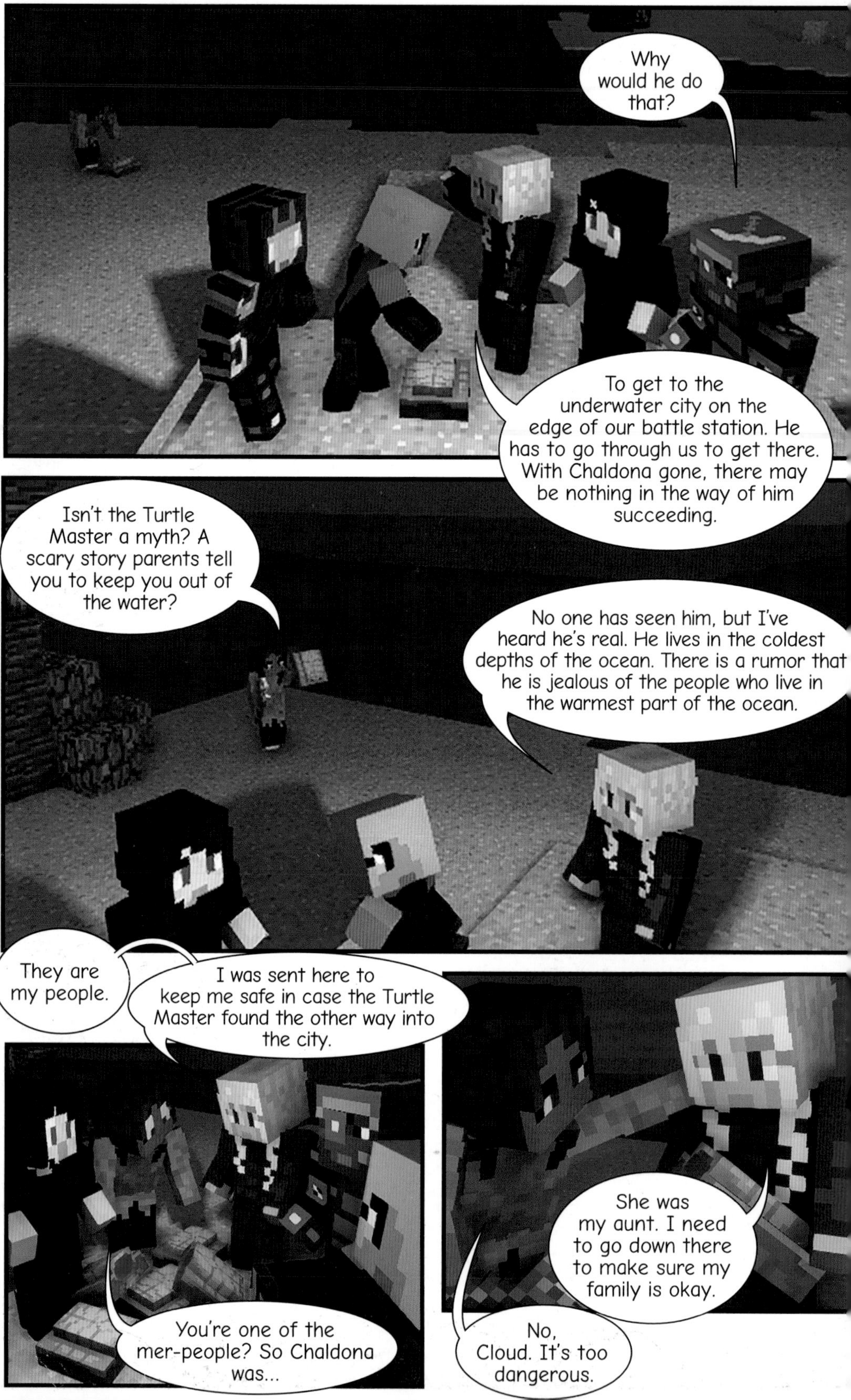
Why would he do that?
To get to the underwater city on the edge of our battle station. He has to go through us to get there. With Chaldona gone, there may be nothing in the way of him succeeding.
Isn't the Turtle Master a myth? A scary story parents tell you to keep you out of the water?
No one has seen him, but I've heard he's real. He lives in the coldest depths of the ocean. There is a rumor that he is jealous of the people who live in the warmest part of the ocean.
They are my people.
I was sent here to keep me safe in case the Turtle Master found the other way into the city.
You're one of the mer-people? So Chaldona was...
She was my aunt. I need to go down there to make sure my family is okay.
No, Cloud. It's too dangerous.

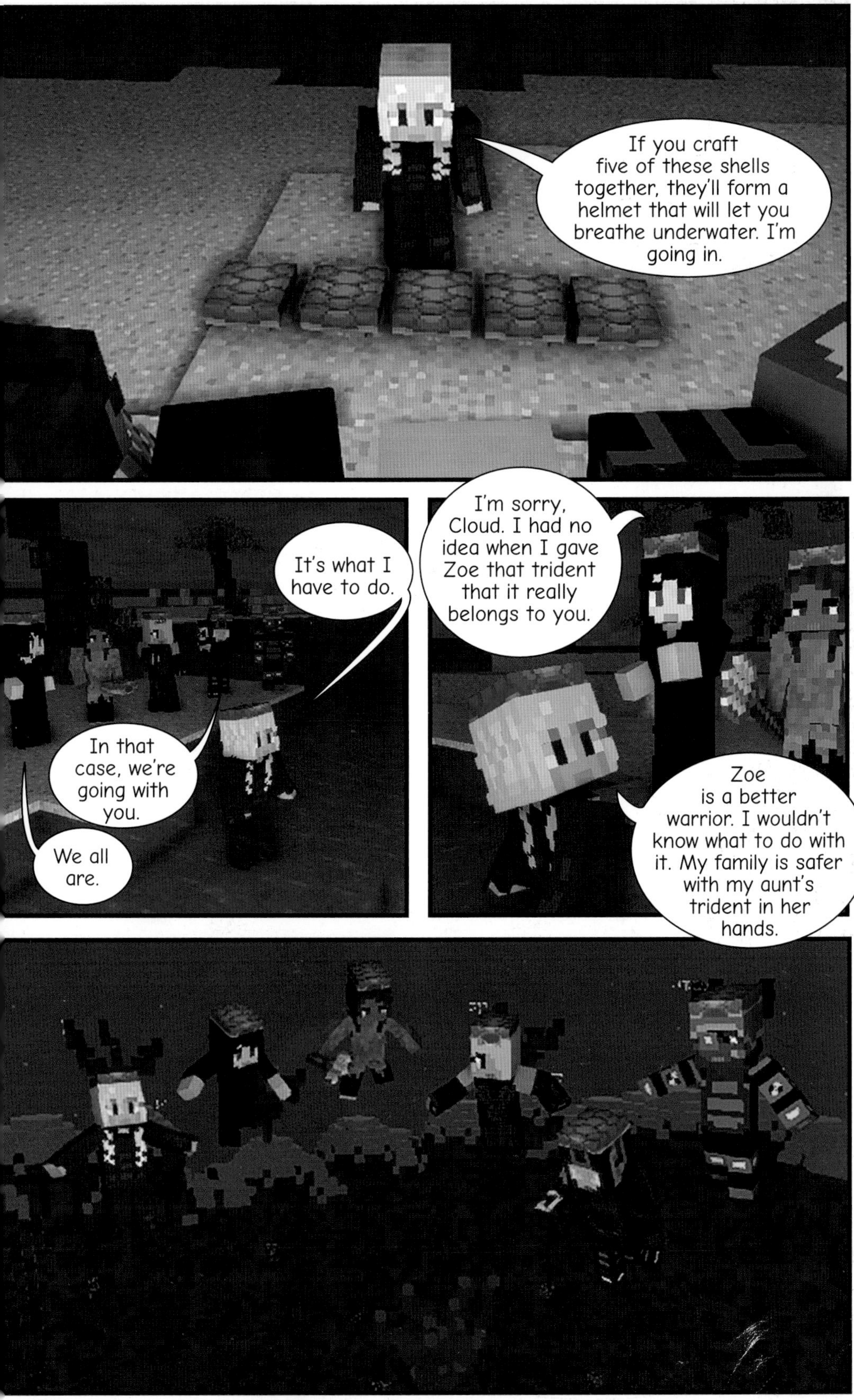

If you craft five of these shells together, they'll form a helmet that will let you breathe underwater. I'm going in.
It's what I have to do.
In that case, we're going with you.
We all are.
I'm sorry, Cloud. I had no idea when I gave Zoe that trident that it really belongs to you.
Zoe is a better warrior. I wouldn't know what to do with it. My family is safer with my aunt's trident in her hands.

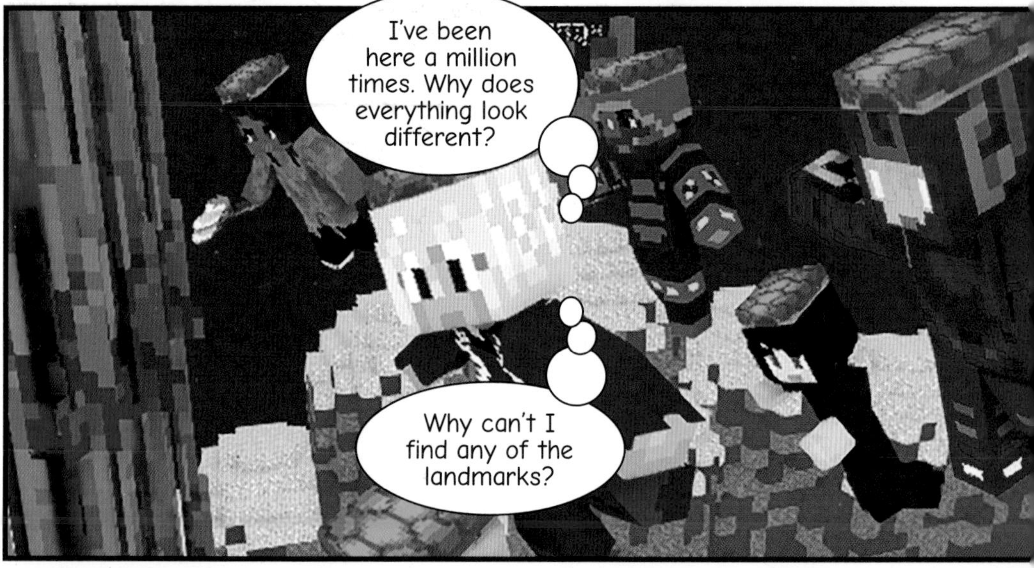
I've been here a million times. Why does everything look different?
Why can't I find any of the landmarks?

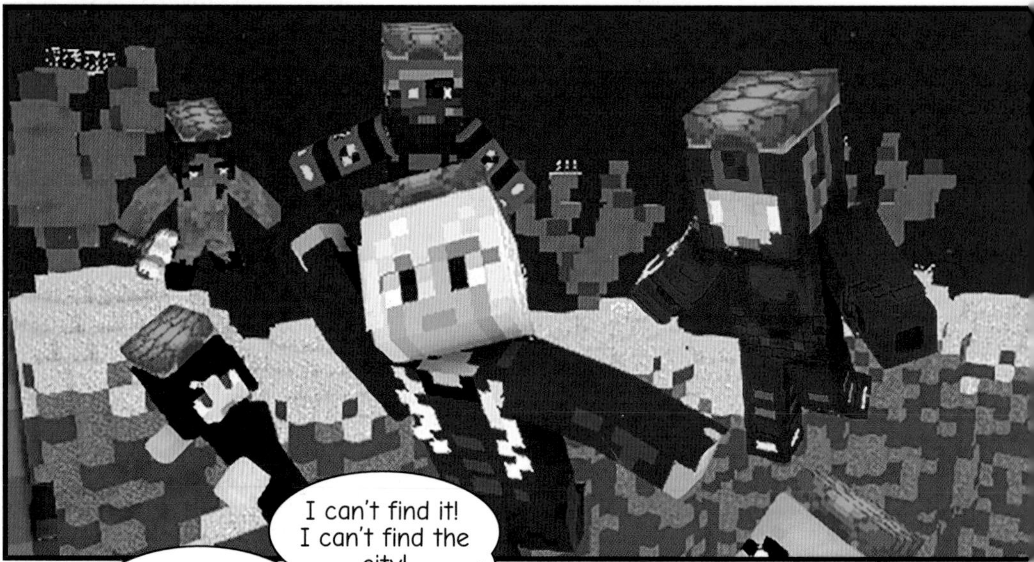
I can't find it! I can't find the city!

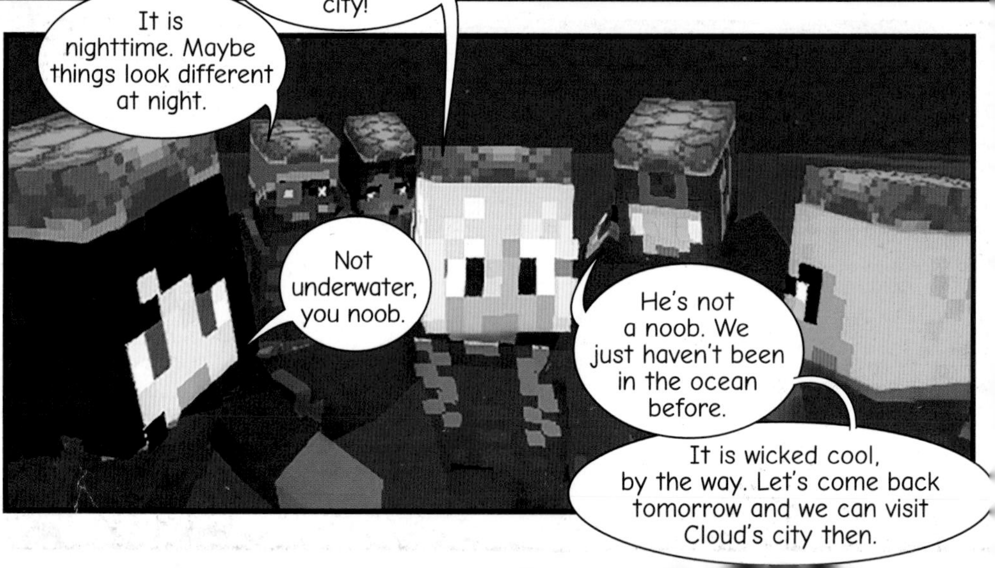
It is nighttime. Maybe things look different at night.
Not underwater, you noob.
He's not a noob. We just haven't been in the ocean before.
It is wicked cool, by the way. Let's come back tomorrow and we can visit Cloud's city then.

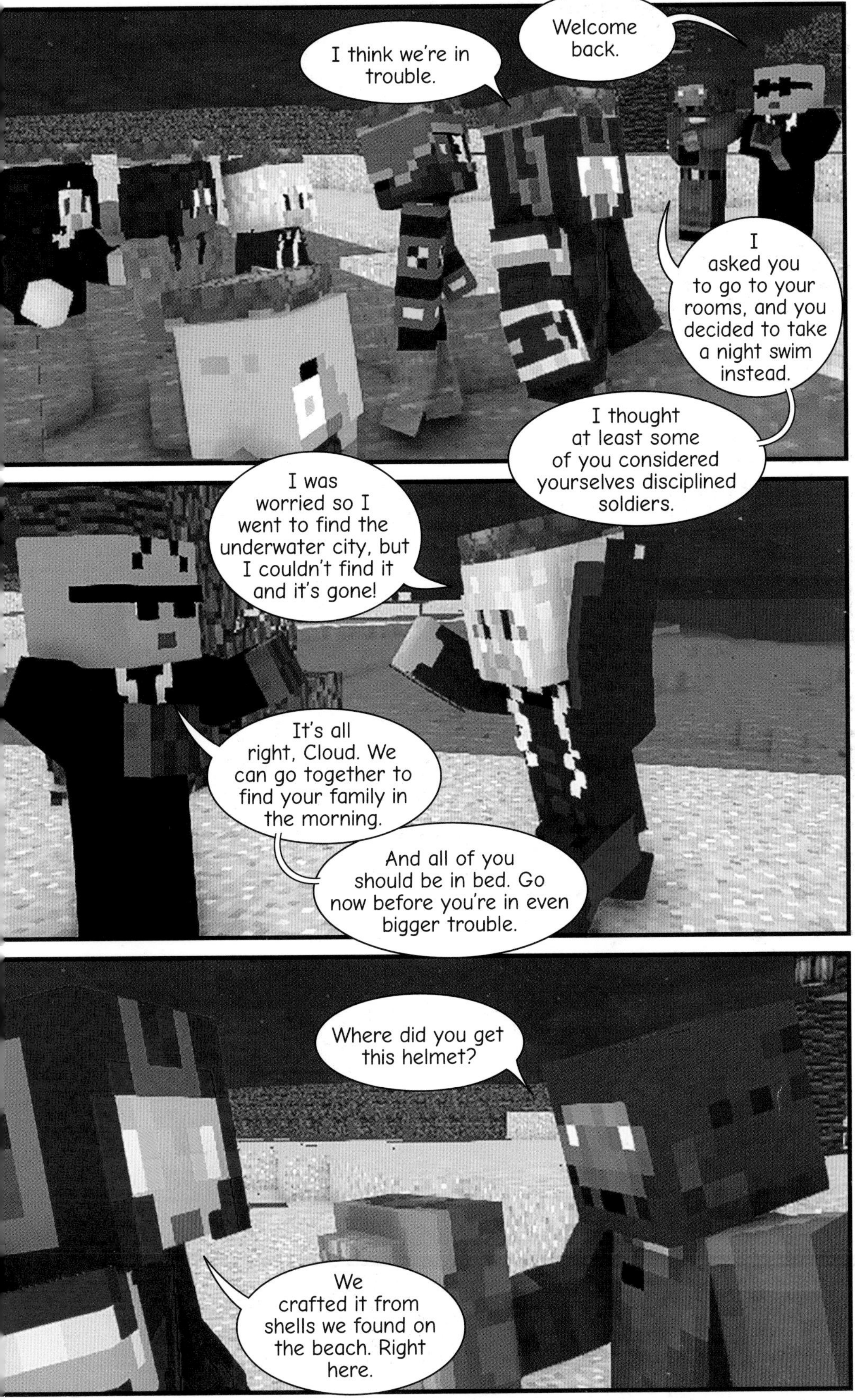
I think we're in trouble.
Welcome back.
I asked you to go to your rooms, and you decided to take a night swim instead.
I thought at least some of you considered yourselves disciplined soldiers.
I was worried so I went to find the underwater city, but I couldn't find it and it's gone!
It's all right, Cloud. We can go together to find your family in the morning.
And all of you should be in bed. Go now before you're in even bigger trouble.
Where did you get this helmet?
We crafted it from shells we found on the beach. Right here.

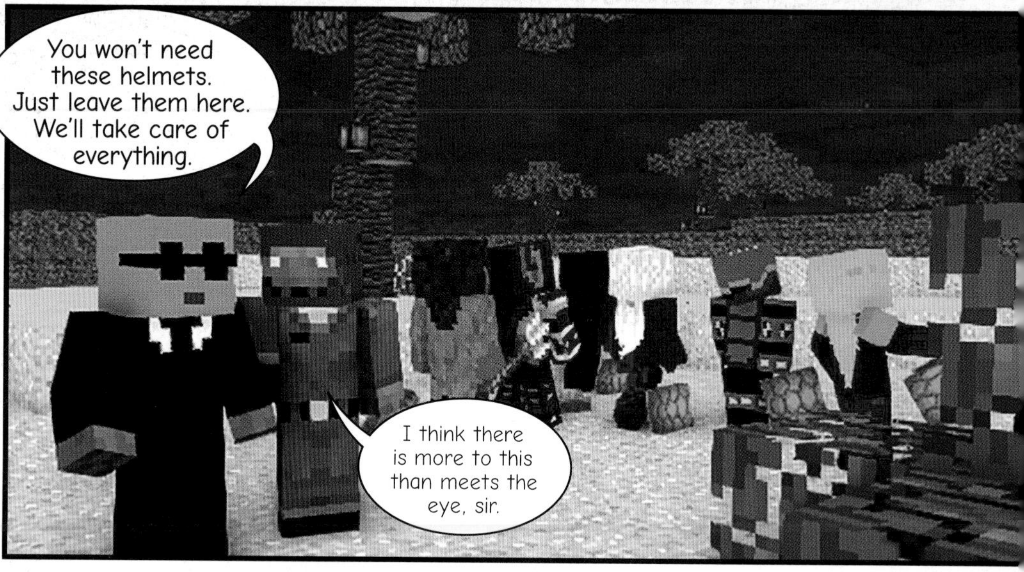
You won't need these helmets. Just leave them here. We'll take care of everything.
I think there is more to this than meets the eye, sir.

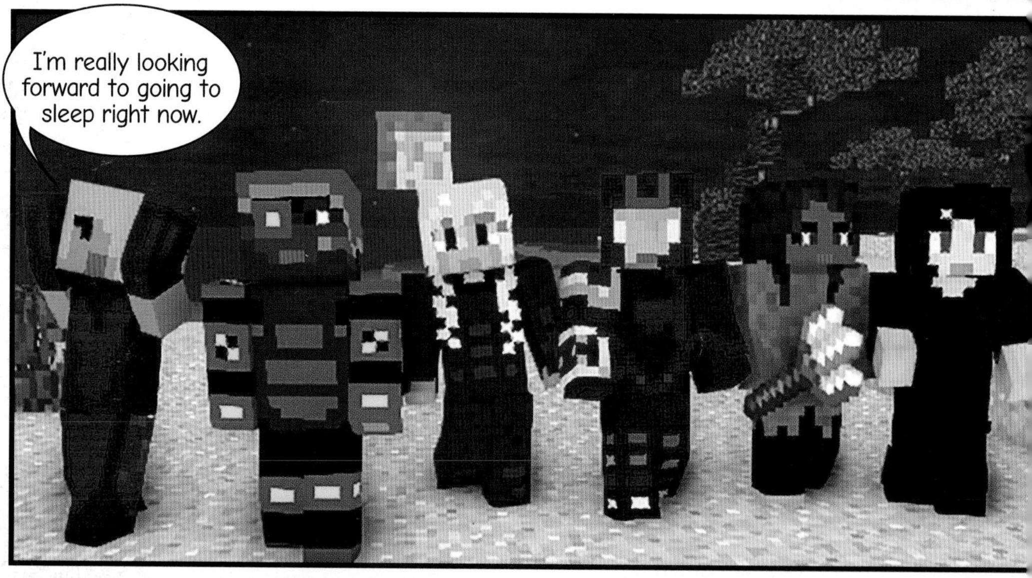
I'm really looking forward to going to sleep right now.

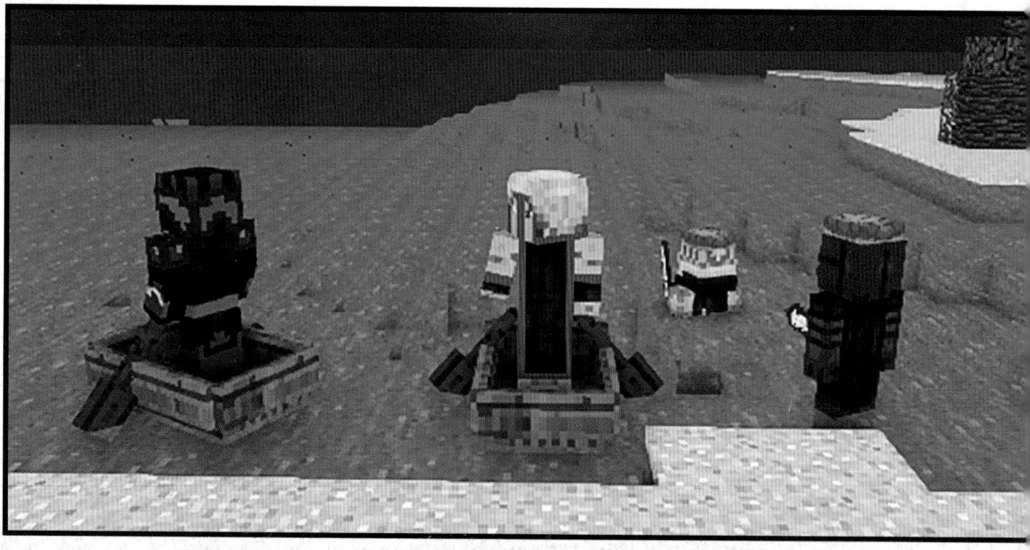

CHAPTER 4

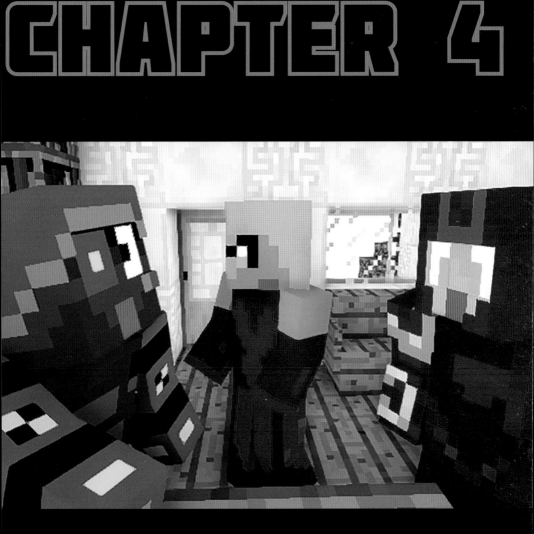

ADVENTURE CALLS

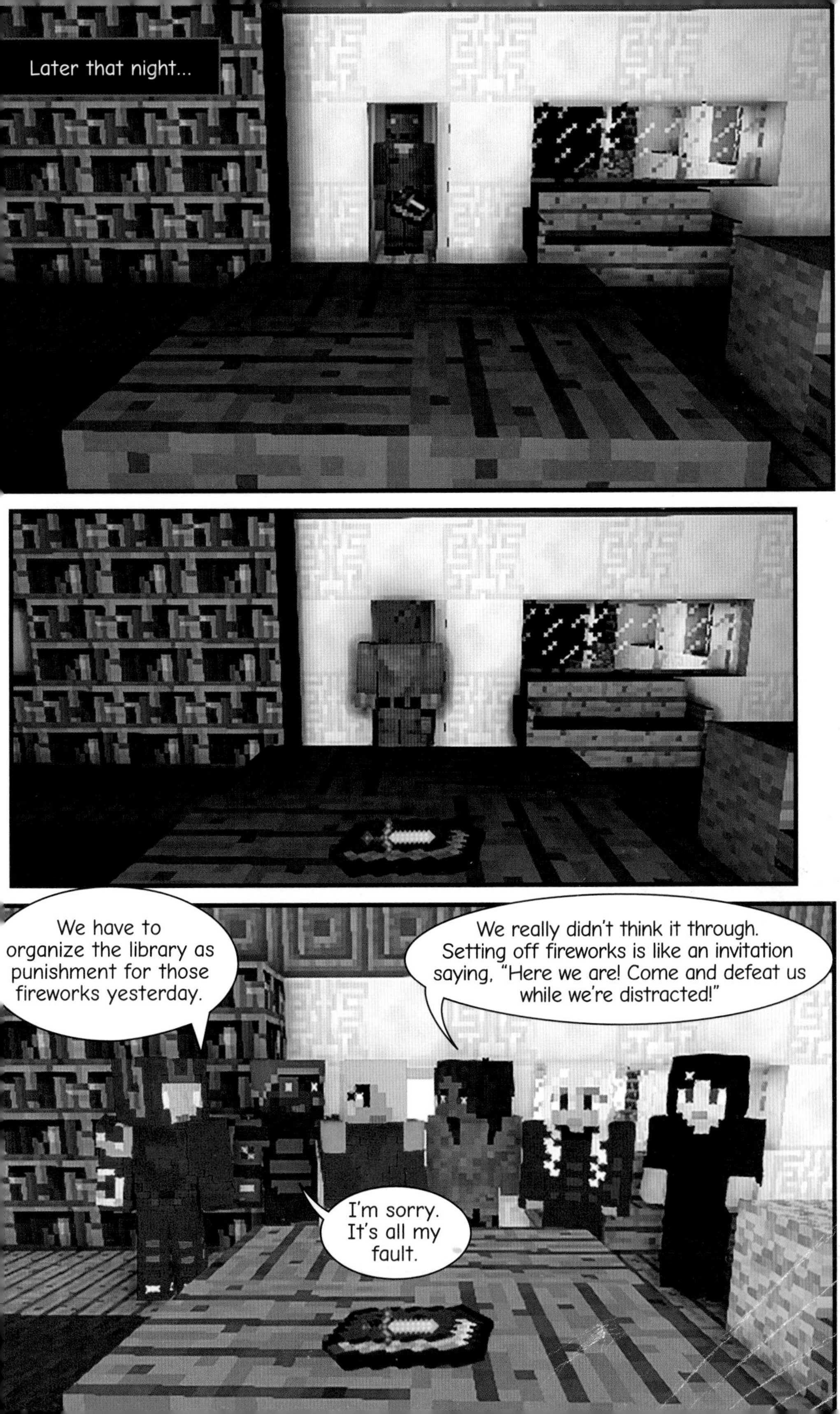
Later that night...
We have to organize the library as punishment for those fireworks yesterday.
We really didn't think it through. Setting off fireworks is like an invitation saying, "Here we are! Come and defeat us while we're distracted!"
I'm sorry. It's all my fault.

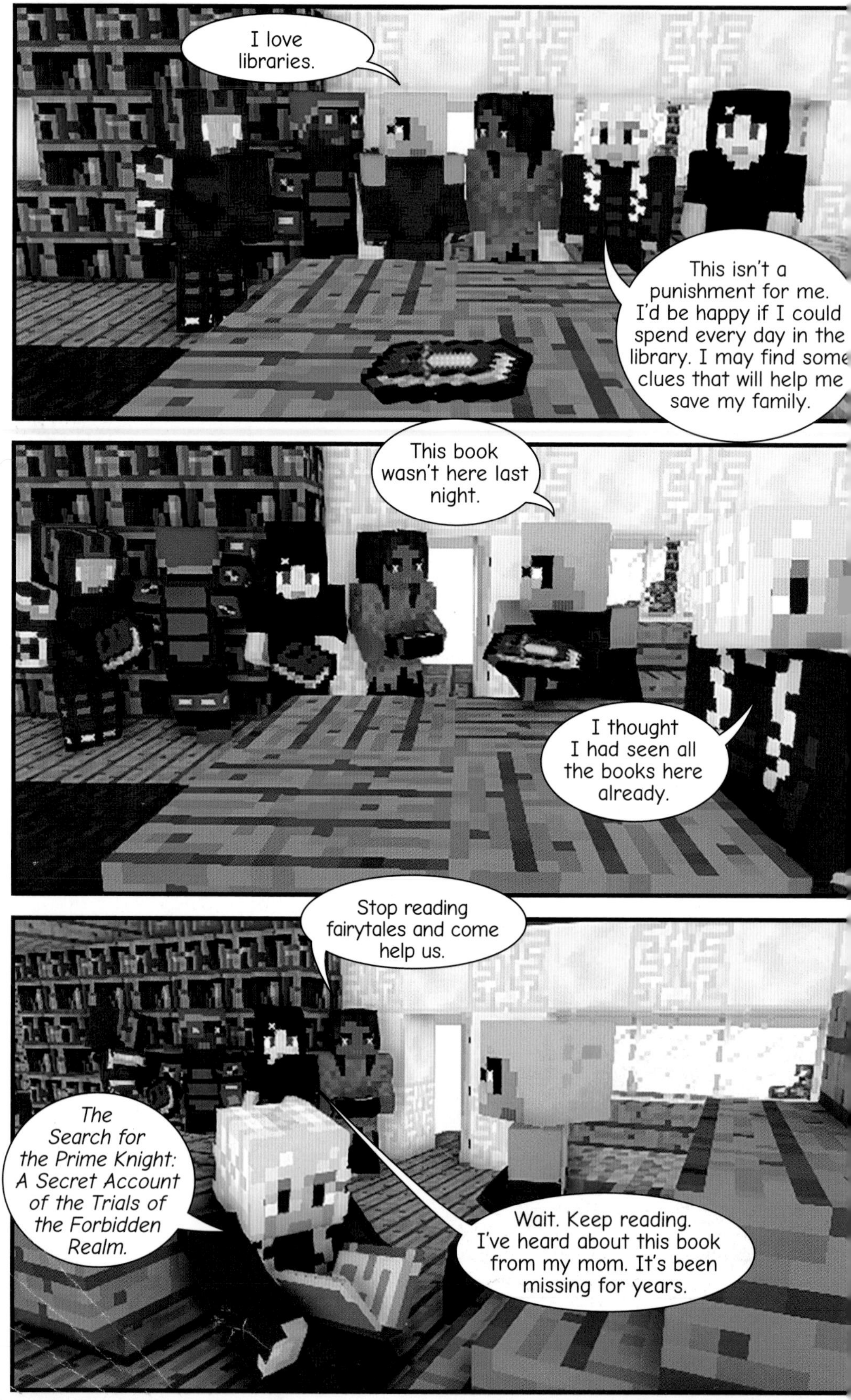
I love libraries.
This isn't a punishment for me. I'd be happy if I could spend every day in the library. I may find some clues that will help me save my family.
This book wasn't here last night.
I thought I had seen all the books here already.
Stop reading fairytales and come help us.
The Search for the Prime Knight: A Secret Account of the Trials of the Forbidden Realm.
Wait. Keep reading. I've heard about this book from my mom. It's been missing for years.

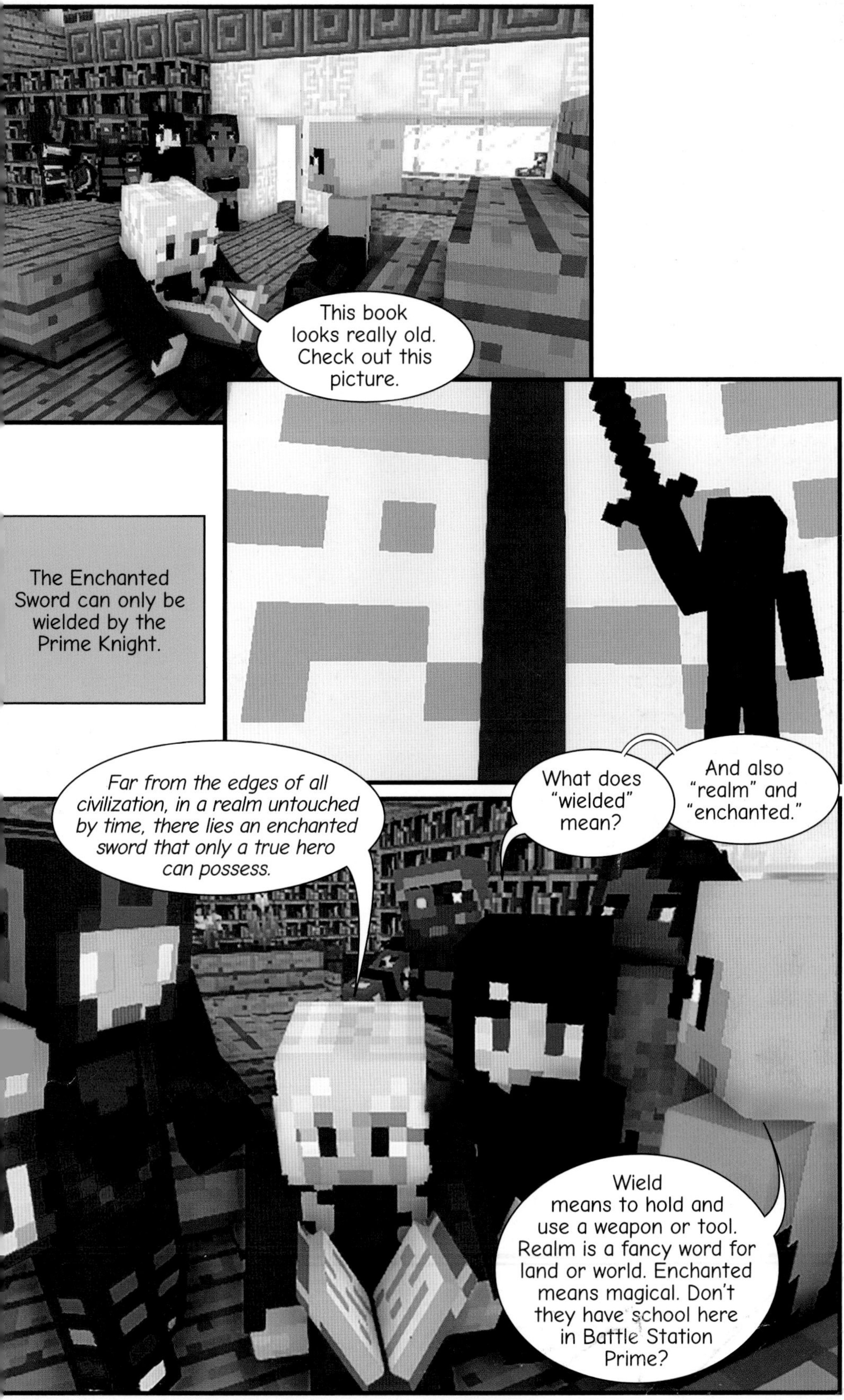
This book looks really old. Check out this picture.
The Enchanted Sword can only be wielded by the Prime Knight.
Far from the edges of all civilization, in a realm untouched by time, there lies an enchanted sword that only a true hero can possess.
What does "wielded" mean?
And also "realm" and "enchanted."
Wield means to hold and use a weapon or tool. Realm is a fancy word for land or world. Enchanted means magical. Don't they have school here in Battle Station Prime?

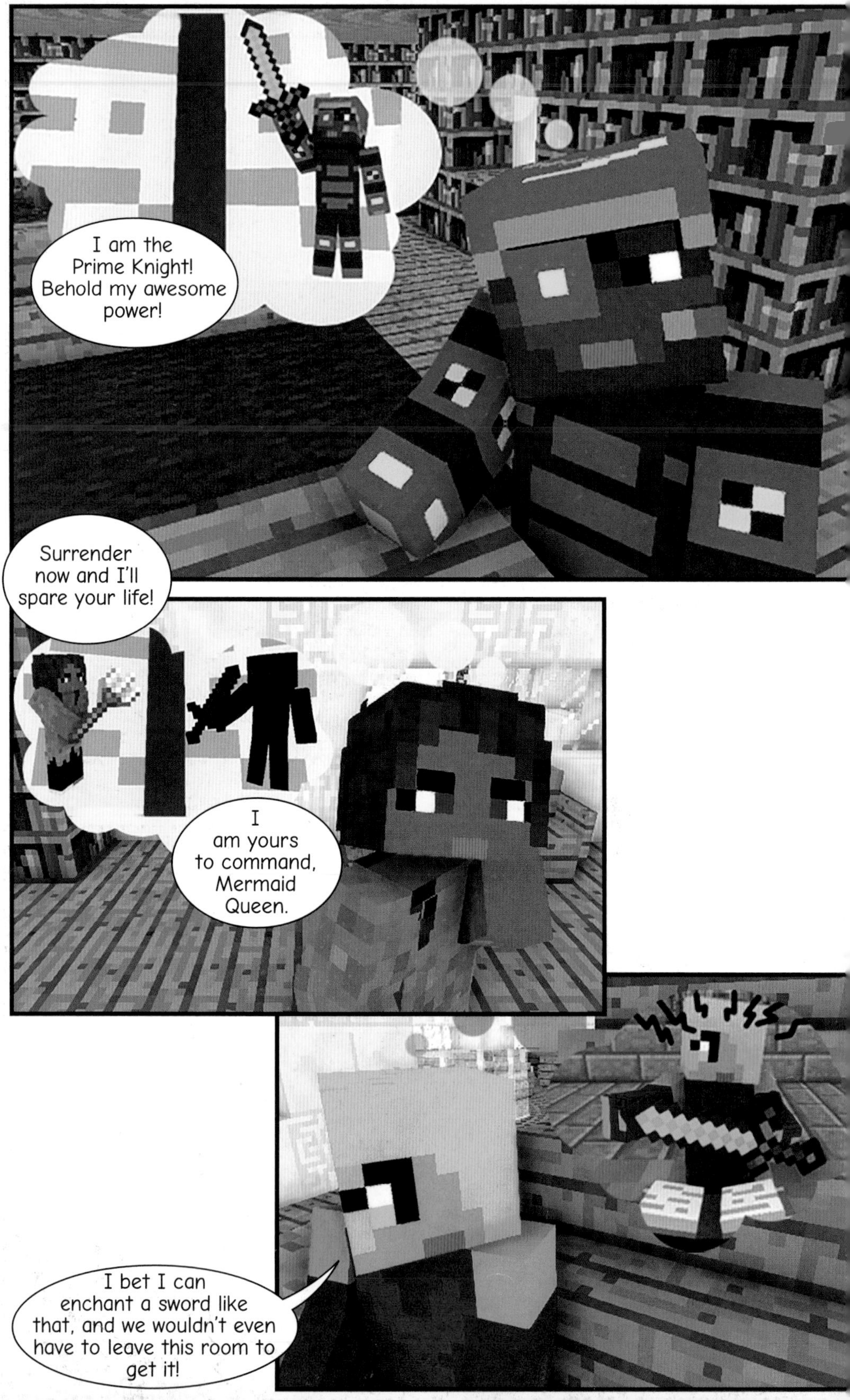

I am the Prime Knight! Behold my awesome power!
Surrender now and I'll spare your life!
I am yours to command, Mermaid Queen.
I bet I can enchant a sword like that, and we wouldn't even have to leave this room to get it!

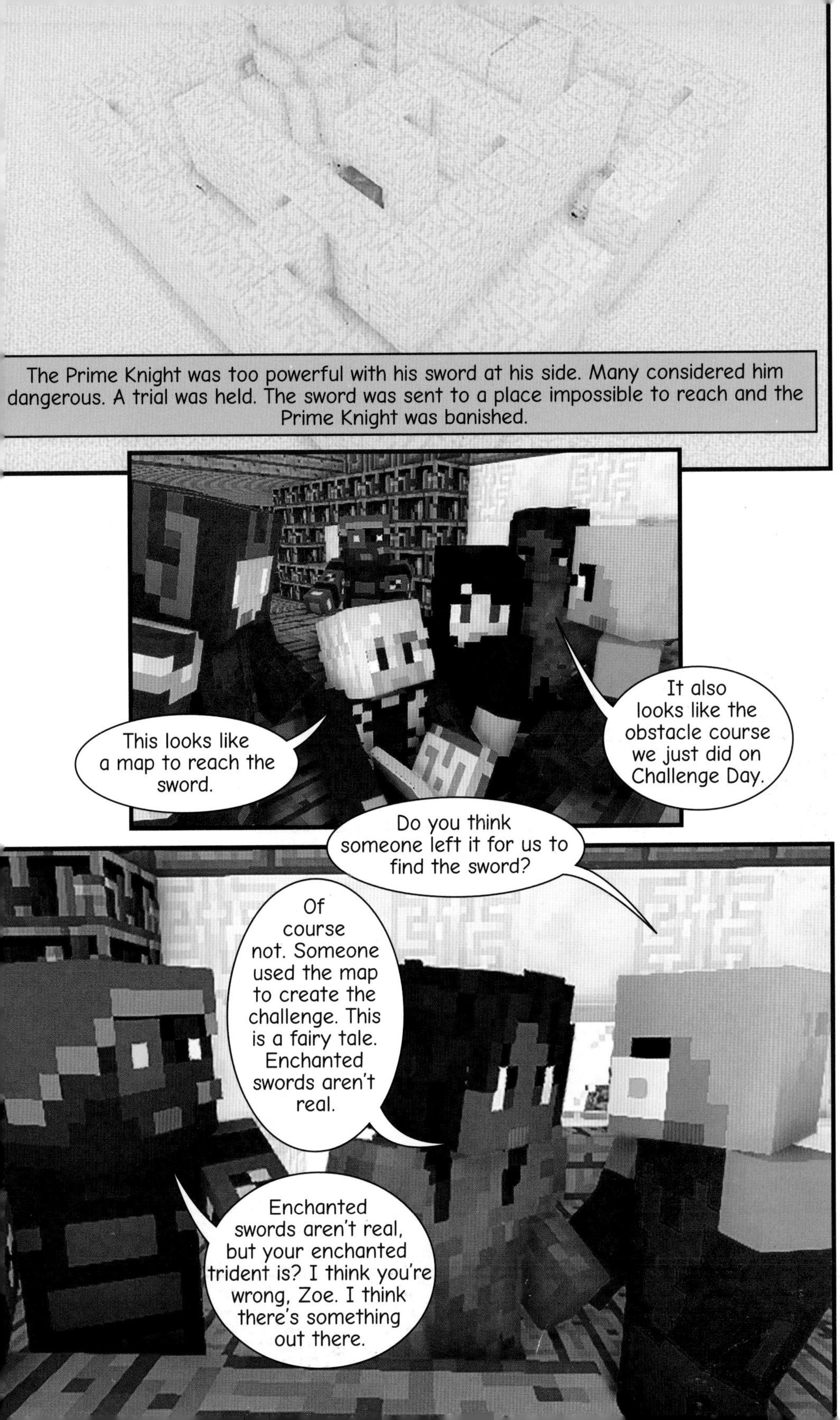

The Prime Knight was too powerful with his sword at his side. Many considered him dangerous. A trial was held. The sword was sent to a place impossible to reach and the Prime Knight was banished.
This looks like a map to reach the sword.
It also looks like the obstacle course we just did on Challenge Day.
Do you think someone left it for us to find the sword?
Of course not. Someone used the map to create the challenge. This is a fairy tale. Enchanted swords aren't real.
Enchanted swords aren't real, but your enchanted trident is? I think you're wrong, Zoe. I think there's something out there.

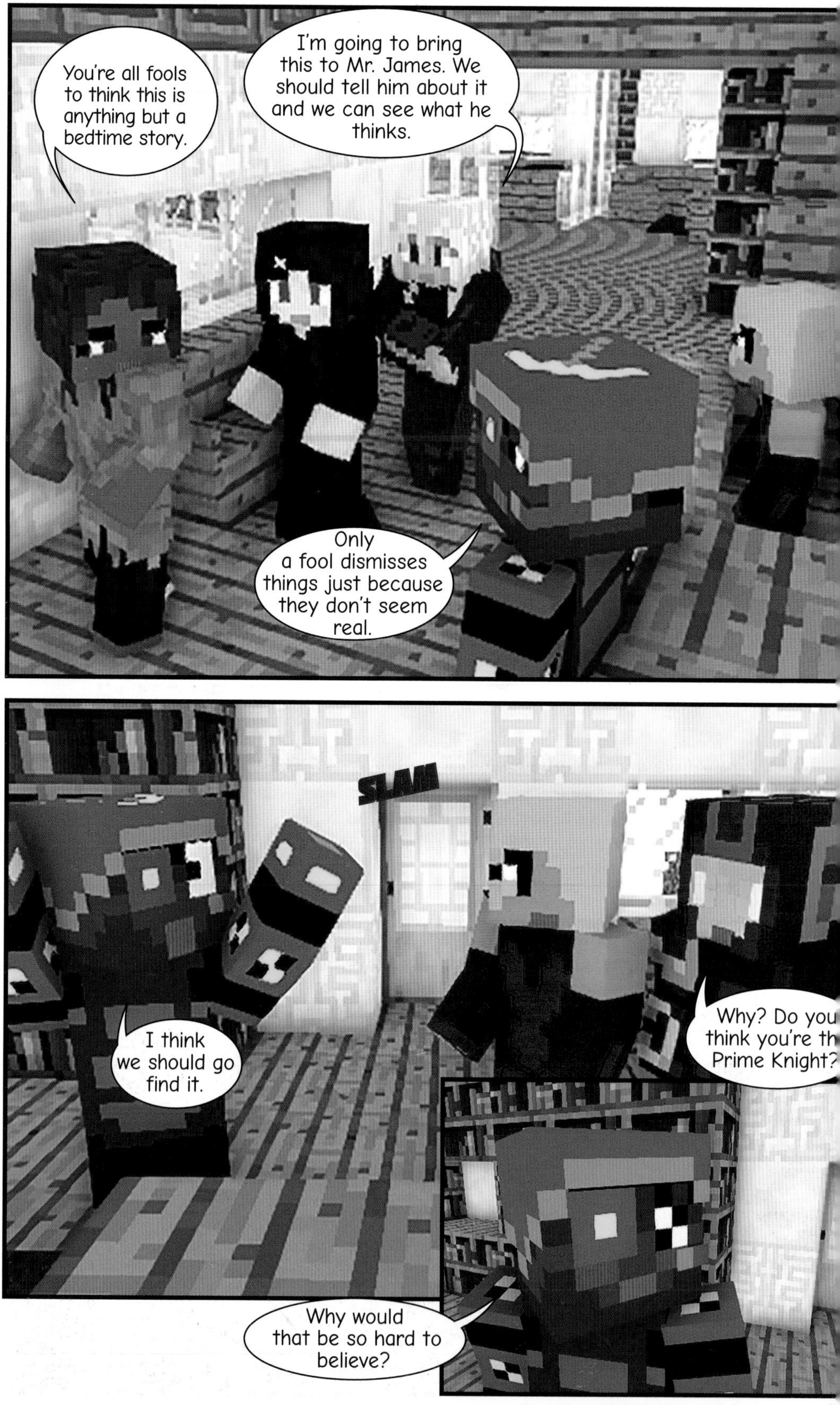

You're all fools to think this is anything but a bedtime story.
I'm going to bring this to Mr. James. We should tell him about it and we can see what he thinks.
Only a fool dismisses things just because they don't seem real.
SLAM
I think we should go find it.
Why? Do you think you're th Prime Knight?
Why would that be so hard to believe?

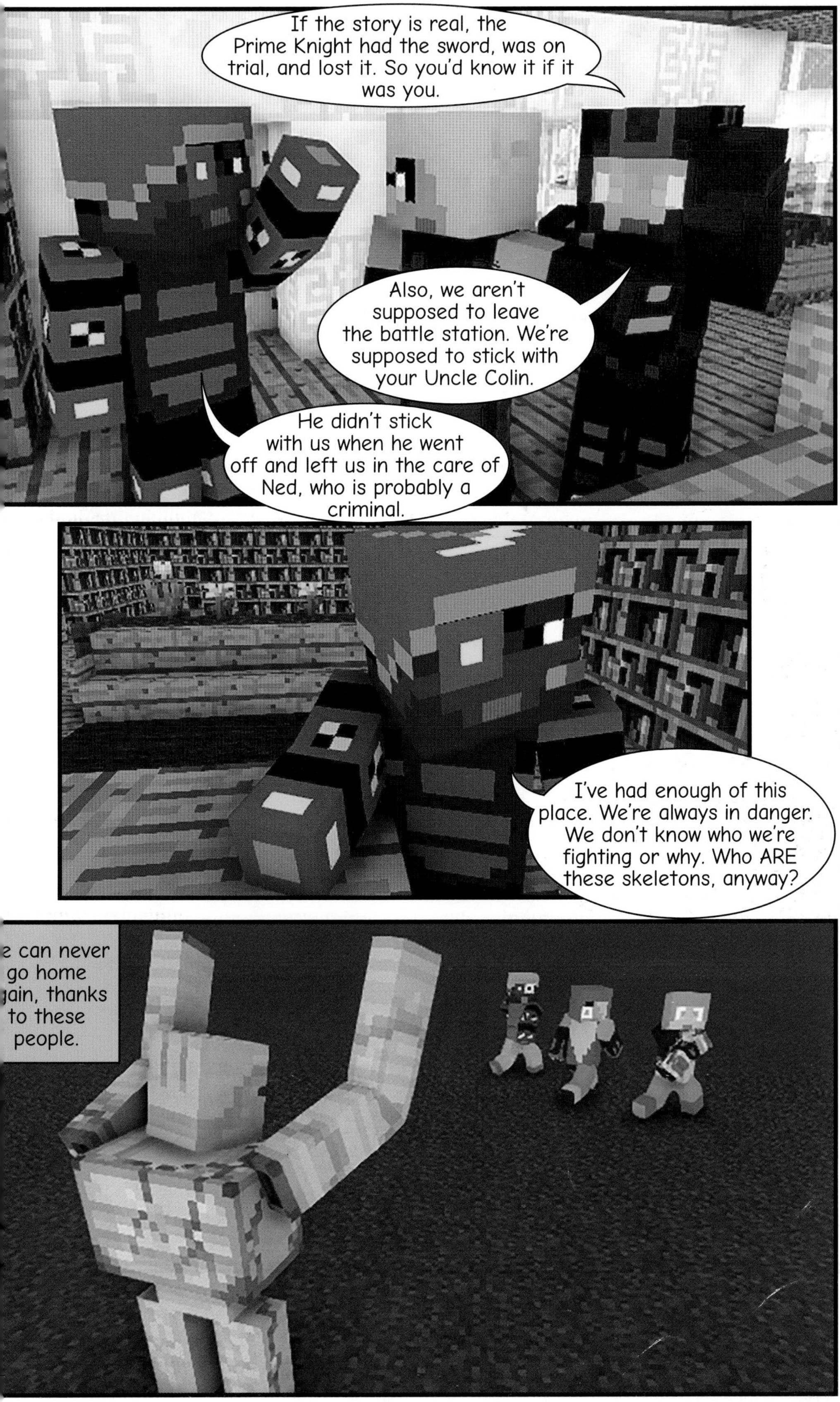
If the story is real, the Prime Knight had the sword, was on trial, and lost it. So you'd know it if it was you.
Also, we aren't supposed to leave the battle station. We're supposed to stick with your Uncle Colin.
He didn't stick with us when he went off and left us in the care of Ned, who is probably a criminal.
I've had enough of this place. We're always in danger. We don't know who we're fighting or why. Who ARE these skeletons, anyway?
e can never go home ain, thanks to these people.

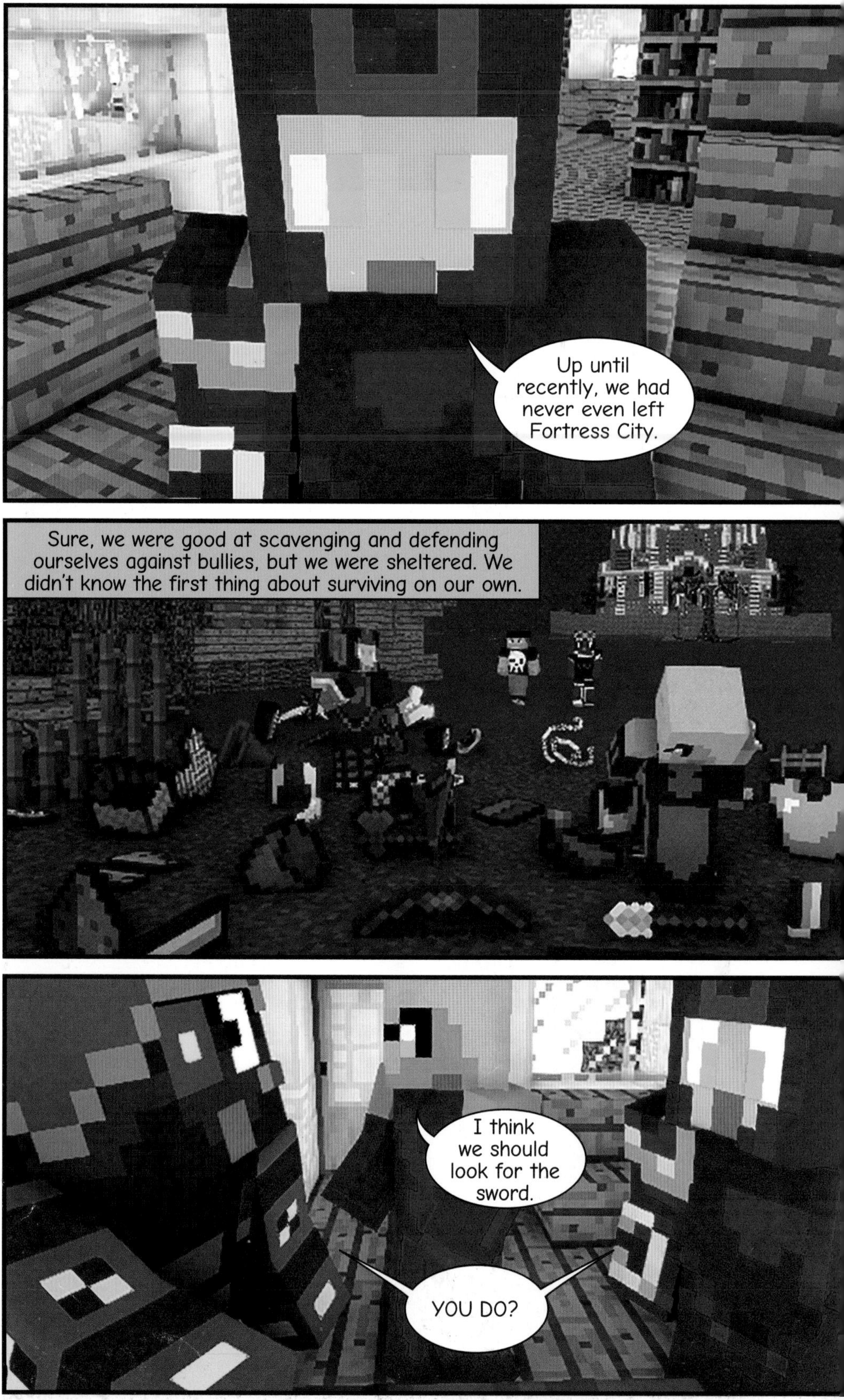
Up until recently, we had never even left Fortress City.
Sure, we were good at scavenging and defending ourselves against bullies, but we were sheltered. We didn't know the first thing about surviving on our own.
I think we should look for the sword.
YOU DO?

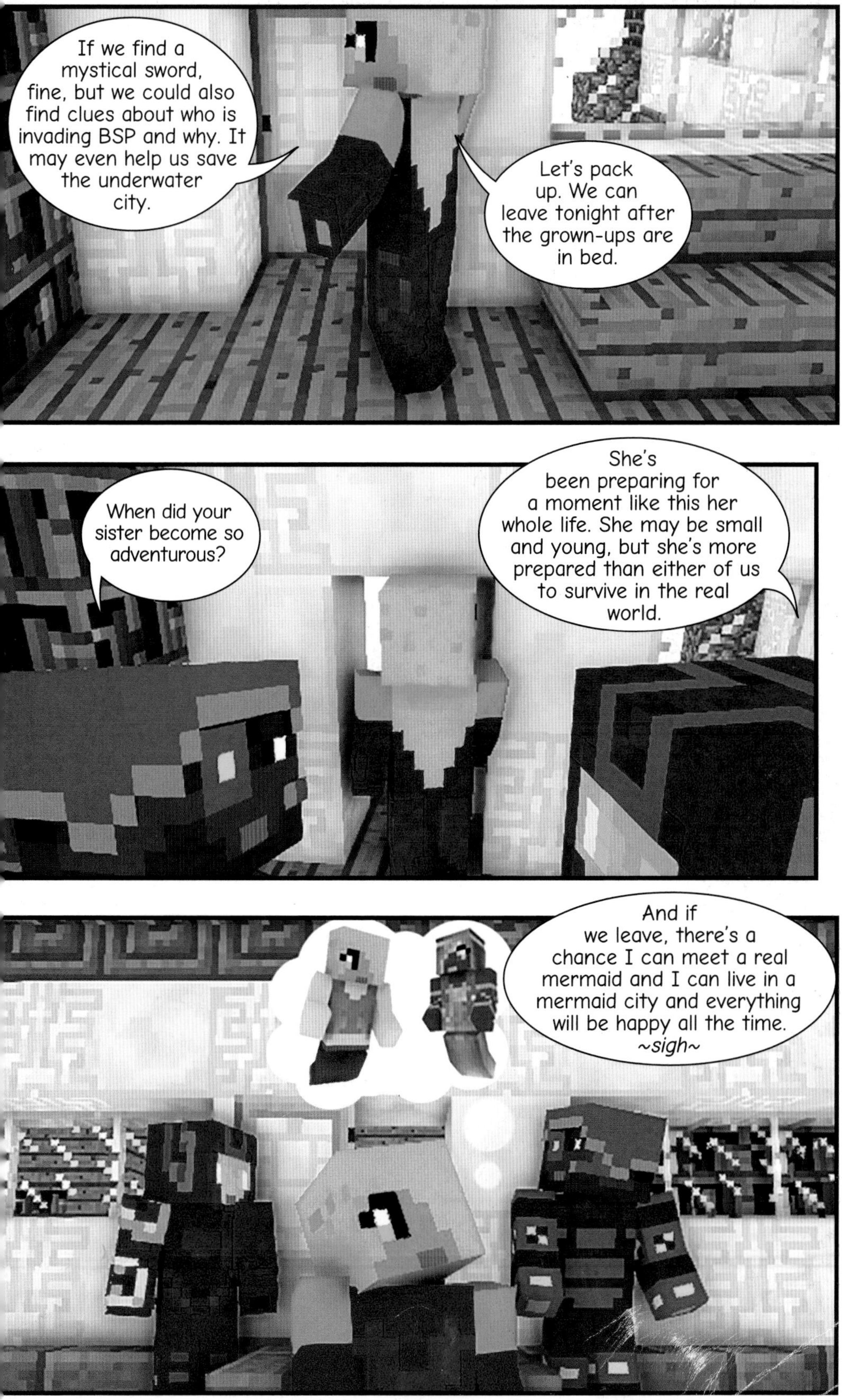
If we find a mystical sword, fine, but we could also find clues about who is invading BSP and why. It may even help us save the underwater city.
Let's pack up. We can leave tonight after the grown-ups are in bed.
When did your sister become so adventurous?
She's been preparing for a moment like this her whole life. She may be small and young, but she's more prepared than either of us to survive in the real world.
And if we leave, there's a chance I can meet a real mermaid and I can live in a mermaid city and everything will be happy all the time.
~sigh~

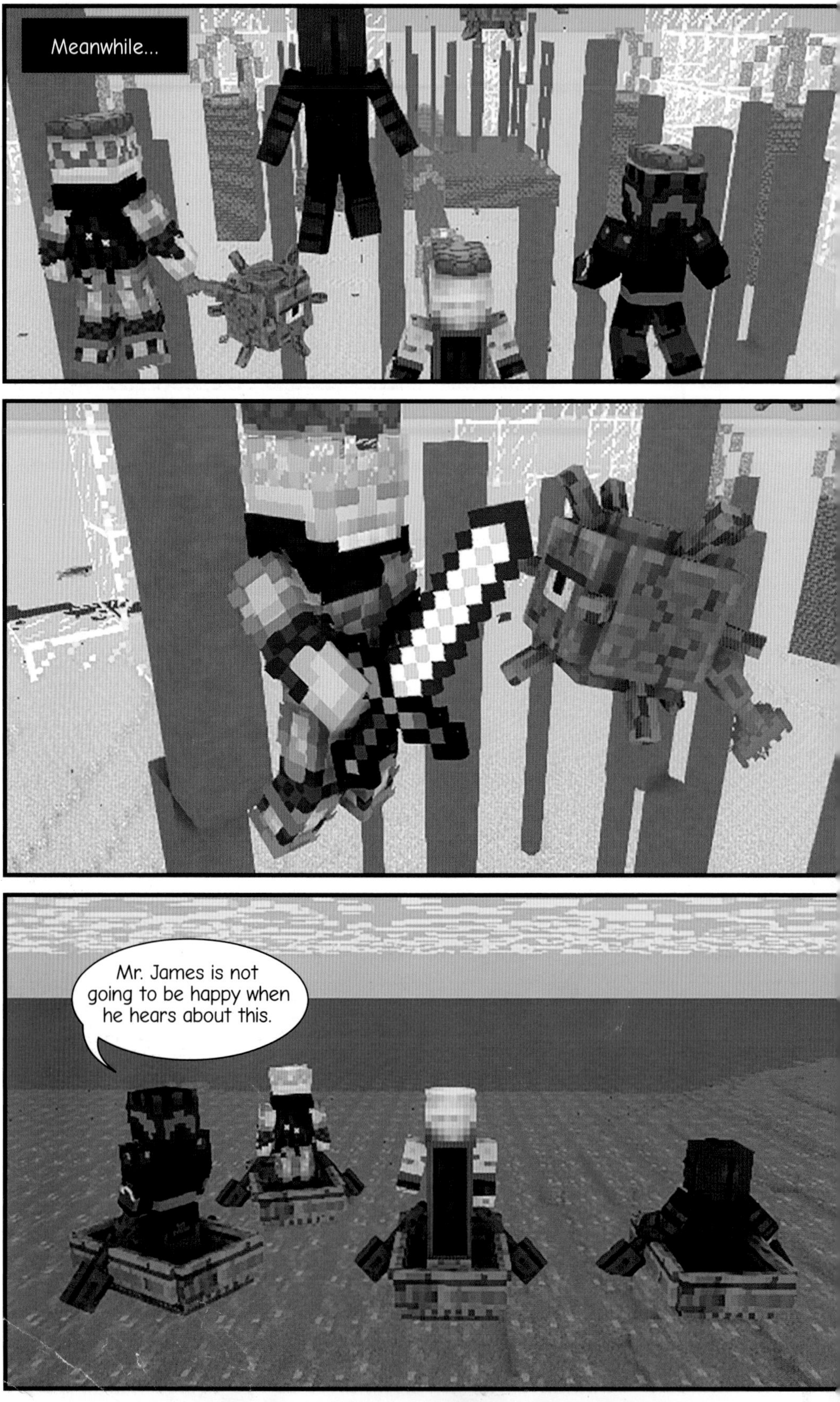
Meanwhile...
Mr. James is not going to be happy when he hears about this.

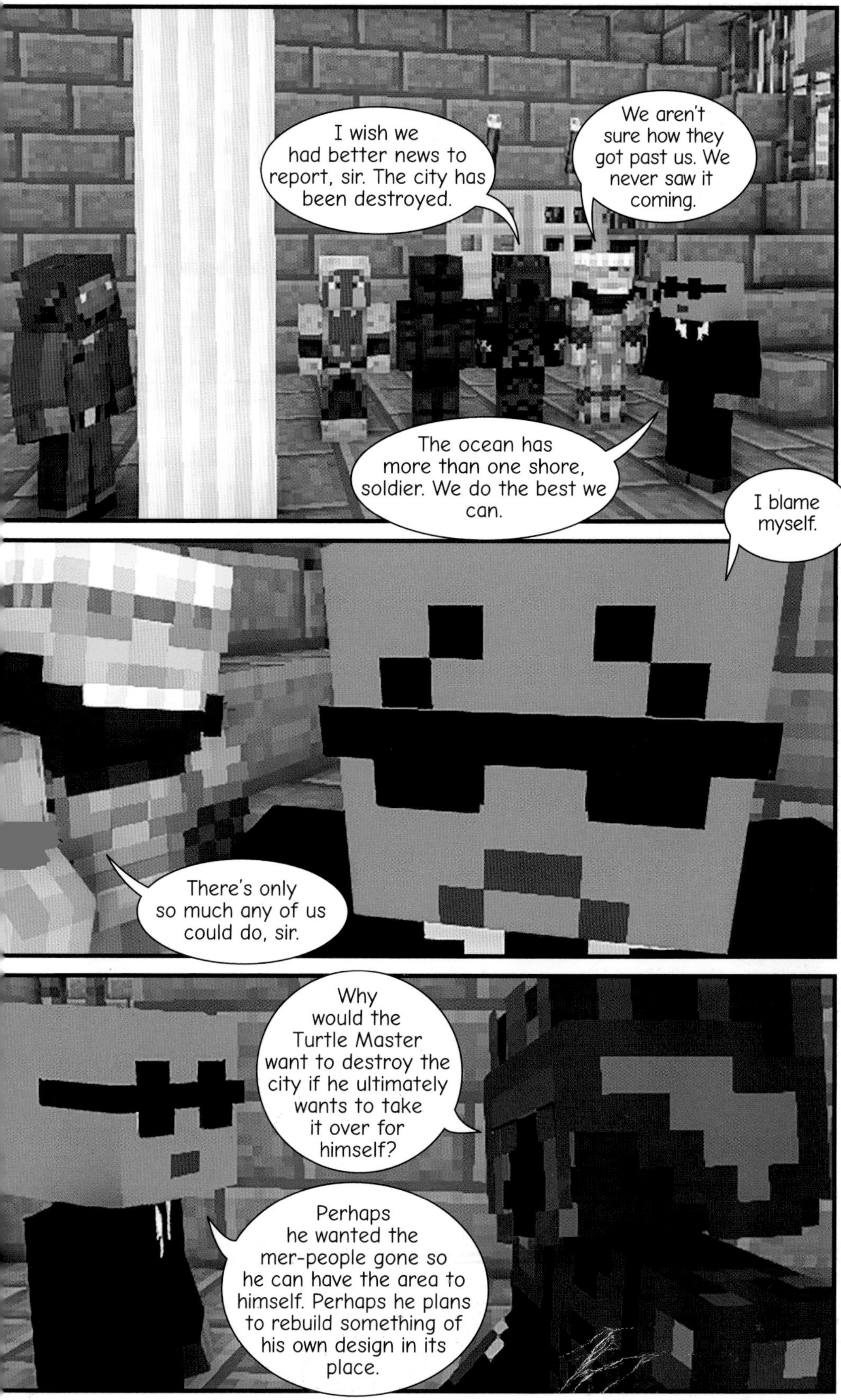
I wish we had better news to report, sir. The city has been destroyed.
We aren't sure how they got past us. We never saw it coming.
The ocean has more than one shore, soldier. We do the best we can.
I blame myself.
There's only so much any of us could do, sir.
Why would the Turtle Master want to destroy the city if he ultimately wants to take it over for himself?
Perhaps he wanted the mer-people gone so he can have the area to himself. Perhaps he plans to rebuild something of his own design in its place.

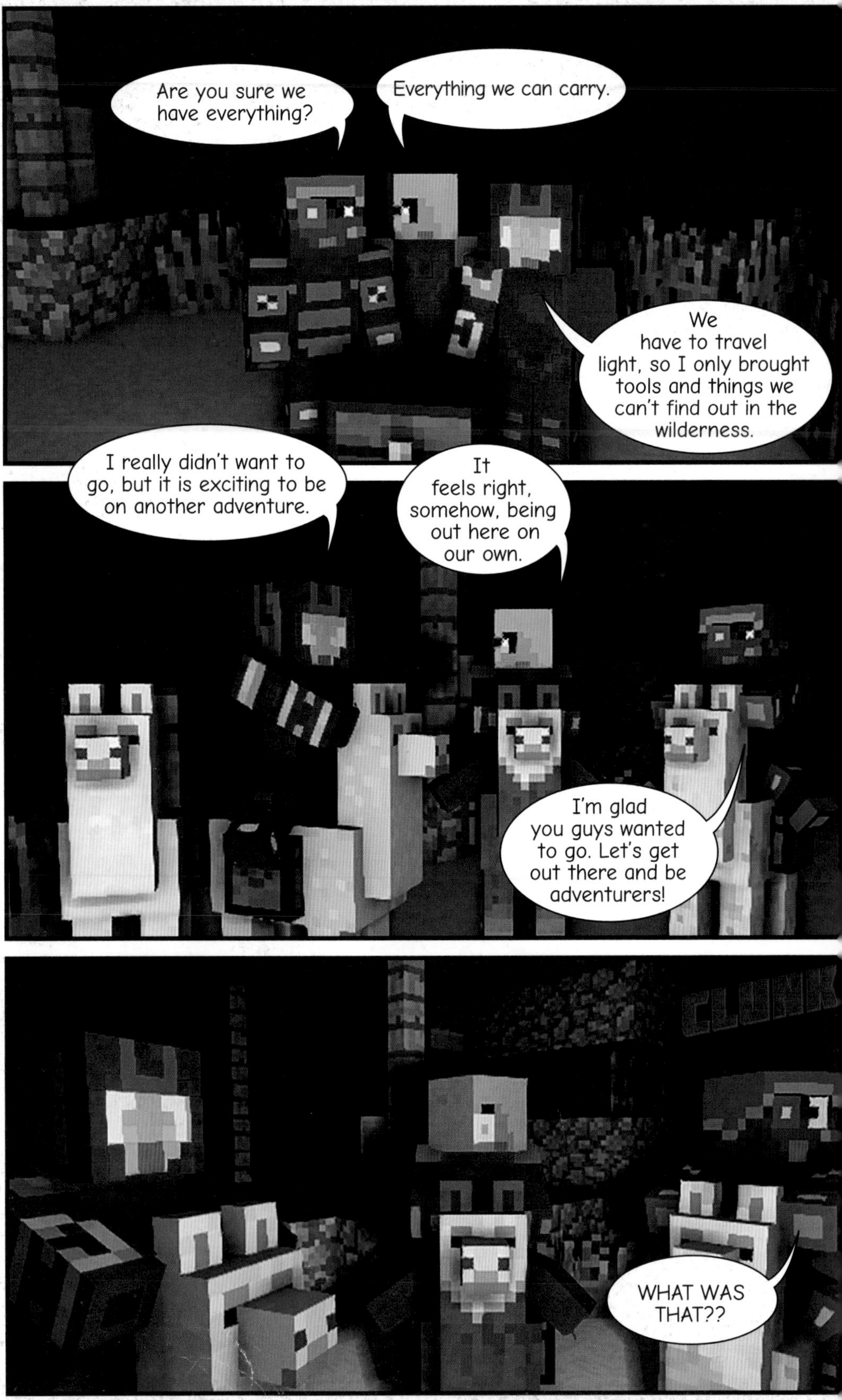
Are you sure we have everything?
Everything we can carry.
We have to travel light, so I only brought tools and things we can't find out in the wilderness.
I really didn't want to go, but it is exciting to be on another adventure.
It feels right, somehow, being out here on our own.
I'm glad you guys wanted to go. Let's get out there and be adventurers!
CLUNK
WHAT WAS THAT??

CHAPTER 5

HERO'S QUEST

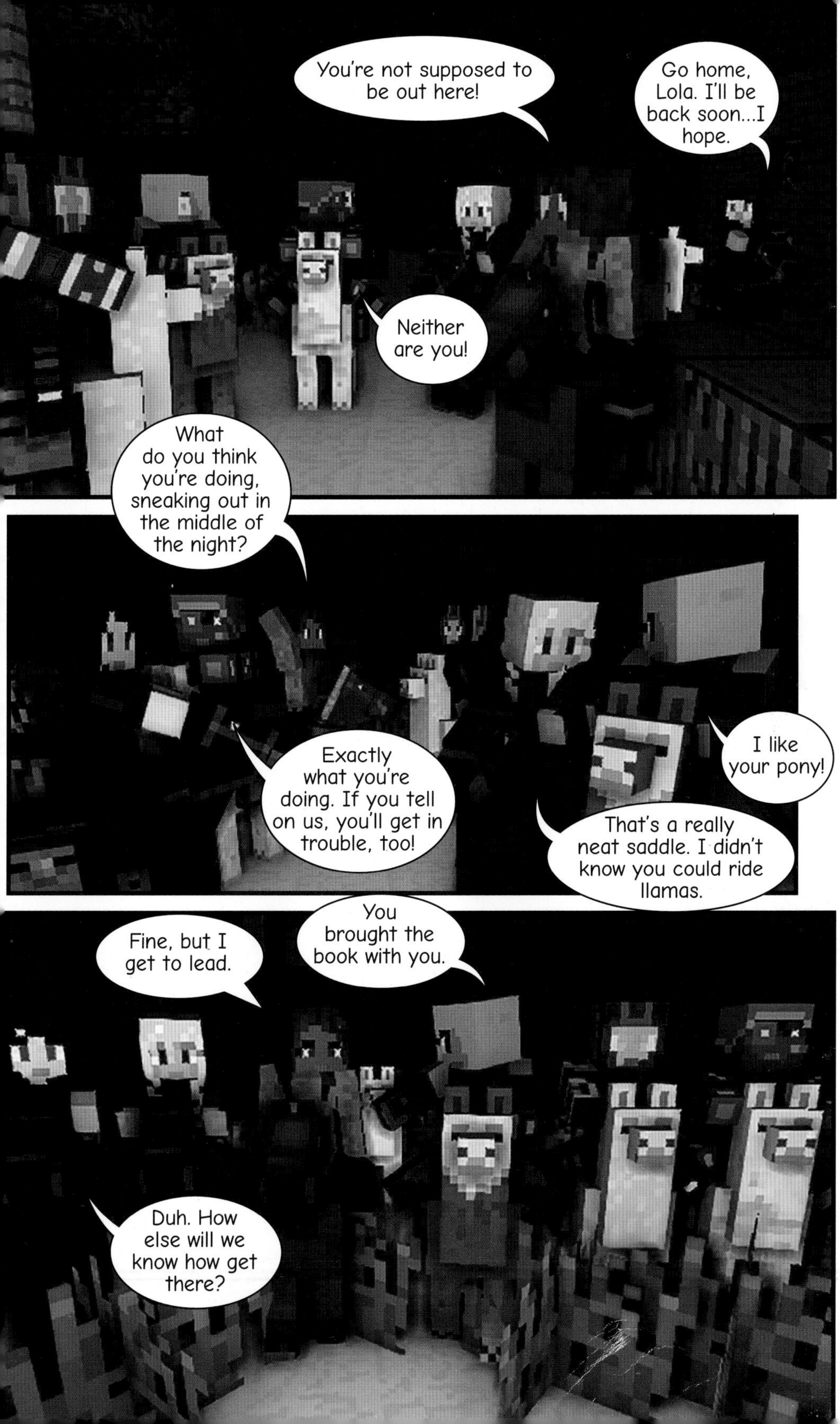
You're not supposed to be out here!
Go home, Lola. I'll be back soon...I hope.
Neither are you!
What do you think you're doing, sneaking out in the middle of the night?
Exactly what you're doing. If you tell on us, you'll get in trouble, too!
I like your pony!
That's a really neat saddle. I didn't know you could ride llamas.
Fine, but I get to lead.
You brought the book with you.
Duh. How else will we know how get there?

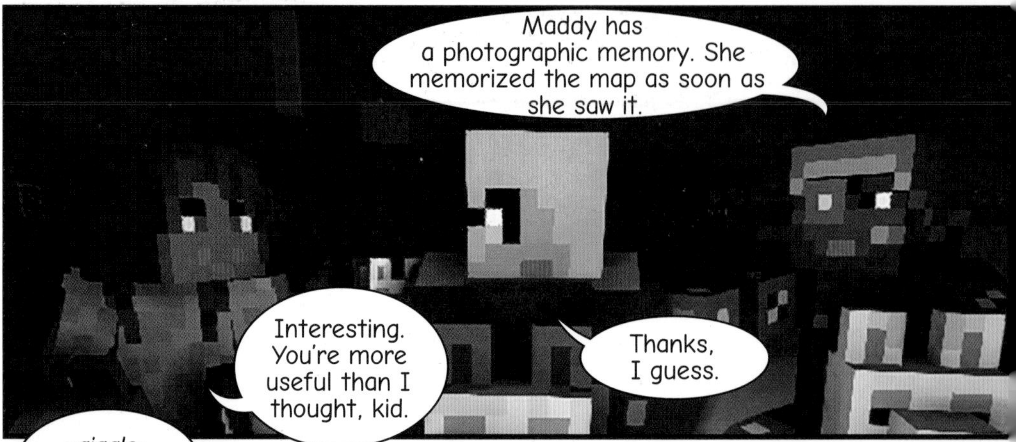
Maddy has a photographic memory. She memorized the map as soon as she saw it.
Interesting. You're more useful than I thought, kid.
Thanks, I guess.

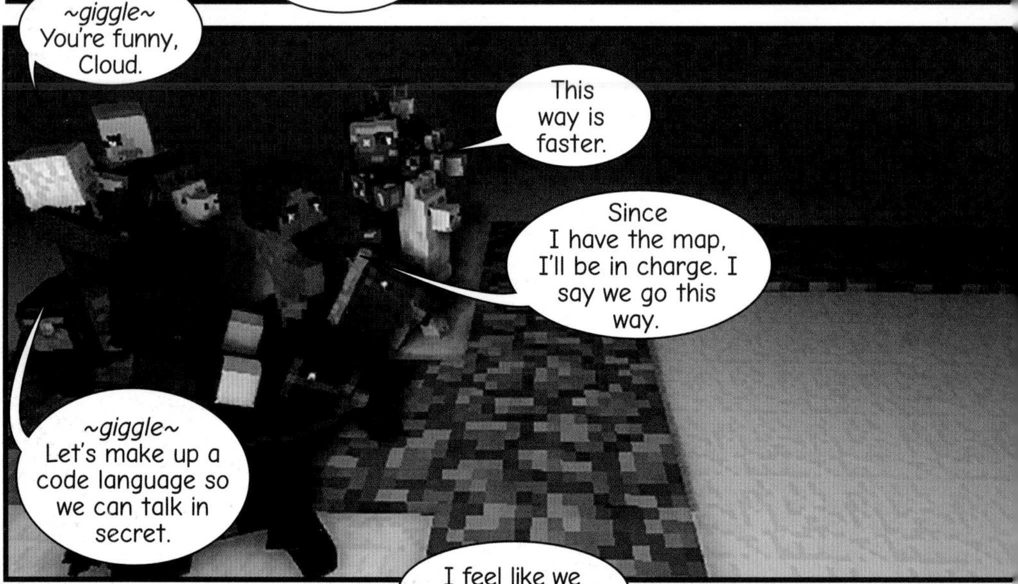
~giggle~ You're funny, Cloud.
This way is faster.
Since I have the map, I'll be in charge. I say we go this way.
~giggle~ Let's make up a code language so we can talk in secret.

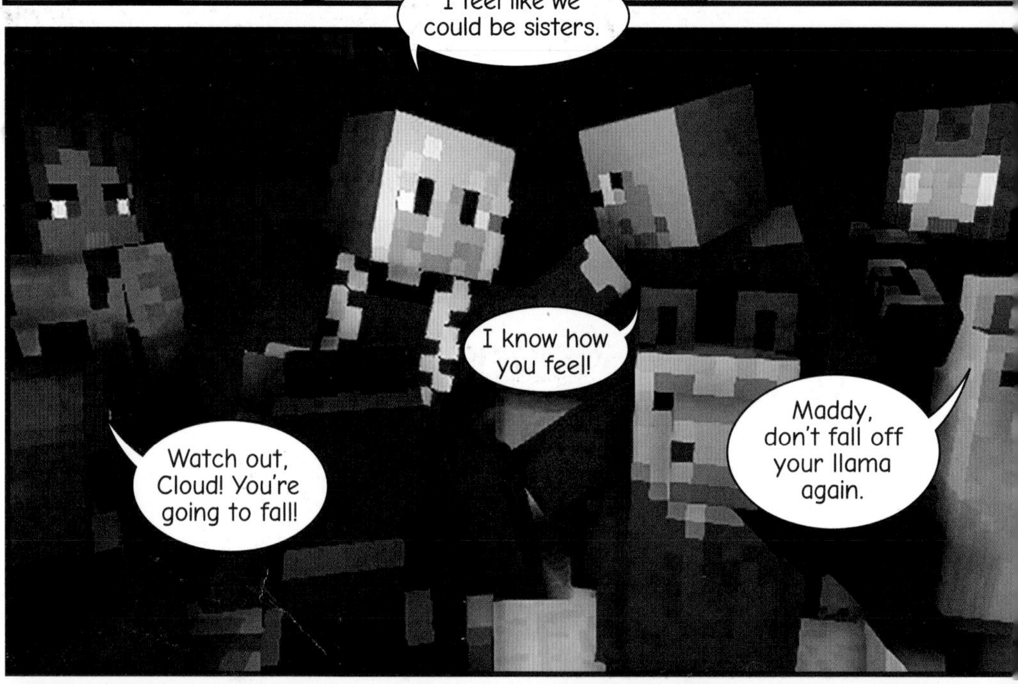
I feel like we could be sisters.
I know how you feel!
Watch out, Cloud! You're going to fall!
Maddy, don't fall off your llama again.

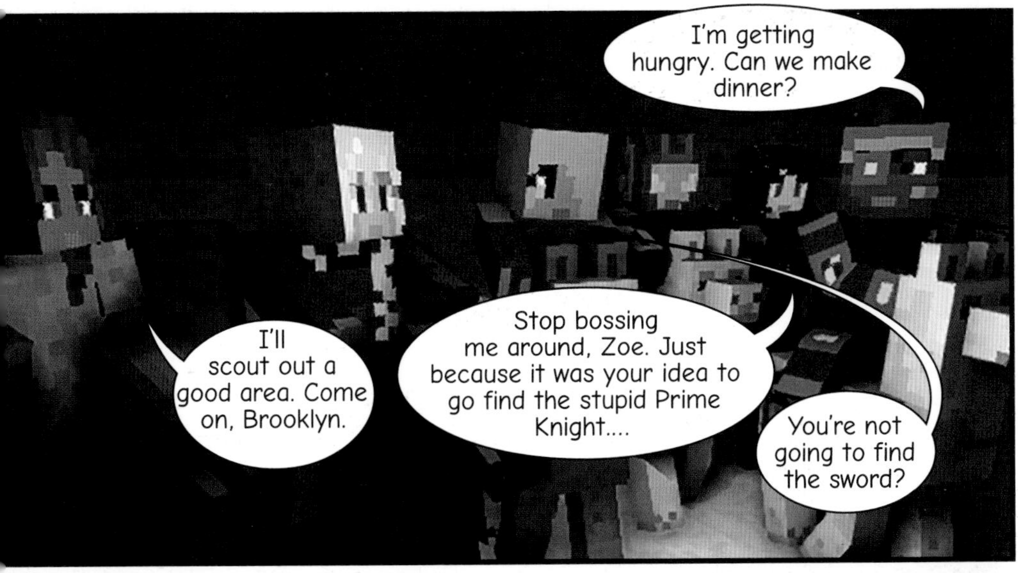
I'm getting hungry. Can we make dinner?
I'll scout out a good area. Come on, Brooklyn.
Stop bossing me around, Zoe. Just because it was your idea to go find the stupid Prime Knight....
You're not going to find the sword?

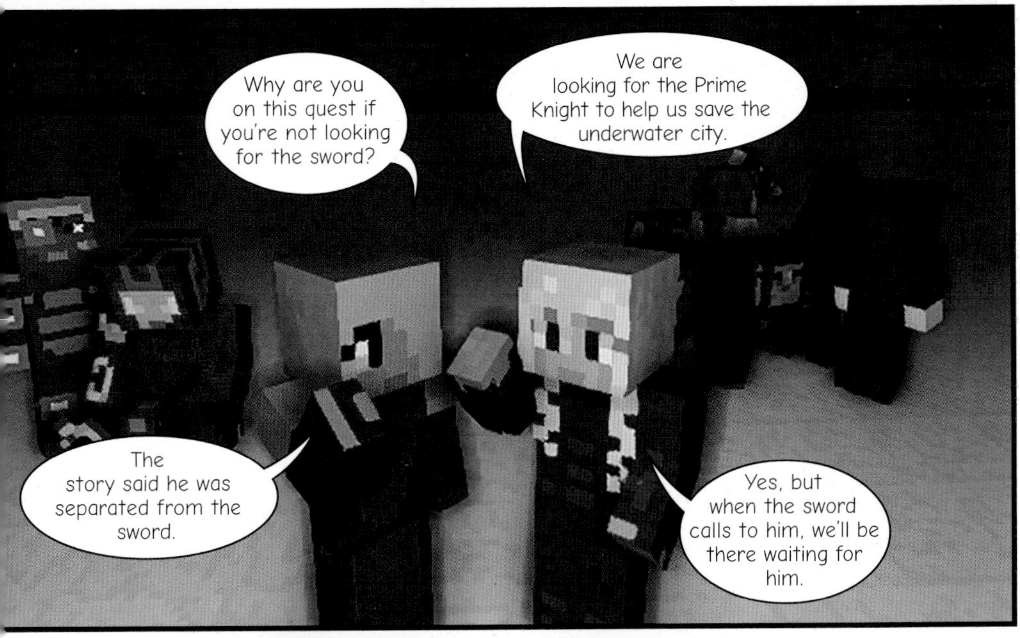
Why are you on this quest if you're not looking for the sword?
We are looking for the Prime Knight to help us save the underwater city.
The story said he was separated from the sword.
Yes, but when the sword calls to him, we'll be there waiting for him.

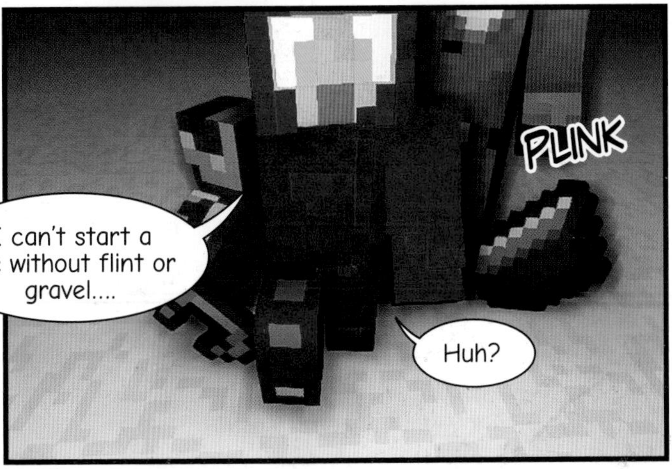
PLINK
I can't start a fire without flint or gravel....
Huh?

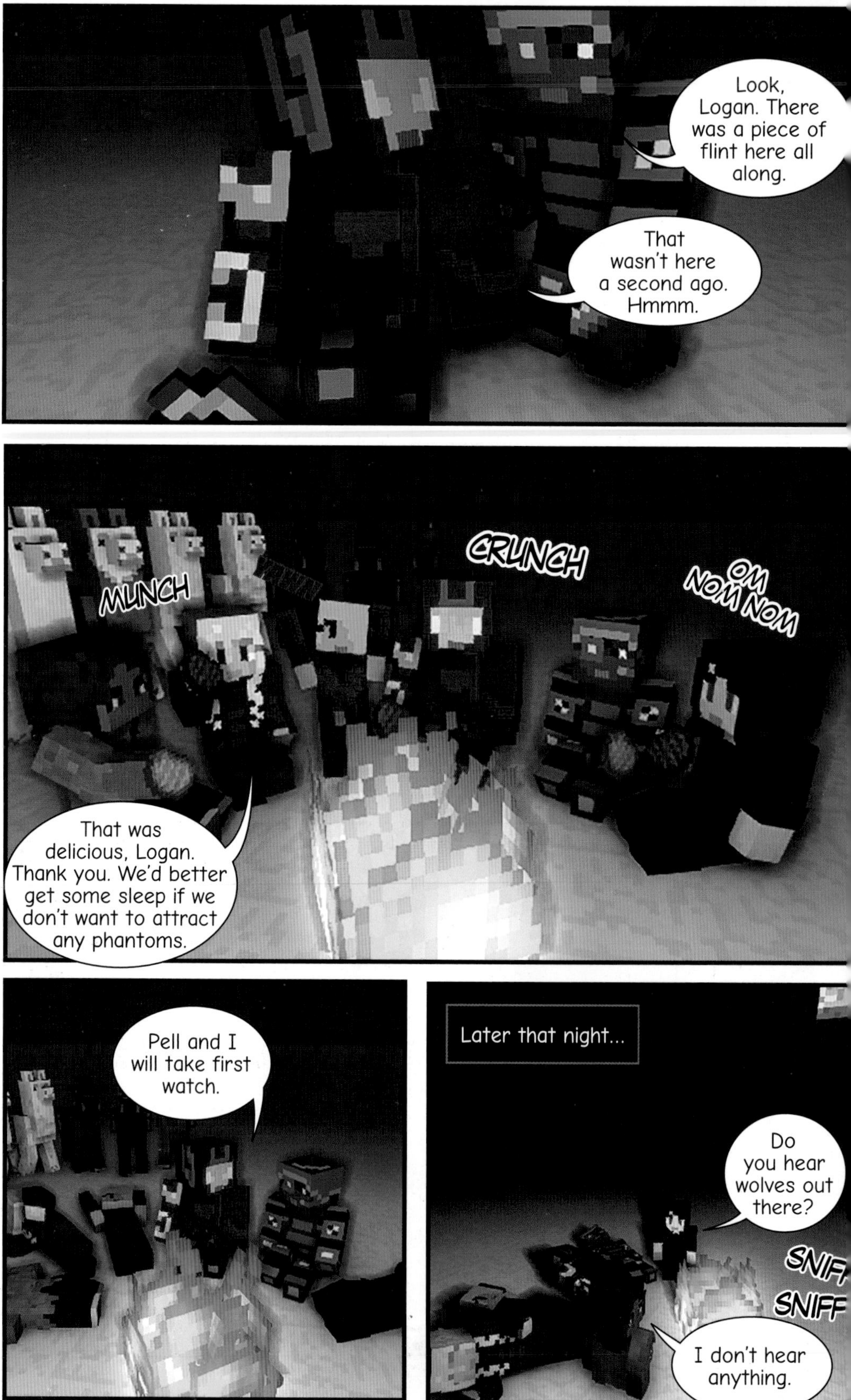

Look, Logan. There was a piece of flint here all along.
That wasn't here a second ago. Hmmm.
MUNCH
CRUNCH
OM NOM NOM
That was delicious, Logan. Thank you. We'd better get some sleep if we don't want to attract any phantoms.
Pell and I will take first watch.
Later that night...
Do you hear wolves out there?
SNIFF,
SNIFF
I don't hear anything.

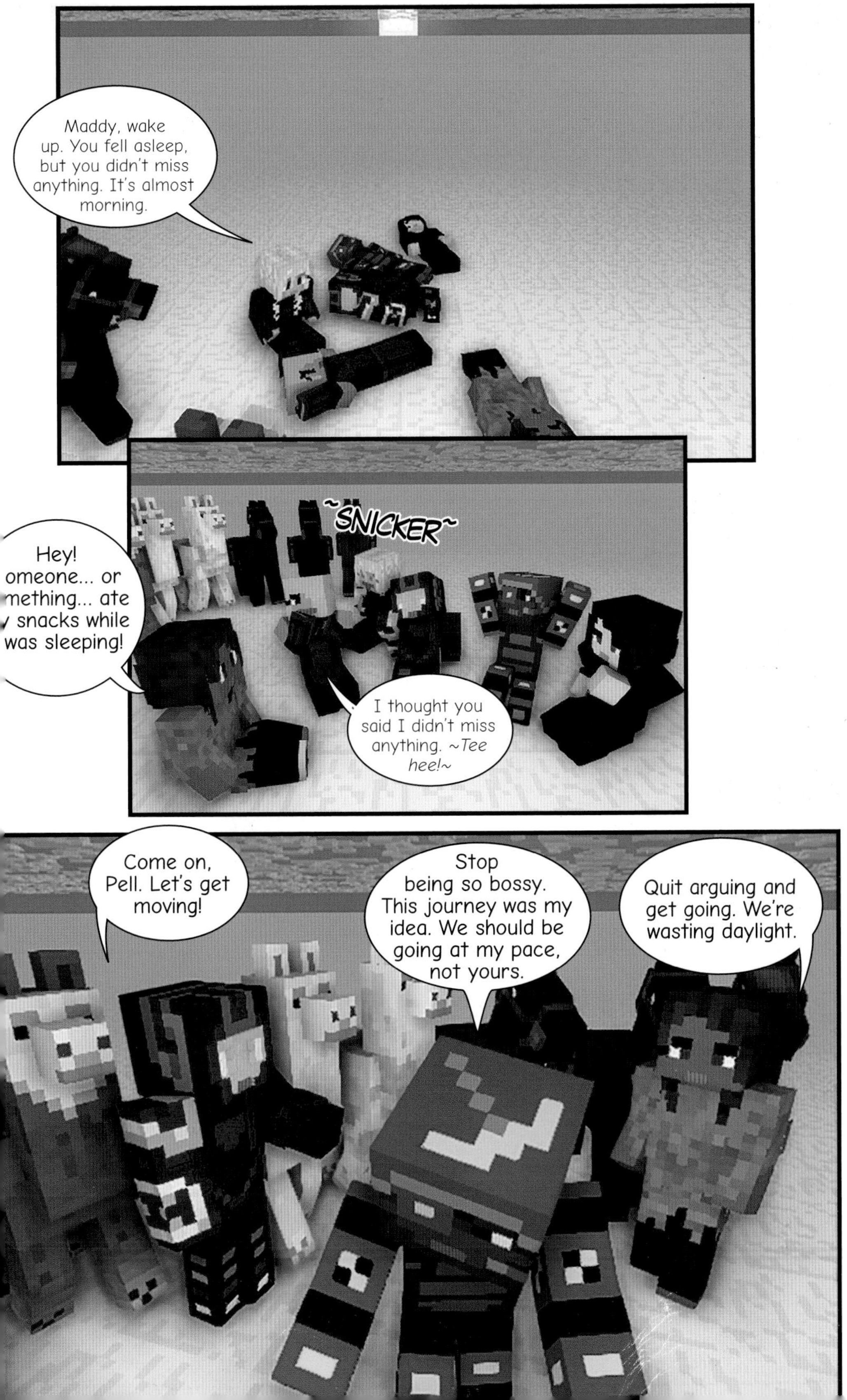

Maddy, wake up. You fell asleep, but you didn't miss anything. It's almost morning.
Hey! omeone... or mething... ate snacks while was sleeping!
~SNICKER~
I thought you said I didn't miss anything. ~Tee hee!~
Come on, Pell. Let's get moving!
Stop being so bossy. This journey was my idea. We should be going at my pace, not yours.
Quit arguing and get going. We're wasting daylight.

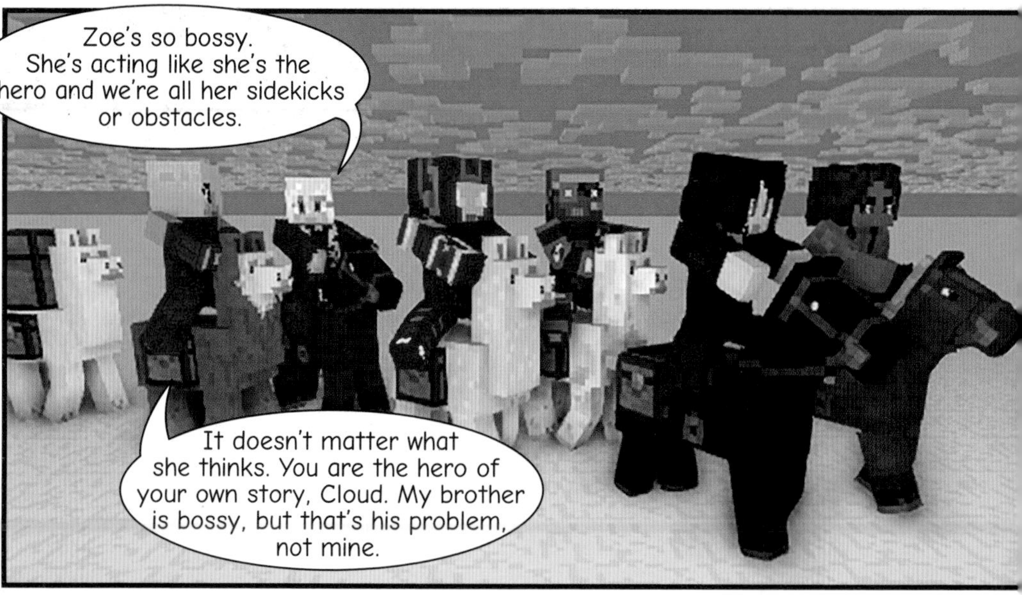
Zoe's so bossy. She's acting like she's the hero and we're all her sidekicks or obstacles.
It doesn't matter what she thinks. You are the hero of your own story, Cloud. My brother is bossy, but that's his problem, not mine.

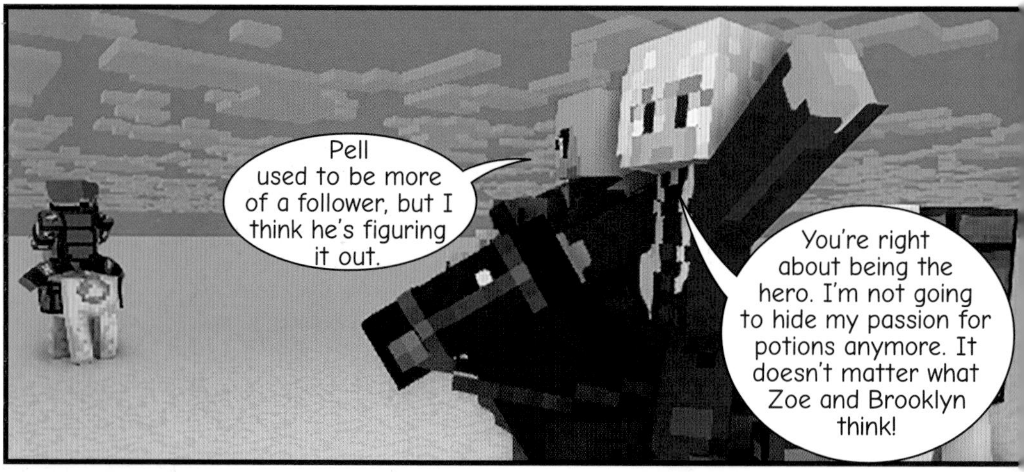
Pell used to be more of a follower, but I think he's figuring it out.
You're right about being the hero. I'm not going to hide my passion for potions anymore. It doesn't matter what Zoe and Brooklyn think!

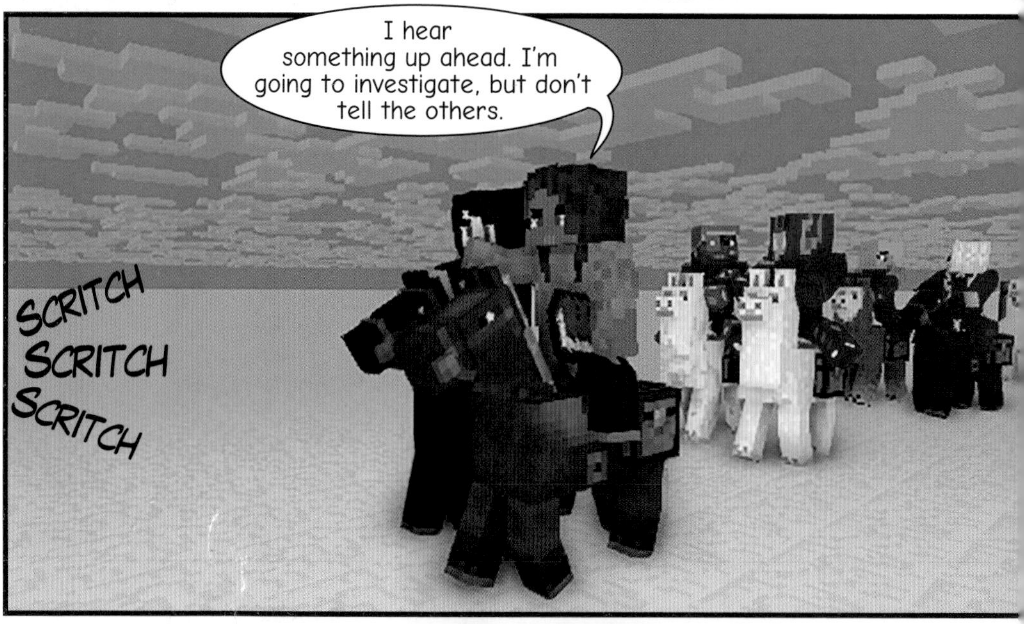
I hear something up ahead. I'm going to investigate, but don't tell the others.
SCRITCH
SCRITCH
SCRITCH

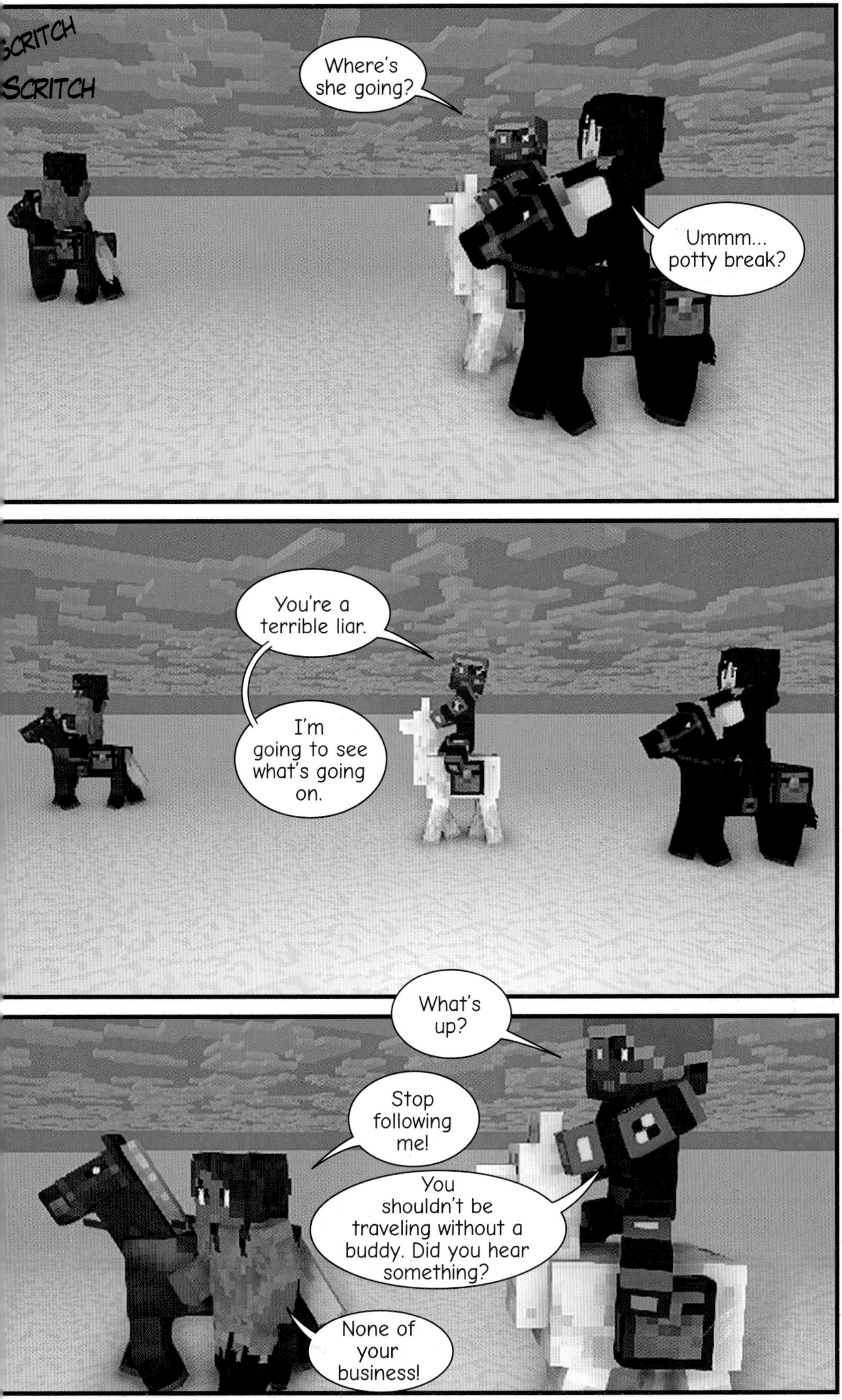
SCRITCH
SCRITCH
Where's she going?
Ummm... potty break?
You're a terrible liar.
I'm going to see what's going on.
What's up?
Stop following me!
You shouldn't be traveling without a buddy. Did you hear something?
None of your business!

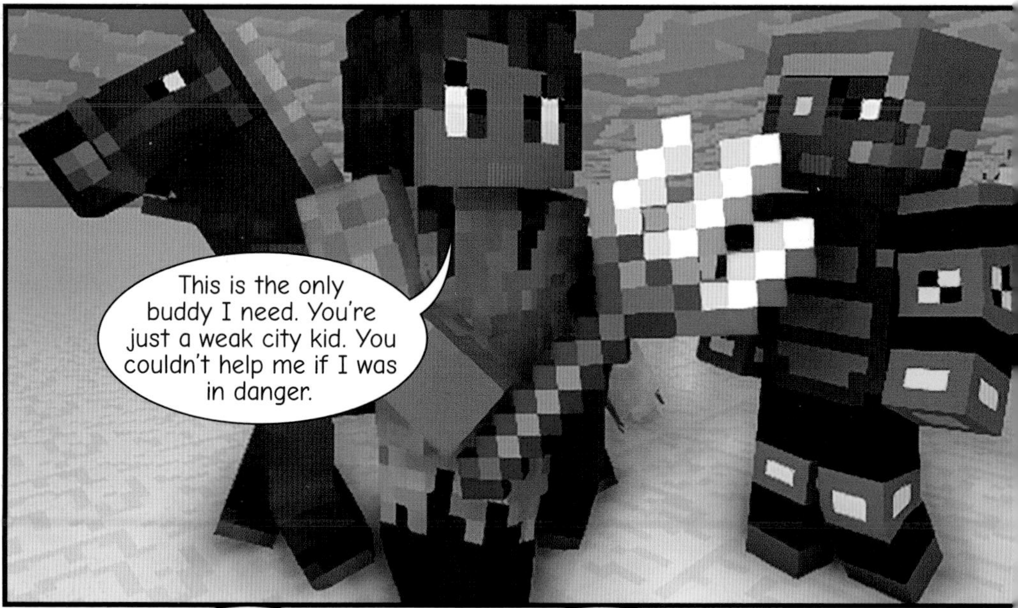
This is the only buddy I need. You're just a weak city kid. You couldn't help me if I was in danger.

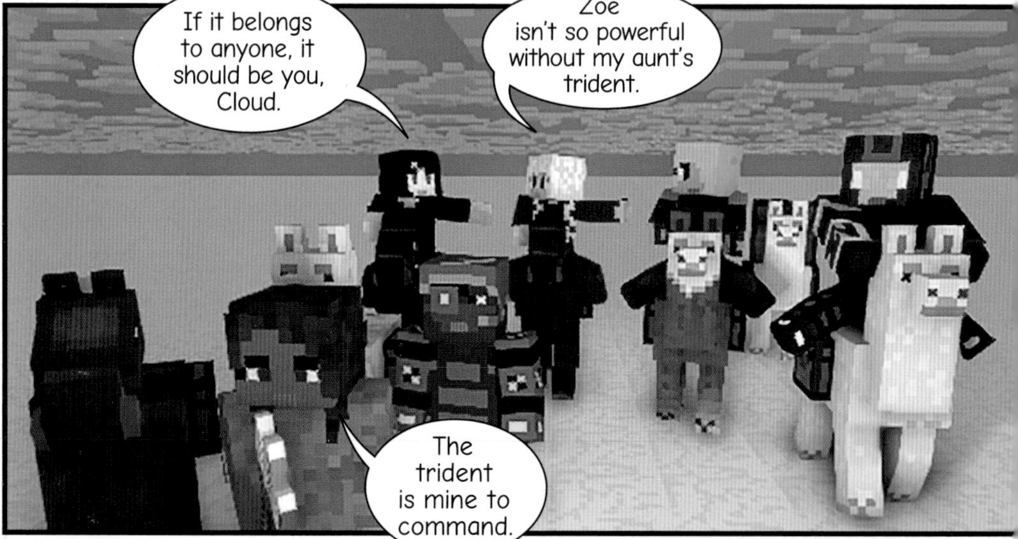
If it belongs to anyone, it should be you, Cloud.
Zoe isn't so powerful without my aunt's trident.
The trident is mine to command.

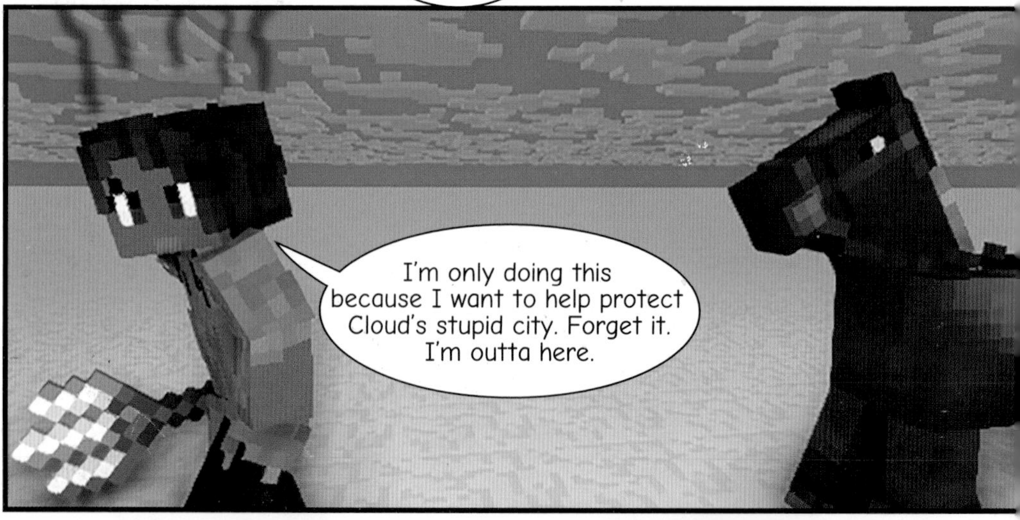
I'm only doing this because I want to help protect Cloud's stupid city. Forget it. I'm outta here.

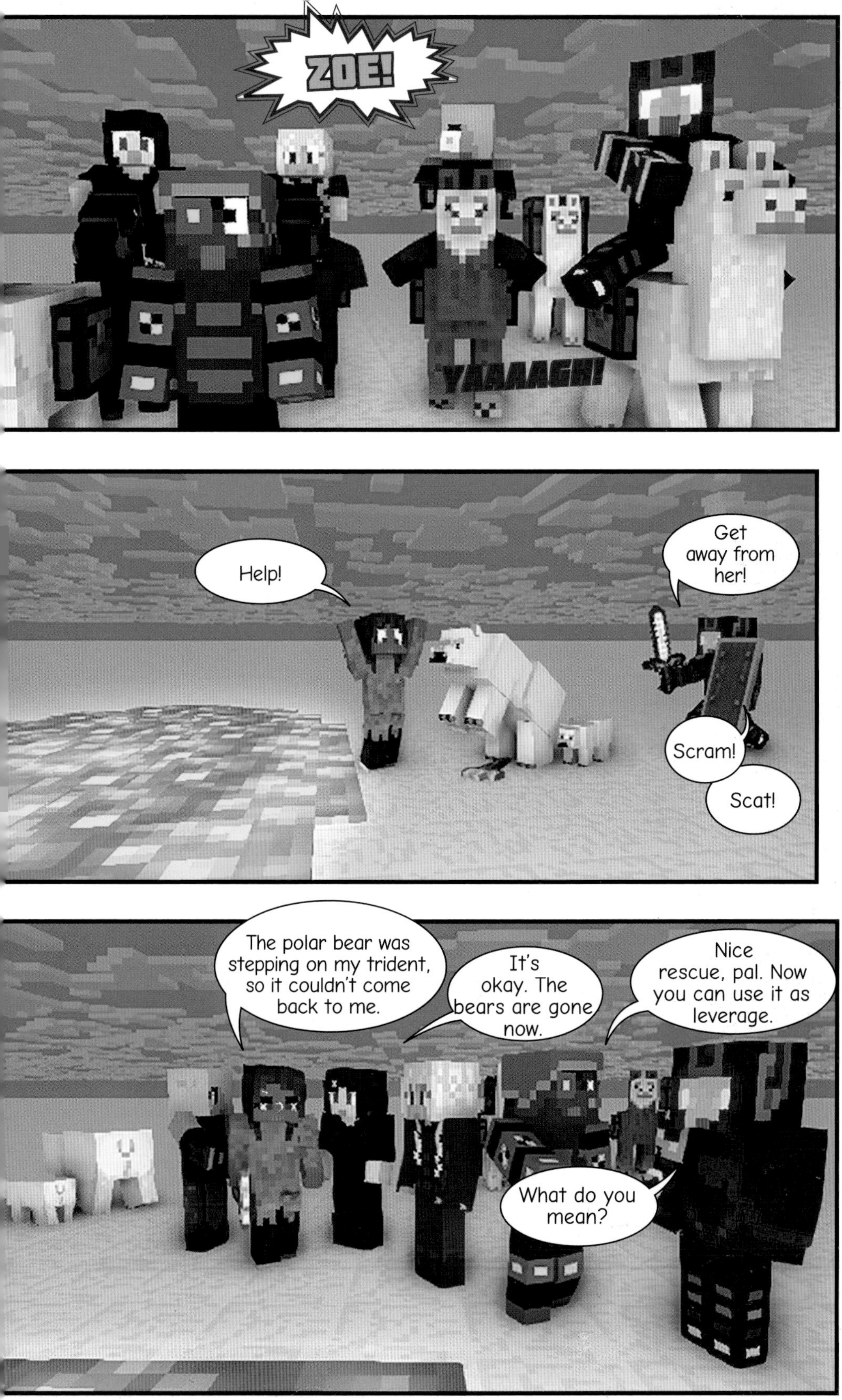
ZOE!
YAAAGH!
Help!
Get away from her!
Scram!
Scat!
The polar bear was stepping on my trident, so it couldn't come back to me.
It's okay. The bears are gone now.
Nice rescue, pal. Now you can use it as leverage.
What do you mean?

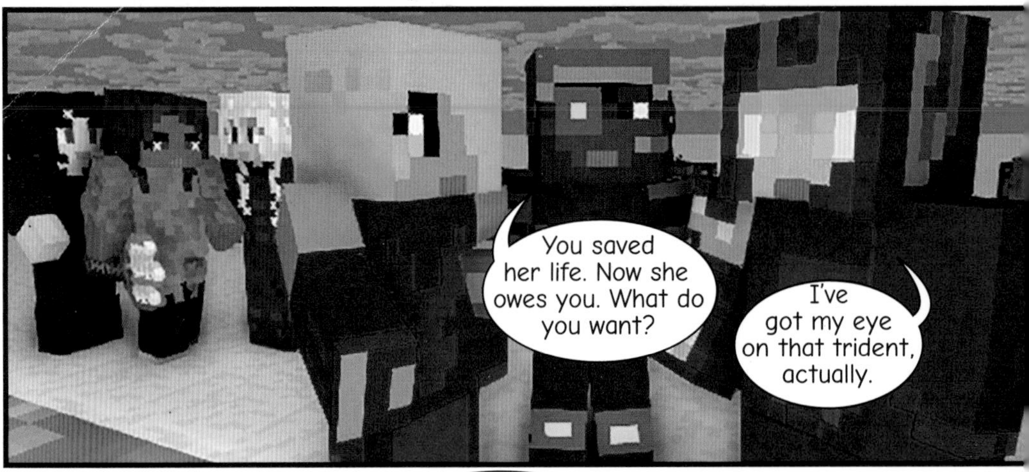
You saved her life. Now she owes you. What do you want?
I've got my eye on that trident, actually.

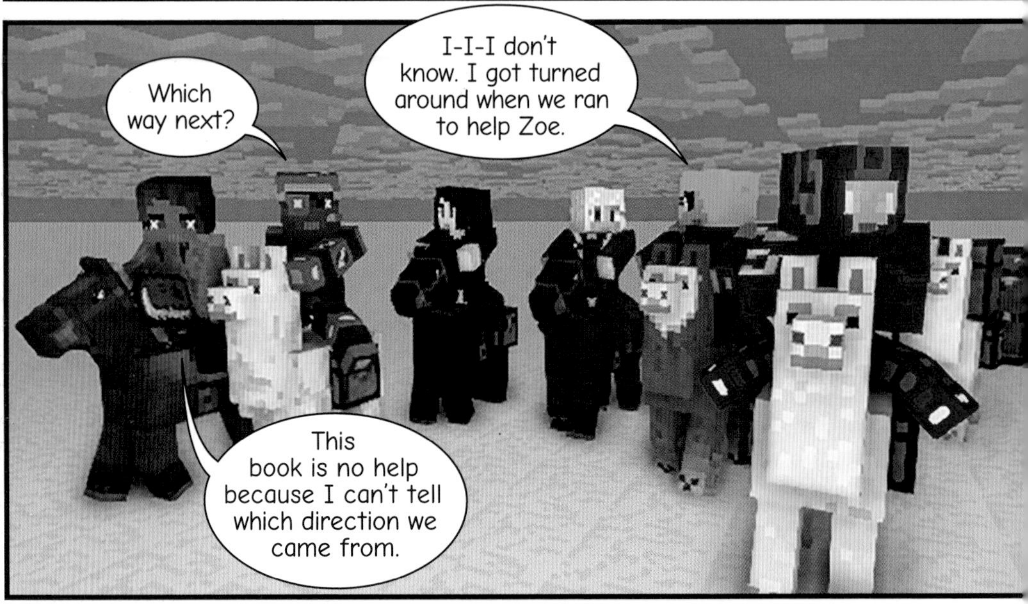
Which way next?
I-I-I don't know. I got turned around when we ran to help Zoe.
This book is no help because I can't tell which direction we came from.

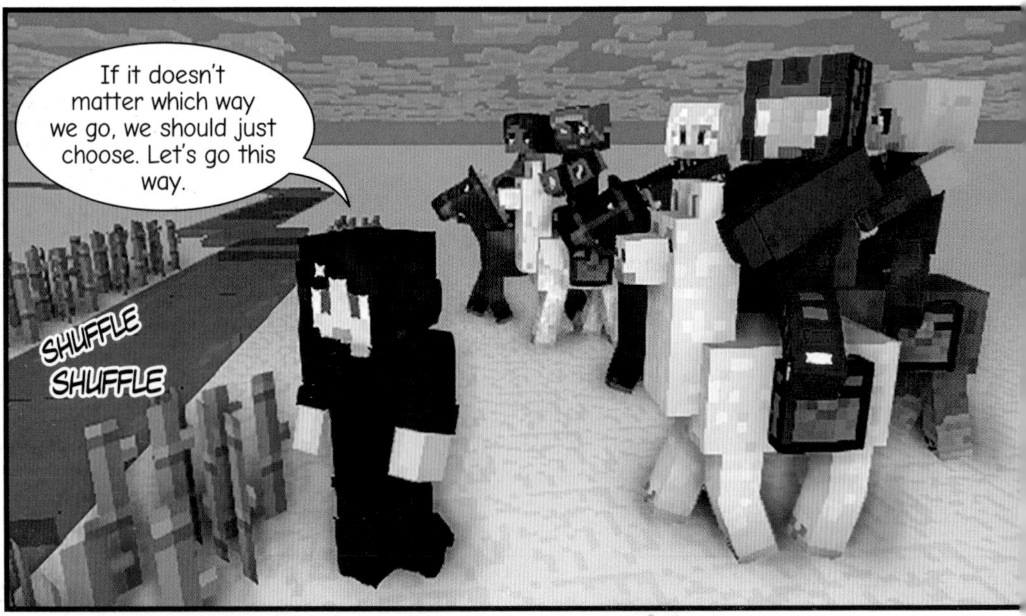
If it doesn't matter which way we go, we should just choose. Let's go this way.
SHUFFLE
SHUFFLE

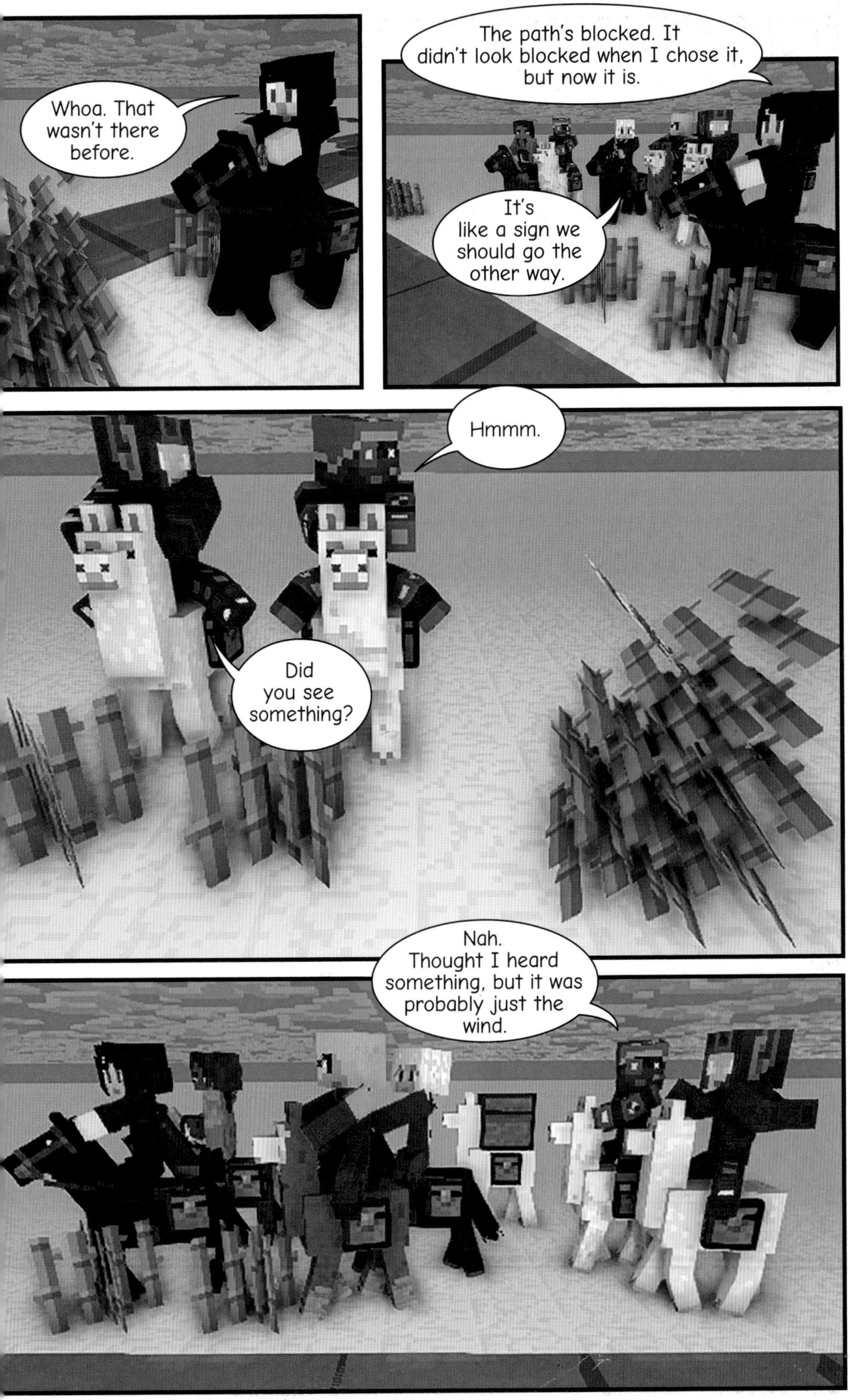
Whoa. That wasn't there before.
The path's blocked. It didn't look blocked when I chose it, but now it is.
It's like a sign we should go the other way.
Hmmm.
Did you see something?
Nah. Thought I heard something, but it was probably just the wind.

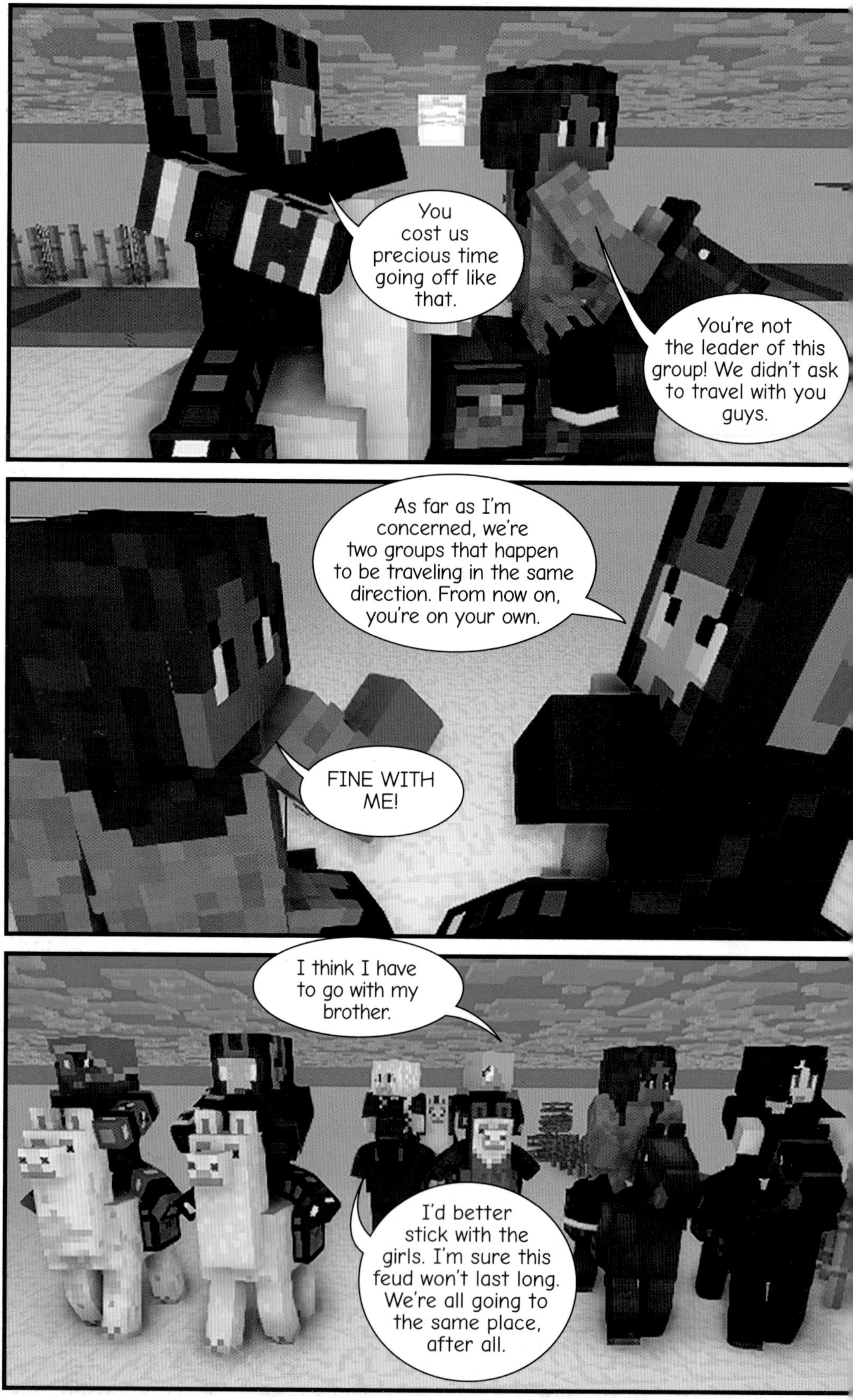
You cost us precious time going off like that.
You're not the leader of this group! We didn't ask to travel with you guys.
As far as I'm concerned, we're two groups that happen to be traveling in the same direction. From now on, you're on your own.
FINE WITH ME!
I think I have to go with my brother.
I'd better stick with the girls. I'm sure this feud won't last long. We're all going to the same place, after all.

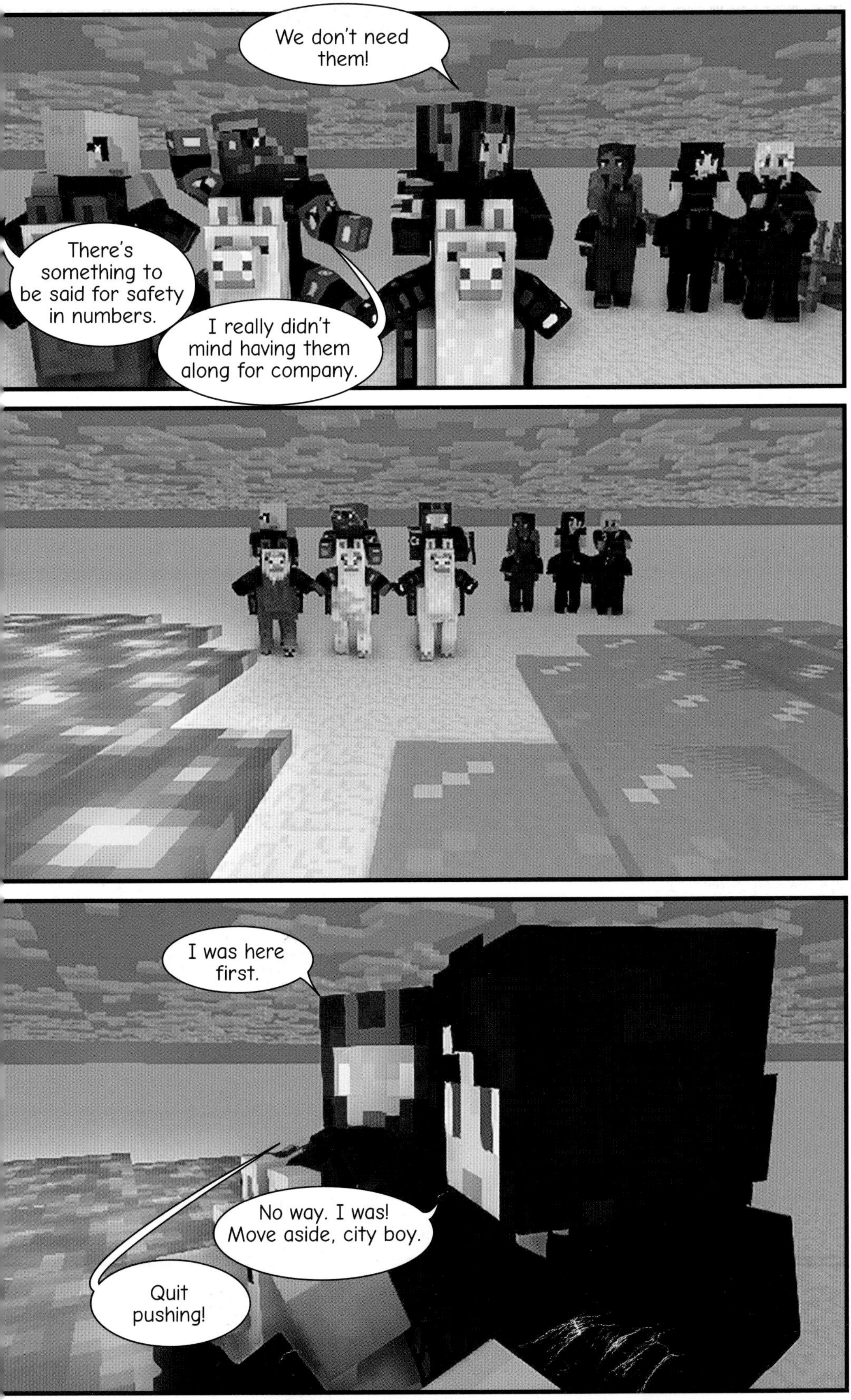
We don't need them!
There's something to be said for safety in numbers.
I really didn't mind having them along for company.
I was here first.
No way. I was! Move aside, city boy.
Quit pushing!

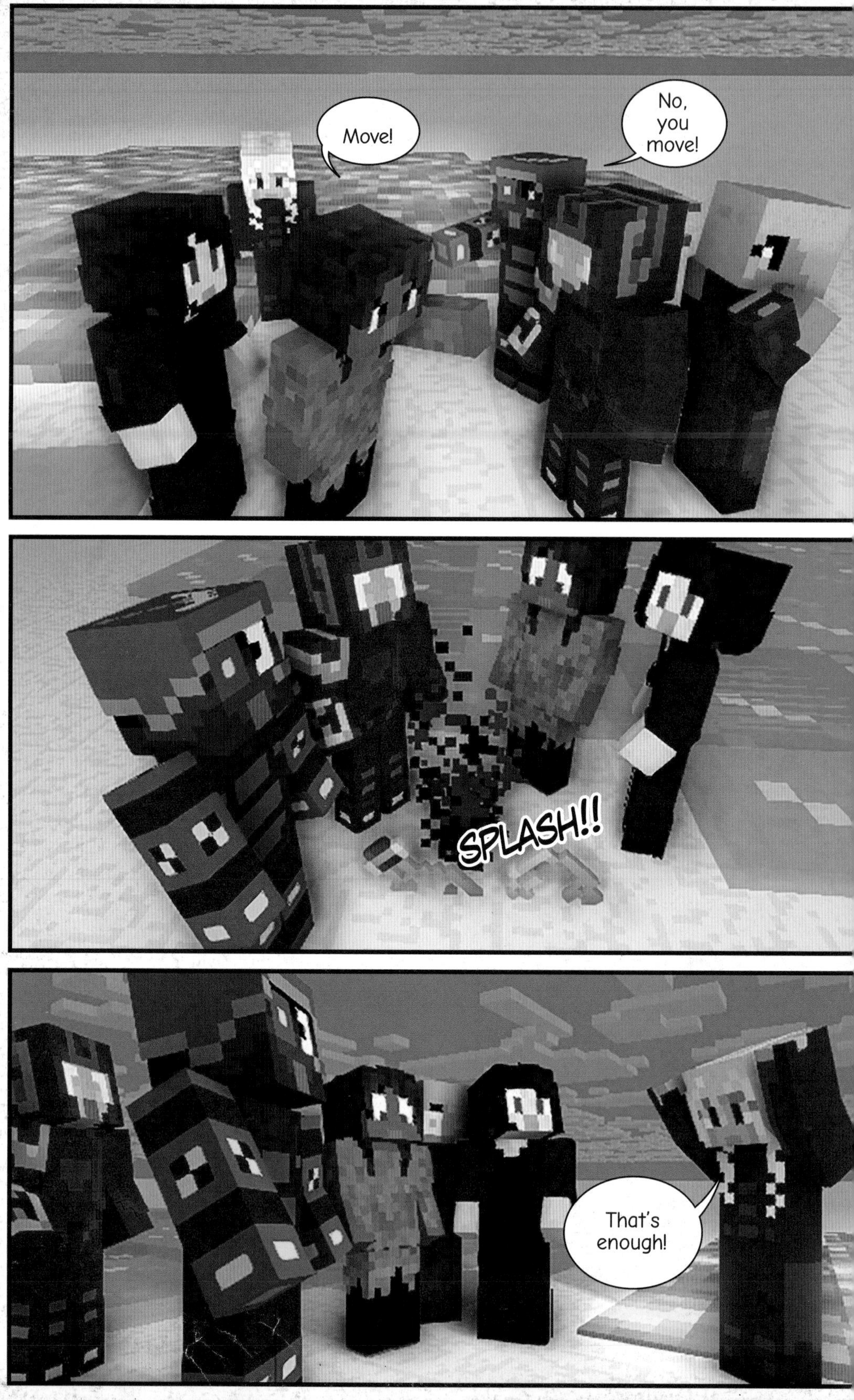
Move!
No, you move!
SPLASH!!
That's enough!

CHAPTER 6

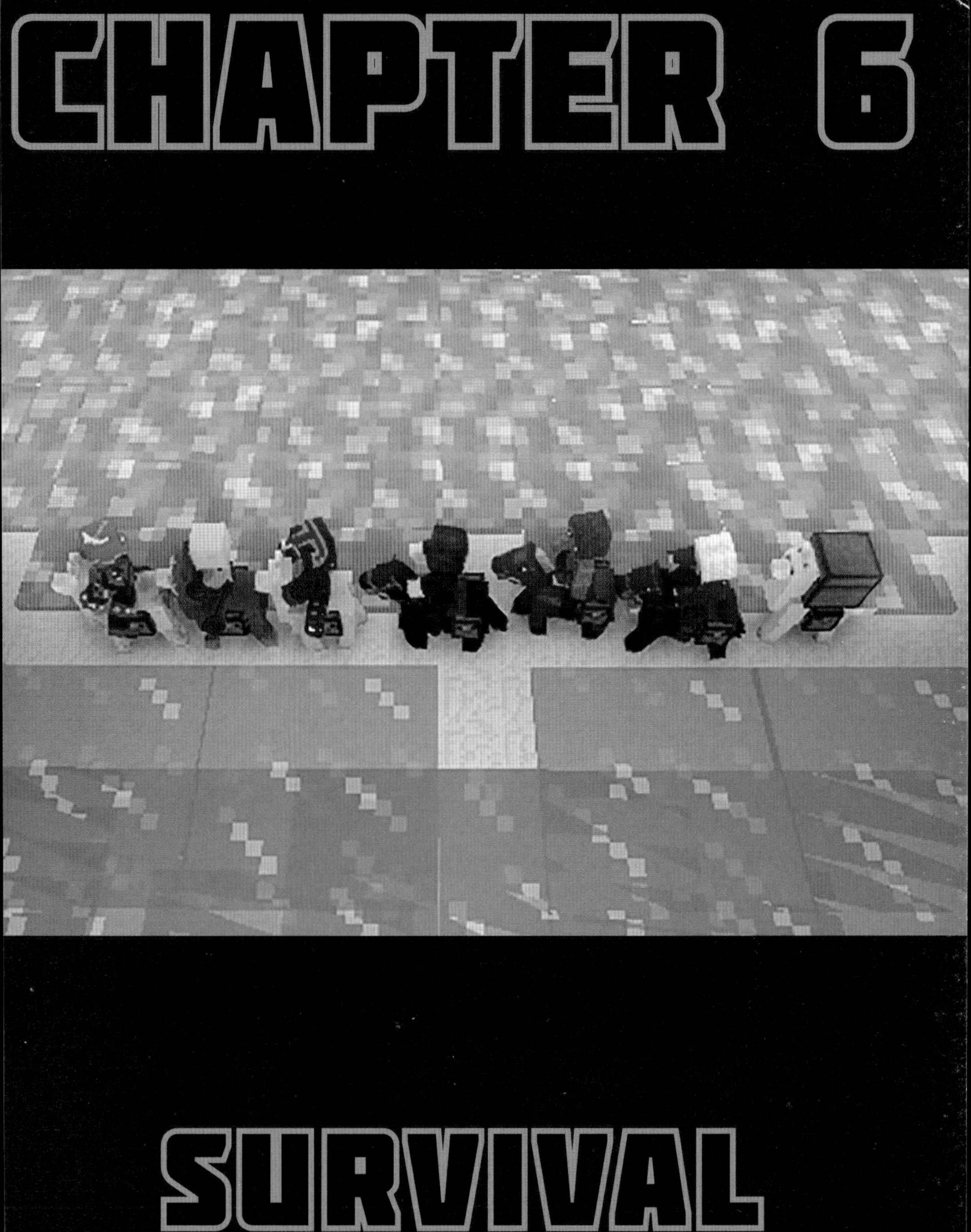

SURVIVAL

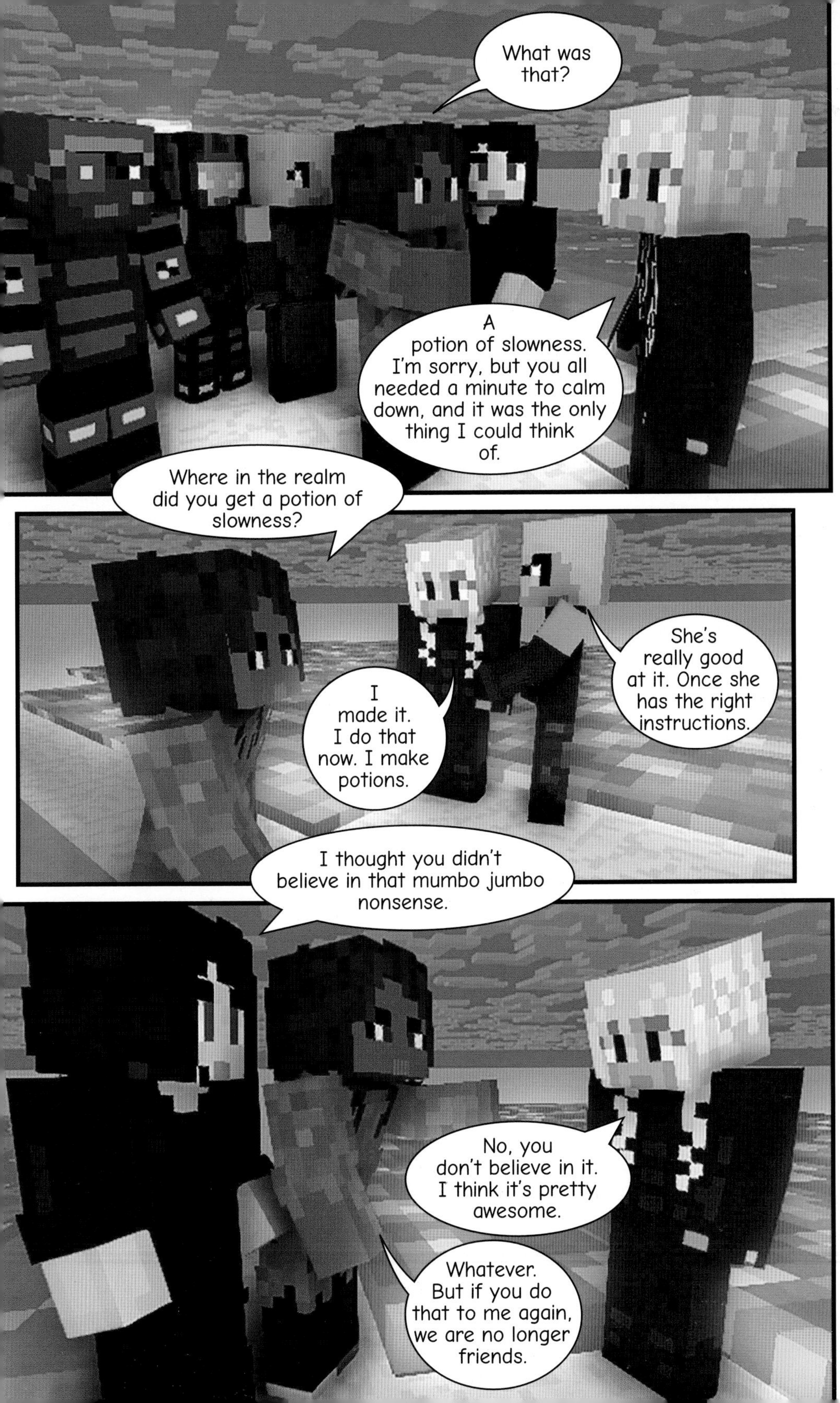
What was that?
A potion of slowness. I'm sorry, but you all needed a minute to calm down, and it was the only thing I could think of.
Where in the realm did you get a potion of slowness?
I made it. I do that now. I make potions.
She's really good at it. Once she has the right instructions.
I thought you didn't believe in that mumbo jumbo nonsense.
No, you don't believe in it. I think it's pretty awesome.
Whatever. But if you do that to me again, we are no longer friends.

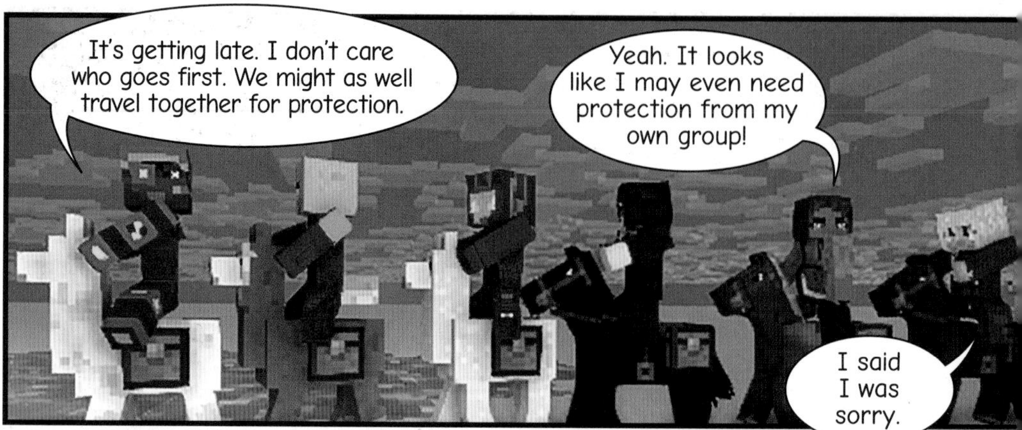
It's getting late. I don't care who goes first. We might as well travel together for protection.
Yeah. It looks like I may even need protection from my own group!
I said I was sorry.

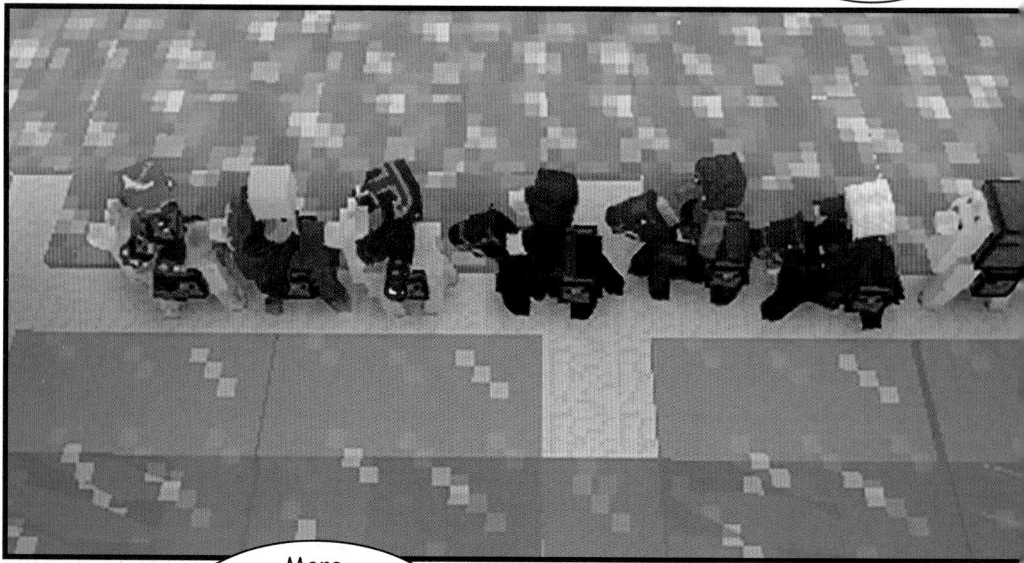

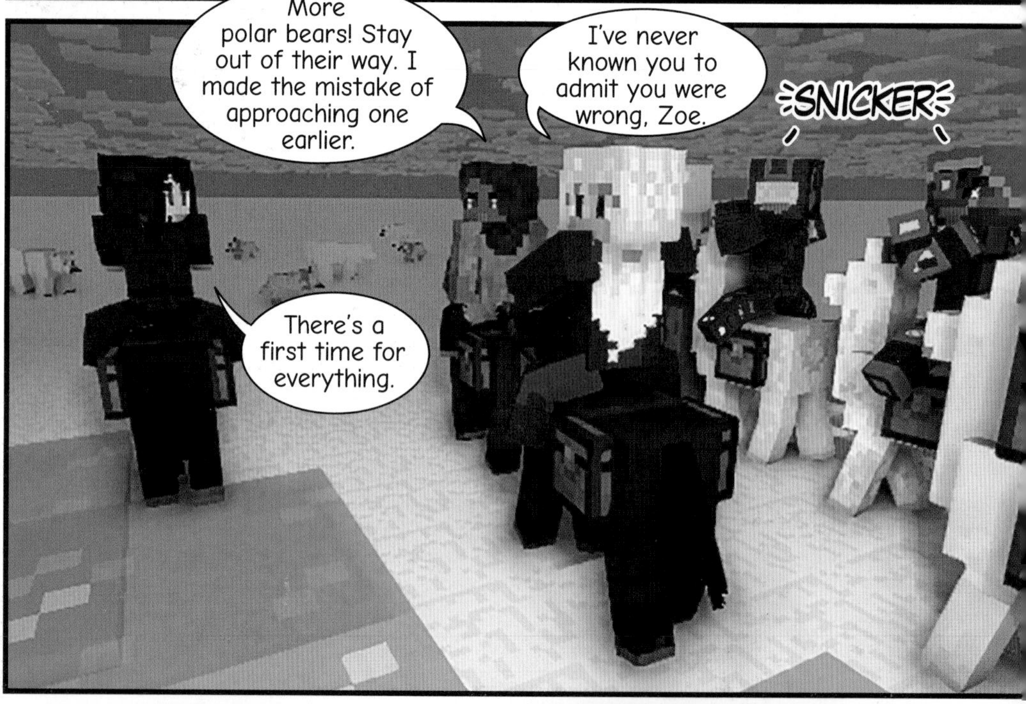
More polar bears! Stay out of their way. I made the mistake of approaching one earlier.
I've never known you to admit you were wrong, Zoe.
SNICKER
There's a first time for everything.

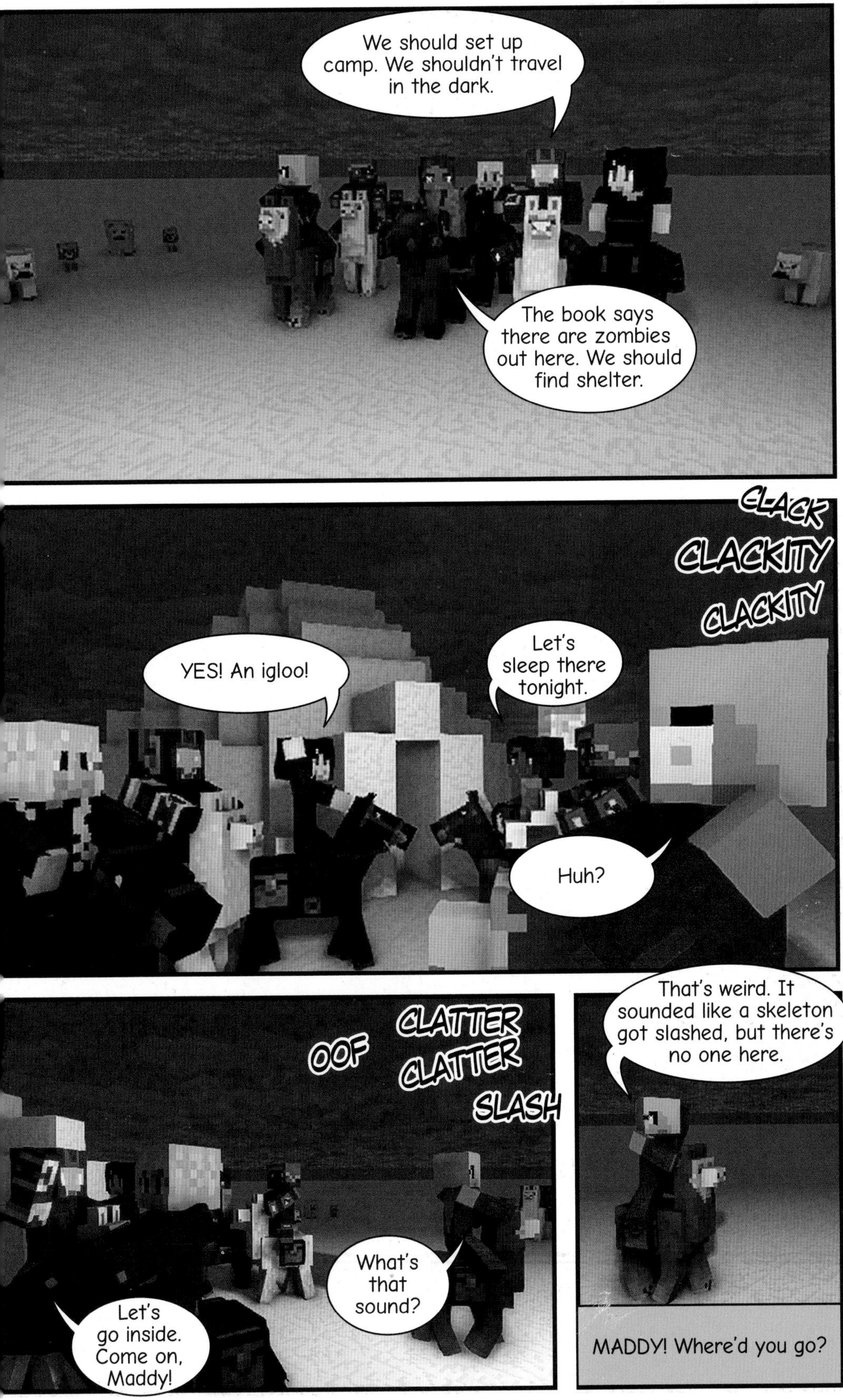

We should set up camp. We shouldn't travel in the dark.
The book says there are zombies out here. We should find shelter.
CLACK
CLACKITY
CLACKITY
YES! An igloo!
Let's sleep there tonight.
Huh?
OOF
CLATTER
CLATTER
SLASH
What's that sound?
Let's go inside. Come on, Maddy!
That's weird. It sounded like a skeleton got slashed, but there's no one here.
MADDY! Where'd you go?

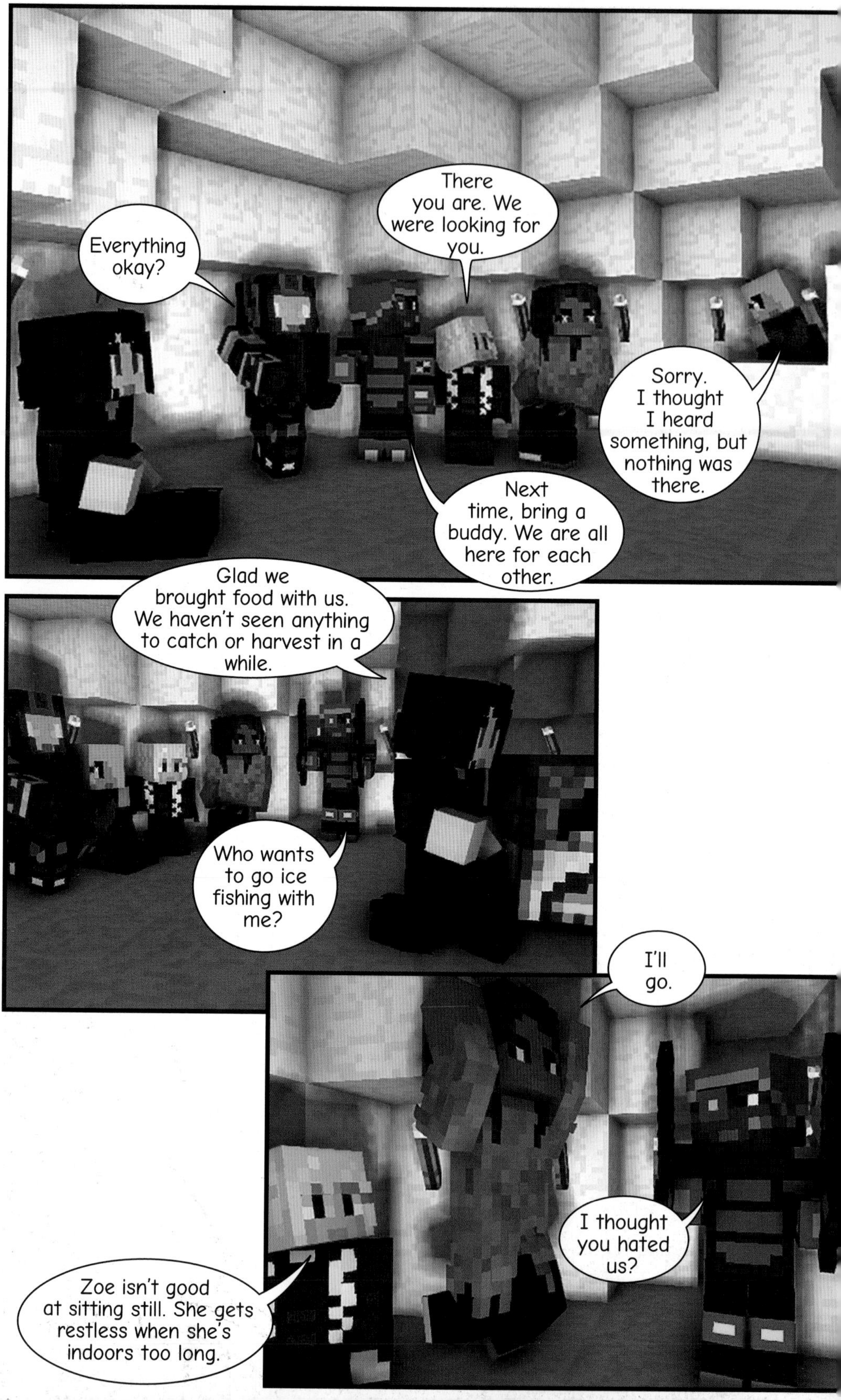
Everything okay?
There you are. We were looking for you.
Sorry. I thought I heard something, but nothing was there.
Next time, bring a buddy. We are all here for each other.
Glad we brought food with us. We haven't seen anything to catch or harvest in a while.
Who wants to go ice fishing with me?
I'll go.
I thought you hated us?
Zoe isn't good at sitting still. She gets restless when she's indoors too long.

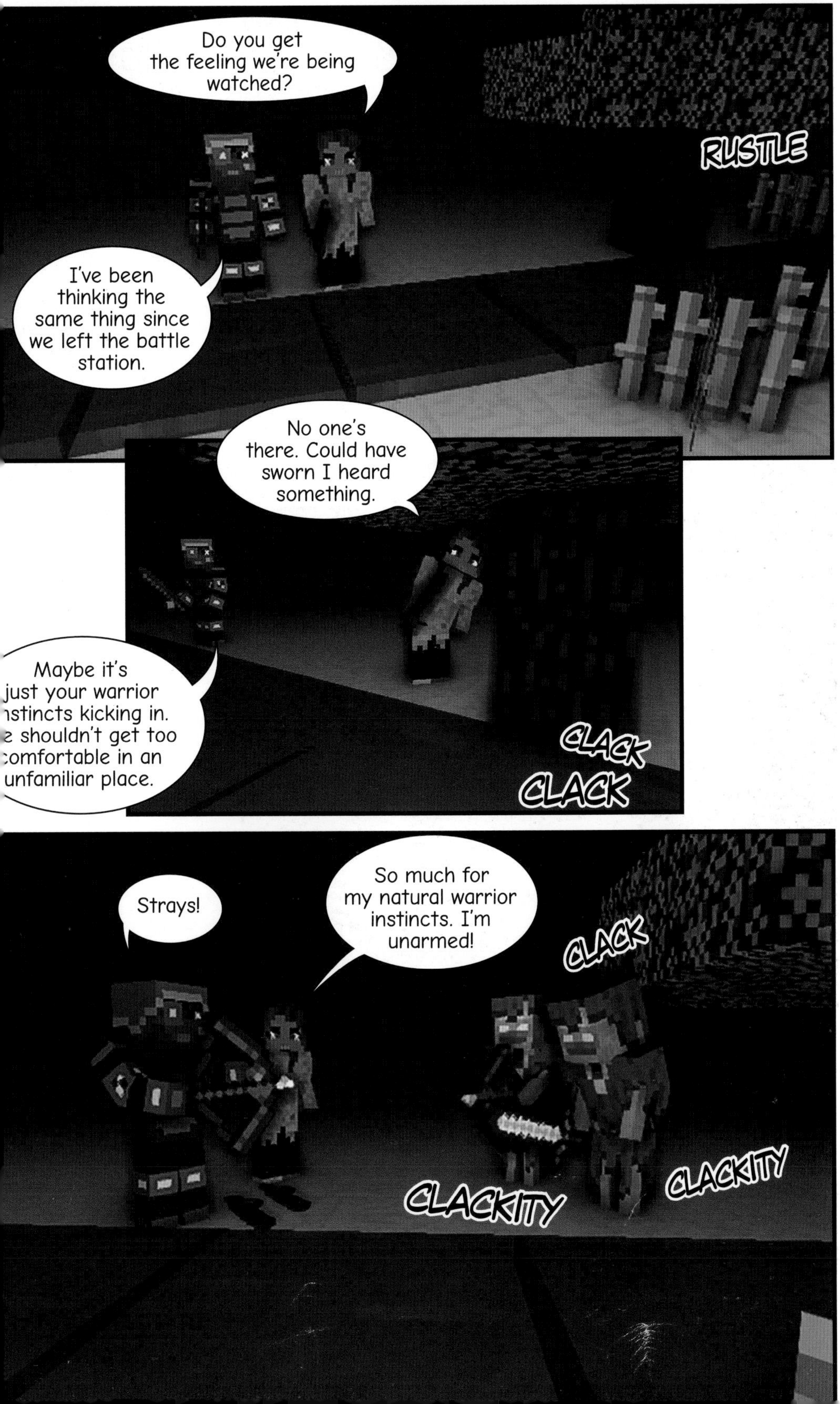
Do you get the feeling we're being watched?
RUSTLE
I've been thinking the same thing since we left the battle station.
No one's there. Could have sworn I heard something.
Maybe it's just your warrior nstincts kicking in. shouldn't get too omfortable in an unfamiliar place.
CLACK
CLACK
Strays!
So much for my natural warrior instincts. I'm unarmed!
CLACK
CLACKITY
CLACKITY

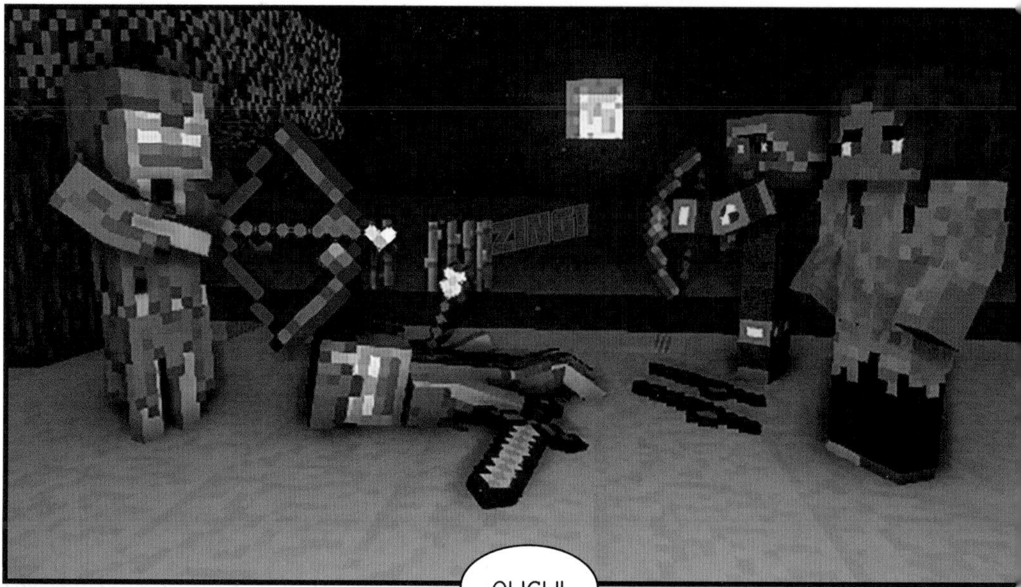

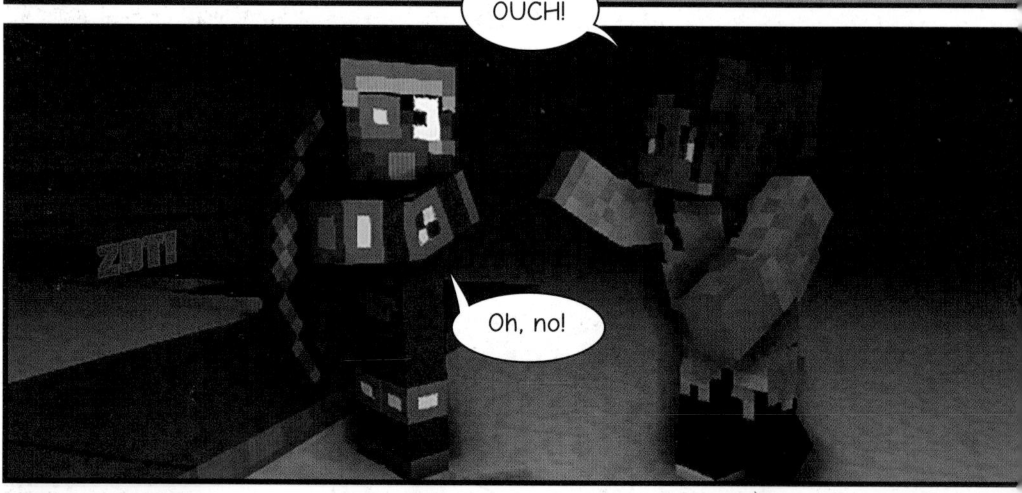
OUCH!
Oh, no!

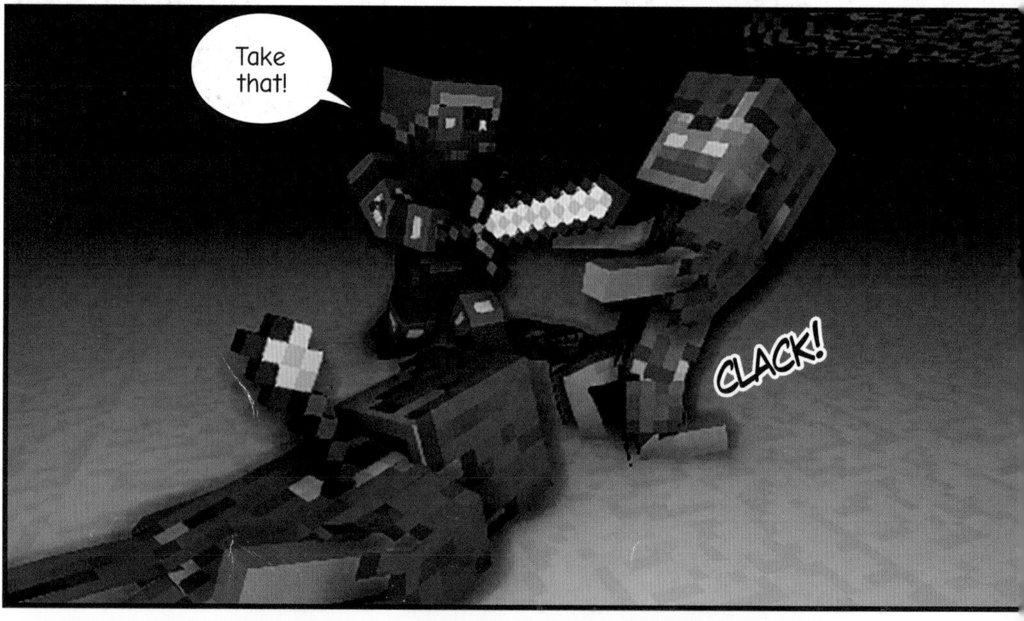
Take that!
CLACK!

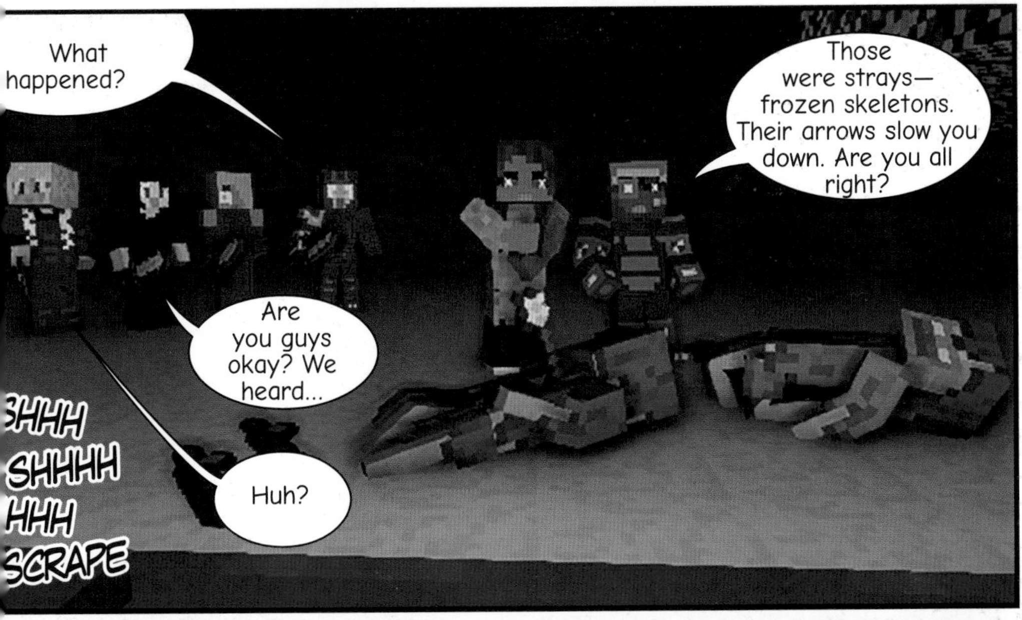
What happened?
Those were strays—frozen skeletons. Their arrows slow you down. Are you all right?
Are you guys okay? We heard...
Huh?
SHHH
SHHHH
HHH
SCRAPE

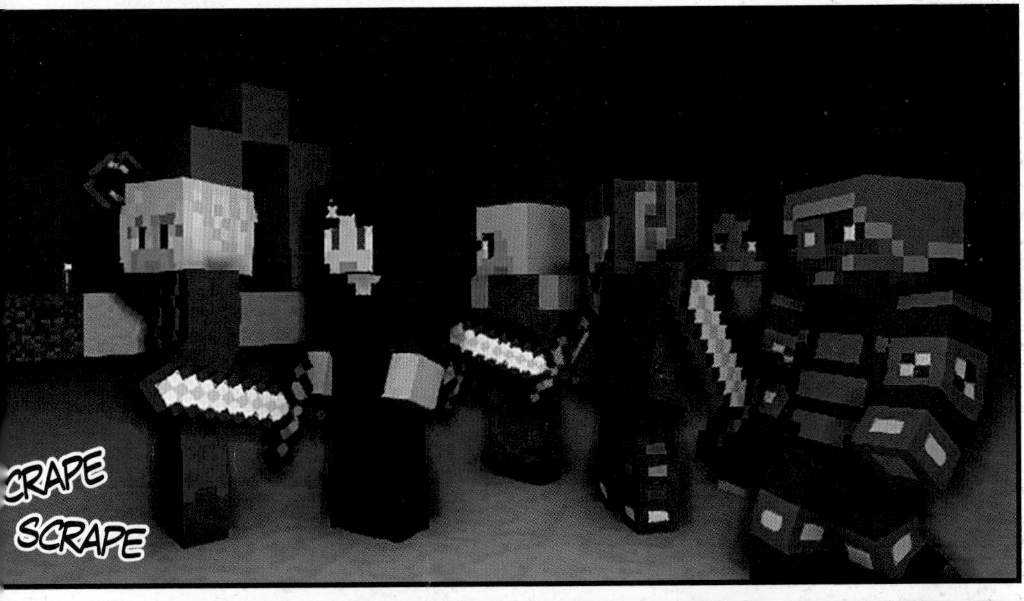
CRAPE
SCRAPE

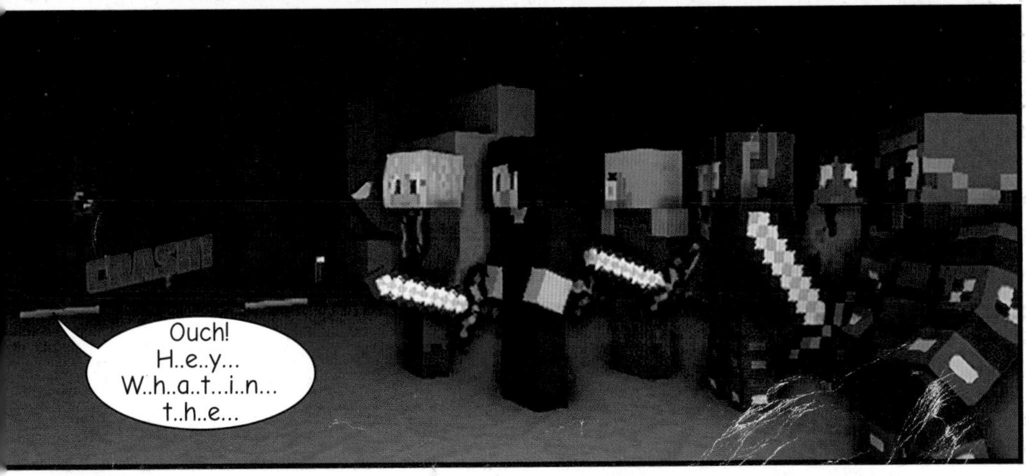
Ouch! H..e..y... W..h..a..t...i..n... t..h..e...

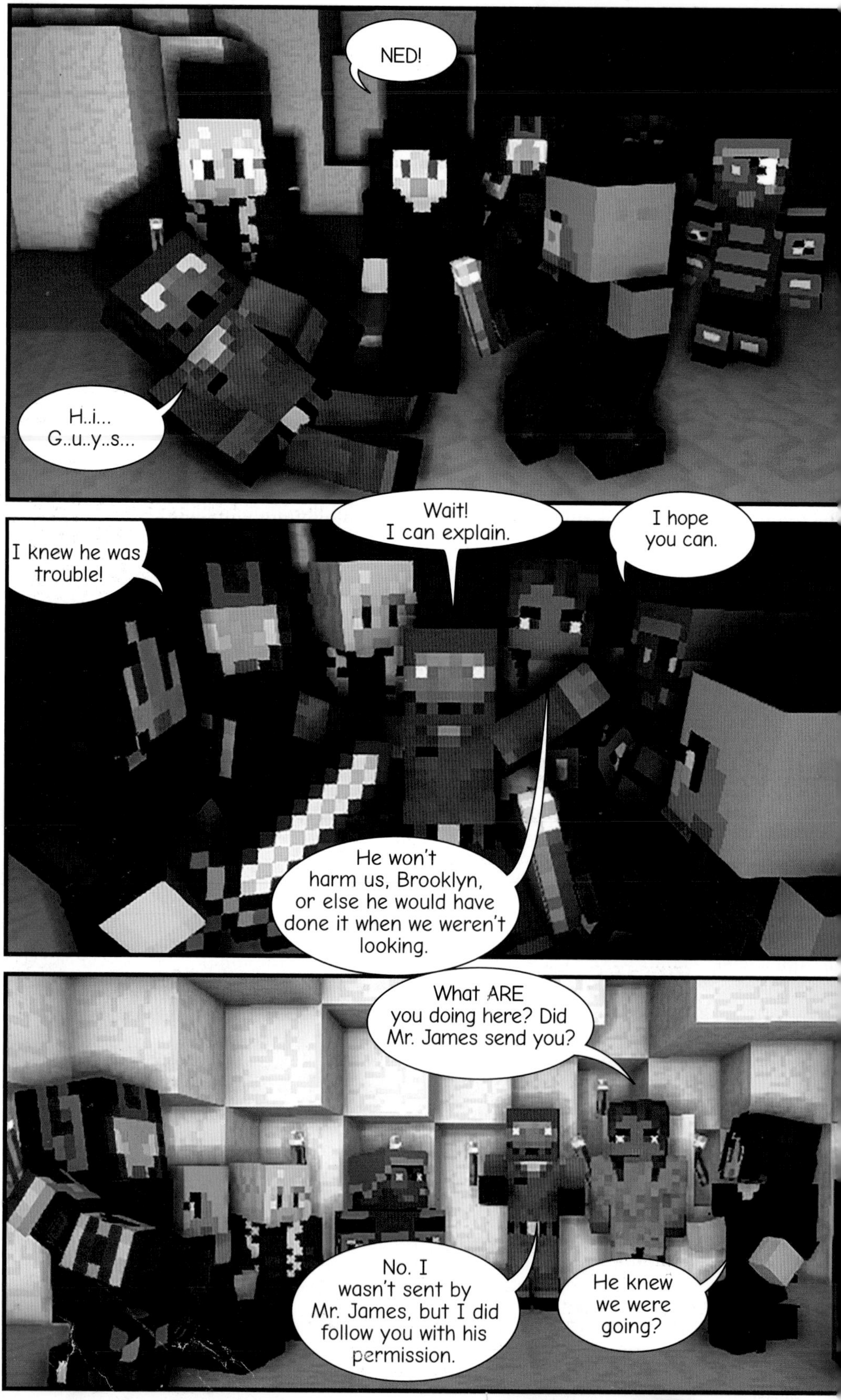
NED!
H..i... G..u..y..s...
I knew he was trouble!
Wait! I can explain.
I hope you can.
He won't harm us, Brooklyn, or else he would have done it when we weren't looking.
What ARE you doing here? Did Mr. James send you?
No. I wasn't sent by Mr. James, but I did follow you with his permission.
He knew we were going?

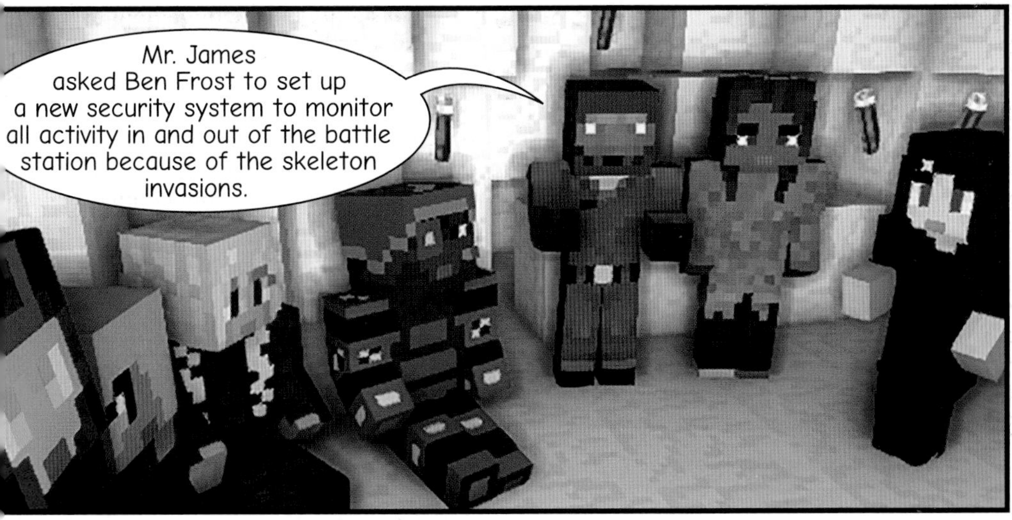
Mr. James asked Ben Frost to set up a new security system to monitor all activity in and out of the battle station because of the skeleton invasions.

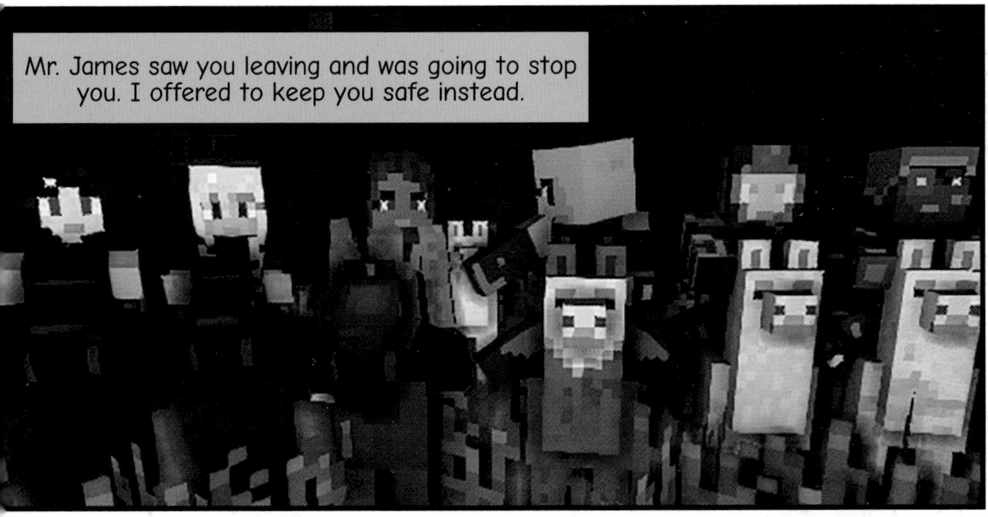
Mr. James saw you leaving and was going to stop you. I offered to keep you safe instead.

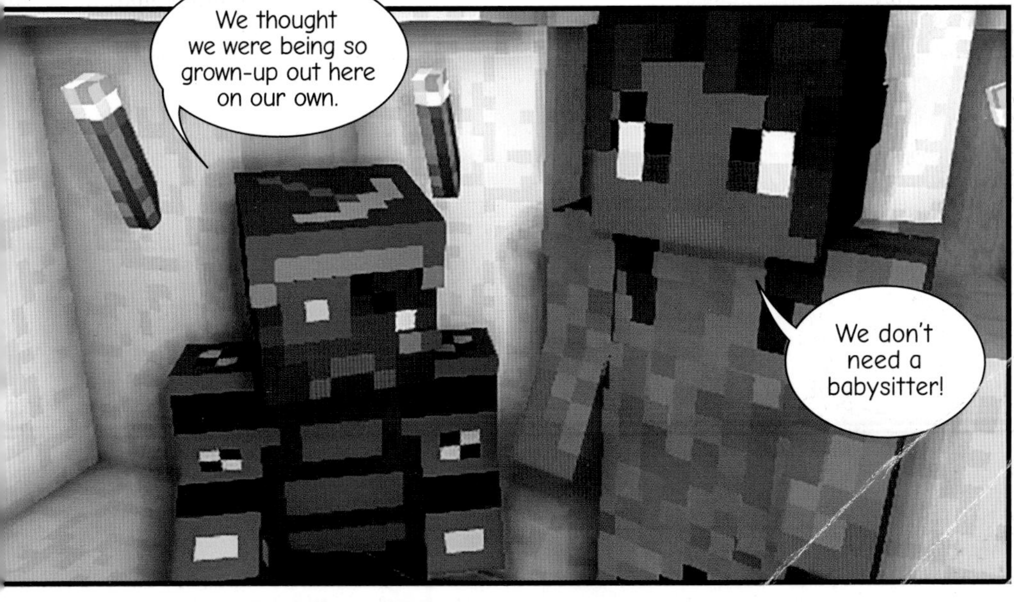
We thought we were being so grown-up out here on our own.
We don't need a babysitter!

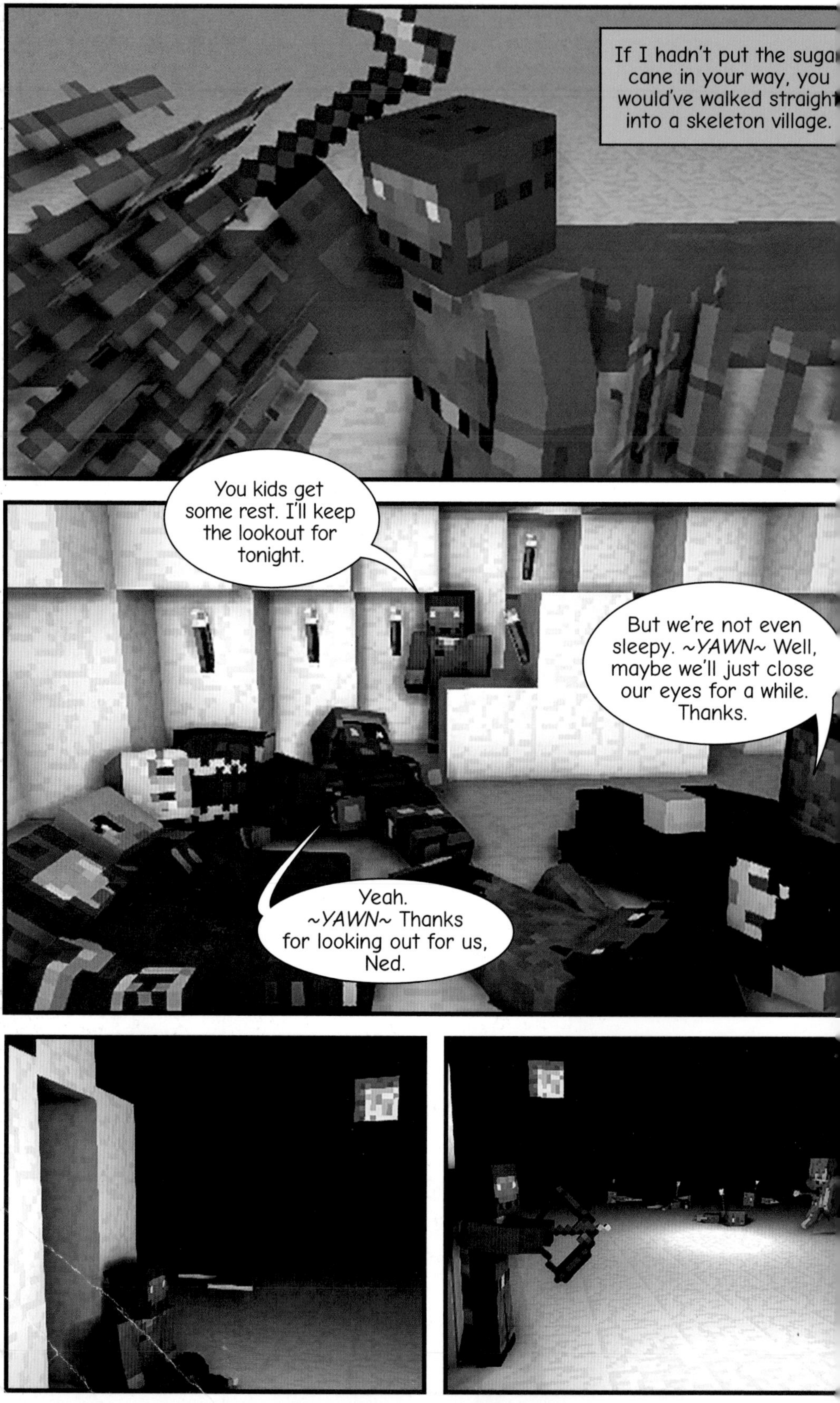
If I hadn't put the suga cane in your way, you would've walked straigh into a skeleton village.
You kids get some rest. I'll keep the lookout for tonight.
But we're not even sleepy. ~*YAWN*~ Well, maybe we'll just close our eyes for a while. Thanks.
Yeah. ~*YAWN*~ Thanks for looking out for us, Ned.

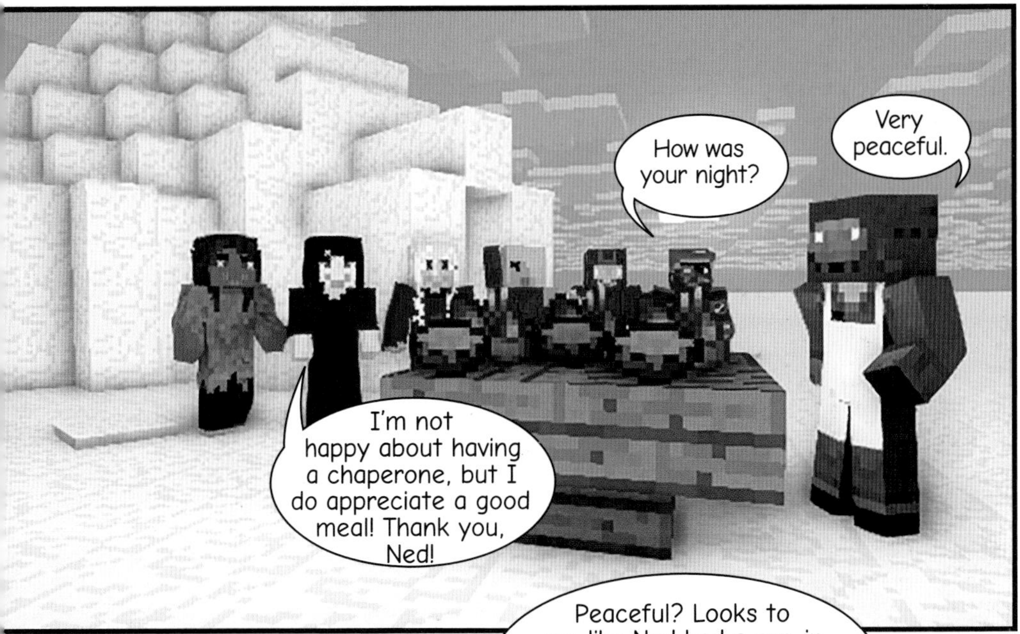
How was your night?
Very peaceful.
I'm not happy about having a chaperone, but I do appreciate a good meal! Thank you, Ned!

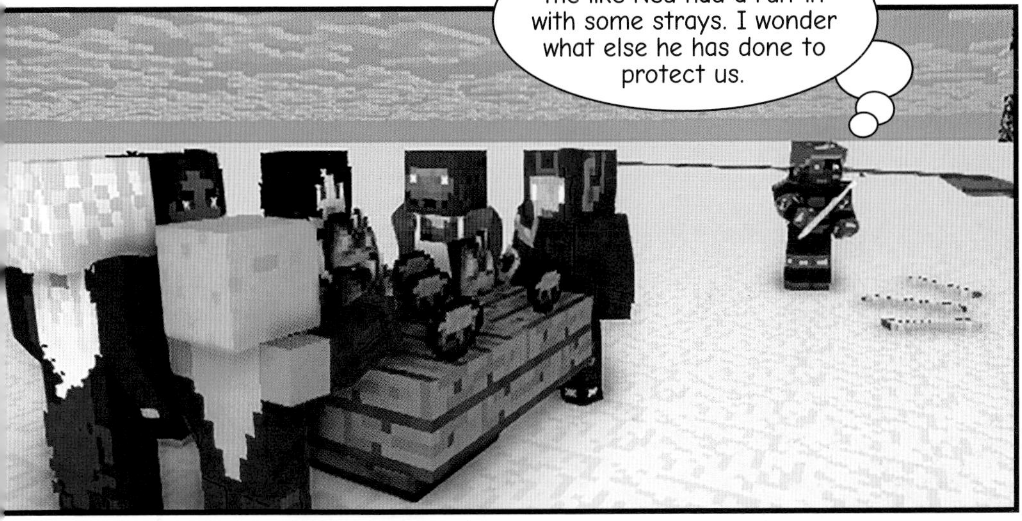
Peaceful? Looks to me like Ned had a run-in with some strays. I wonder what else he has done to protect us.

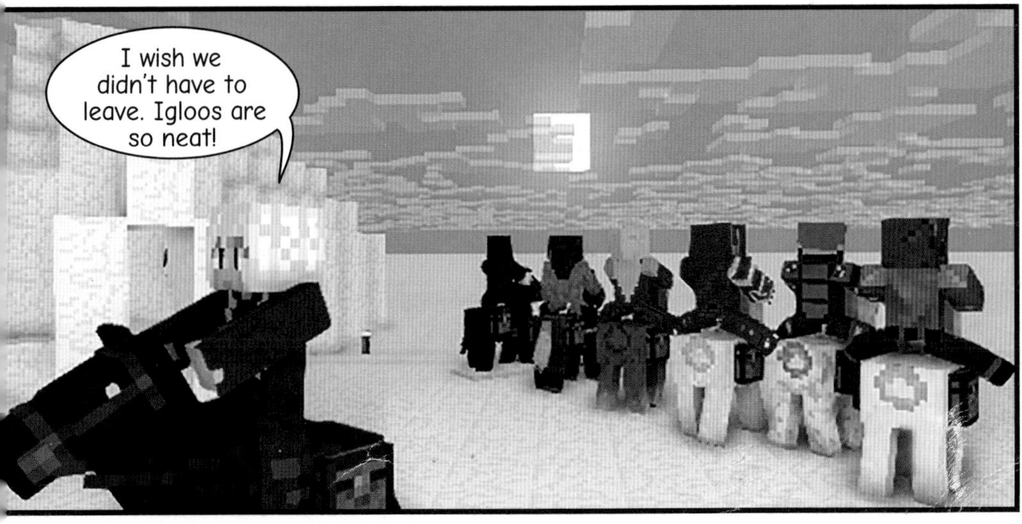
I wish we didn't have to leave. Igloos are so neat!

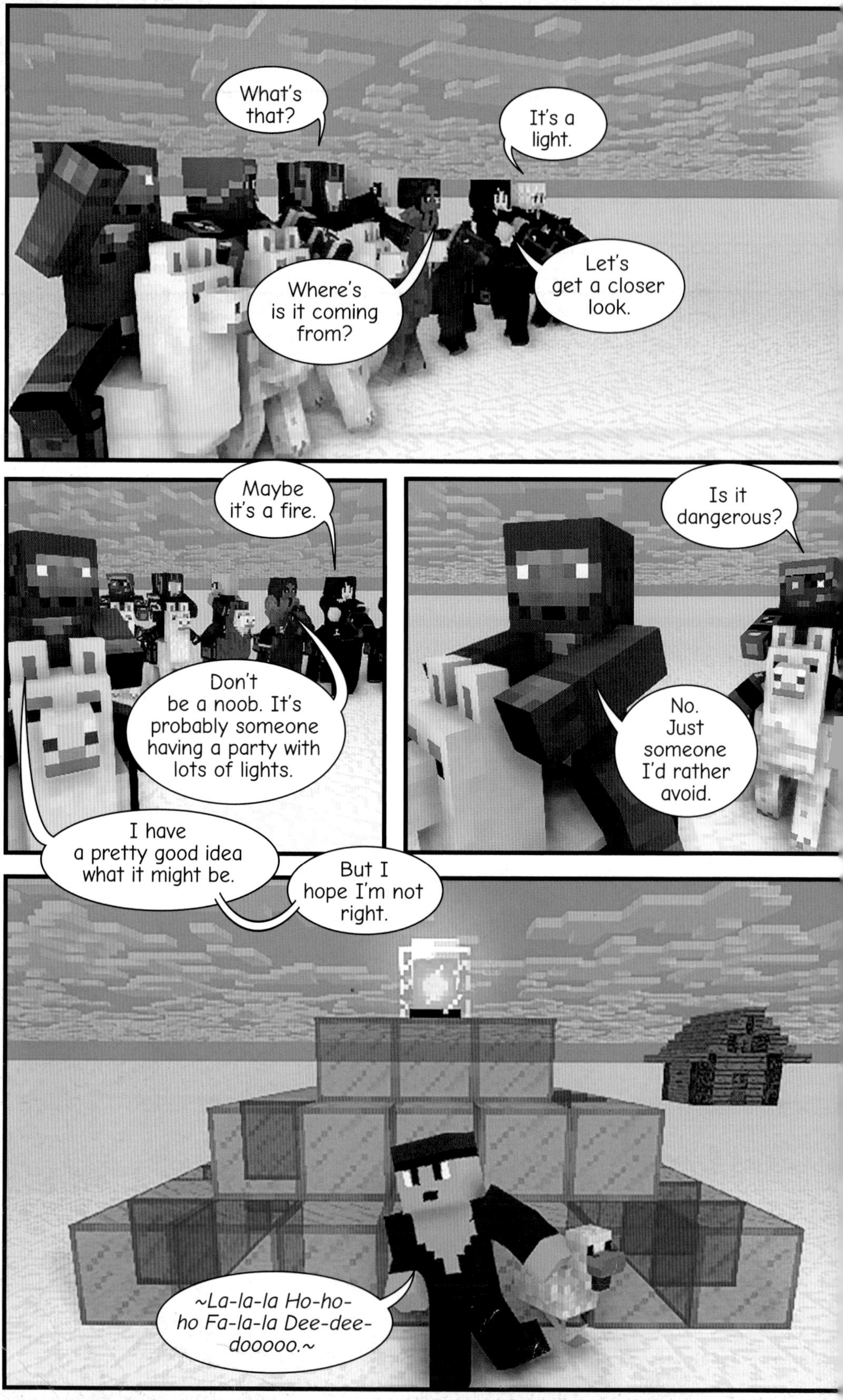
What's that?
It's a light.
Where's is it coming from?
Let's get a closer look.
Maybe it's a fire.
Don't be a noob. It's probably someone having a party with lots of lights.
Is it dangerous?
No. Just someone I'd rather avoid.
I have a pretty good idea what it might be.
But I hope I'm not right.
~La-la-la Ho-ho-ho Fa-la-la Dee-dee-dooooo.~

CHAPTER 7

THE SUMMIT

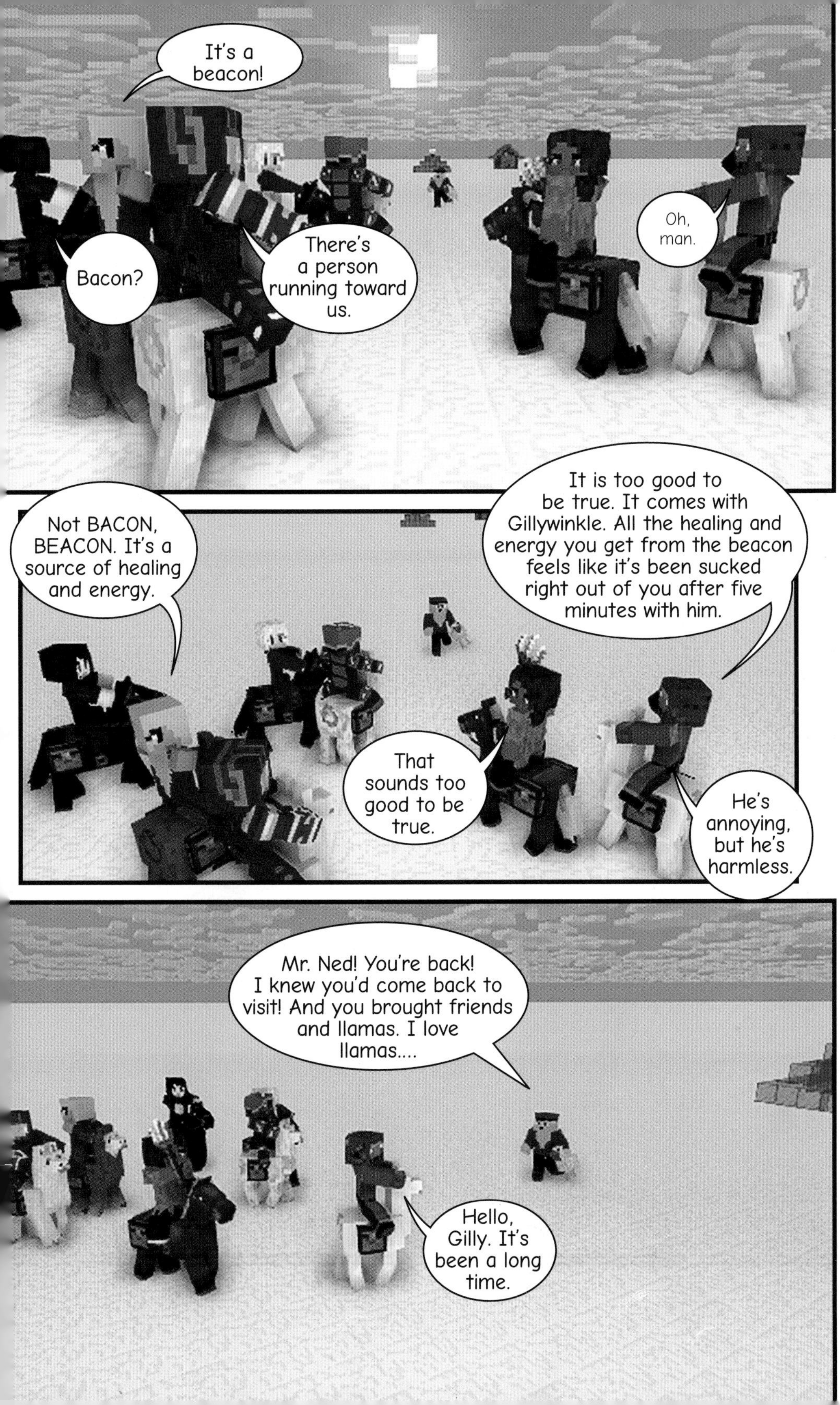
It's a beacon!
Bacon?
There's a person running toward us.
Oh, man.
Not BACON, BEACON. It's a source of healing and energy.
That sounds too good to be true.
It is too good to be true. It comes with Gillywinkle. All the healing and energy you get from the beacon feels like it's been sucked right out of you after five minutes with him.
He's annoying, but he's harmless.
Mr. Ned! You're back! I knew you'd come back to visit! And you brought friends and llamas. I love llamas....
Hello, Gilly. It's been a long time.

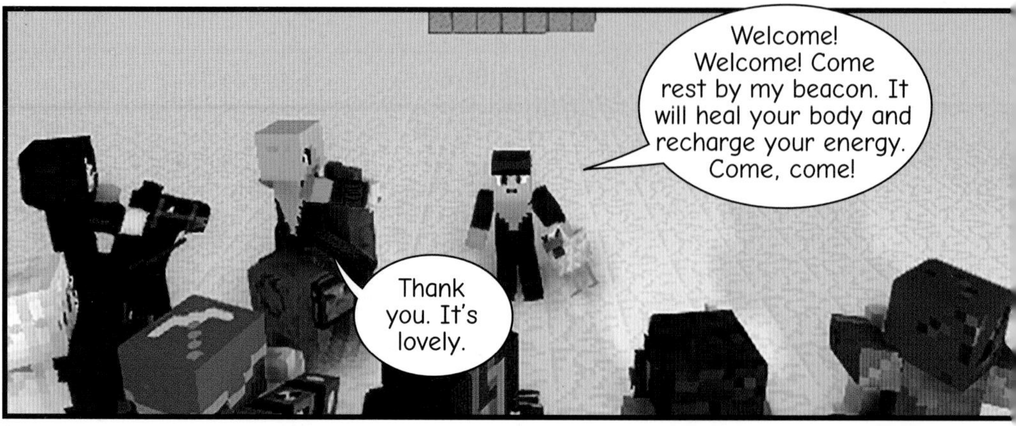
Welcome! Welcome! Come rest by my beacon. It will heal your body and recharge your energy. Come, come!
Thank you. It's lovely.

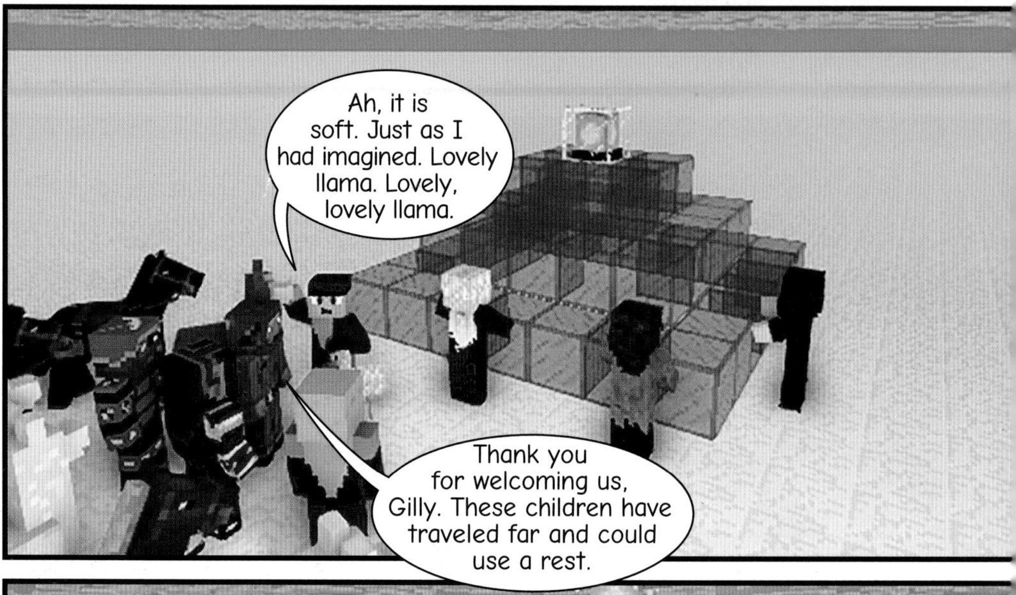
Ah, it is soft. Just as I had imagined. Lovely llama. Lovely, lovely llama.
Thank you for welcoming us, Gilly. These children have traveled far and could use a rest.

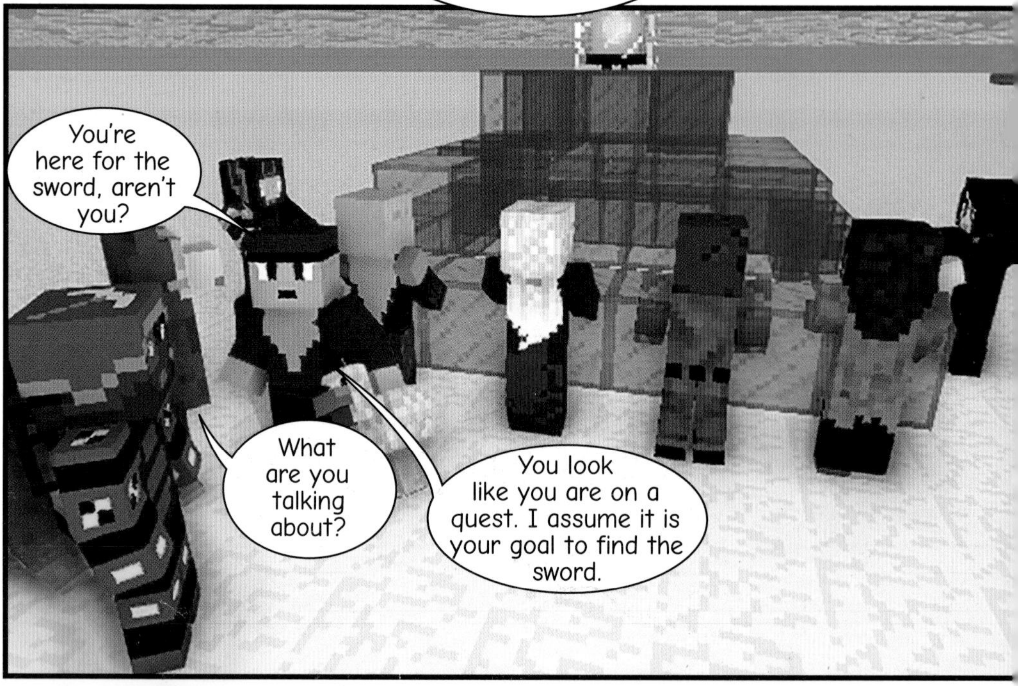
You're here for the sword, aren't you?
What are you talking about?
You look like you are on a quest. I assume it is your goal to find the sword.

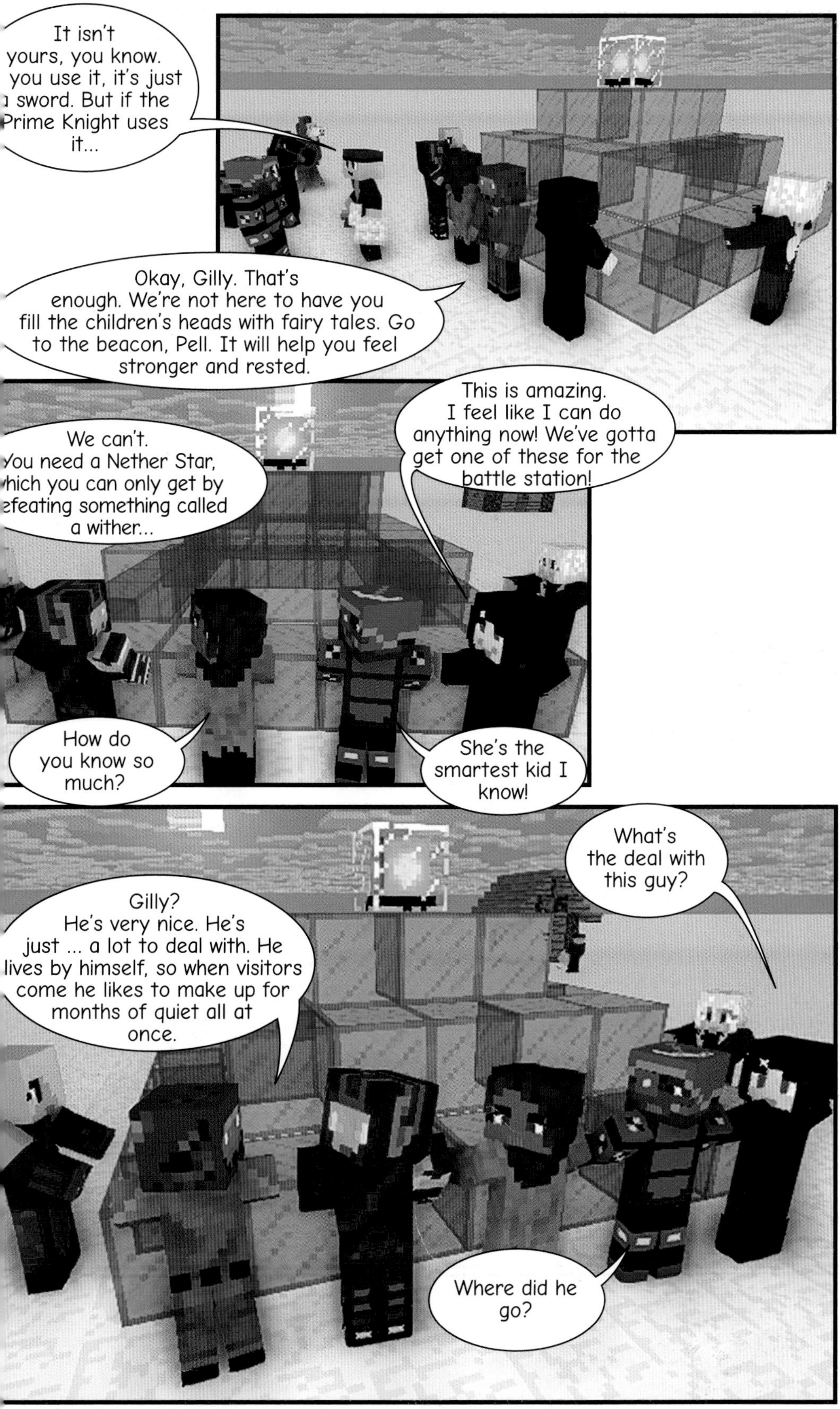
It isn't yours, you know. you use it, it's just sword. But if the Prime Knight uses it...
Okay, Gilly. That's enough. We're not here to have you fill the children's heads with fairy tales. Go to the beacon, Pell. It will help you feel stronger and rested.
This is amazing. I feel like I can do anything now! We've gotta get one of these for the battle station!
We can't. You need a Nether Star, hich you can only get by efeating something called a wither...
How do you know so much?
She's the smartest kid I know!
Gilly? He's very nice. He's just ... a lot to deal with. He lives by himself, so when visitors come he likes to make up for months of quiet all at once.
What's the deal with this guy?
Where did he go?

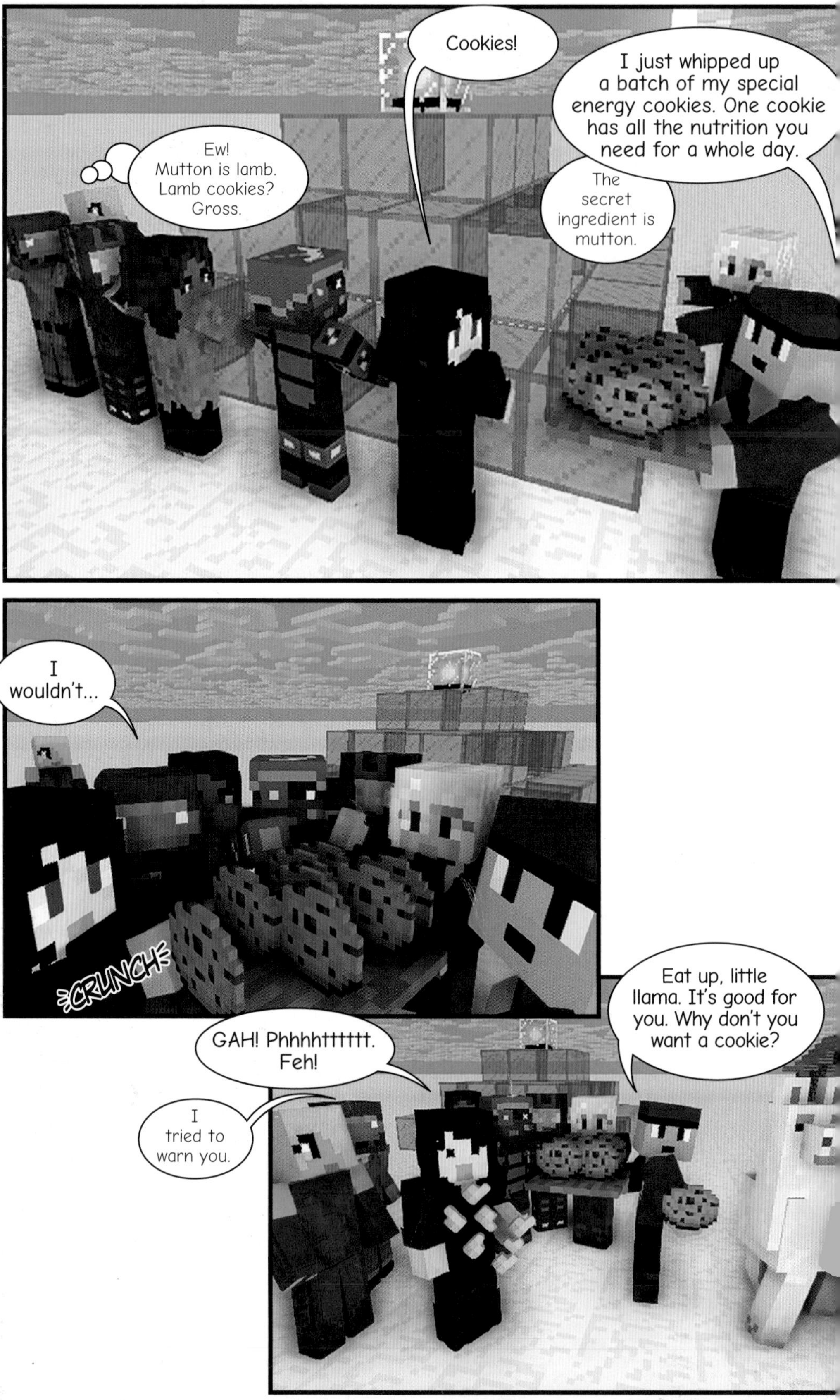
I just whipped up a batch of my special energy cookies. One cookie has all the nutrition you need for a whole day.
The secret ingredient is mutton.
Cookies!
Ew! Mutton is lamb. Lamb cookies? Gross.
I wouldn't...
CRUNCH
GAH! Phhhhtttttt. Feh!
I tried to warn you.
Eat up, little llama. It's good for you. Why don't you want a cookie?

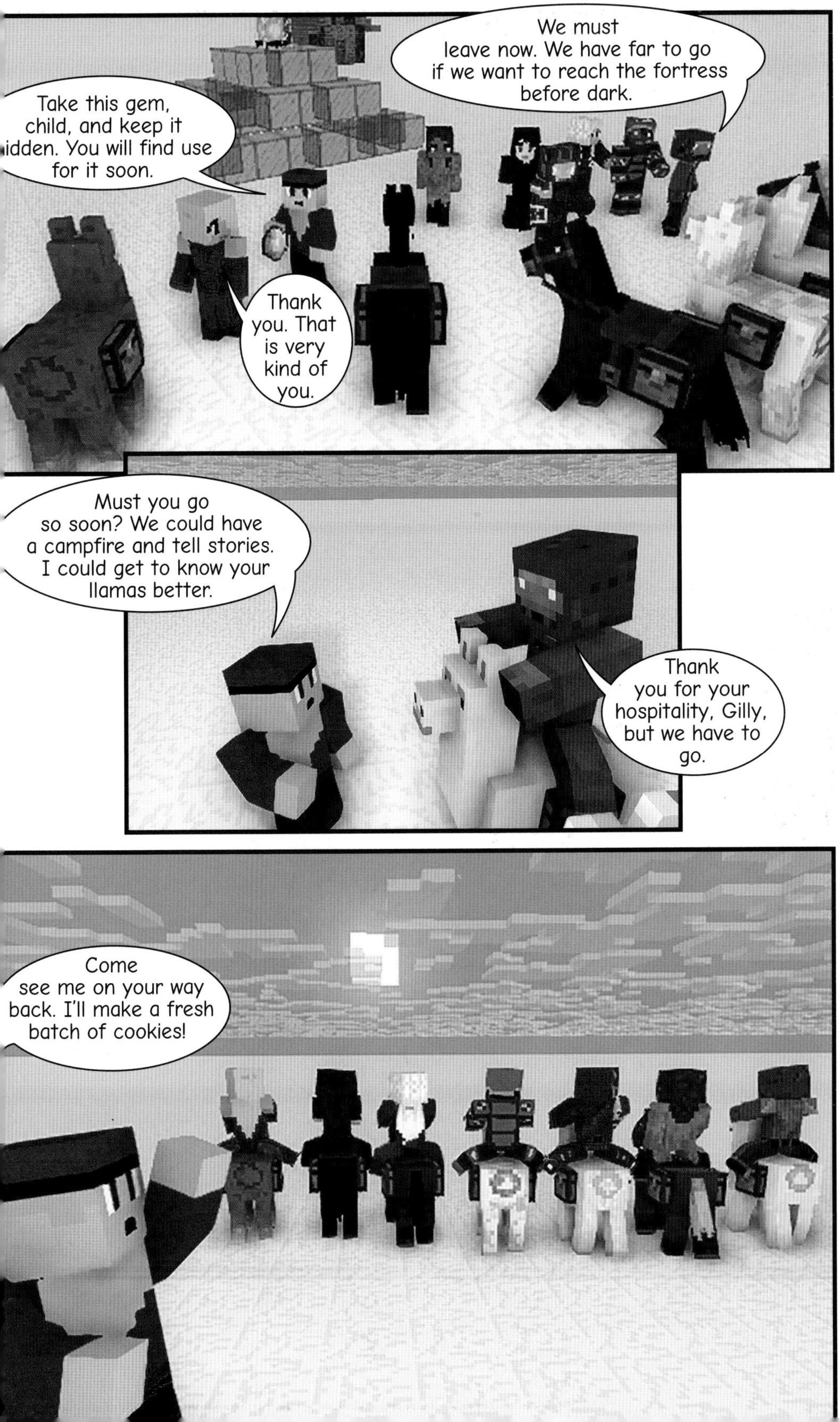

Take this gem, child, and keep it idden. You will find use for it soon.
Thank you. That is very kind of you.
We must leave now. We have far to go if we want to reach the fortress before dark.
Must you go so soon? We could have a campfire and tell stories. I could get to know your llamas better.
Thank you for your hospitality, Gilly, but we have to go.
Come see me on your way back. I'll make a fresh batch of cookies!

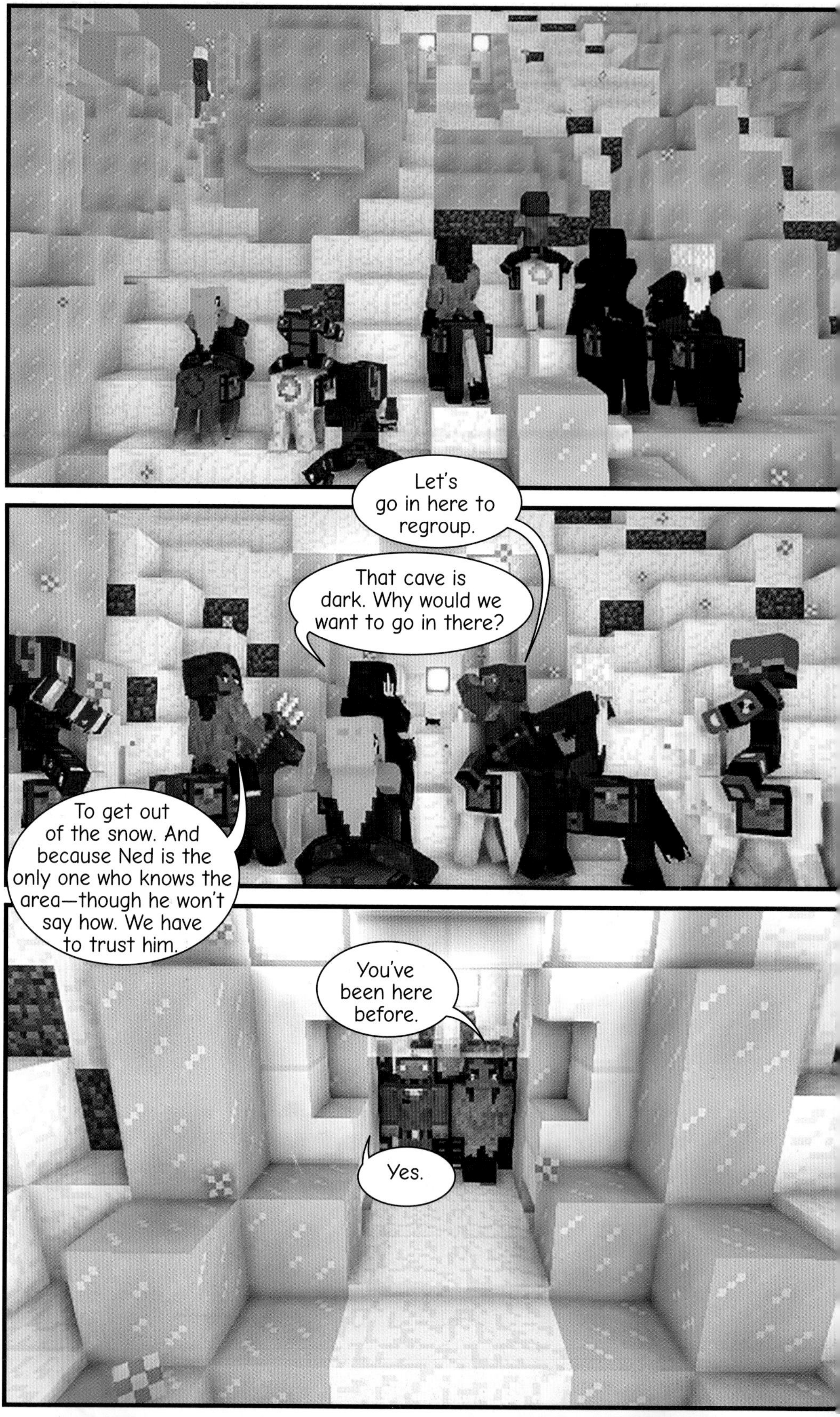
Let's go in here to regroup.
That cave is dark. Why would we want to go in there?
To get out of the snow. And because Ned is the only one who knows the area—though he won't say how. We have to trust him.
You've been here before.
Yes.

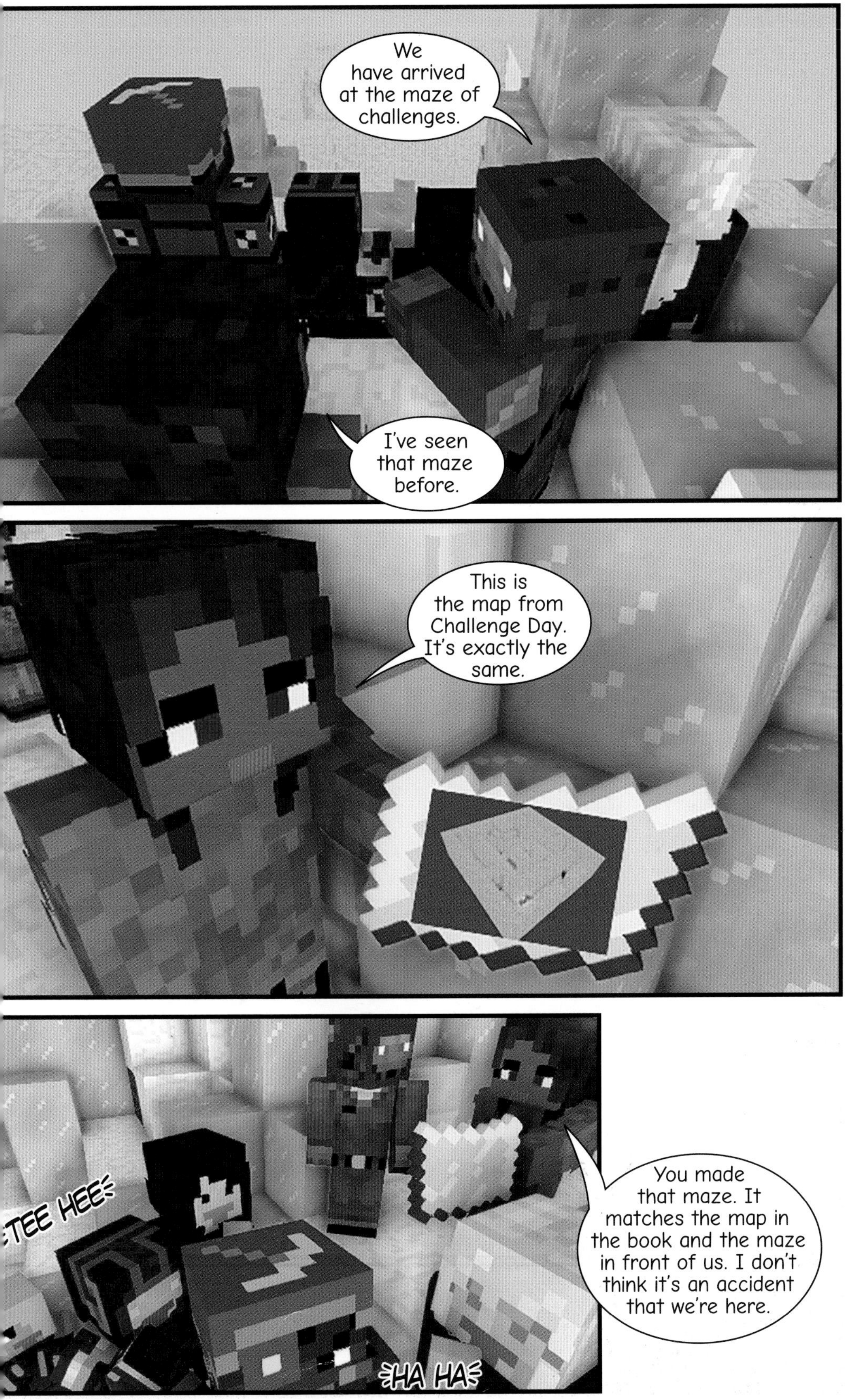
We have arrived at the maze of challenges.
I've seen that maze before.
This is the map from Challenge Day. It's exactly the same.
TEE HEE
You made that maze. It matches the map in the book and the maze in front of us. I don't think it's an accident that we're here.
HA HA

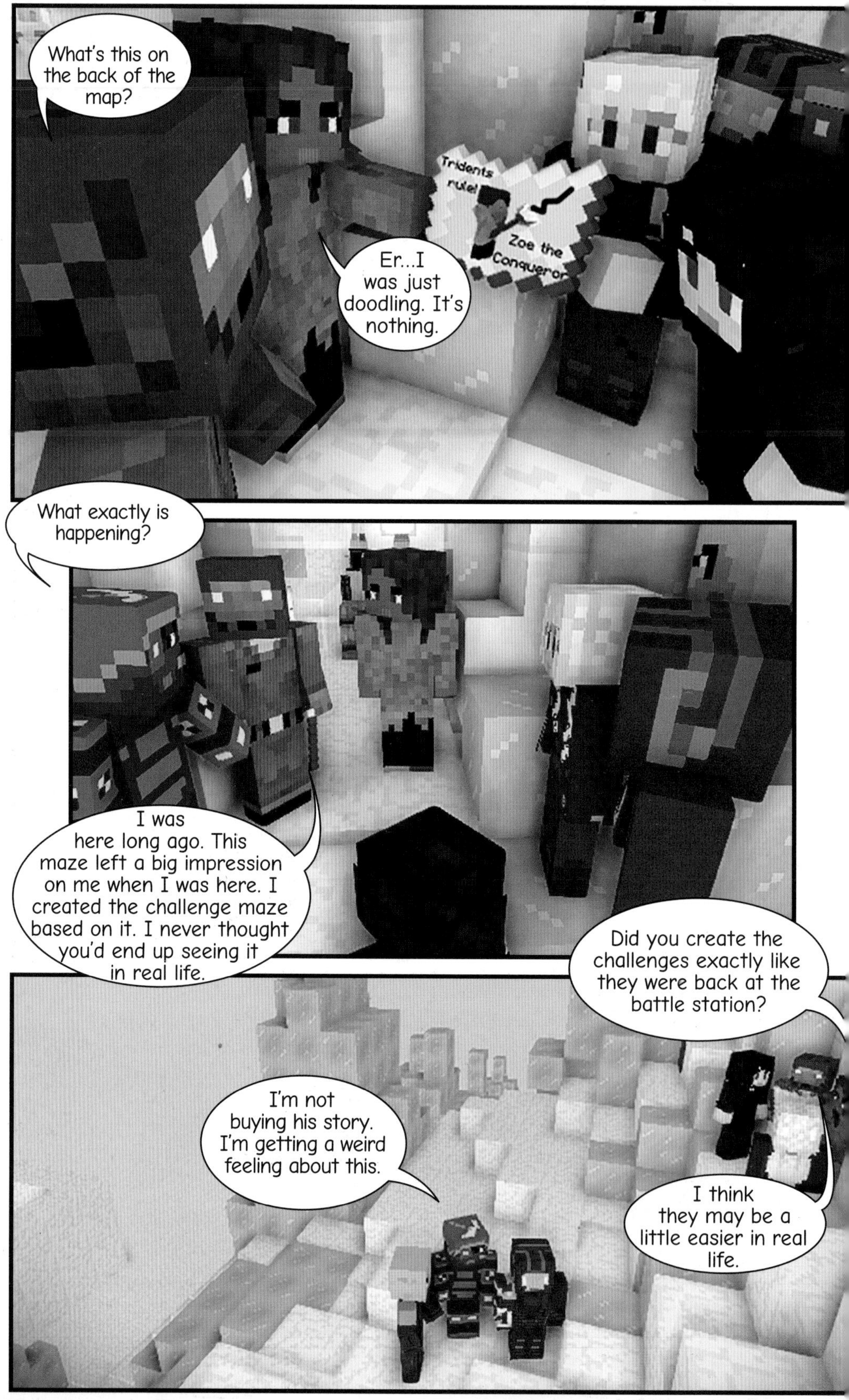
What's this on the back of the map?
Tridents rule!
Zoe the Conqueror
Er...I was just doodling. It's nothing.
What exactly is happening?
I was here long ago. This maze left a big impression on me when I was here. I created the challenge maze based on it. I never thought you'd end up seeing it in real life.
Did you create the challenges exactly like they were back at the battle station?
I think they may be a little easier in real life.
I'm not buying his story. I'm getting a weird feeling about this.

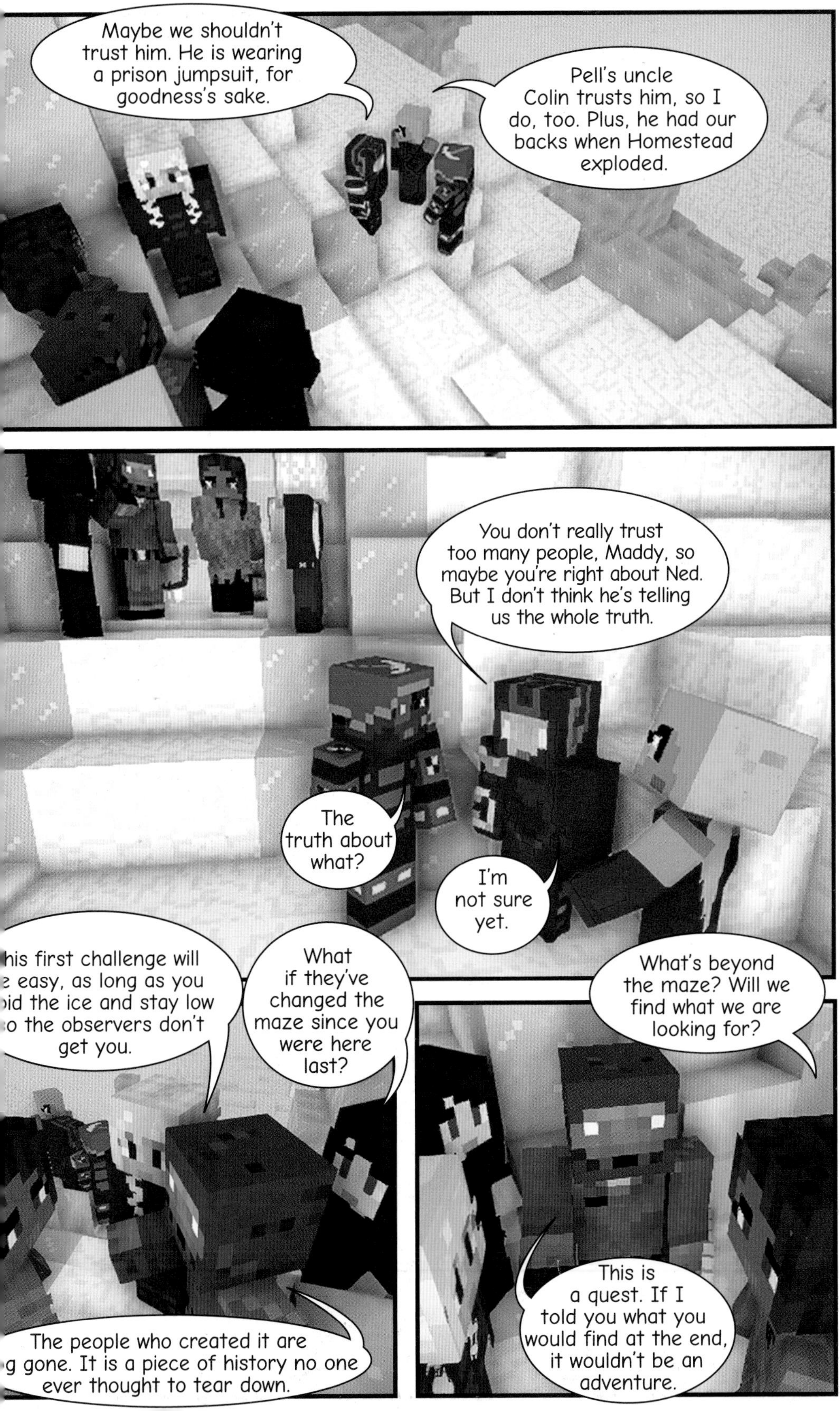
Maybe we shouldn't trust him. He is wearing a prison jumpsuit, for goodness's sake.
Pell's uncle Colin trusts him, so I do, too. Plus, he had our backs when Homestead exploded.
You don't really trust too many people, Maddy, so maybe you're right about Ned. But I don't think he's telling us the whole truth.
The truth about what?
I'm not sure yet.
his first challenge will e easy, as long as you oid the ice and stay low o the observers don't get you.
What if they've changed the maze since you were here last?
The people who created it are g gone. It is a piece of history no one ever thought to tear down.
What's beyond the maze? Will we find what we are looking for?
This is a quest. If I told you what you would find at the end, it wouldn't be an adventure.

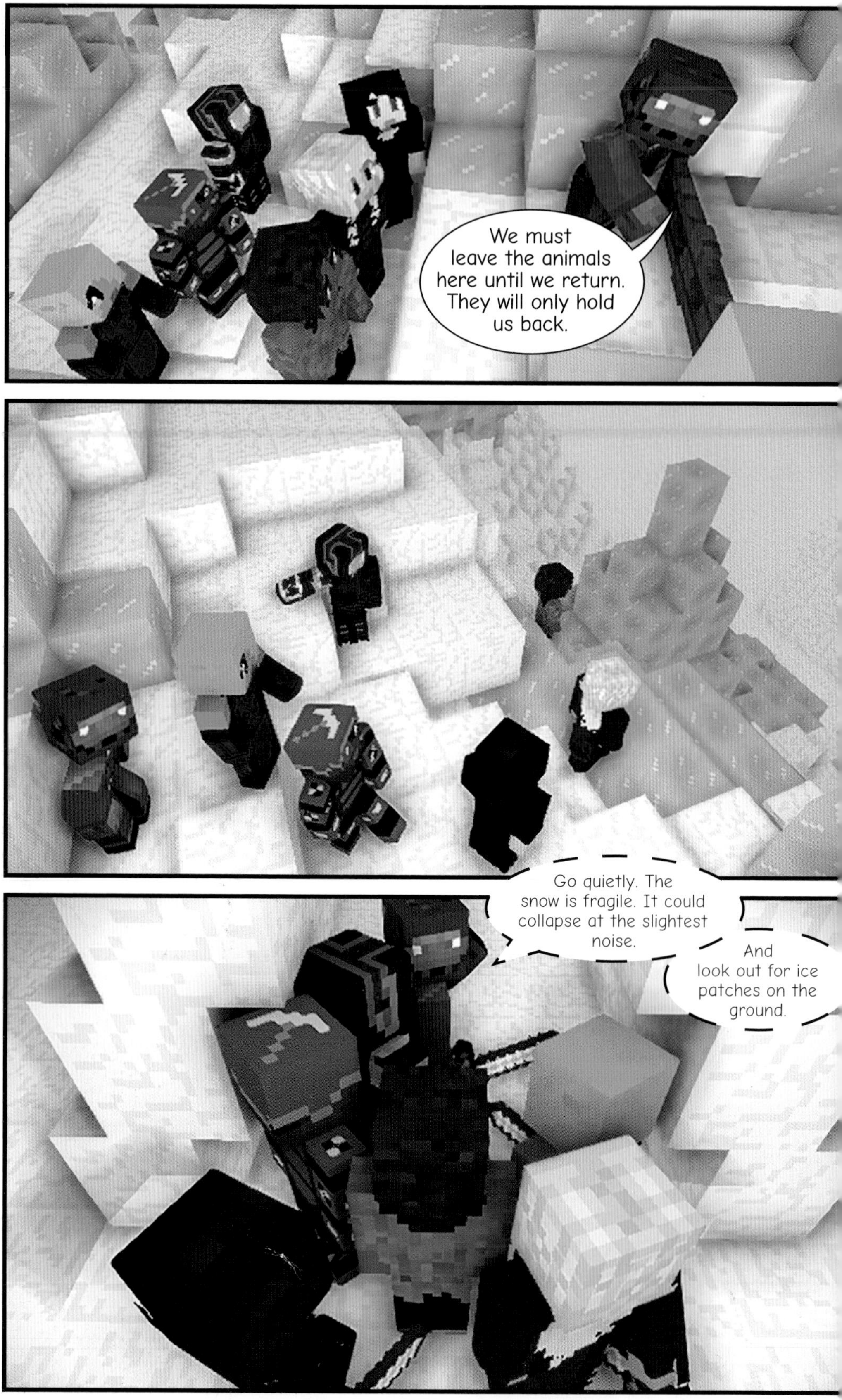
We must leave the animals here until we return. They will only hold us back.
Go quietly. The snow is fragile. It could collapse at the slightest noise.
And look out for ice patches on the ground.

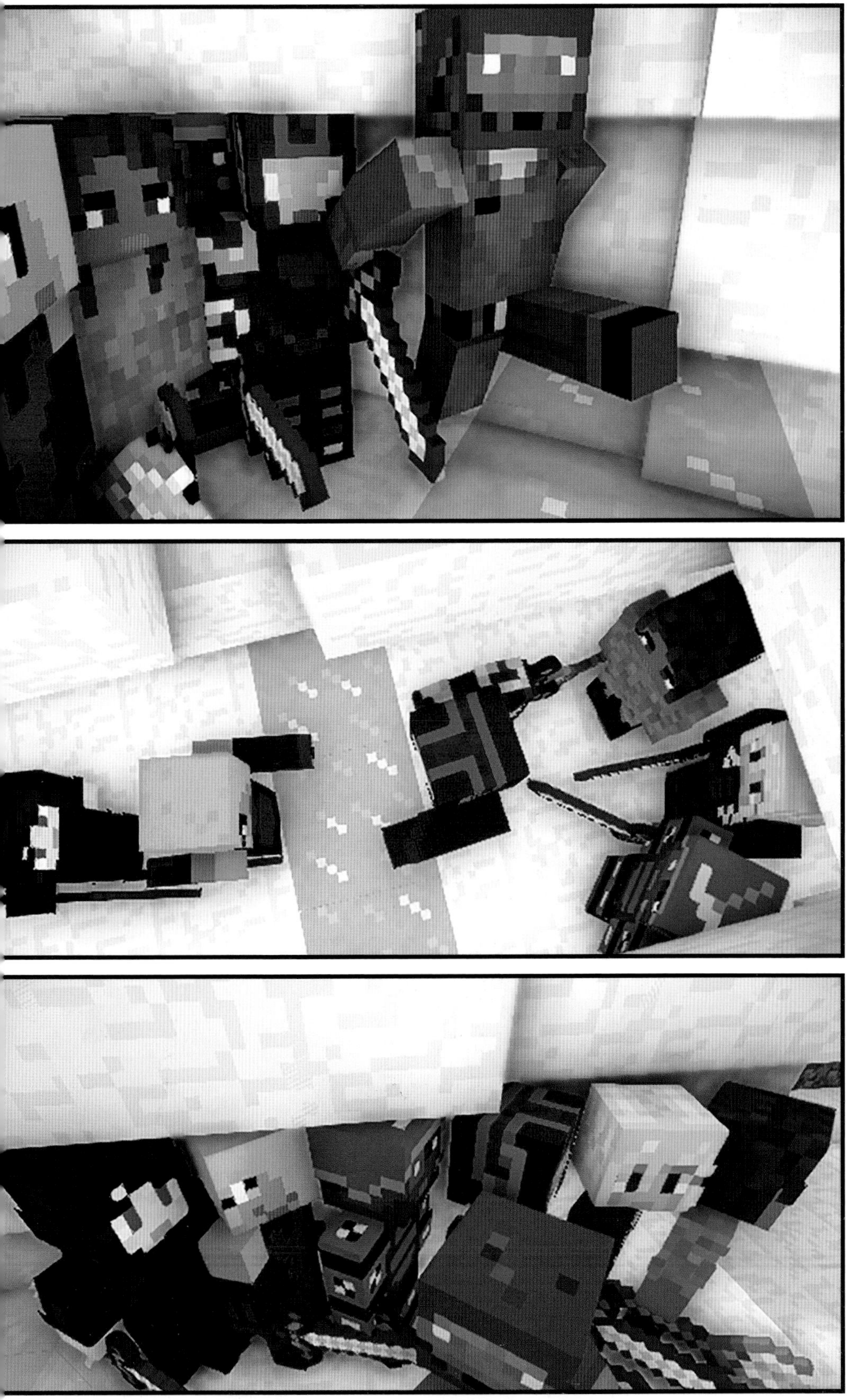

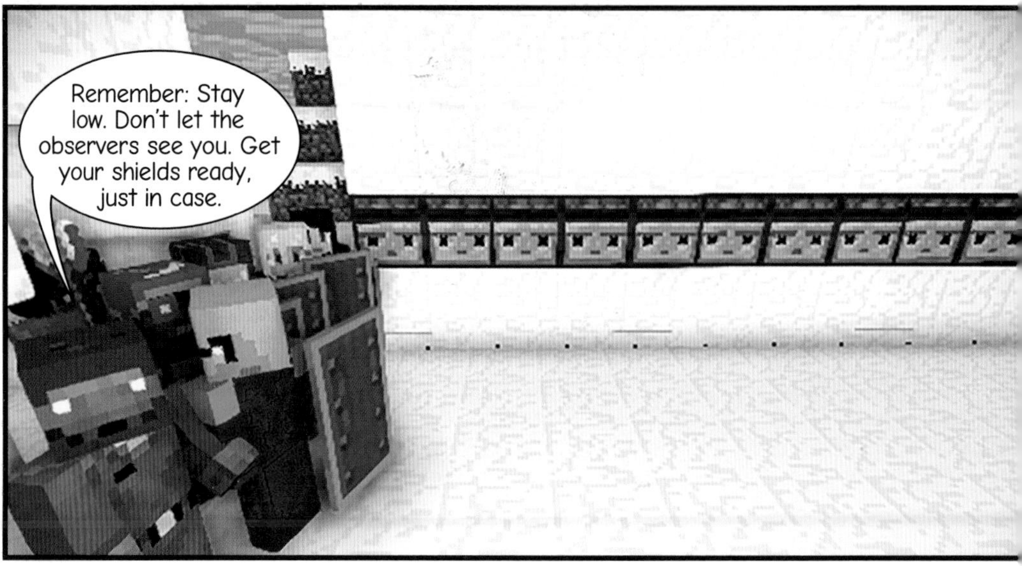
Remember: Stay low. Don't let the observers see you. Get your shields ready, just in case.

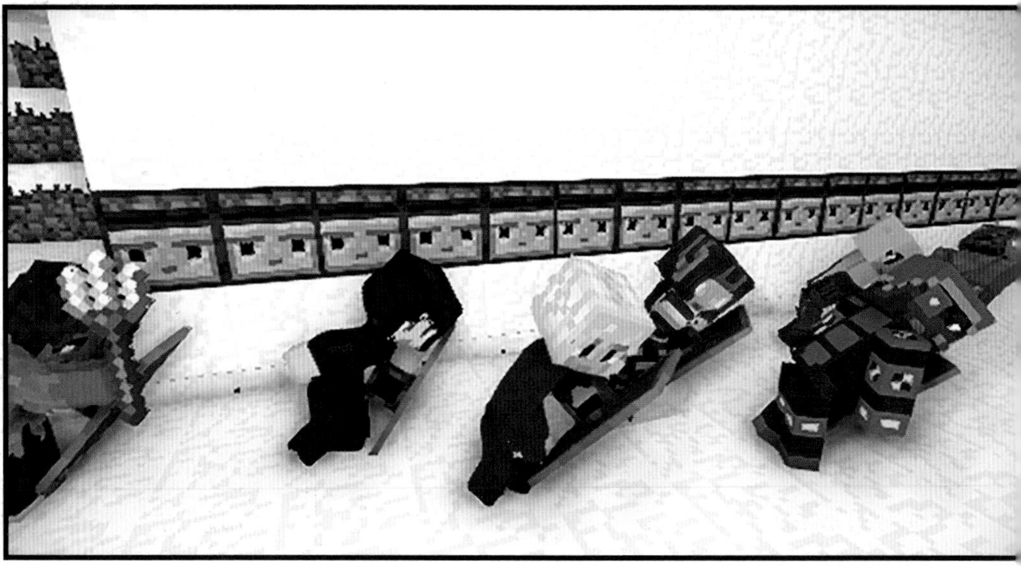

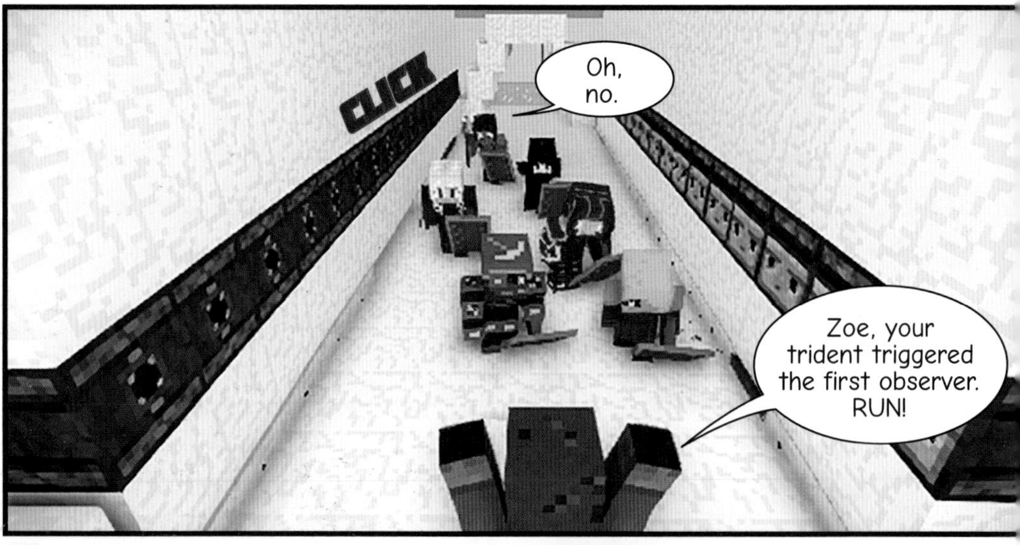
CLICK
Oh, no.
Zoe, your trident triggered the first observer. RUN!

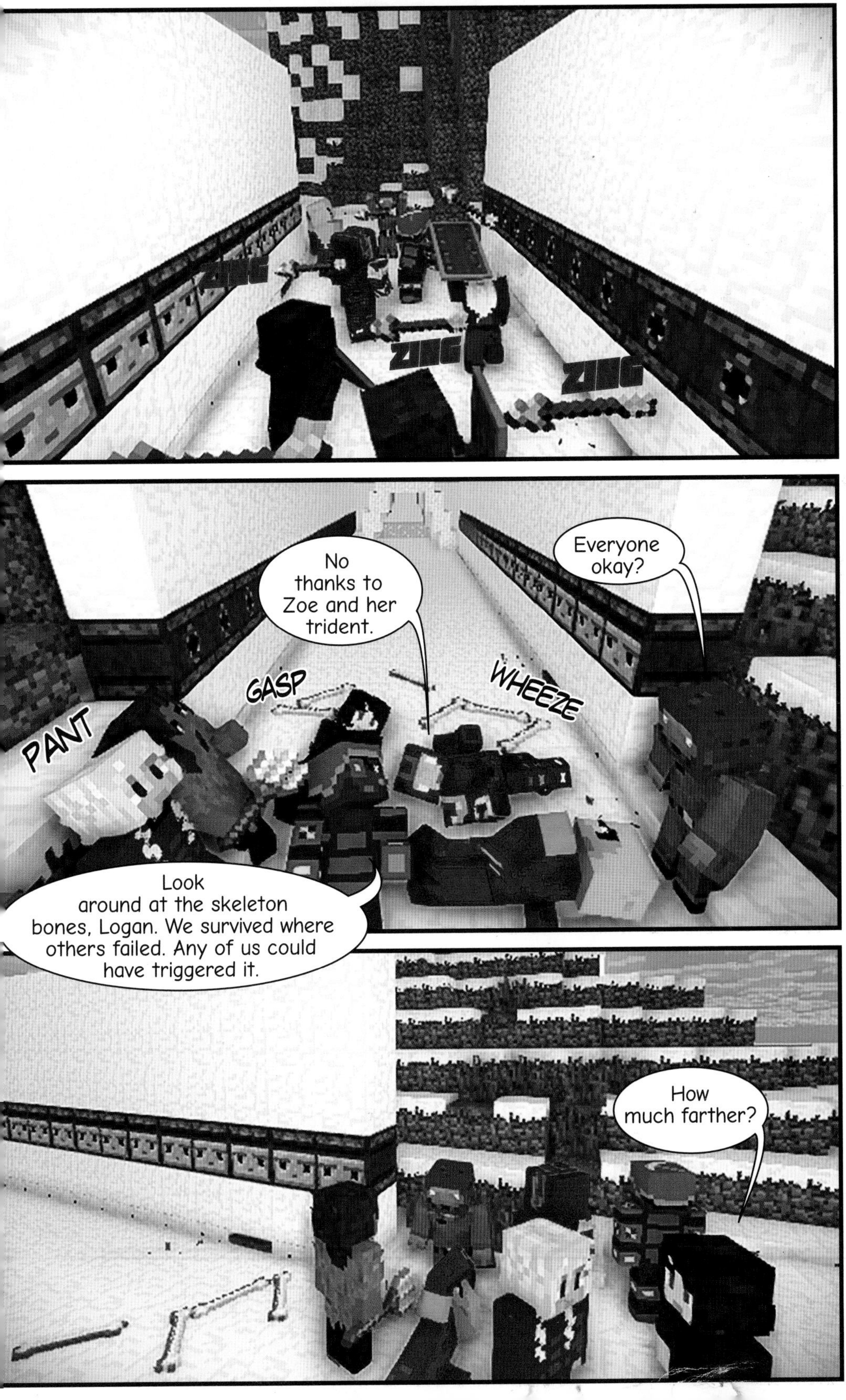
ZING
ZING
ZING
No thanks to Zoe and her trident.
Everyone okay?
GASP
WHEEZE
PANT
Look around at the skeleton bones, Logan. We survived where others failed. Any of us could have triggered it.
How much farther?

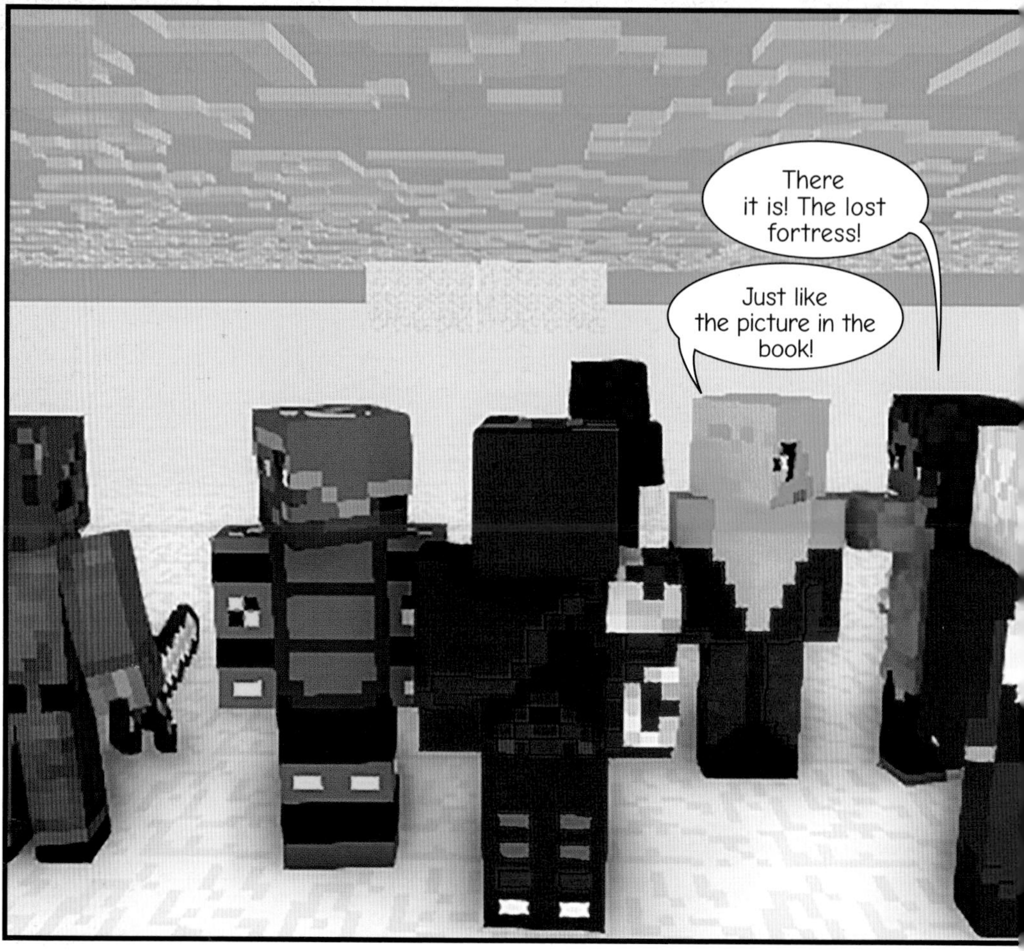
There it is! The lost fortress!
Just like the picture in the book!

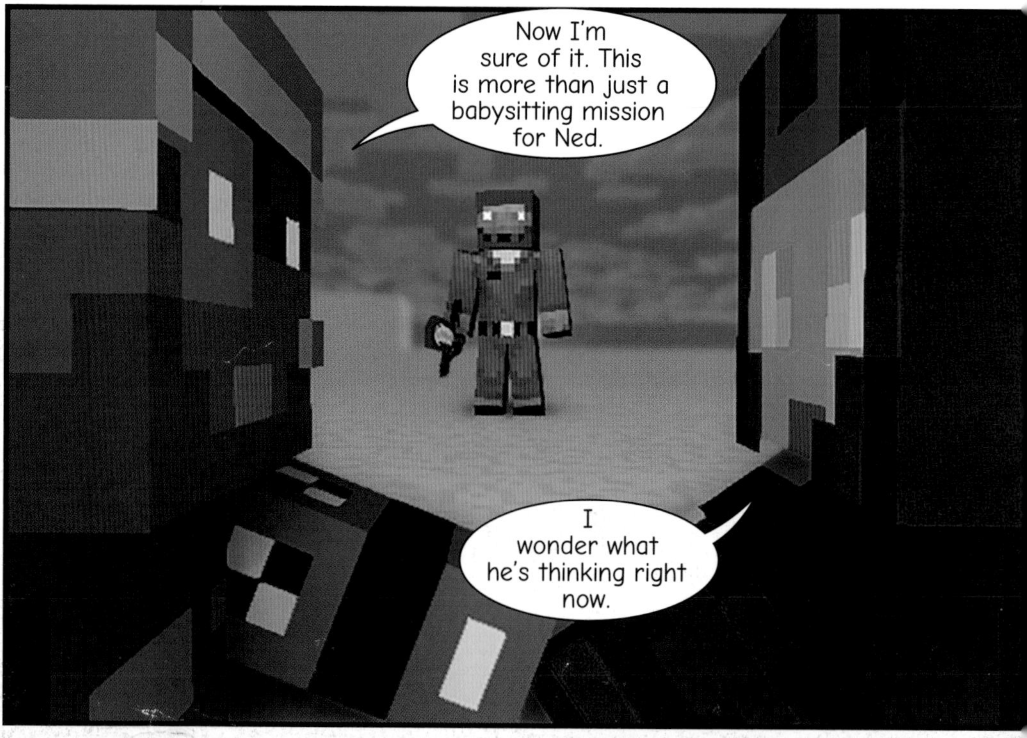
Now I'm sure of it. This is more than just a babysitting mission for Ned.
I wonder what he's thinking right now.

CHAPTER 8

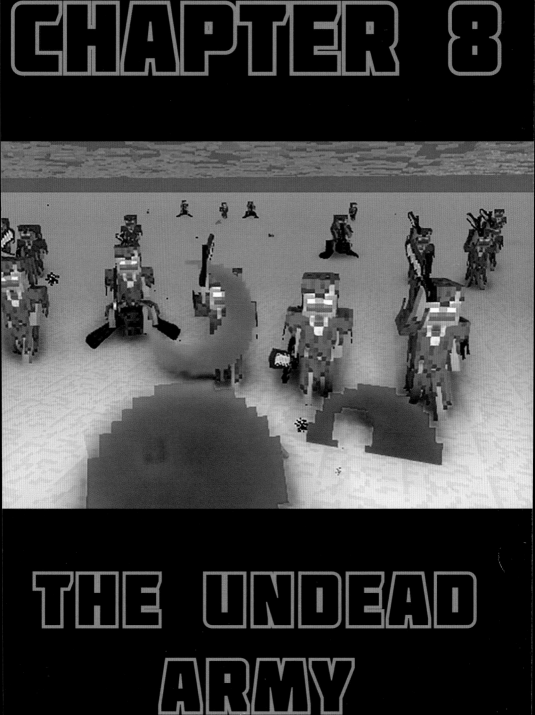

THE UNDEAD
ARMY

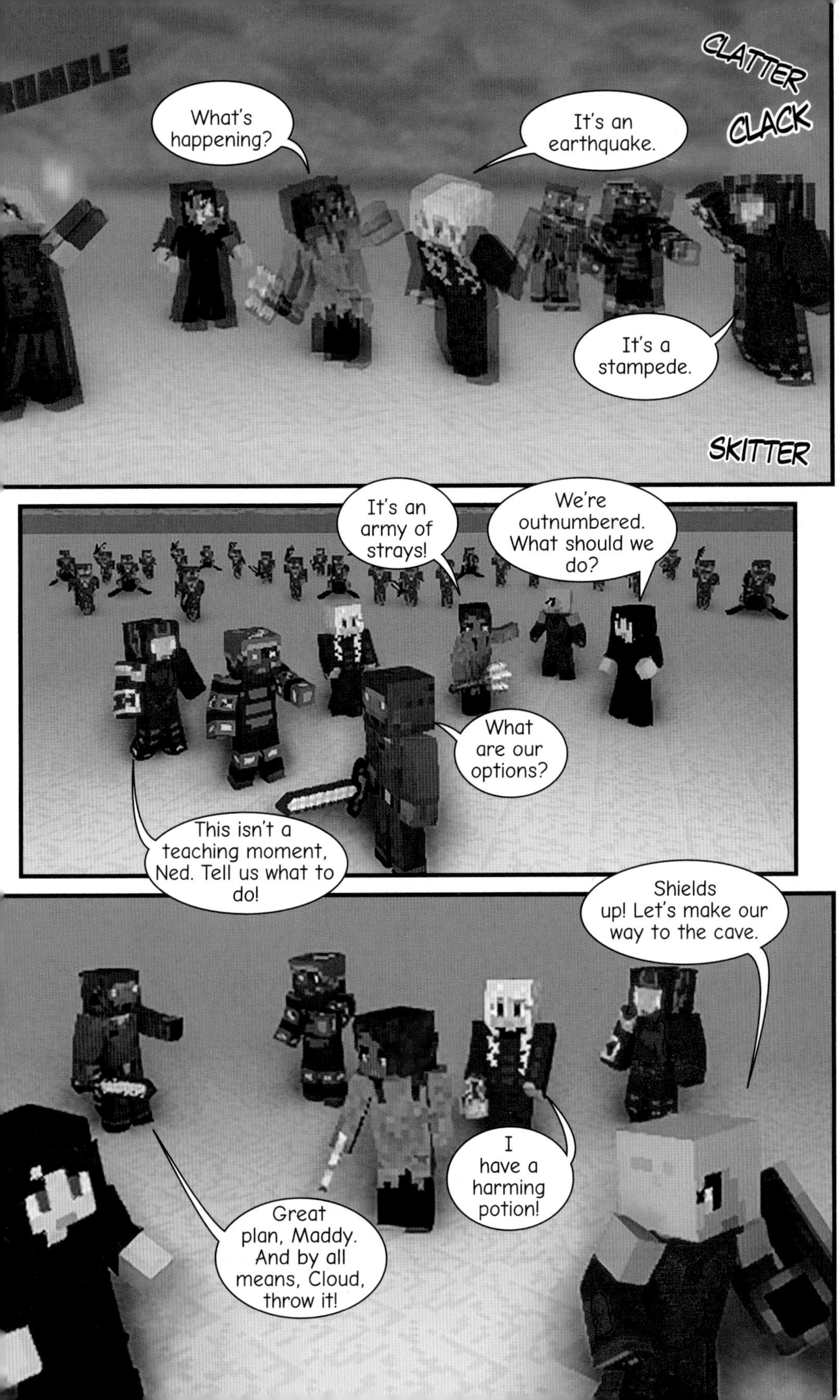
RUMBLE
CLATTER
CLACK
What's happening?
It's an earthquake.
It's a stampede.
SKITTER
It's an army of strays!
We're outnumbered. What should we do?
What are our options?
This isn't a teaching moment, Ned. Tell us what to do!
Shields up! Let's make our way to the cave.
I have a harming potion!
Great plan, Maddy. And by all means, Cloud, throw it!

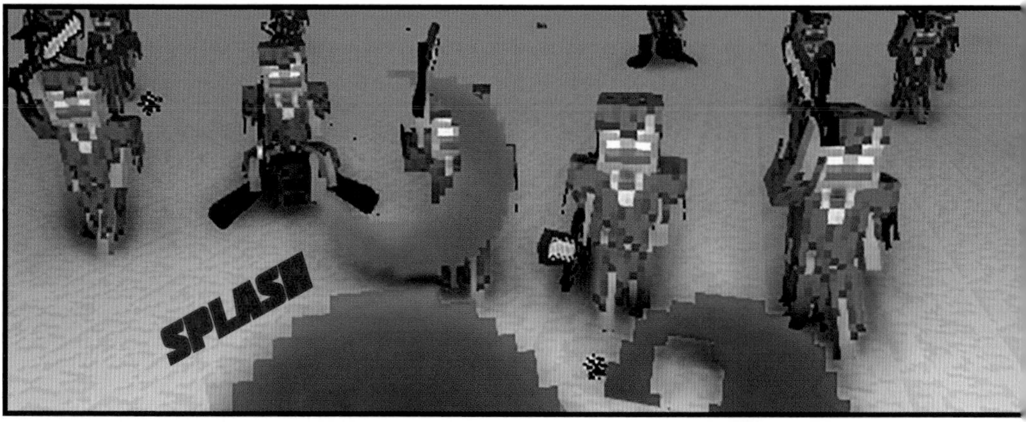
SPLASH

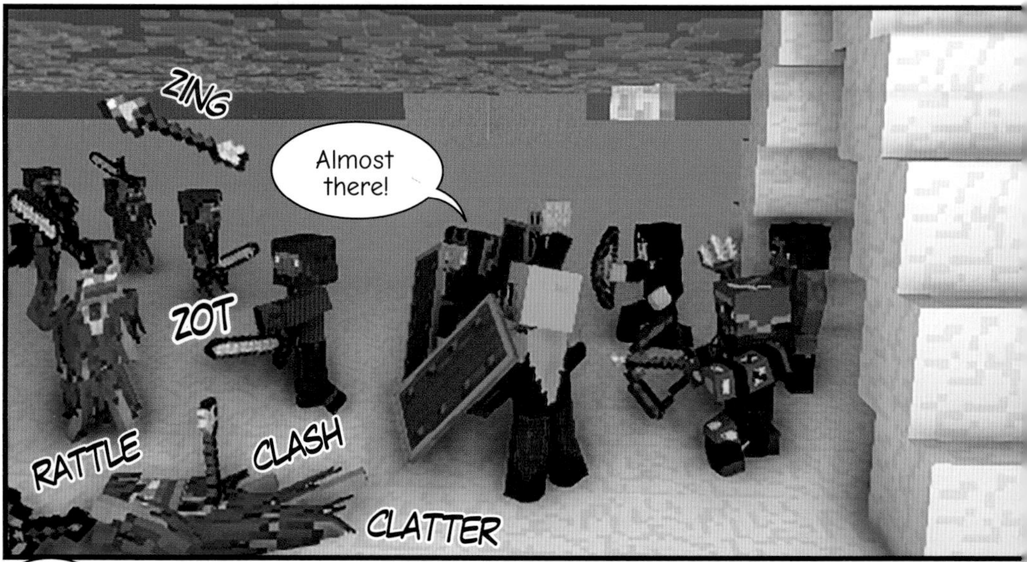
ZING
Almost there!
ZOT
RATTLE
CLASH
CLATTER

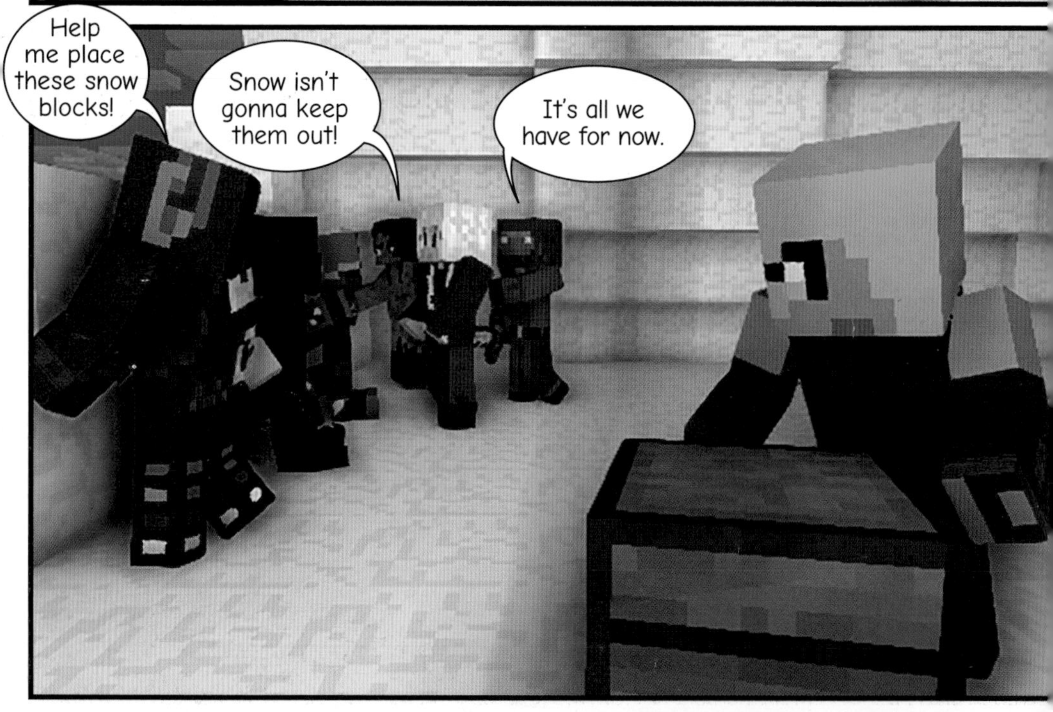
Help me place these snow blocks!
Snow isn't gonna keep them out!
It's all we have for now.

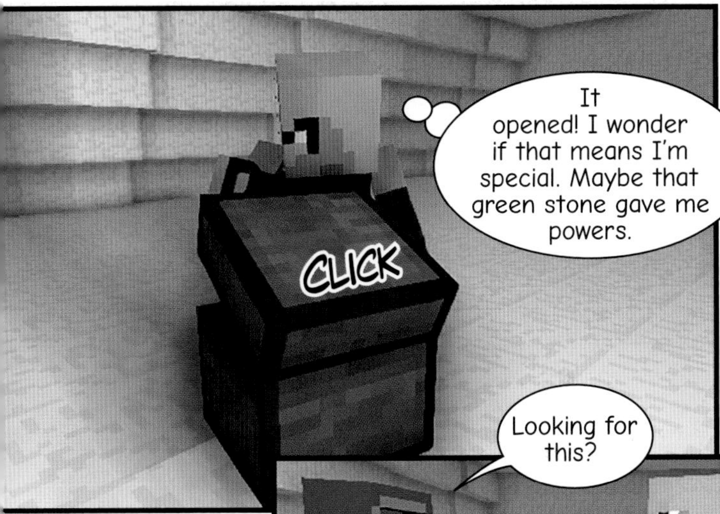
It opened! I wonder if that means I'm special. Maybe that green stone gave me powers.
CLICK

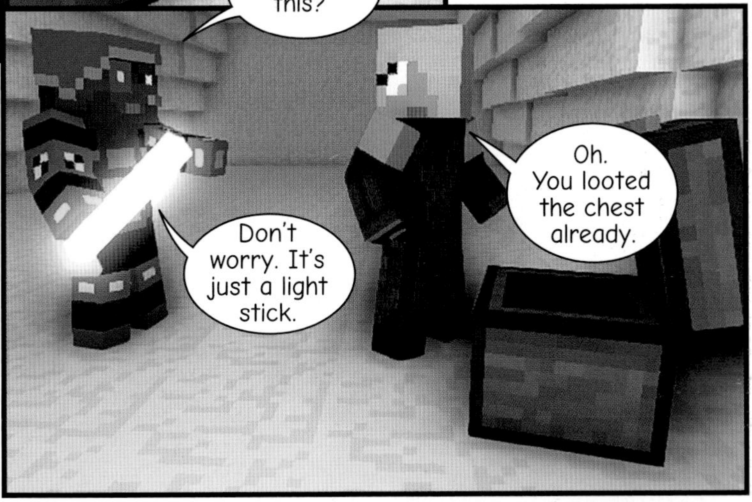
Looking for this?
Oh. You looted the chest already.
Don't worry. It's just a light stick.

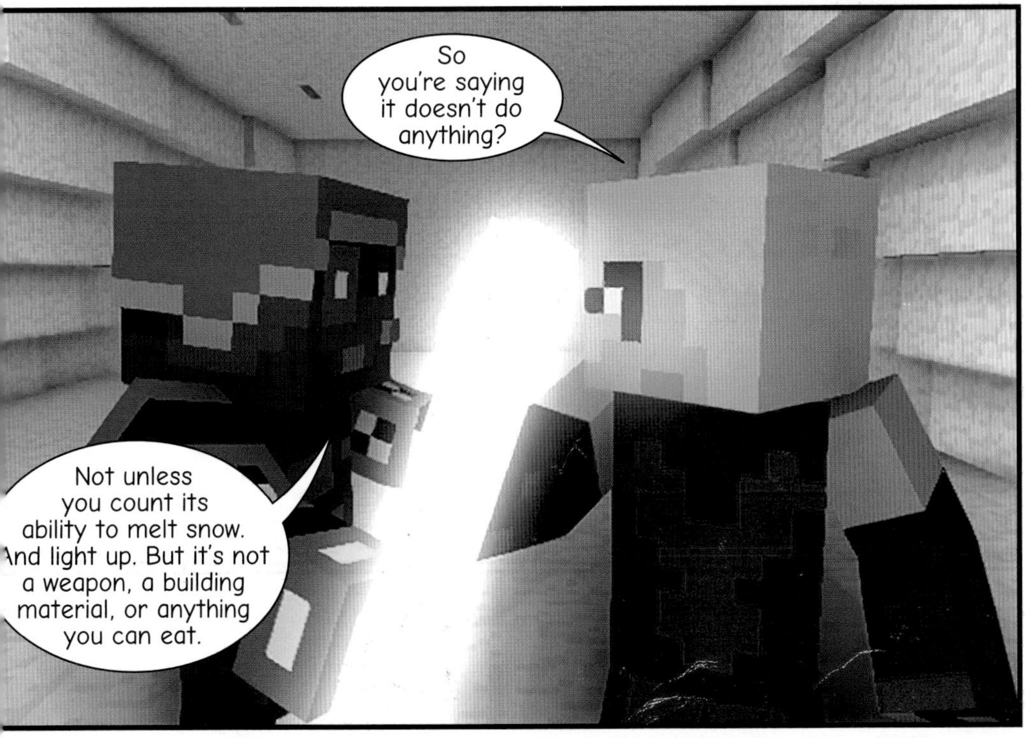
So you're saying it doesn't do anything?
Not unless you count its ability to melt snow. And light up. But it's not a weapon, a building material, or anything you can eat.

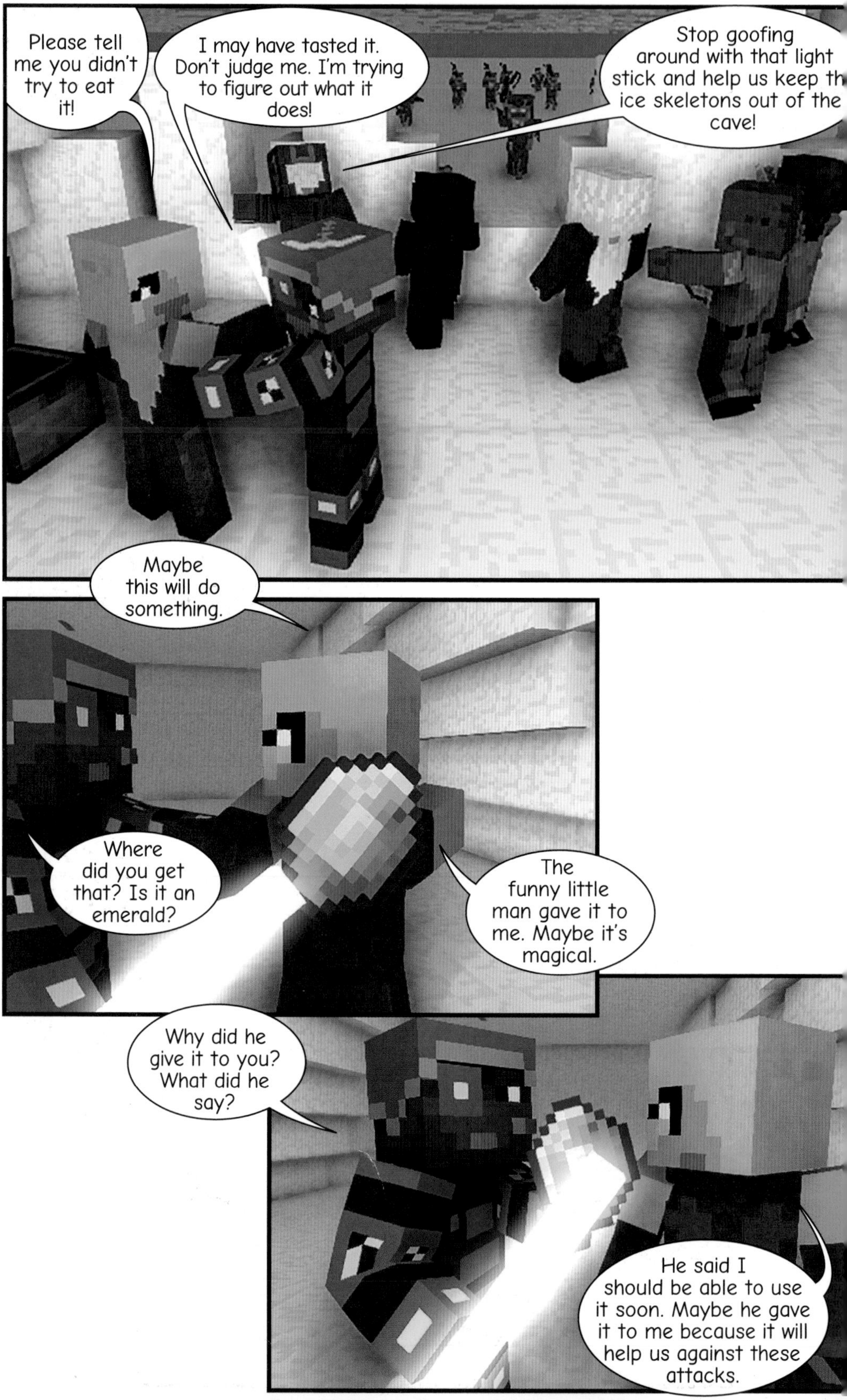
Please tell me you didn't try to eat it!
I may have tasted it. Don't judge me. I'm trying to figure out what it does!
Stop goofing around with that light stick and help us keep th ice skeletons out of the cave!
Maybe this will do something.
Where did you get that? Is it an emerald?
The funny little man gave it to me. Maybe it's magical.
Why did he give it to you? What did he say?
He said I should be able to use it soon. Maybe he gave it to me because it will help us against these attacks.

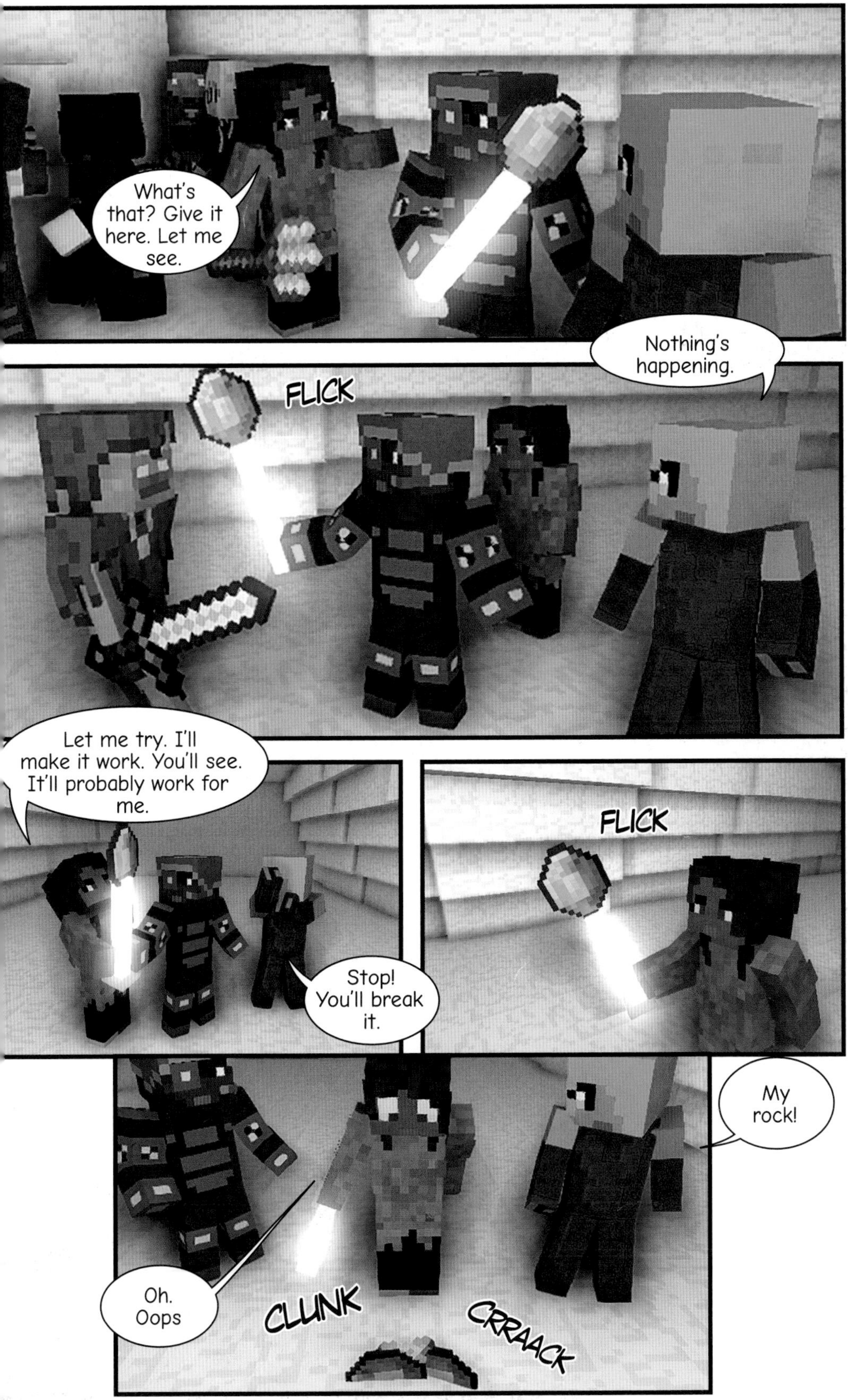
What's that? Give it here. Let me see.
FLICK
Nothing's happening.
Let me try. I'll make it work. You'll see. It'll probably work for me.
Stop! You'll break it.
FLICK
My rock!
Oh. Oops
CLUNK
CRRAACK

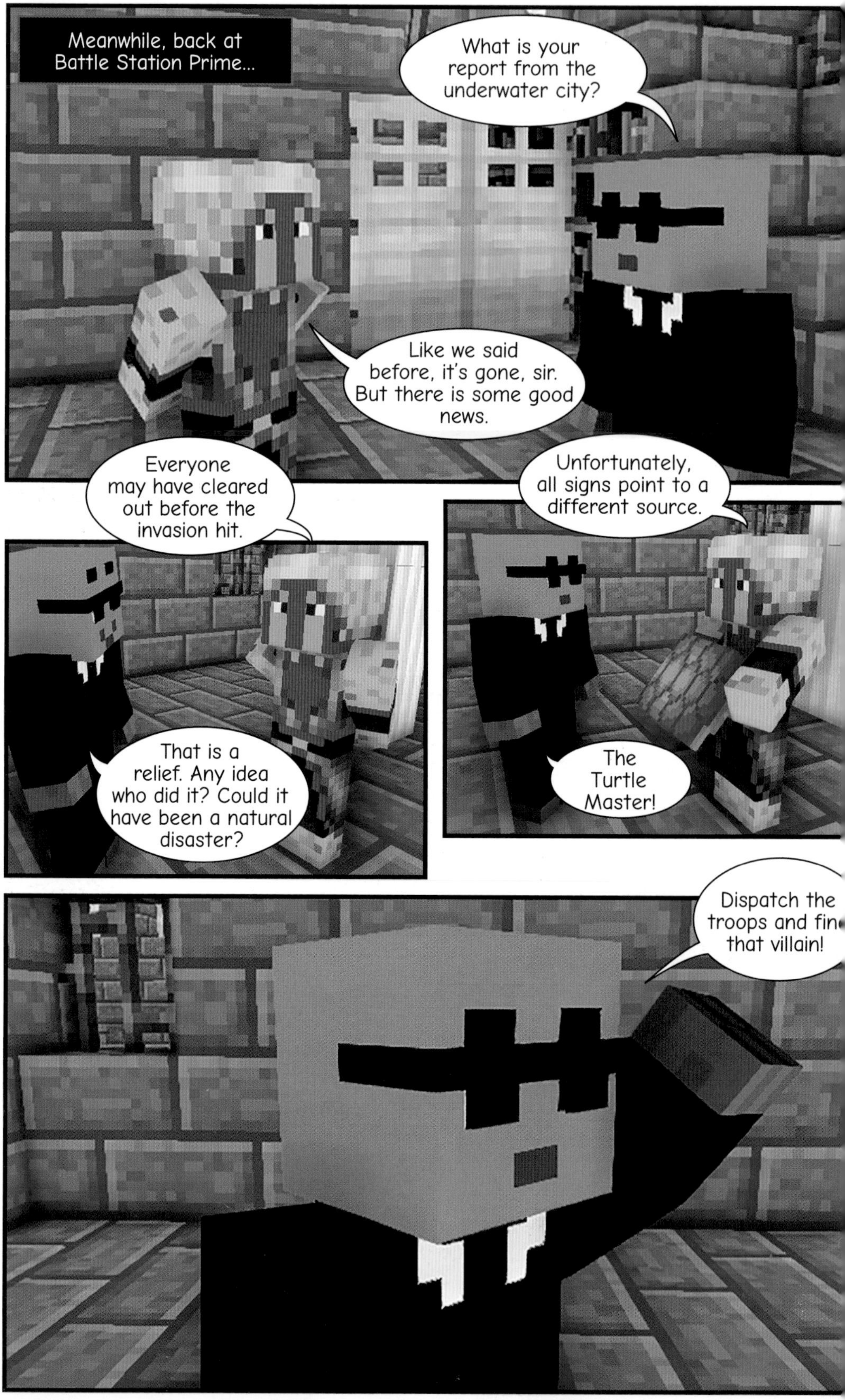
Meanwhile, back at Battle Station Prime...
What is your report from the underwater city?
Like we said before, it's gone, sir. But there is some good news.
Everyone may have cleared out before the invasion hit.
That is a relief. Any idea who did it? Could it have been a natural disaster?
Unfortunately, all signs point to a different source.
The Turtle Master!
Dispatch the troops and fin
that villain!

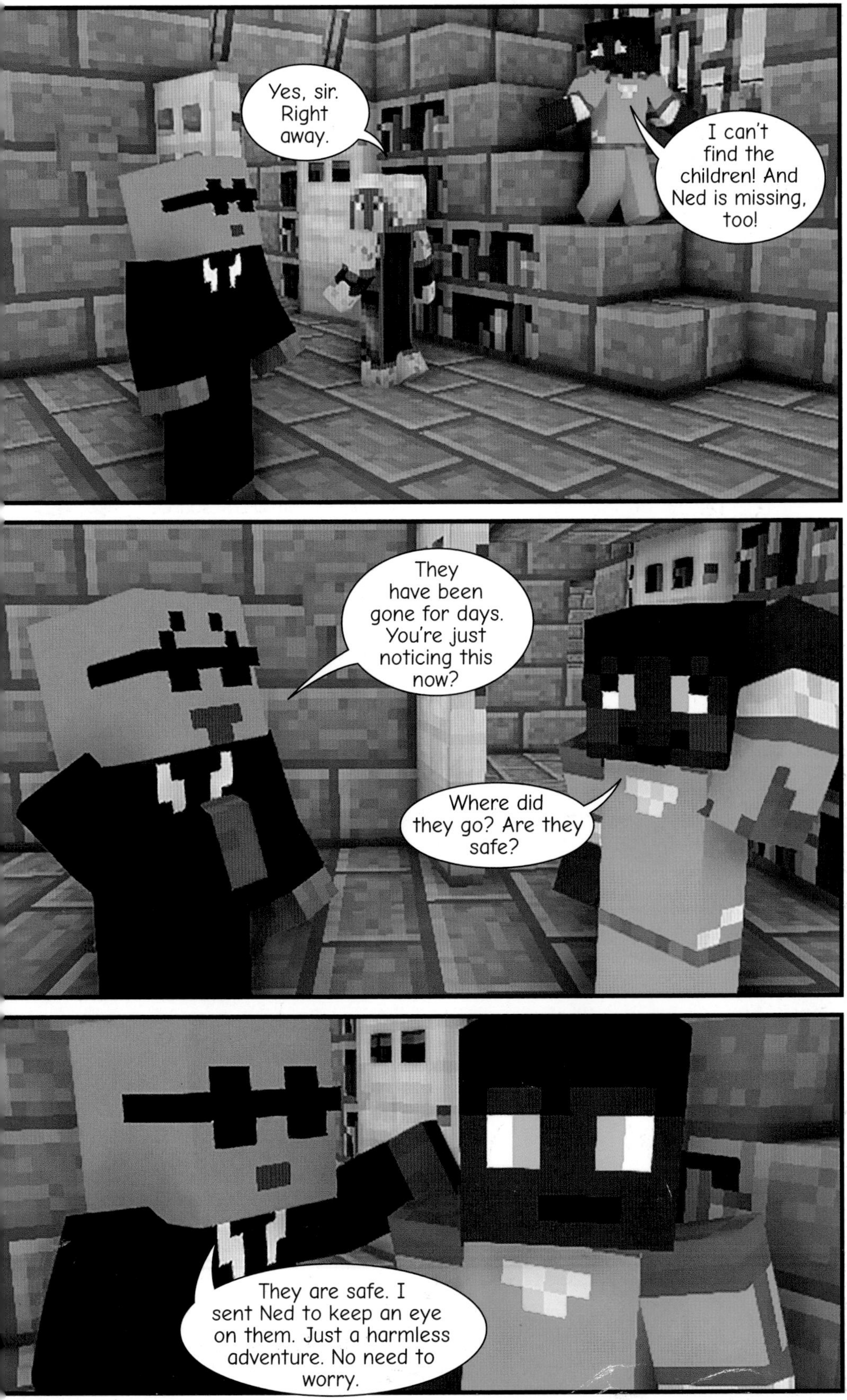
Yes, sir. Right away.
I can't find the children! And Ned is missing, too!
They have been gone for days. You're just noticing this now?
Where did they go? Are they safe?
They are safe. I sent Ned to keep an eye on them. Just a harmless adventure. No need to worry.

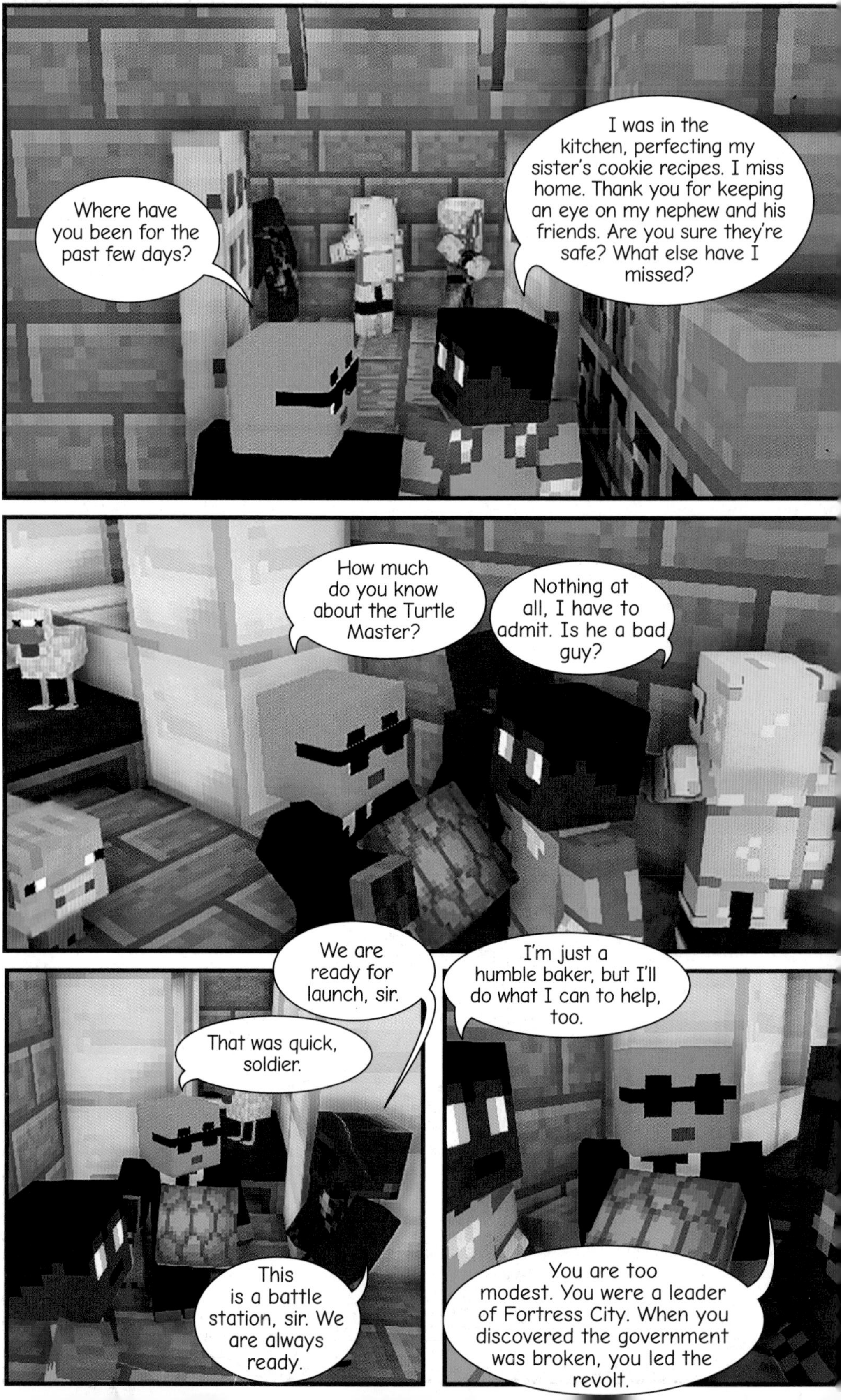
Where have you been for the past few days?
I was in the kitchen, perfecting my sister's cookie recipes. I miss home. Thank you for keeping an eye on my nephew and his friends. Are you sure they're safe? What else have I missed?
How much do you know about the Turtle Master?
Nothing at all, I have to admit. Is he a bad guy?
That was quick, soldier.
We are ready for launch, sir.
This is a battle station, sir. We are always ready.
I'm just a humble baker, but I'll do what I can to help, too.
You are too modest. You were a leader of Fortress City. When you discovered the government was broken, you led the revolt.

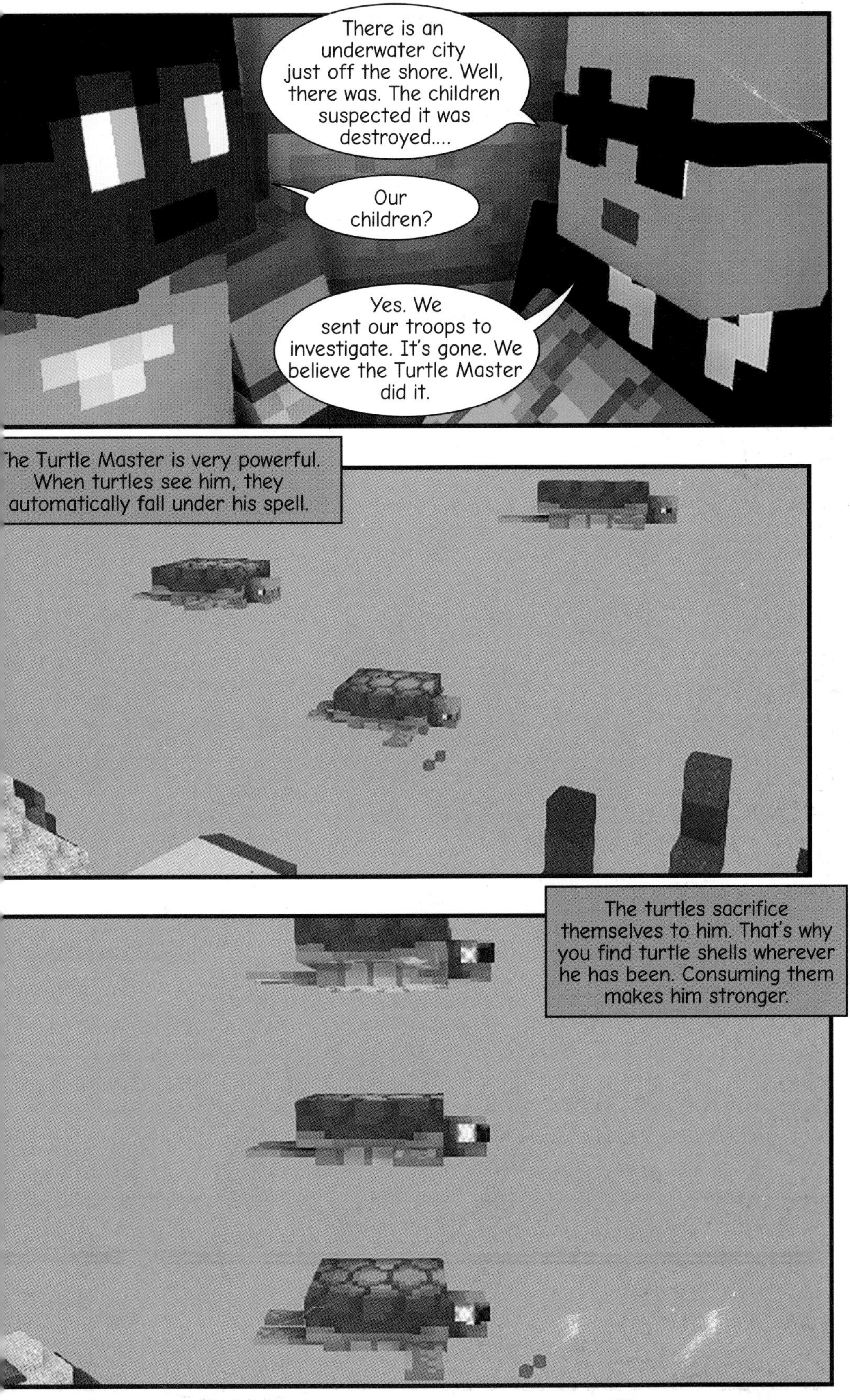
There is an underwater city just off the shore. Well, there was. The children suspected it was destroyed....
Our children?
Yes. We sent our troops to investigate. It's gone. We believe the Turtle Master did it.
he Turtle Master is very powerful. When turtles see him, they automatically fall under his spell.
The turtles sacrifice themselves to him. That's why you find turtle shells wherever he has been. Consuming them makes him stronger.

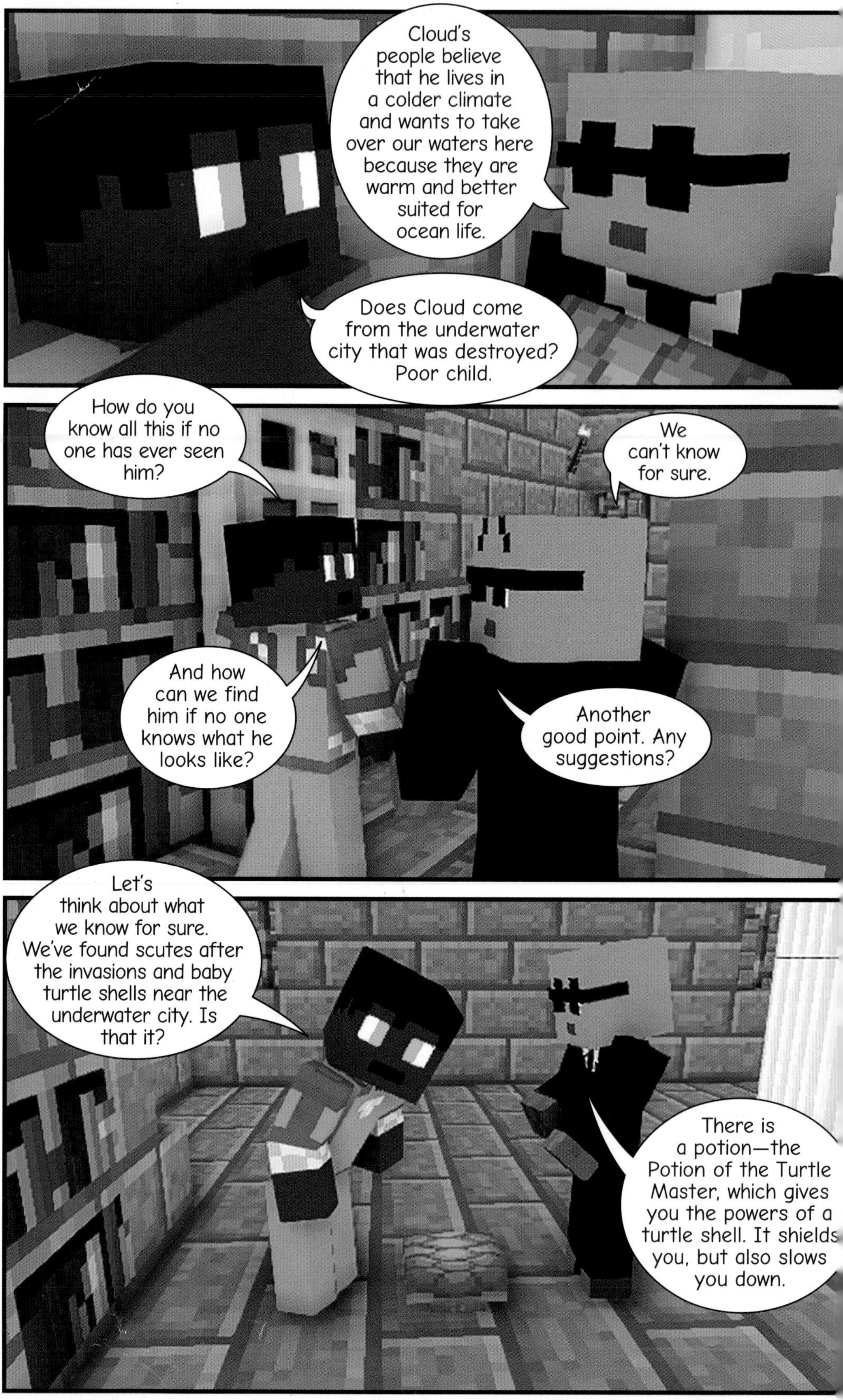
Cloud's people believe that he lives in a colder climate and wants to take over our waters here because they are warm and better suited for ocean life.
Does Cloud come from the underwater city that was destroyed? Poor child.
How do you know all this if no one has ever seen him?
We can't know for sure.
And how can we find him if no one knows what he looks like?
Another good point. Any suggestions?
Let's think about what we know for sure. We've found scutes after the invasions and baby turtle shells near the underwater city. Is that it?
There is a potion—the Potion of the Turtle Master, which gives you the powers of a turtle shell. It shields you, but also slows you down.

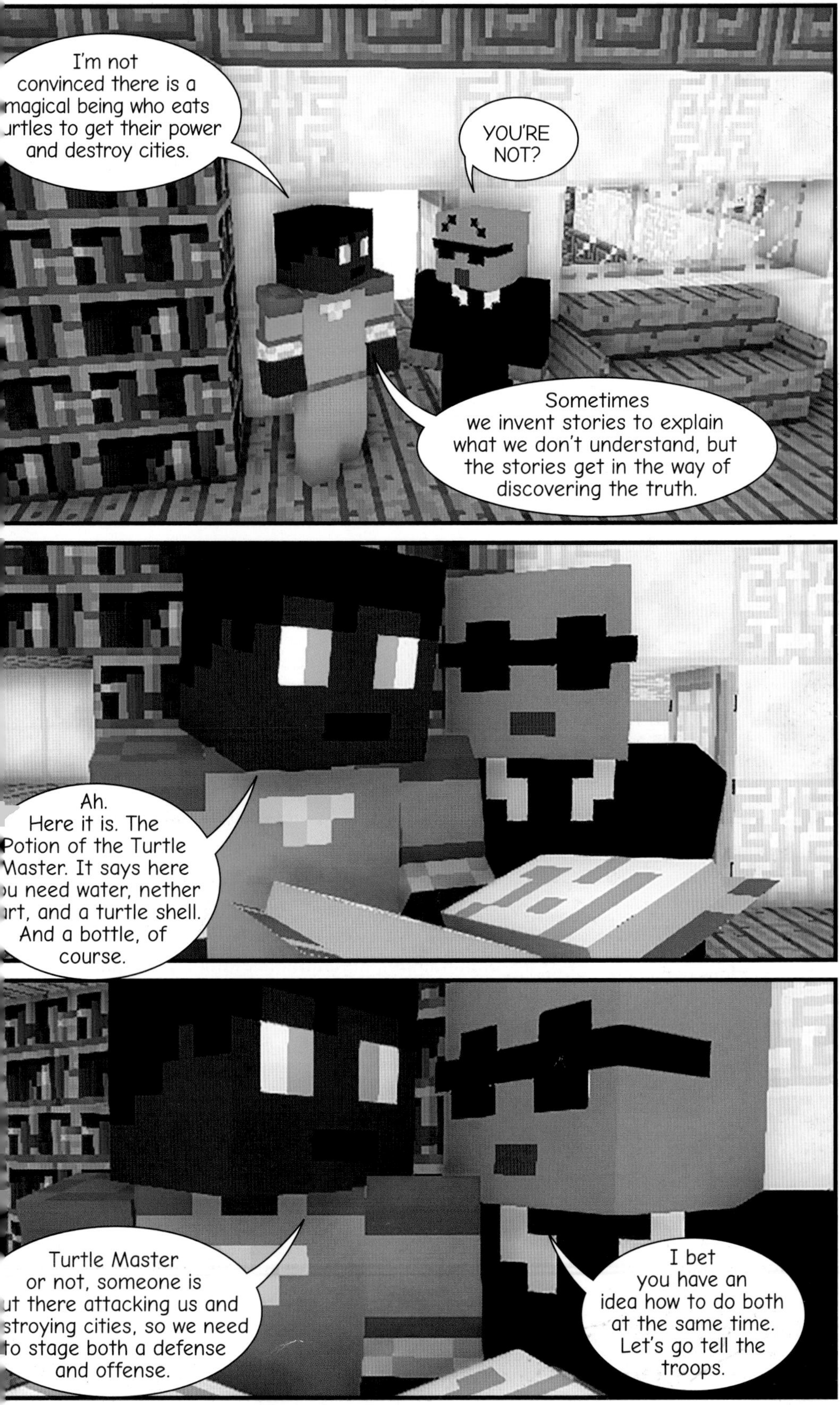
I'm not convinced there is a magical being who eats urtles to get their power and destroy cities.
YOU'RE NOT?
Sometimes we invent stories to explain what we don't understand, but the stories get in the way of discovering the truth.
Ah. Here it is. The Potion of the Turtle Master. It says here u need water, nether rt, and a turtle shell. And a bottle, of course.
Turtle Master or not, someone is ut there attacking us and stroying cities, so we need to stage both a defense and offense.
I bet you have an idea how to do both at the same time. Let's go tell the troops.

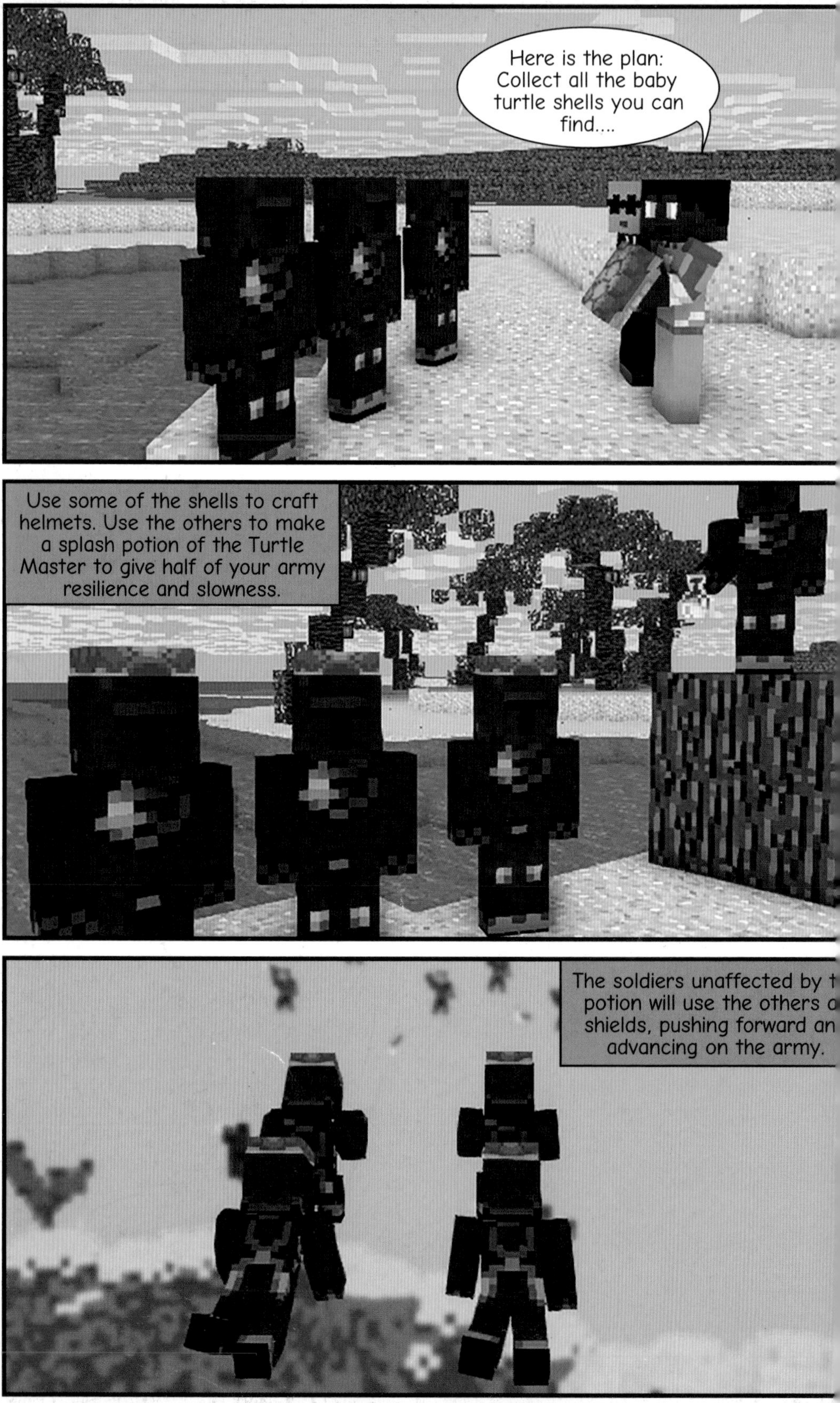
Here is the plan: Collect all the baby turtle shells you can find....
Use some of the shells to craft helmets. Use the others to make a splash potion of the Turtle Master to give half of your army resilience and slowness.
The soldiers unaffected by t
potion will use the others a
shields, pushing forward an
advancing on the army.

CHAPTER 9

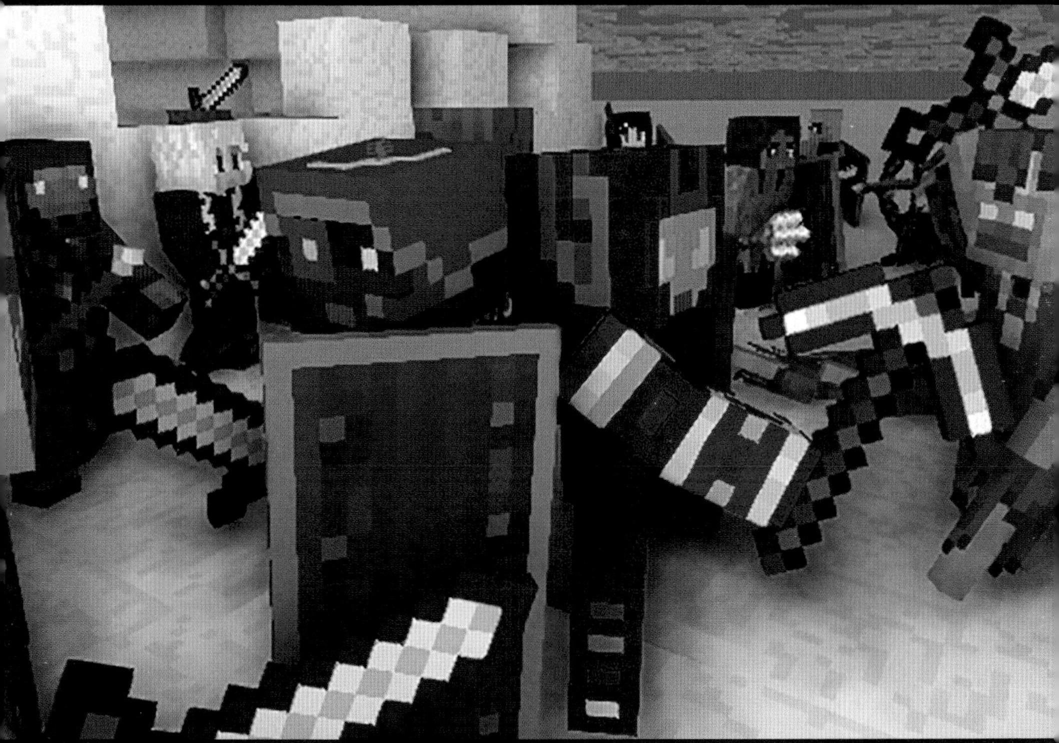

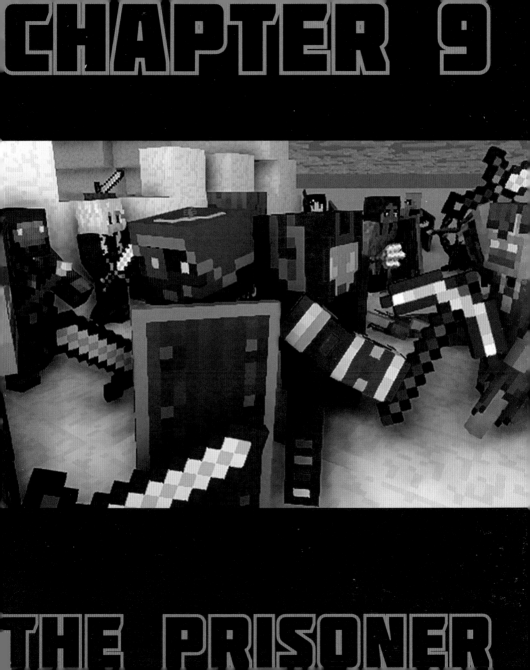

THE PRISONER

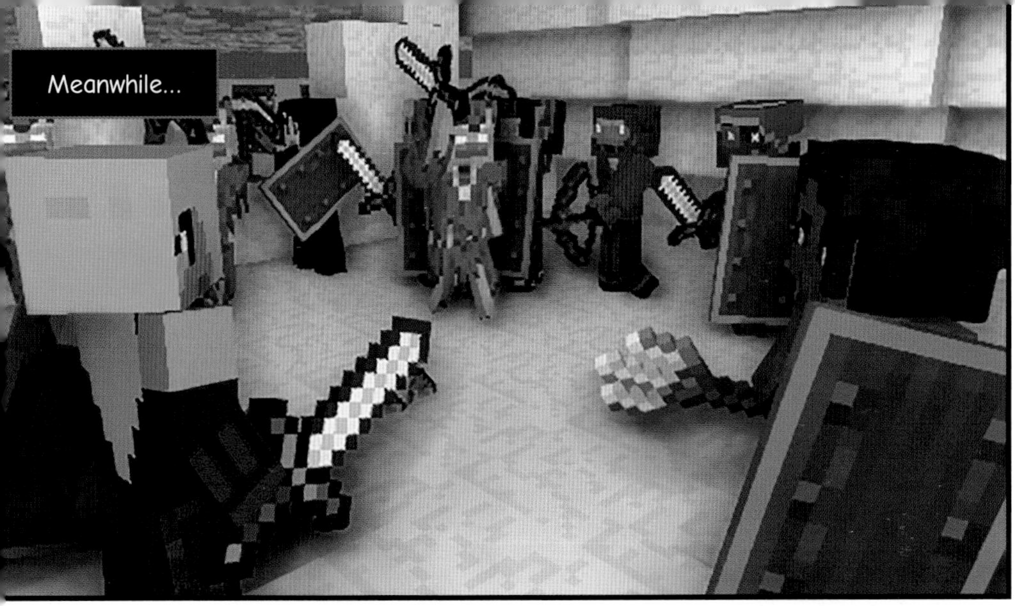
Meanwhile...

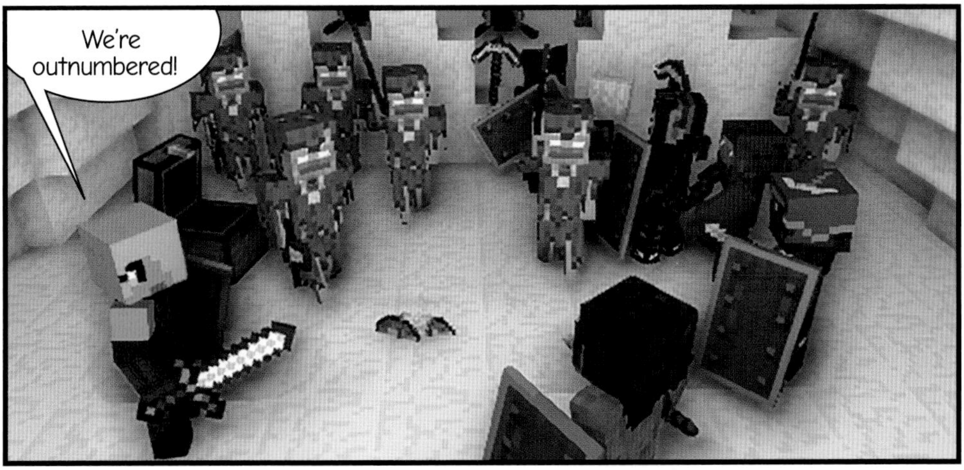
We're outnumbered!

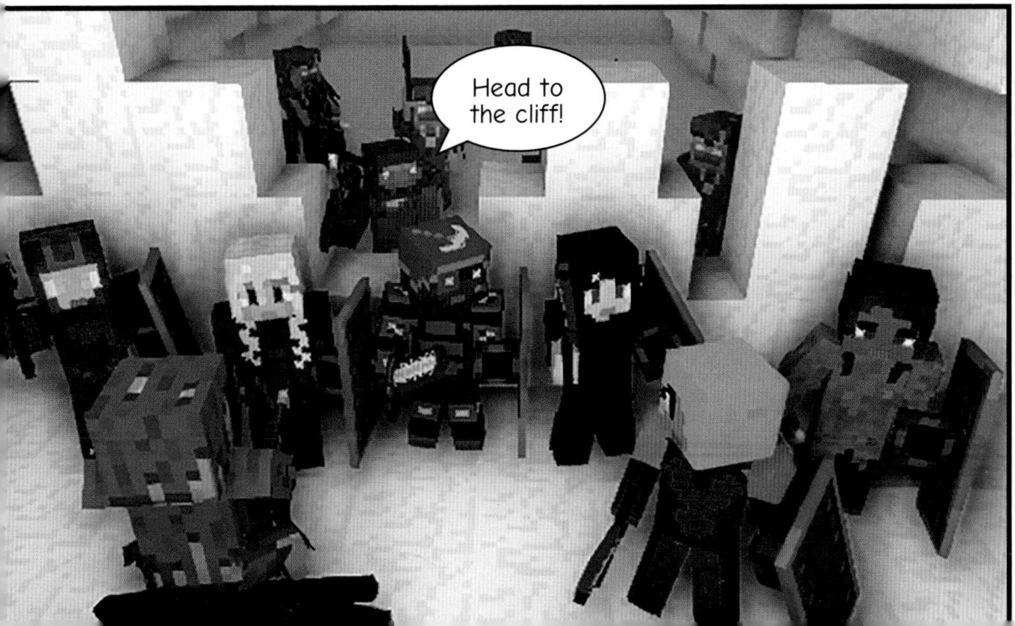
Head to the cliff!

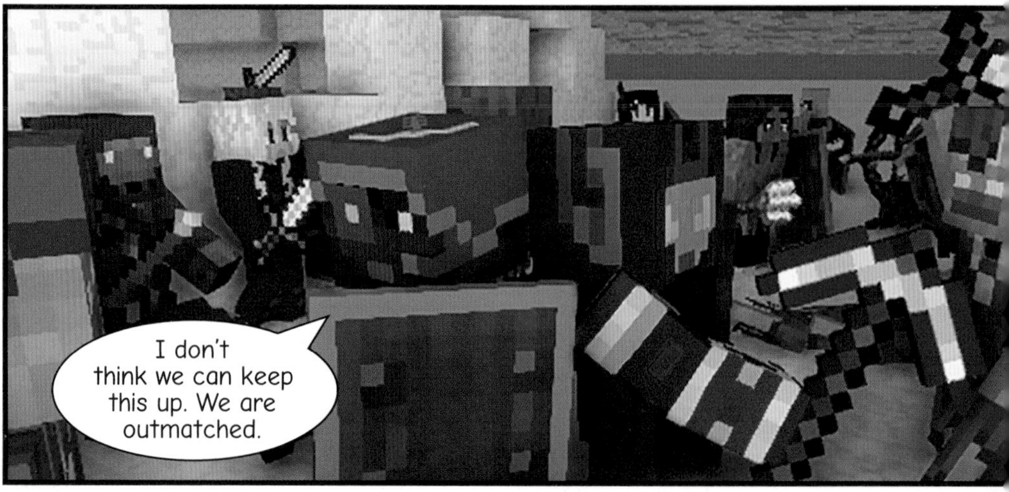
I don't think we can keep this up. We are outmatched.

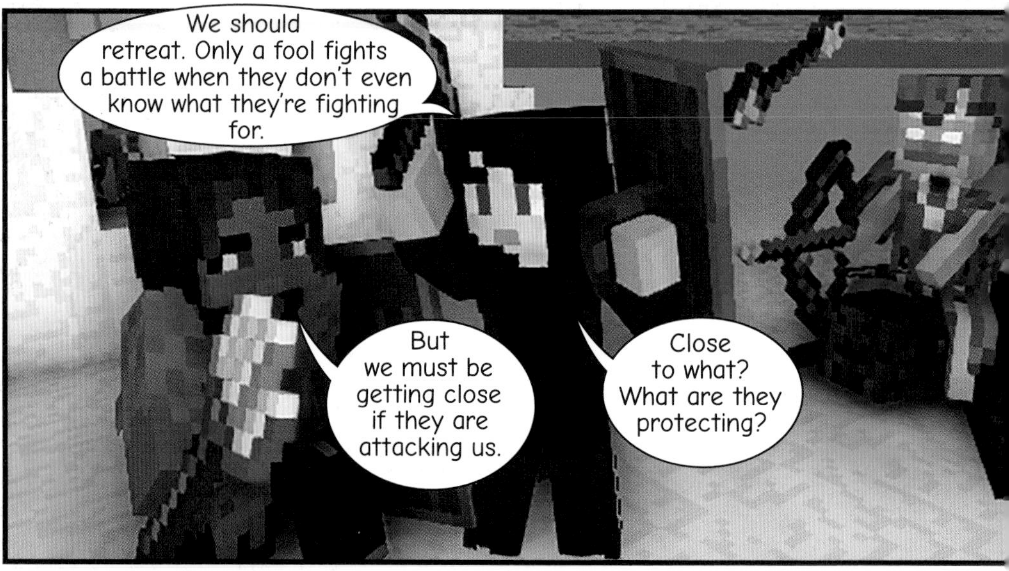
We should retreat. Only a fool fights a battle when they don't even know what they're fighting for.
But we must be getting close if they are attacking us.
Close to what? What are they protecting?

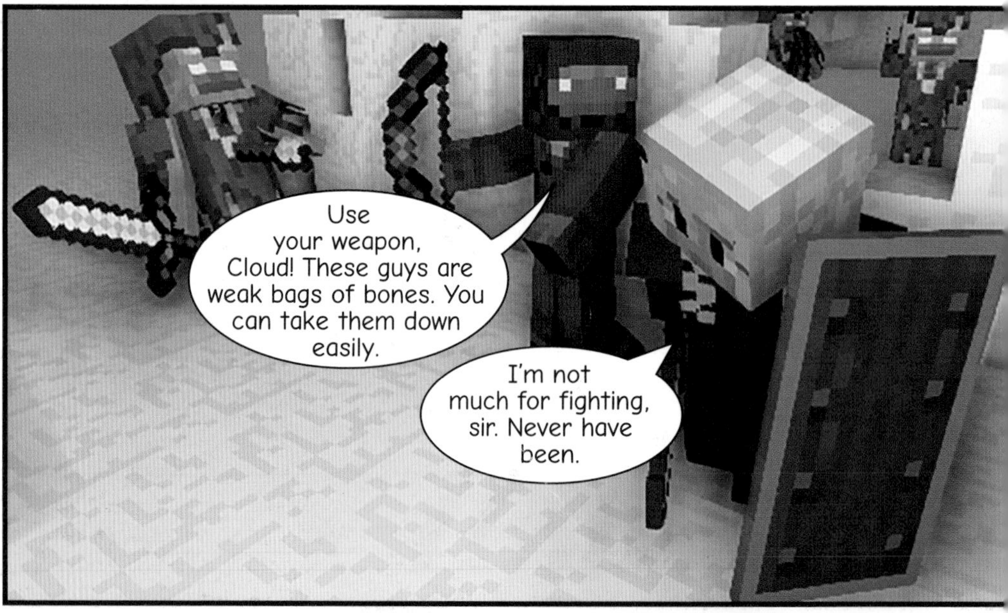
Use your weapon, Cloud! These guys are weak bags of bones. You can take them down easily.
I'm not much for fighting, sir. Never have been.

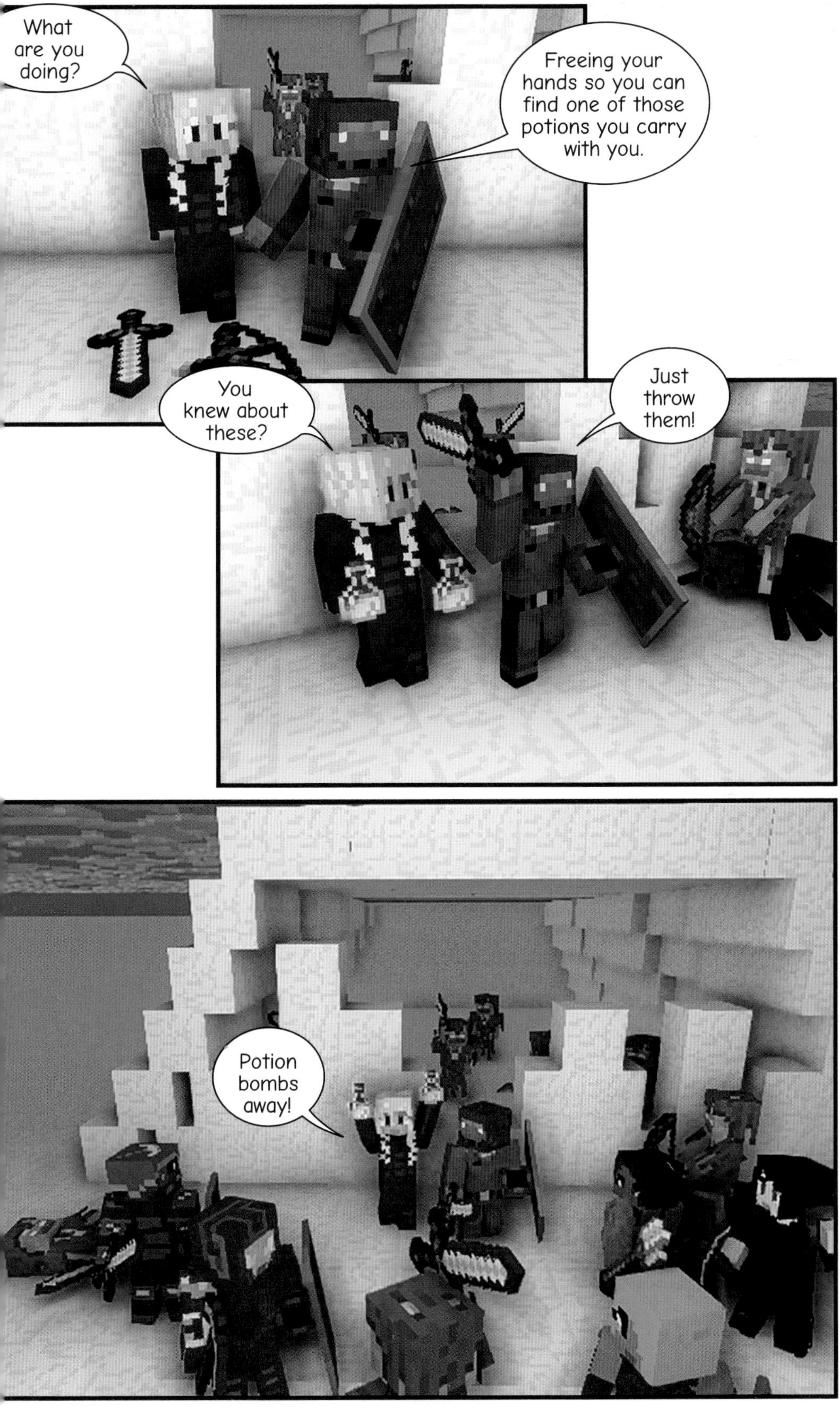
What are you doing?
Freeing your hands so you can find one of those potions you carry with you.
You knew about these?
Just throw them!
Potion bombs away!

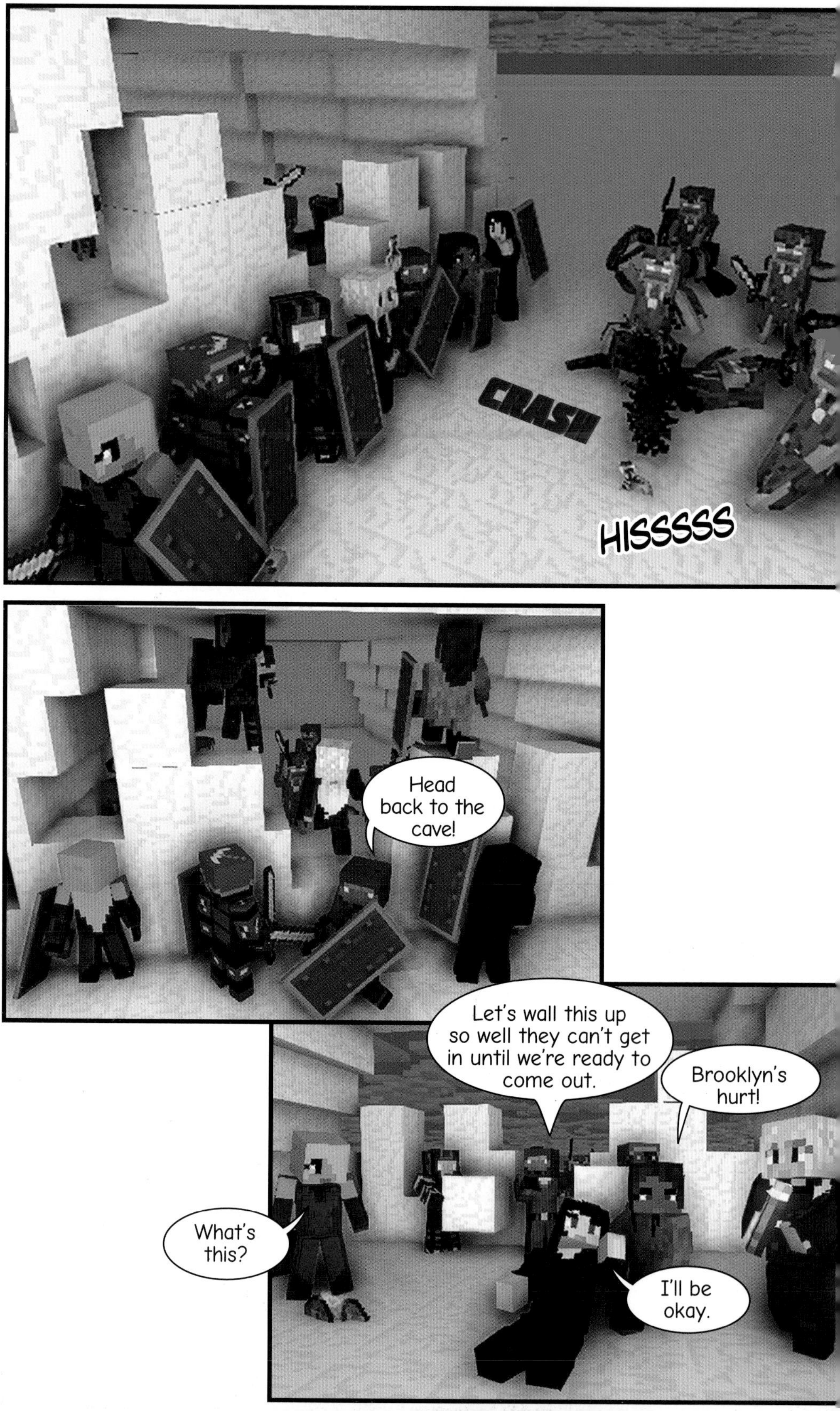
CRASH
HISSSSS
Head back to the cave!
Let's wall this up so well they can't get in until we're ready to come out.
Brooklyn's hurt!
What's this?
I'll be okay.

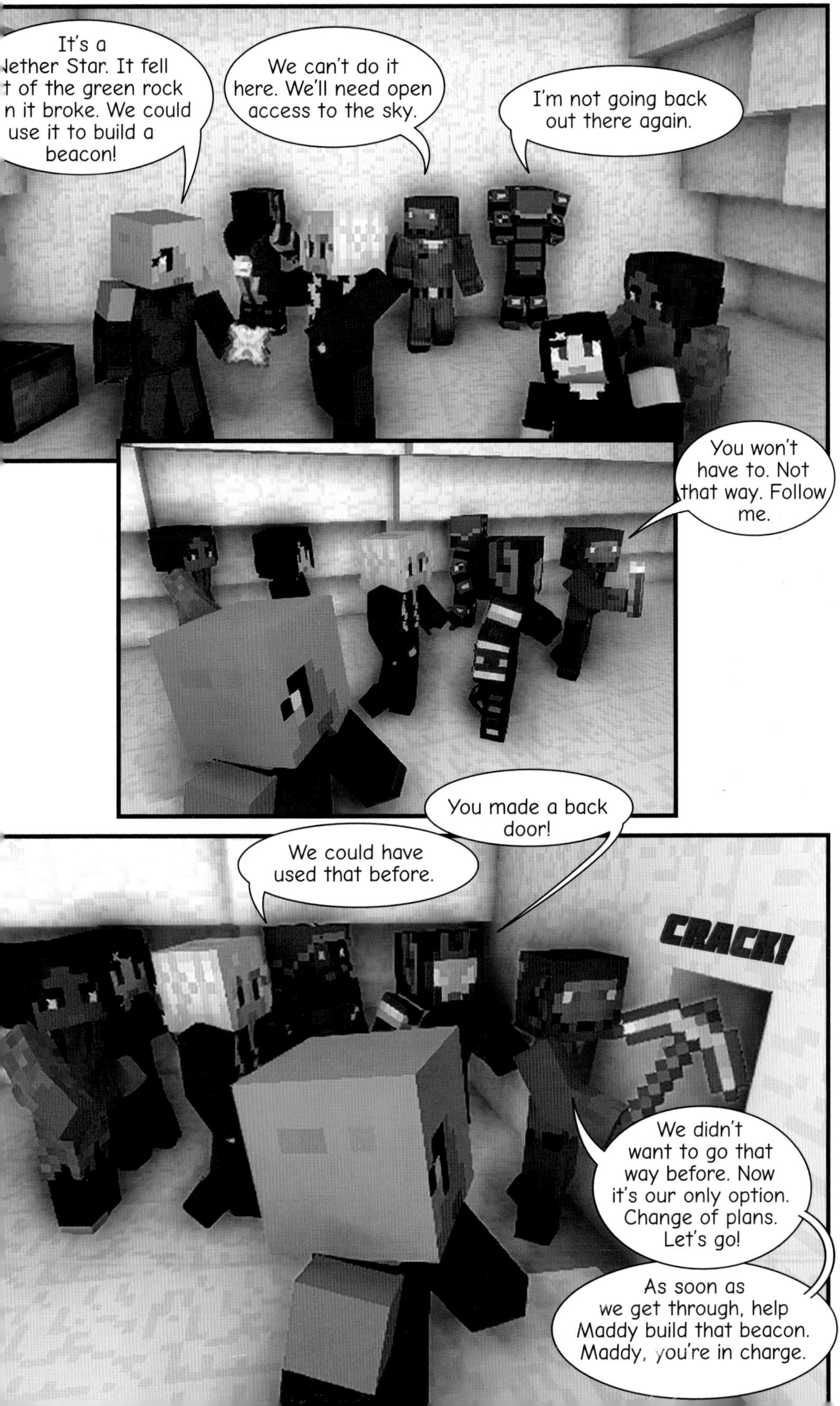
It's a lether Star. It fell t of the green rock n it broke. We could use it to build a beacon!
We can't do it here. We'll need open access to the sky.
I'm not going back out there again.
You won't have to. Not that way. Follow me.
You made a back door!
We could have used that before.
CRACK!
We didn't want to go that way before. Now it's our only option. Change of plans. Let's go!
As soon as we get through, help Maddy build that beacon. Maddy, you're in charge.

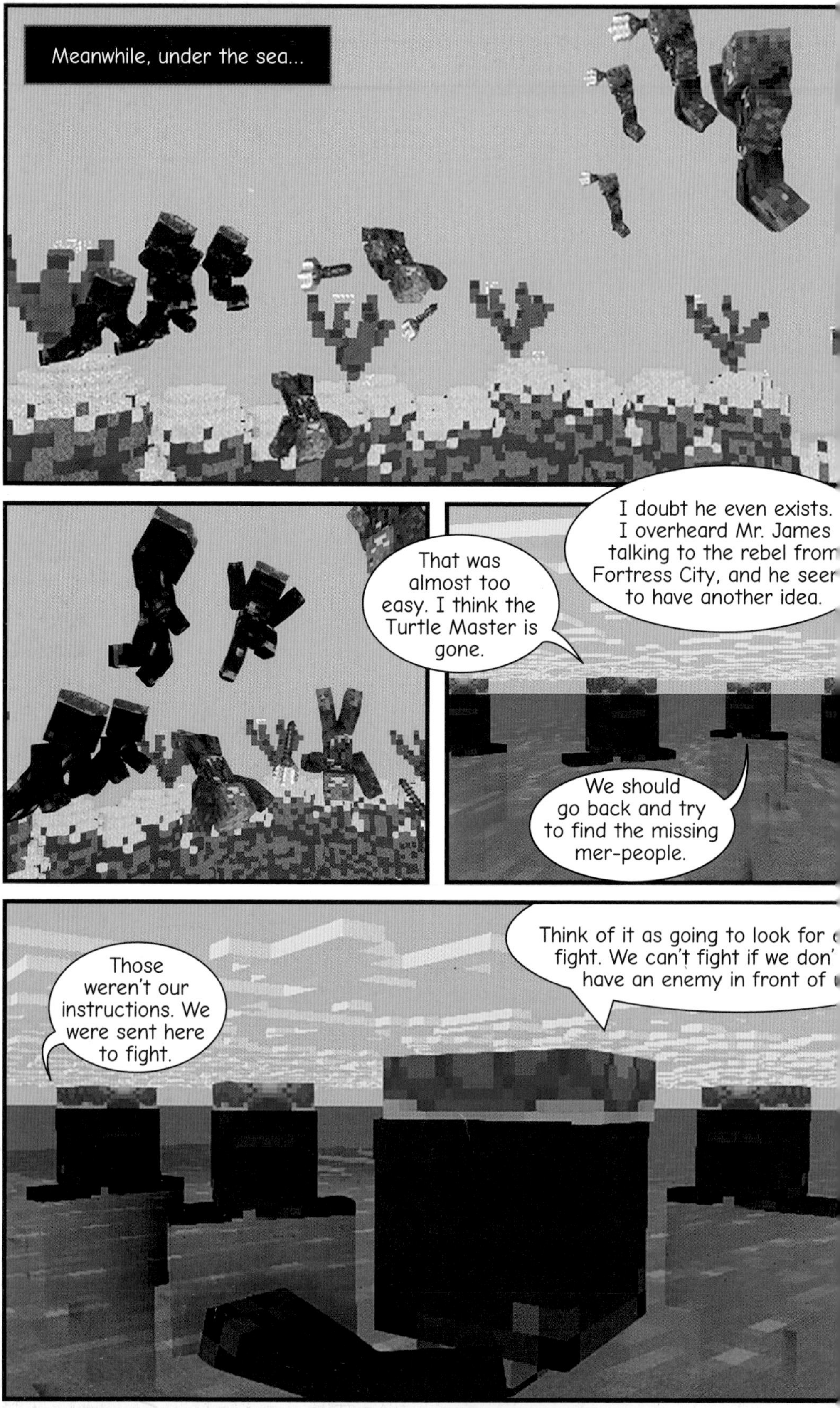
Meanwhile, under the sea...
That was almost too easy. I think the Turtle Master is gone.
I doubt he even exists. I overheard Mr. James talking to the rebel from Fortress City, and he seem to have another idea.
We should go back and try to find the missing mer-people.
Those weren't our instructions. We were sent here to fight.
Think of it as going to look for fight. We can't fight if we don' have an enemy in front of

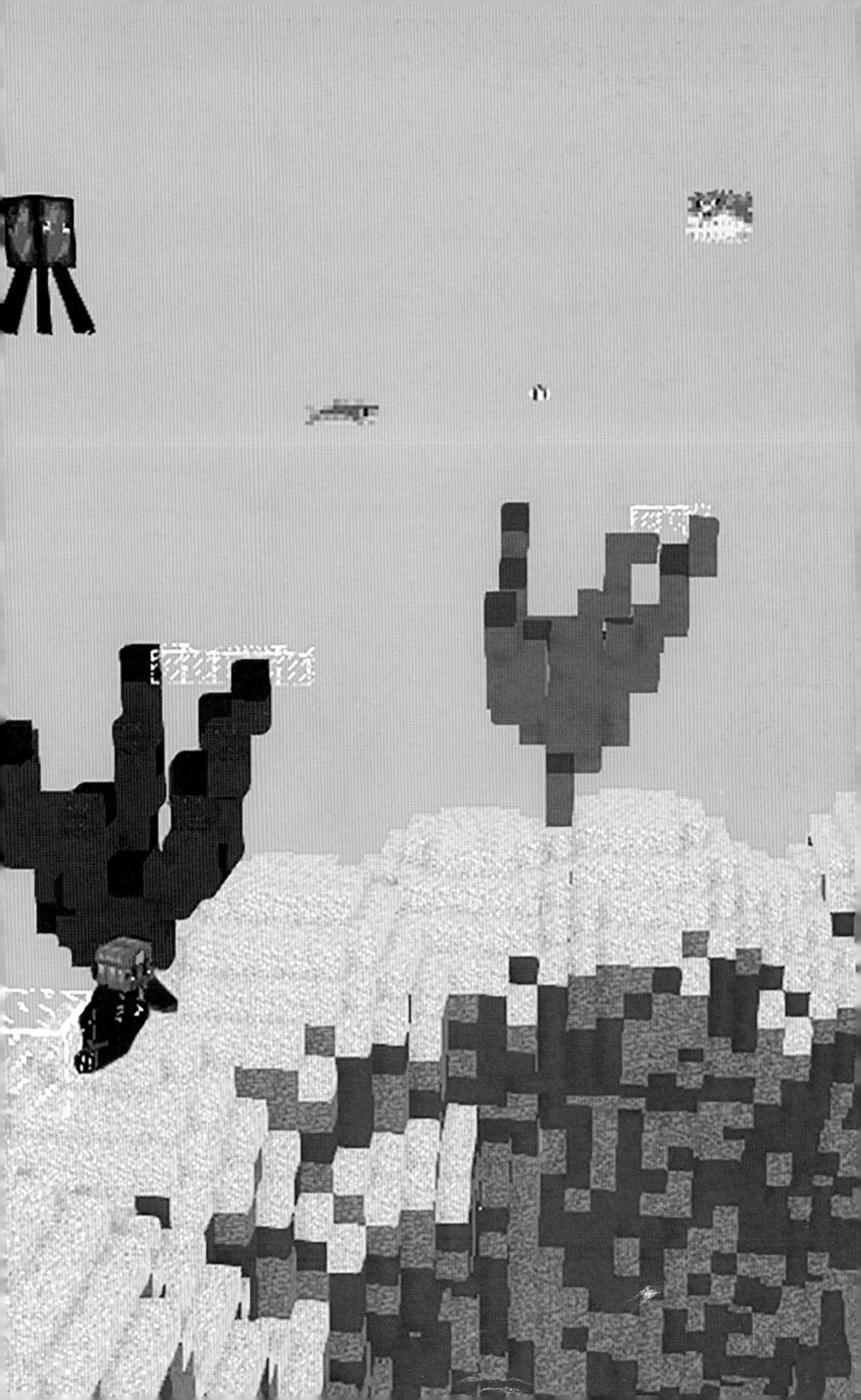

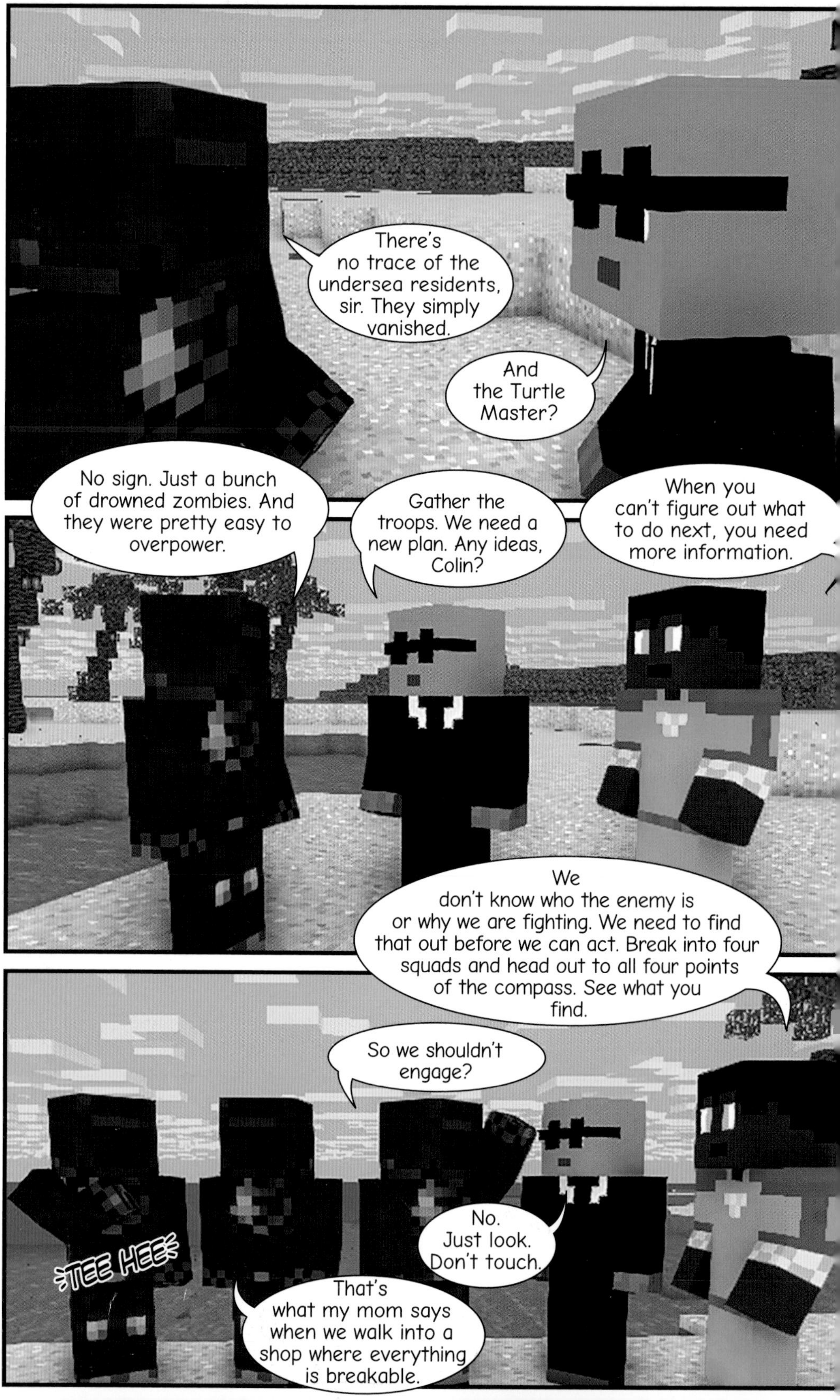
There's no trace of the undersea residents, sir. They simply vanished.
And the Turtle Master?
No sign. Just a bunch of drowned zombies. And they were pretty easy to overpower.
Gather the troops. We need a new plan. Any ideas, Colin?
When you can't figure out what to do next, you need more information.
We don't know who the enemy is or why we are fighting. We need to find that out before we can act. Break into four squads and head out to all four points of the compass. See what you find.
So we shouldn't engage?
No. Just look. Don't touch.
TEE HEE
That's what my mom says when we walk into a shop where everything is breakable.

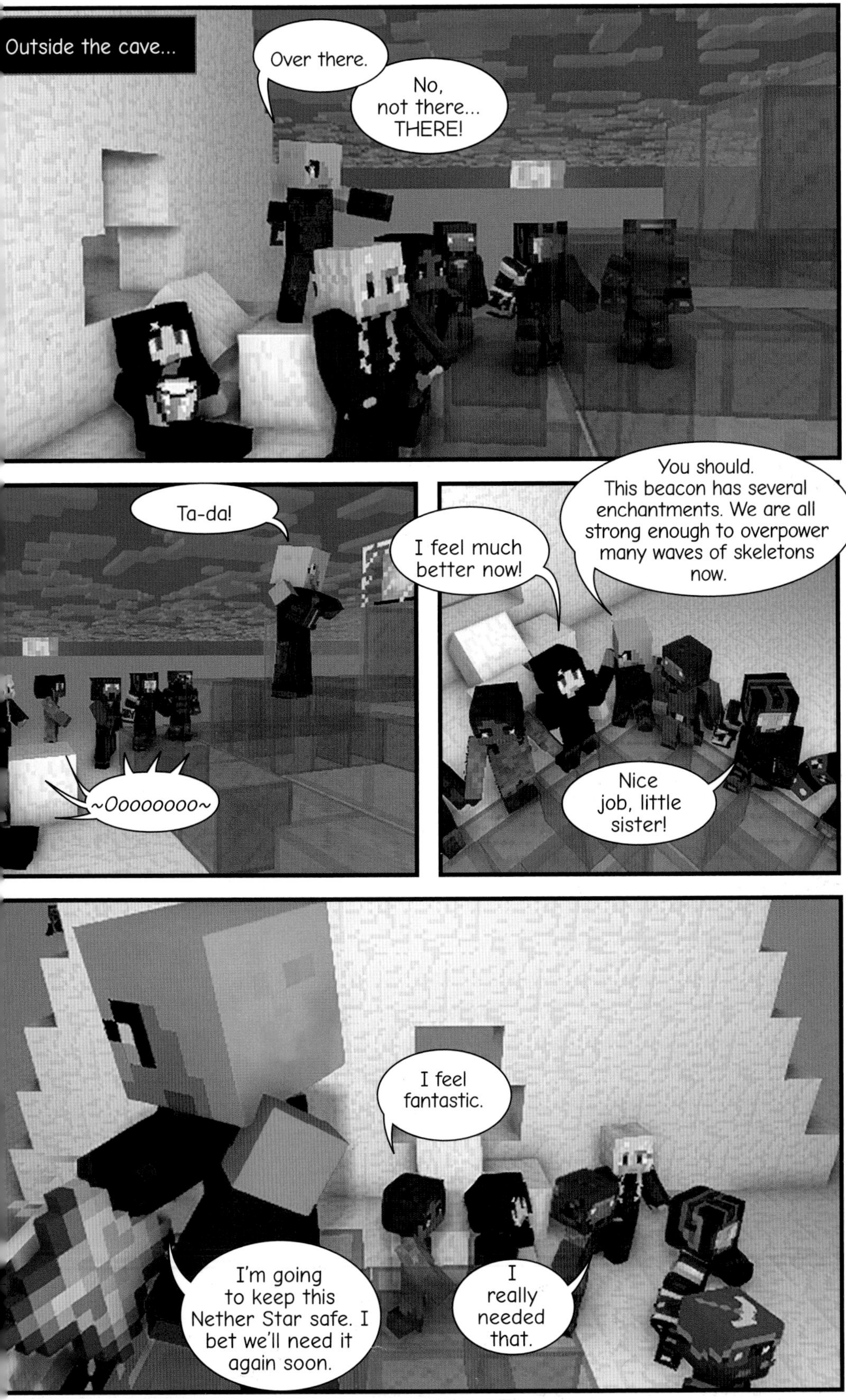

Outside the cave...
Over there.
No, not there... THERE!
Ta-da!
~Oooooooo~
I feel much better now!
You should. This beacon has several enchantments. We are all strong enough to overpower many waves of skeletons now.
Nice job, little sister!
I feel fantastic.
I'm going to keep this Nether Star safe. I bet we'll need it again soon.
I really needed that.

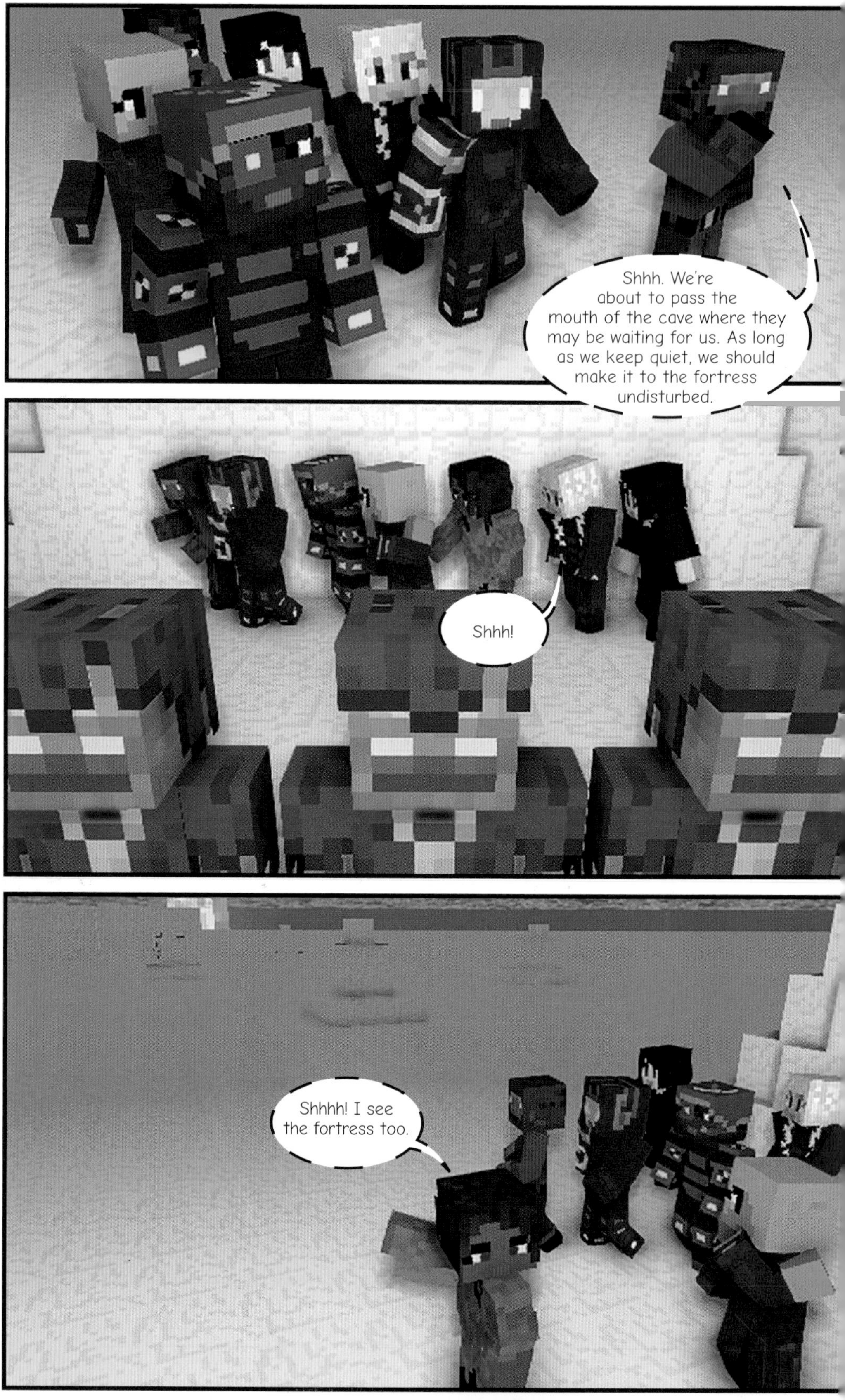
Shhh. We're about to pass the mouth of the cave where they may be waiting for us. As long as we keep quiet, we should make it to the fortress undisturbed.
Shhh!
Shhhh! I see the fortress too.

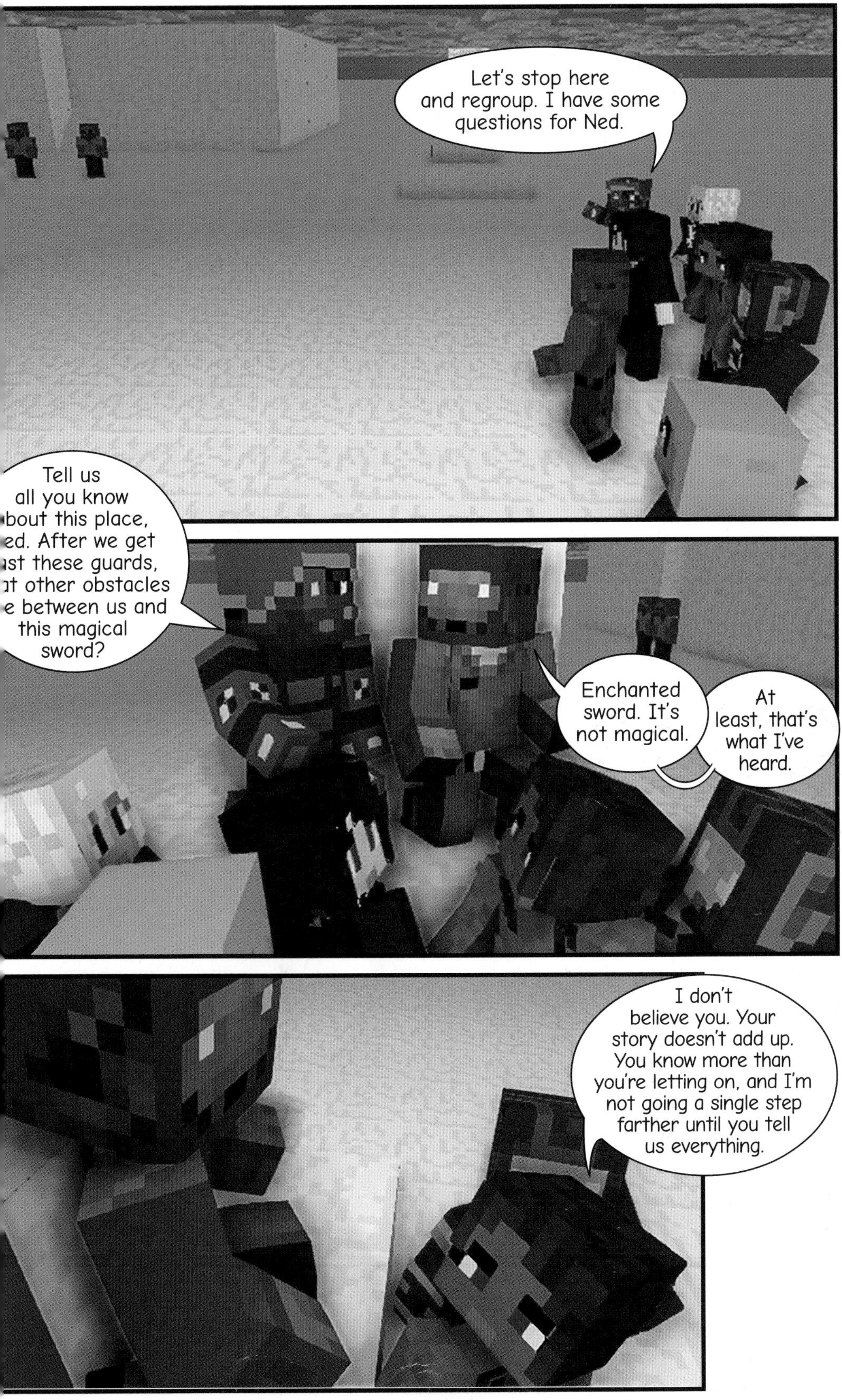
Let's stop here and regroup. I have some questions for Ned.
Tell us all you know bout this place, ed. After we get st these guards, t other obstacles e between us and this magical sword?
Enchanted sword. It's not magical.
At least, that's what I've heard.
I don't believe you. Your story doesn't add up. You know more than you're letting on, and I'm not going a single step farther until you tell us everything.

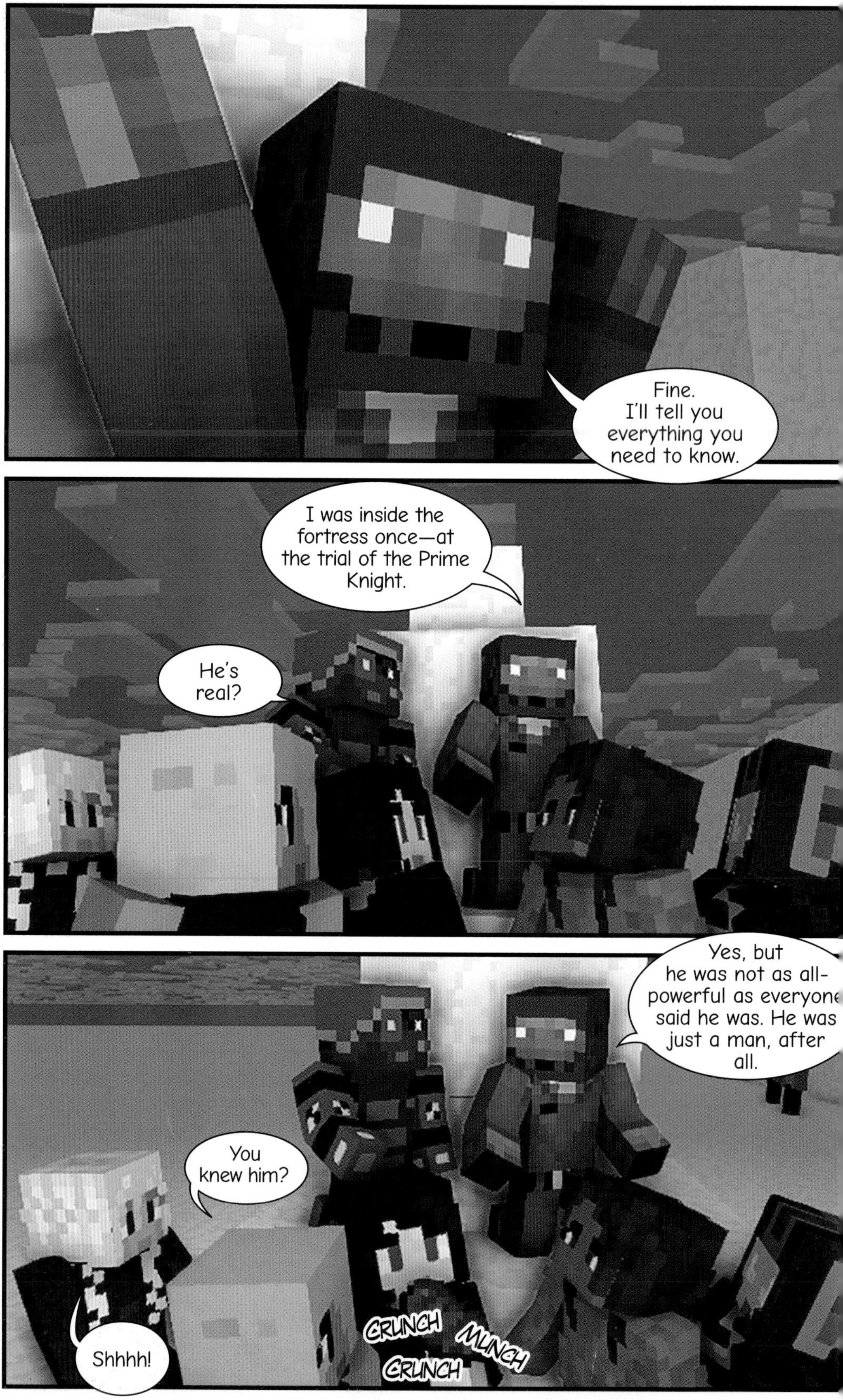
Fine. I'll tell you everything you need to know.
I was inside the fortress once—at the trial of the Prime Knight.
He's real?
Yes, but he was not as all-powerful as everyone said he was. He was just a man, after all.
You knew him?
Shhhh!
CRUNCH
MUNCH
CRUNCH

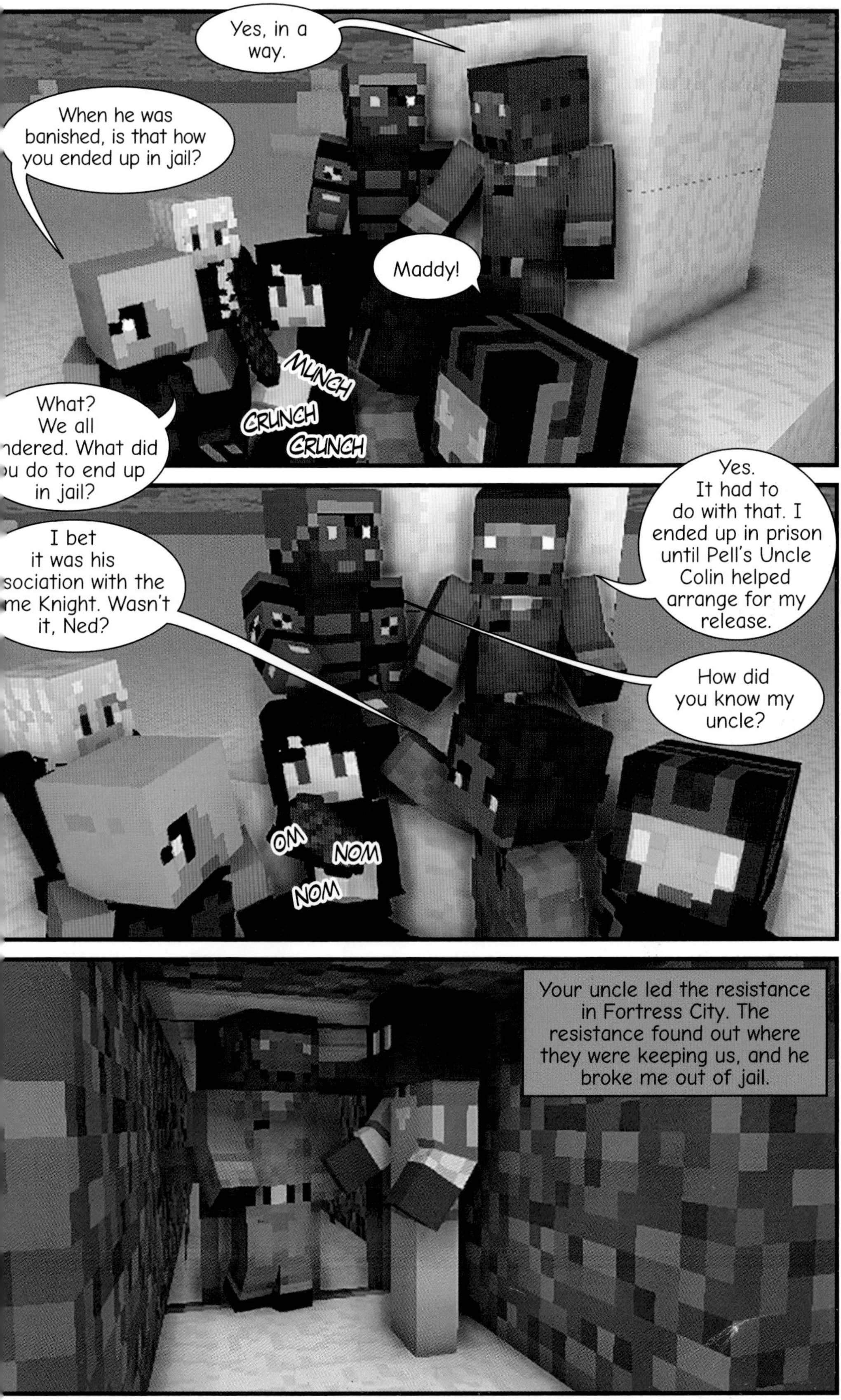
Yes, in a way.
When he was banished, is that how you ended up in jail?
Maddy!
MUNCH
CRUNCH
CRUNCH
What? We all
ndered. What did
u do to end up in jail?
Yes. It had to do with that. I ended up in prison until Pell's Uncle Colin helped arrange for my release.
I bet it was his
sociation with the
me Knight. Wasn't it, Ned?
How did you know my uncle?
OM
NOM
NOM
Your uncle led the resistance in Fortress City. The resistance found out where they were keeping us, and he broke me out of jail.

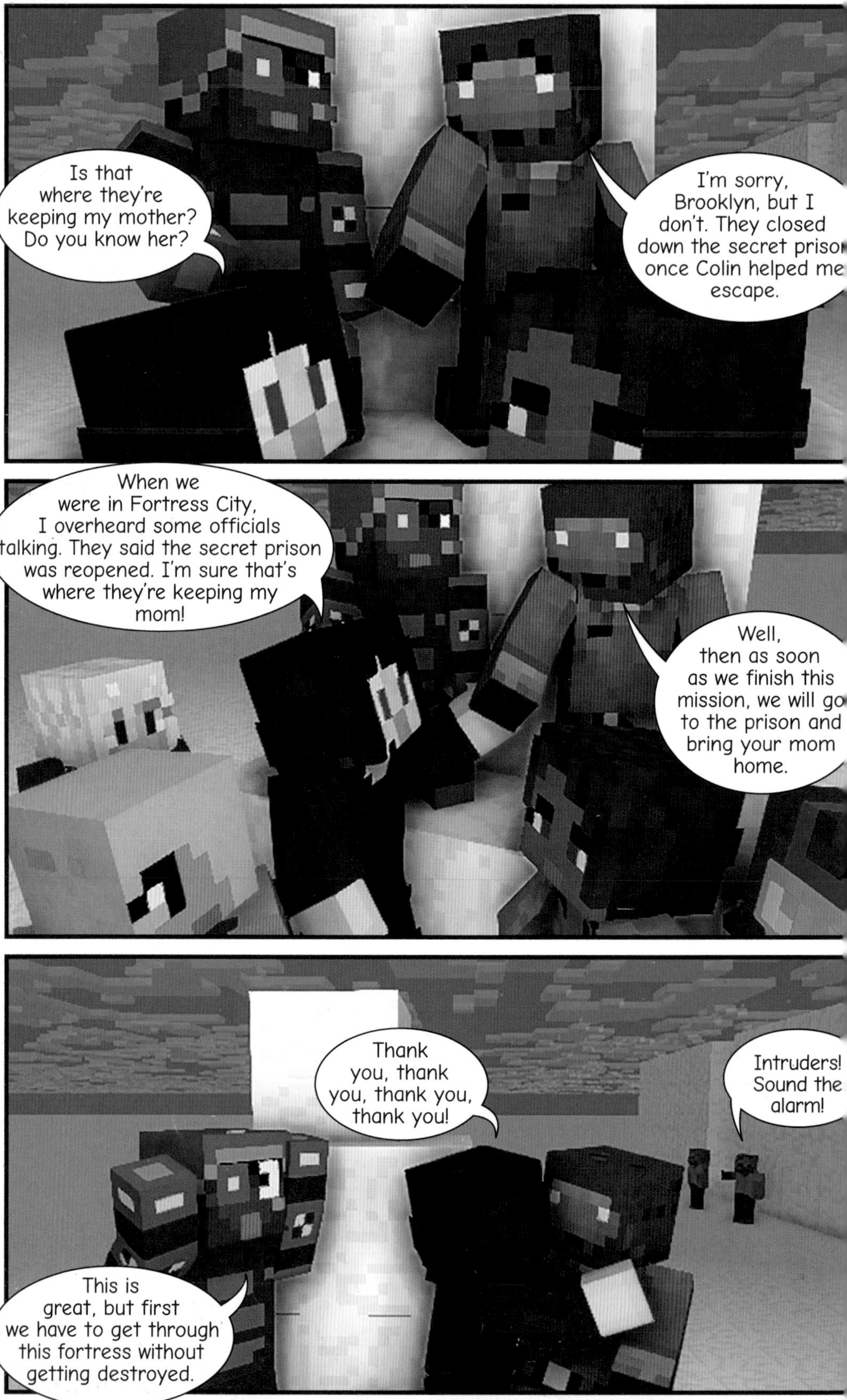
Is that where they're keeping my mother? Do you know her?
I'm sorry, Brooklyn, but I don't. They closed down the secret prison once Colin helped me escape.
When we were in Fortress City, I overheard some officials talking. They said the secret prison was reopened. I'm sure that's where they're keeping my mom!
Well, then as soon as we finish this mission, we will go to the prison and bring your mom home.
Thank you, thank you, thank you, thank you!
Intruders! Sound the alarm!
This is great, but first we have to get through this fortress without getting destroyed.

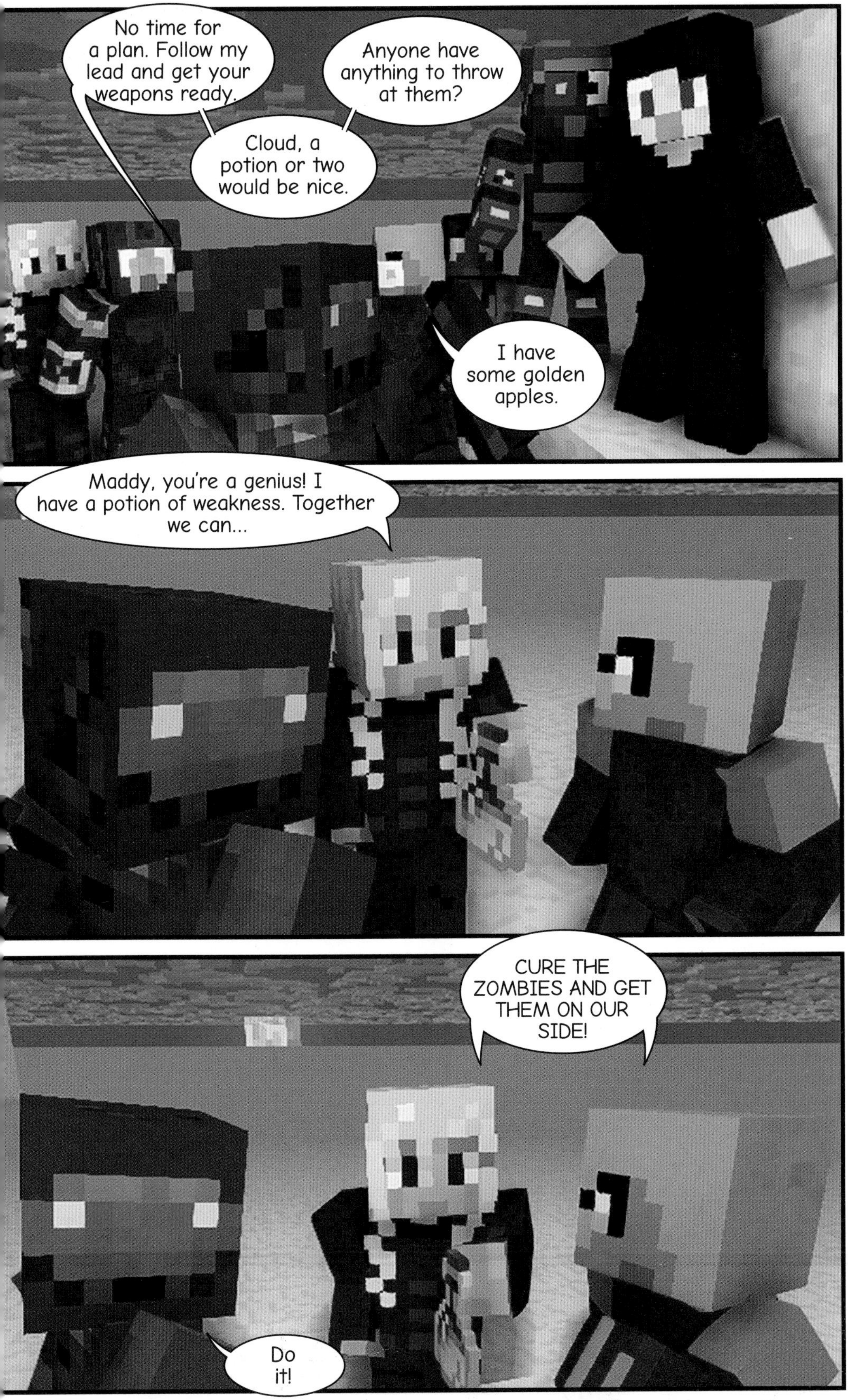
No time for a plan. Follow my lead and get your weapons ready.
Cloud, a potion or two would be nice.
Anyone have anything to throw at them?
I have some golden apples.
Maddy, you're a genius! I have a potion of weakness. Together we can...
CURE THE ZOMBIES AND GET THEM ON OUR SIDE!
Do it!

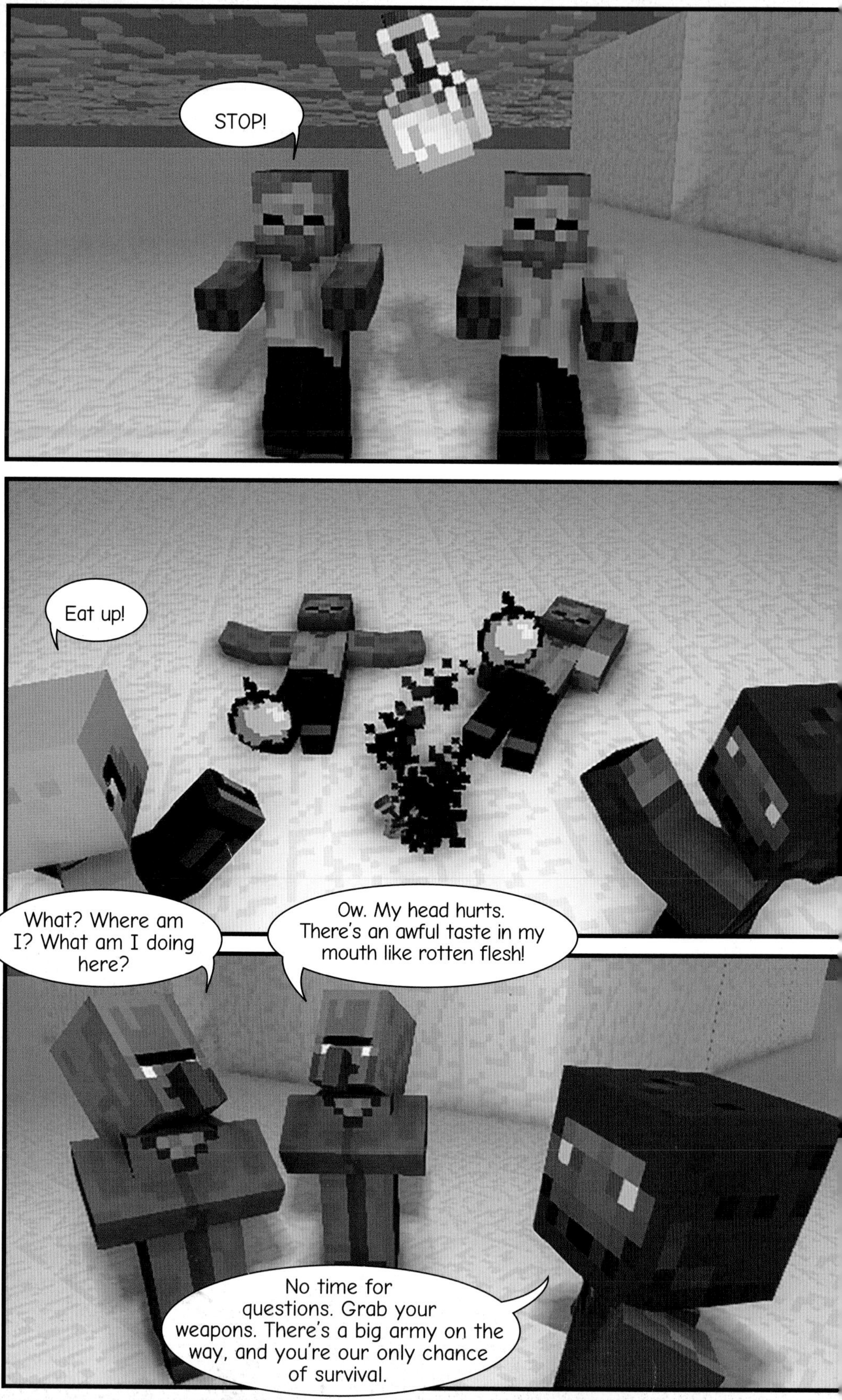
STOP!
Eat up!
What? Where am I? What am I doing here?
Ow. My head hurts. There's an awful taste in my mouth like rotten flesh!
No time for questions. Grab your weapons. There's a big army on the way, and you're our only chance of survival.

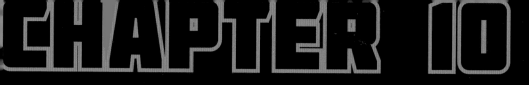

CHAPTER 10

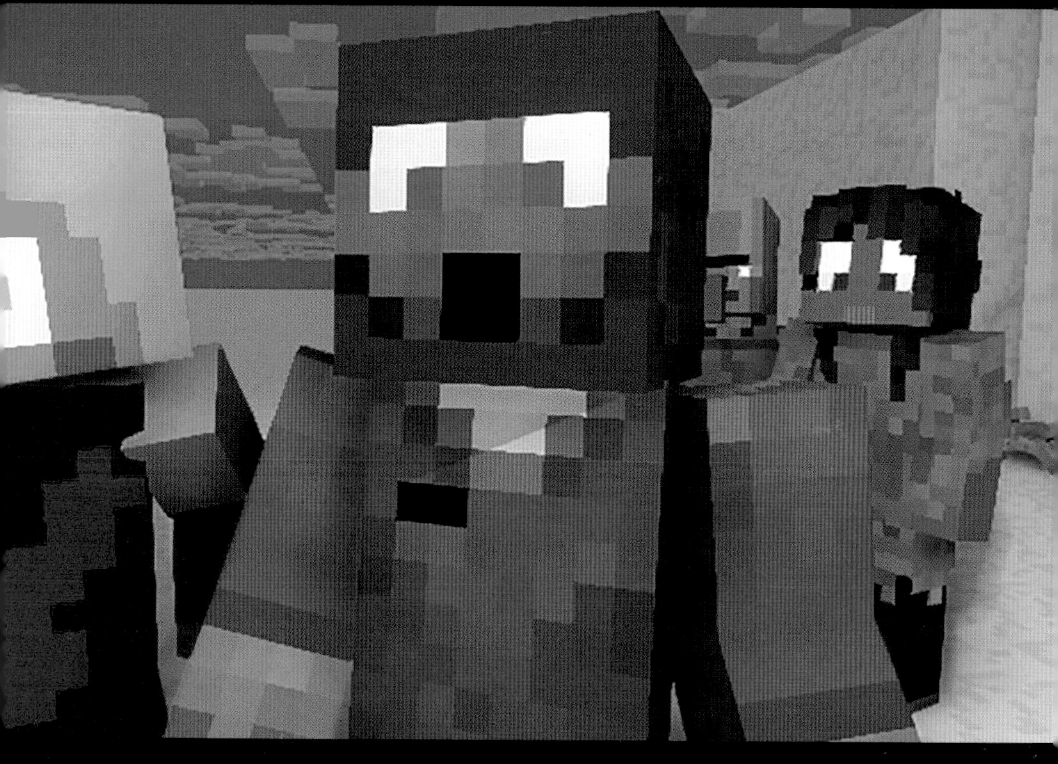

THE PRIME KNIGHT

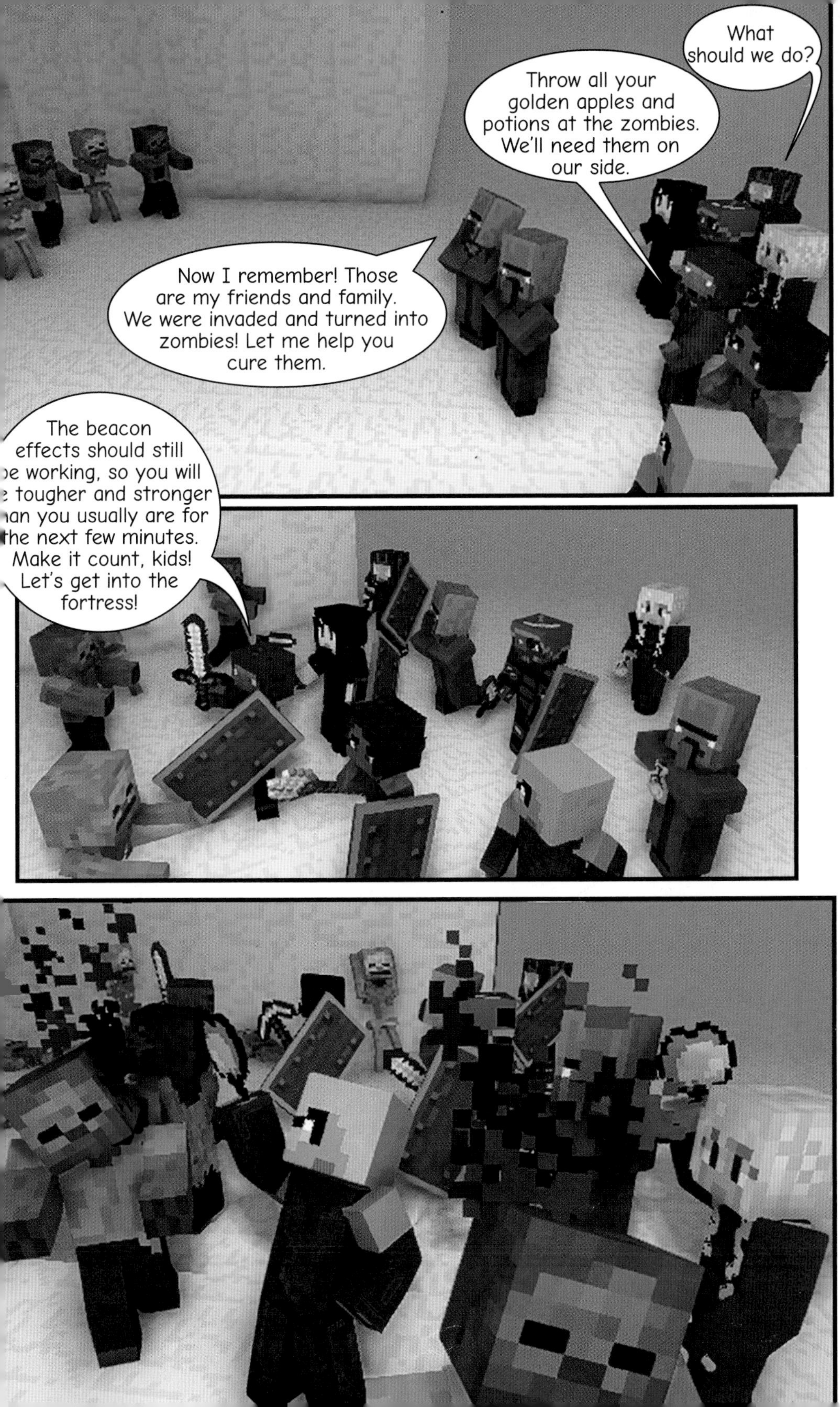
What should we do?
Throw all your golden apples and potions at the zombies. We'll need them on our side.
Now I remember! Those are my friends and family. We were invaded and turned into zombies! Let me help you cure them.
The beacon effects should still e working, so you will tougher and stronger an you usually are for the next few minutes. Make it count, kids! Let's get into the fortress!

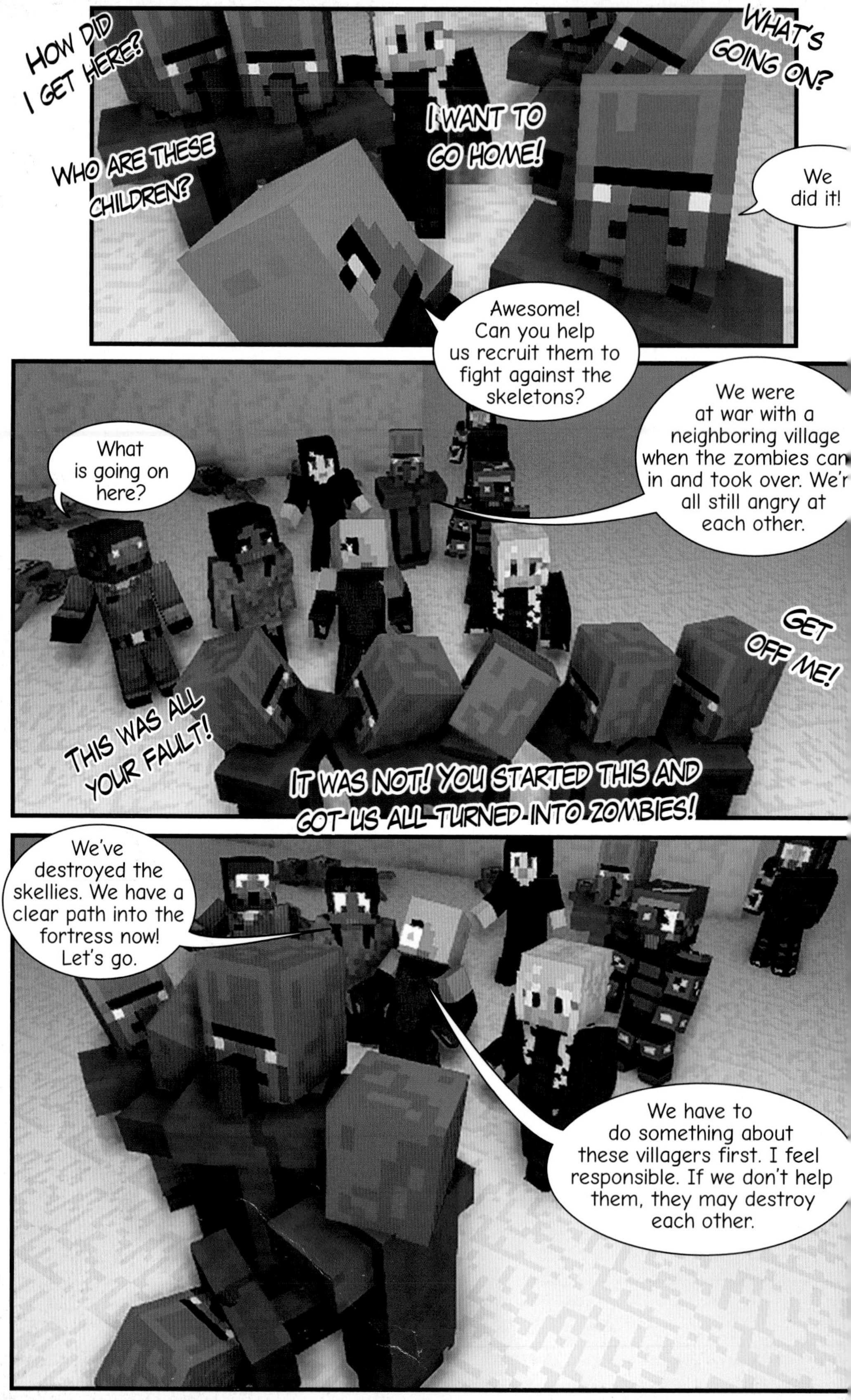

HOW DID I GET HERE?
WHAT'S GOING ON?
I WANT TO GO HOME!
WHO ARE THESE CHILDREN?
We did it!
Awesome! Can you help us recruit them to fight against the skeletons?
What is going on here?
We were at war with a neighboring village when the zombies can in and took over. We'r all still angry at each other.
GET OFF ME!
THIS WAS ALL YOUR FAULT!
IT WAS NOT! YOU STARTED THIS AND GOT US ALL TURNED INTO ZOMBIES!
We've destroyed the skellies. We have a clear path into the fortress now! Let's go.
We have to do something about these villagers first. I feel responsible. If we don't help them, they may destroy each other.

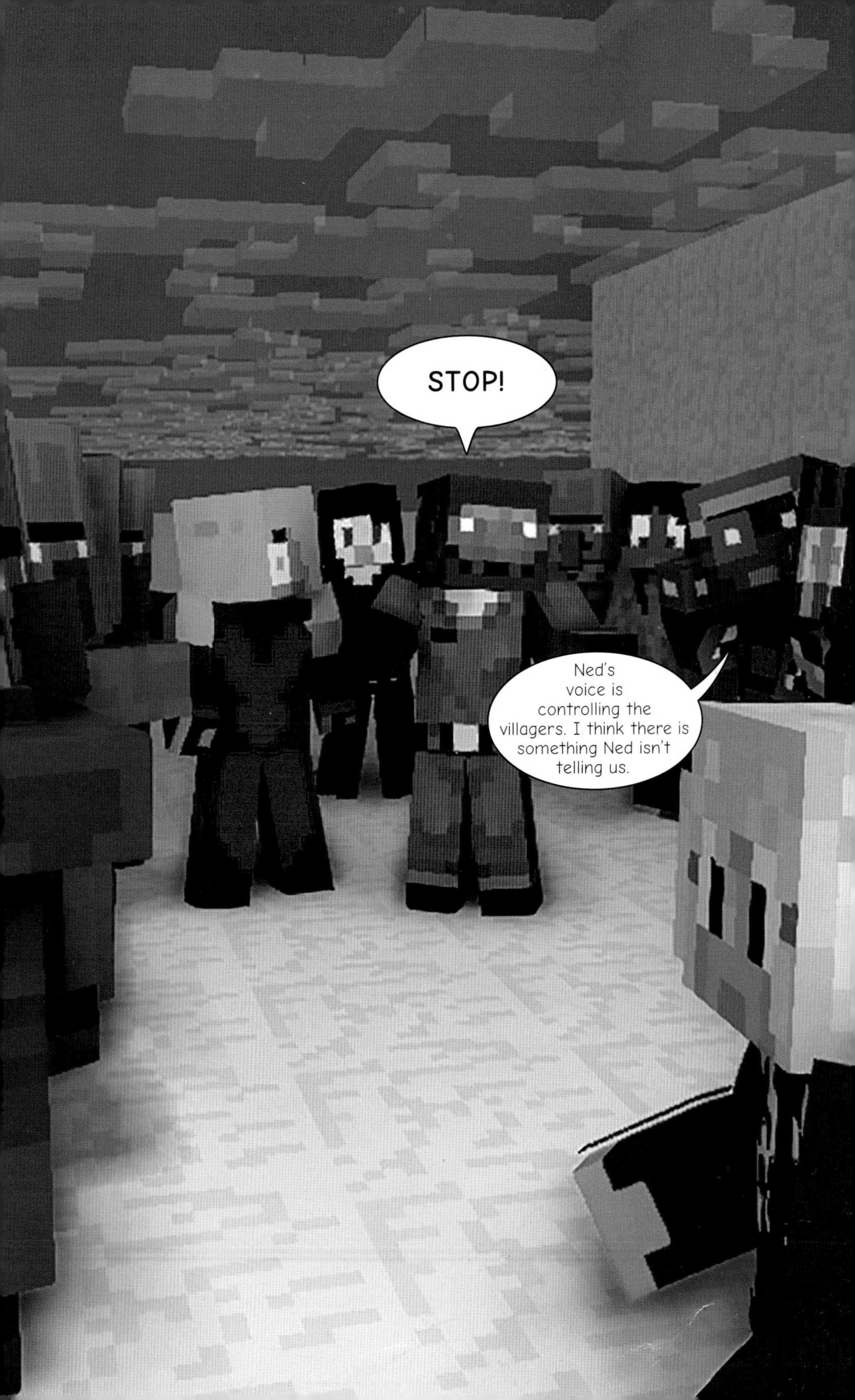
STOP!
Ned's voice is controlling the villagers. I think there is something Ned isn't telling us.

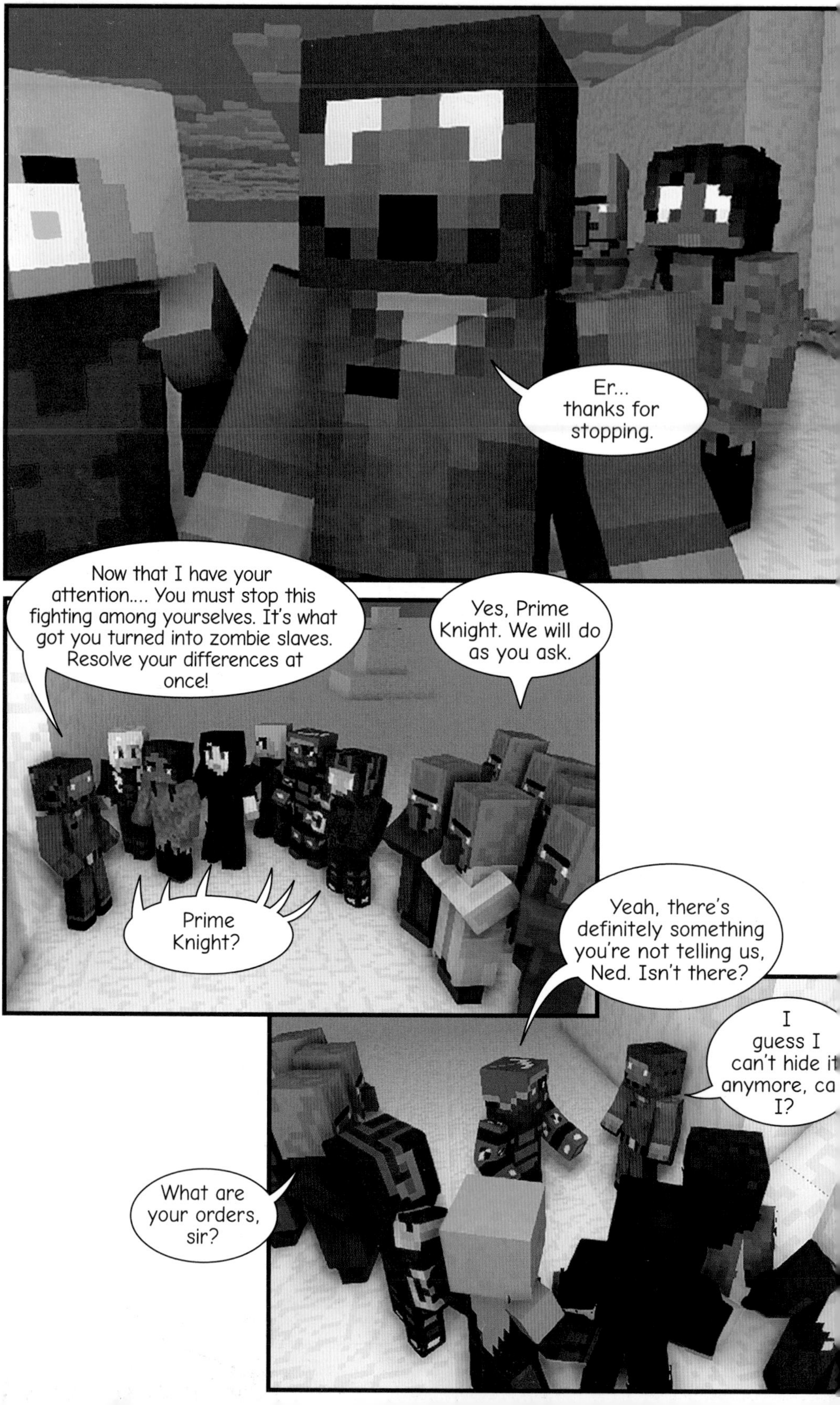
Er...
thanks for
stopping.
Now that I have your attention.... You must stop this fighting among yourselves. It's what got you turned into zombie slaves. Resolve your differences at once!
Yes, Prime Knight. We will do as you ask.
Prime Knight?
Yeah, there's definitely something you're not telling us, Ned. Isn't there?
I guess I can't hide it anymore, ca I?
What are your orders, sir?

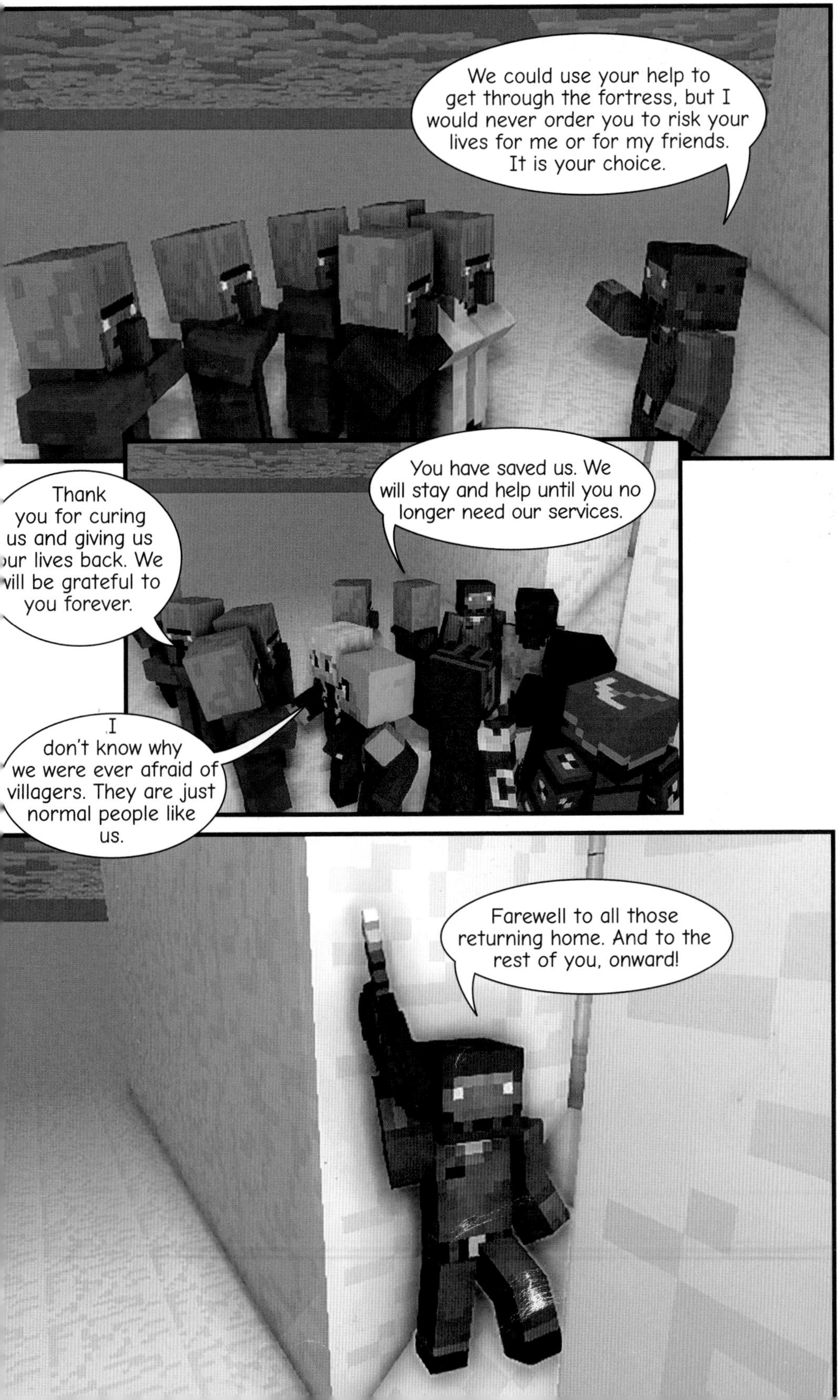
We could use your help to get through the fortress, but I would never order you to risk your lives for me or for my friends. It is your choice.
You have saved us. We will stay and help until you no longer need our services.
Thank you for curing us and giving us our lives back. We will be grateful to you forever.
I don't know why we were ever afraid of villagers. They are just normal people like us.
Farewell to all those returning home. And to the rest of you, onward!

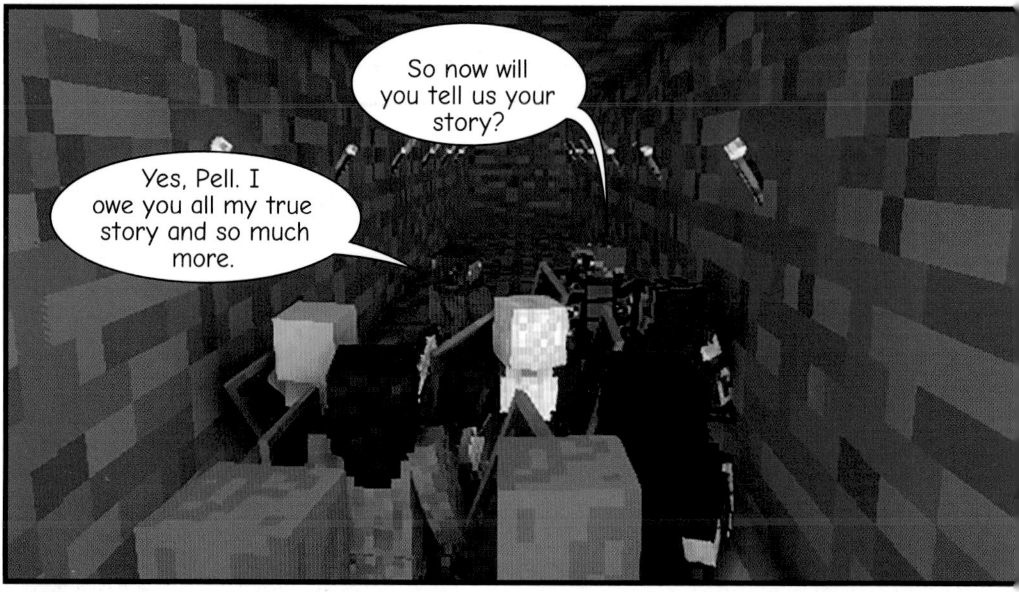
So now will you tell us your story?
Yes, Pell. I owe you all my true story and so much more.

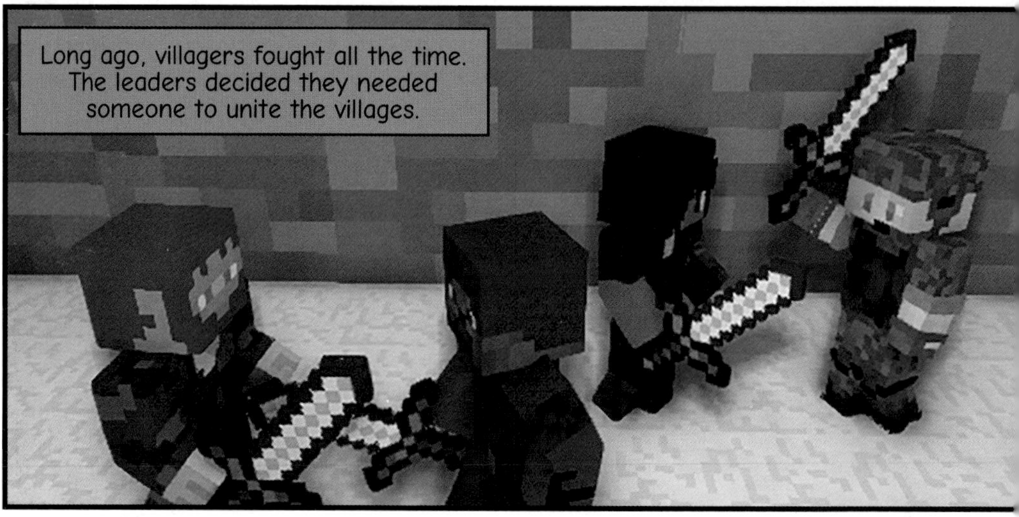
Long ago, villagers fought all the time. The leaders decided they needed someone to unite the villages.

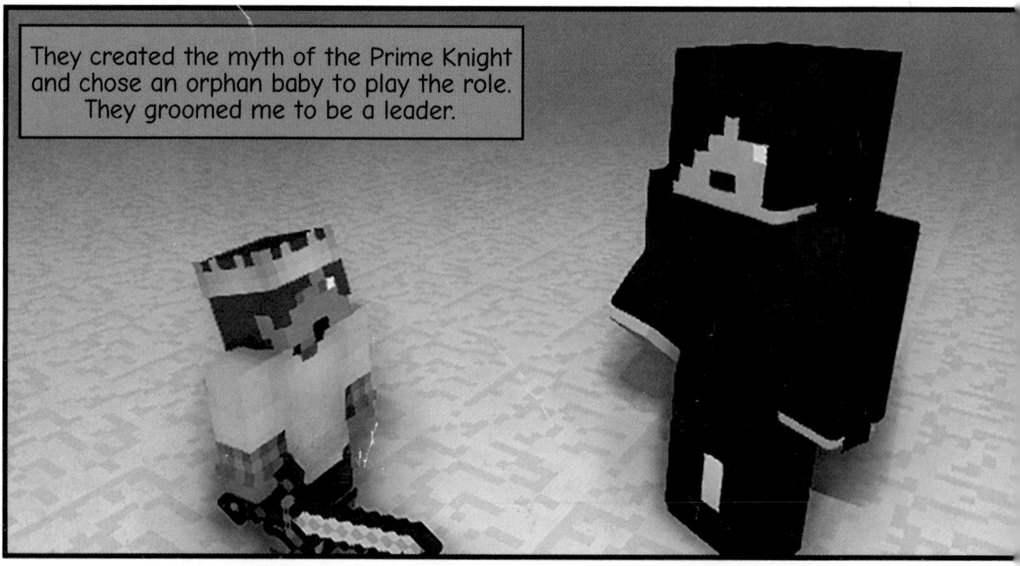
They created the myth of the Prime Knight and chose an orphan baby to play the role. They groomed me to be a leader.

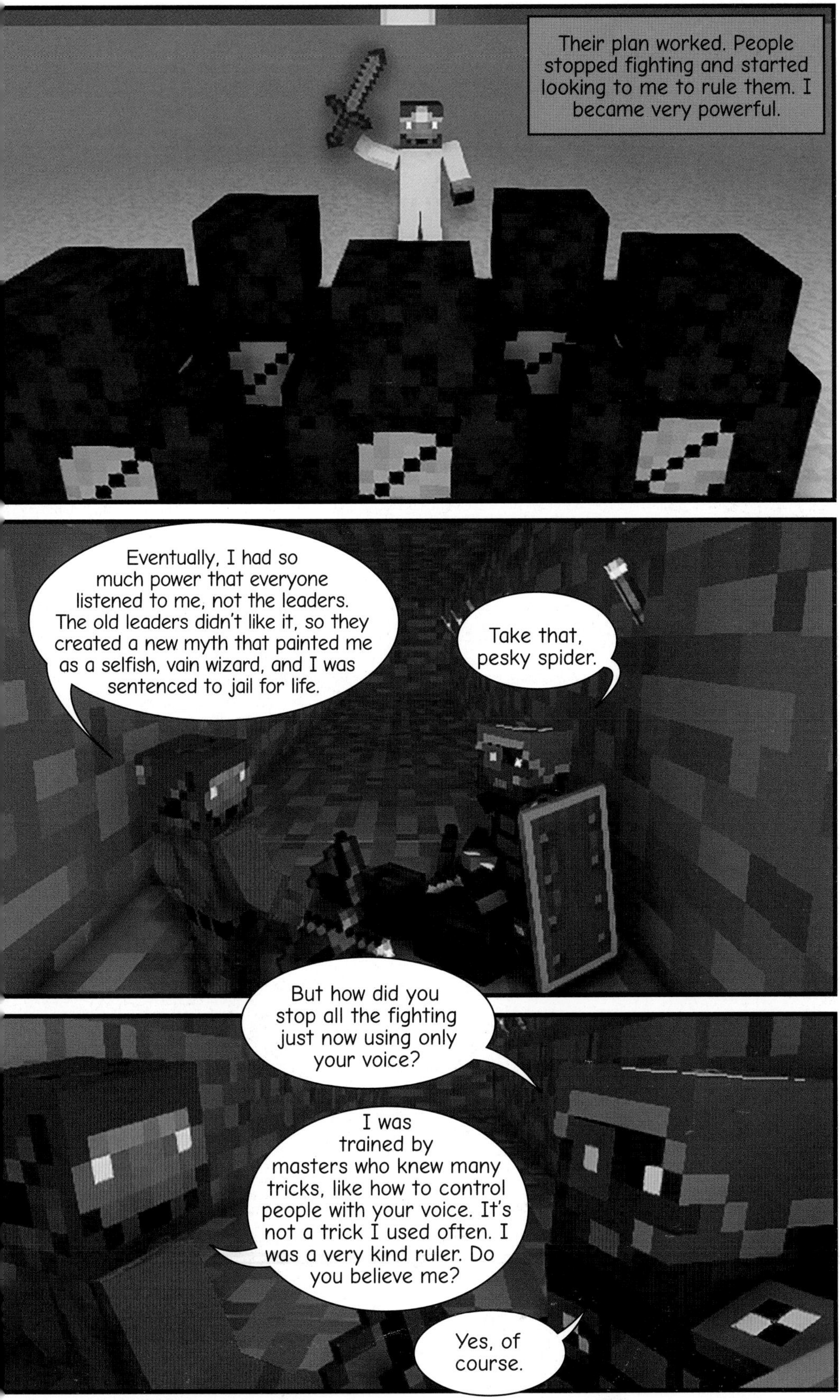
Their plan worked. People stopped fighting and started looking to me to rule them. I became very powerful.
Eventually, I had so much power that everyone listened to me, not the leaders. The old leaders didn't like it, so they created a new myth that painted me as a selfish, vain wizard, and I was sentenced to jail for life.
Take that, pesky spider.
But how did you stop all the fighting just now using only your voice?
I was trained by masters who knew many tricks, like how to control people with your voice. It's not a trick I used often. I was a very kind ruler. Do you believe me?
Yes, of course.

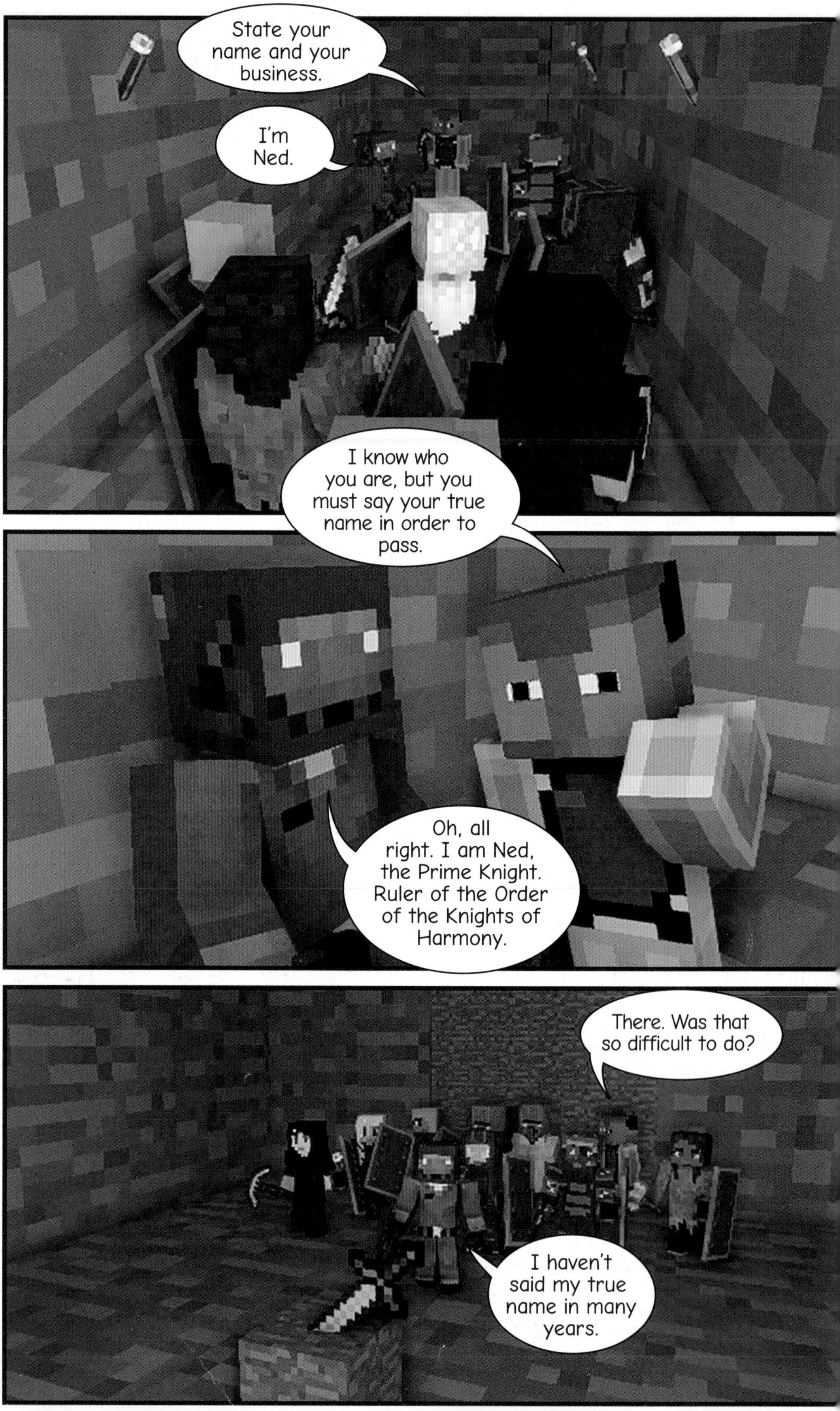
State your name and your business.
I'm Ned.
I know who you are, but you must say your true name in order to pass.
Oh, all right. I am Ned, the Prime Knight. Ruler of the Order of the Knights of Harmony.
There. Was that so difficult to do?
I haven't said my true name in many years.

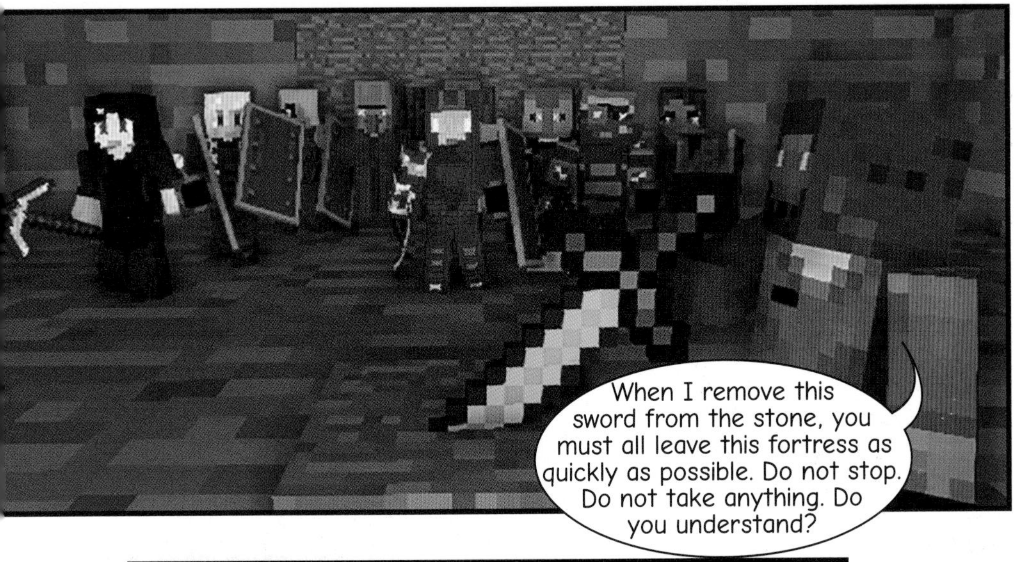
When I remove this sword from the stone, you must all leave this fortress as quickly as possible. Do not stop. Do not take anything. Do you understand?

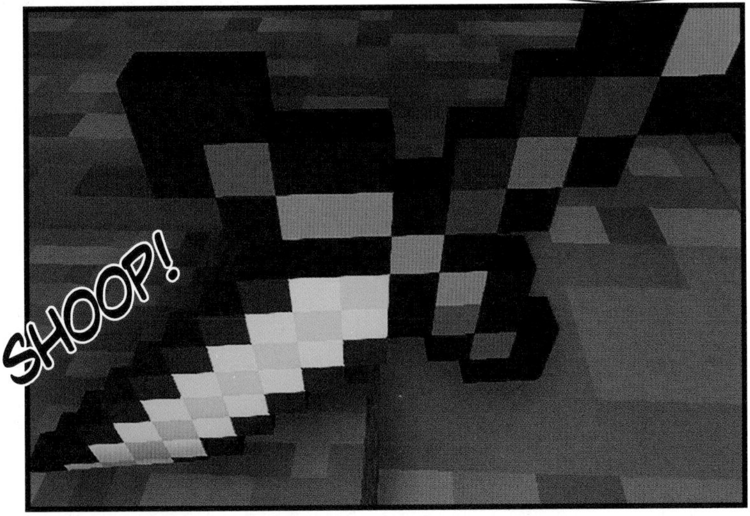
SHOOP!

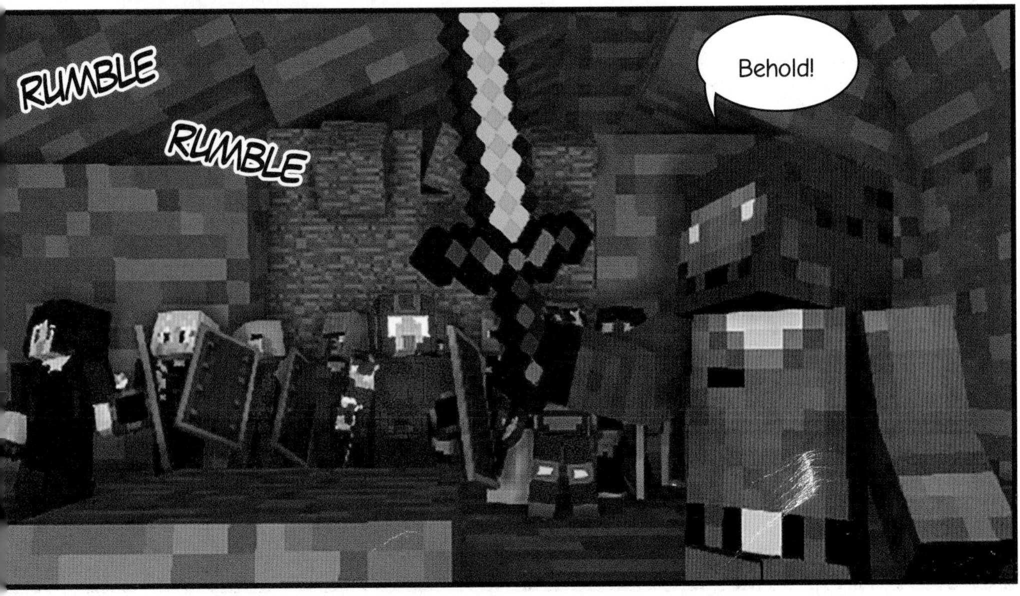
RUMBLE
RUMBLE
Behold!

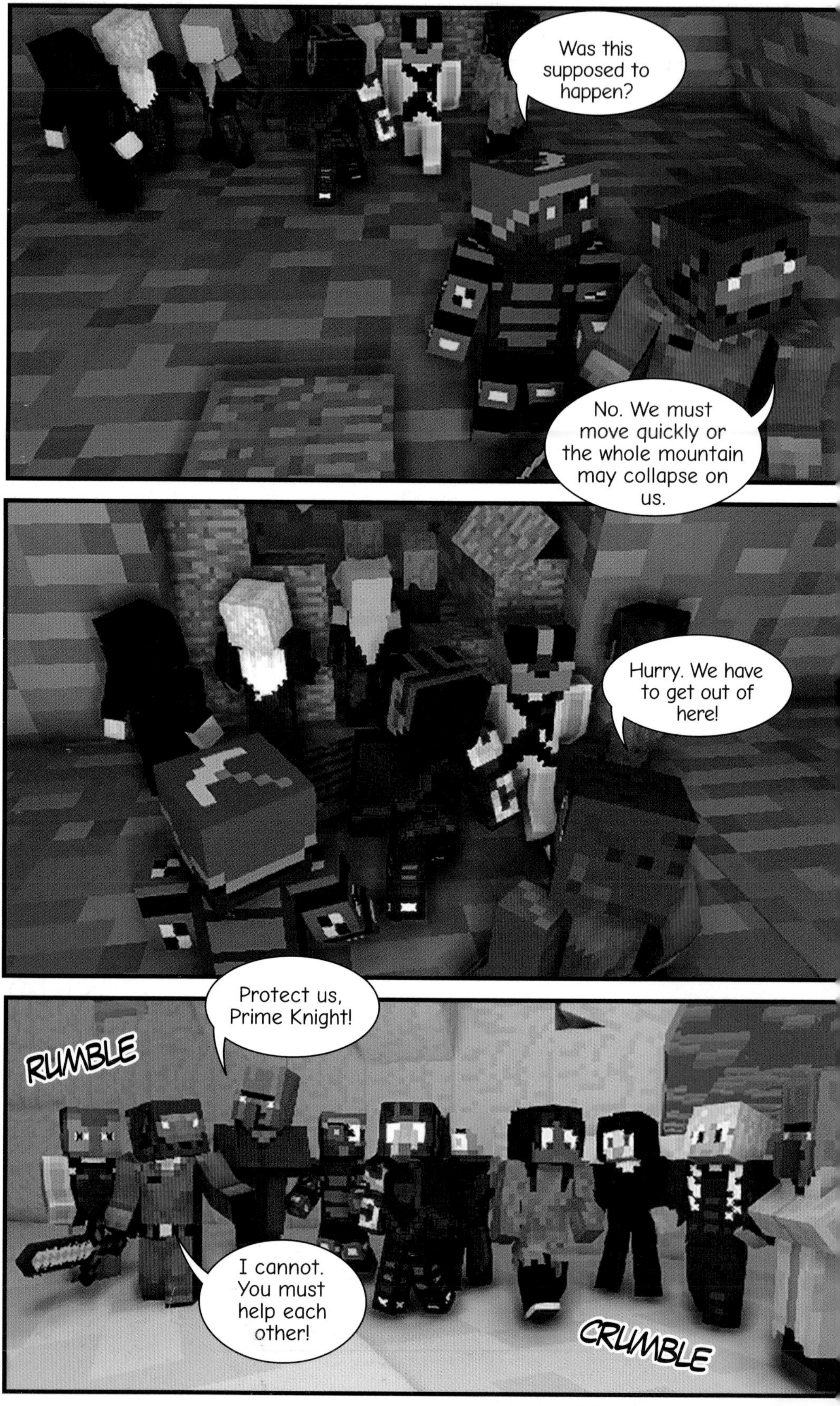
Was this supposed to happen?
No. We must move quickly or the whole mountain may collapse on us.
Hurry. We have to get out of here!
Protect us, Prime Knight!
RUMBLE
I cannot. You must help each other!
CRUMBLE

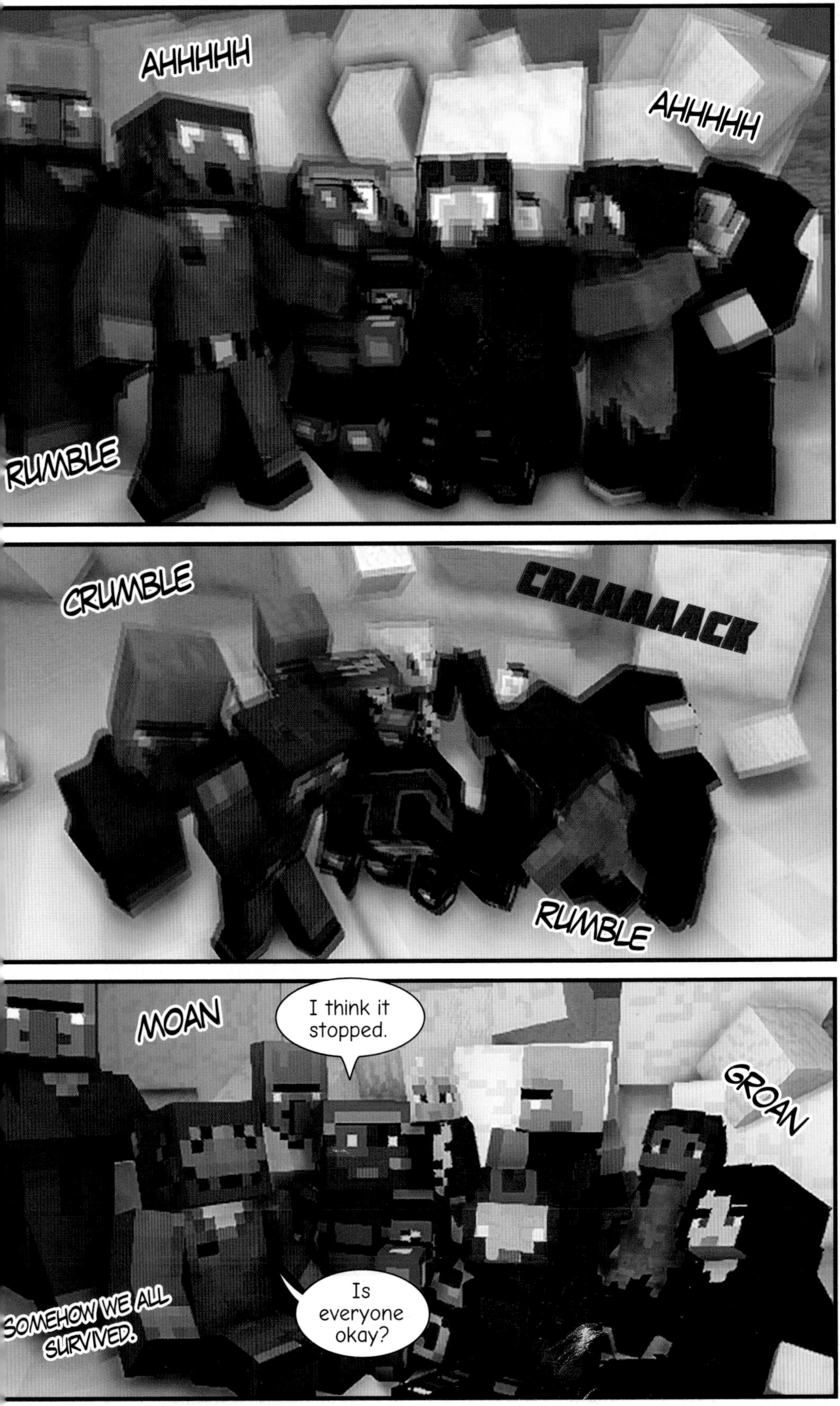
AHHHHH
AHHHHH
RUMBLE
CRUMBLE
CRAAAAACK
RUMBLE
MOAN
I think it stopped.
GROAN
SOMEHOW WE ALL SURVIVED.
Is everyone okay?

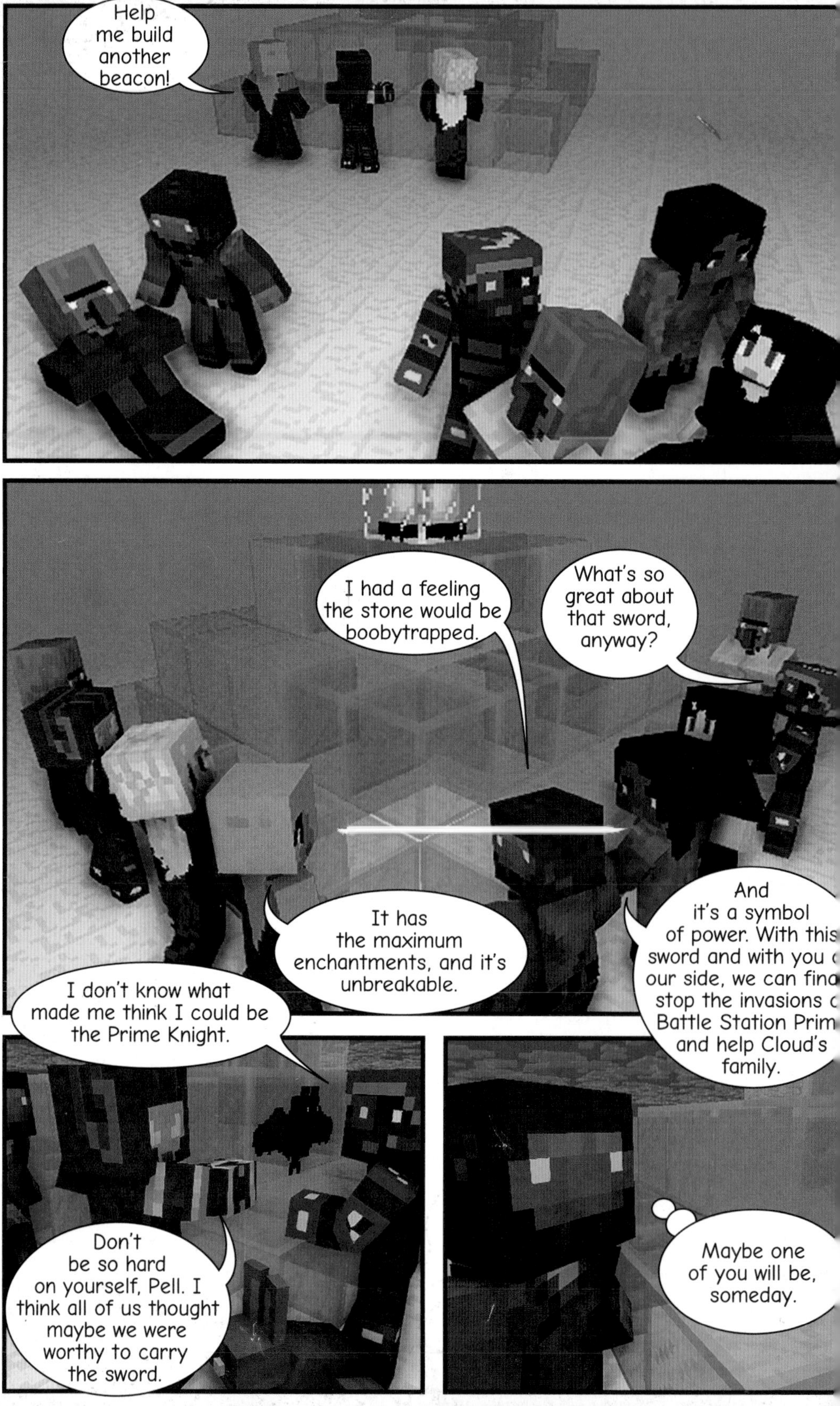
Help me build another beacon!
I had a feeling the stone would be boobytrapped.
What's so great about that sword, anyway?
It has the maximum enchantments, and it's unbreakable.
And it's a symbol of power. With this sword and with you o our side, we can fina stop the invasions o Battle Station Prim and help Cloud's family.
I don't know what made me think I could be the Prime Knight.
Don't be so hard on yourself, Pell. I think all of us thought maybe we were worthy to carry the sword.
Maybe one of you will be, someday.

CHAPTER 11

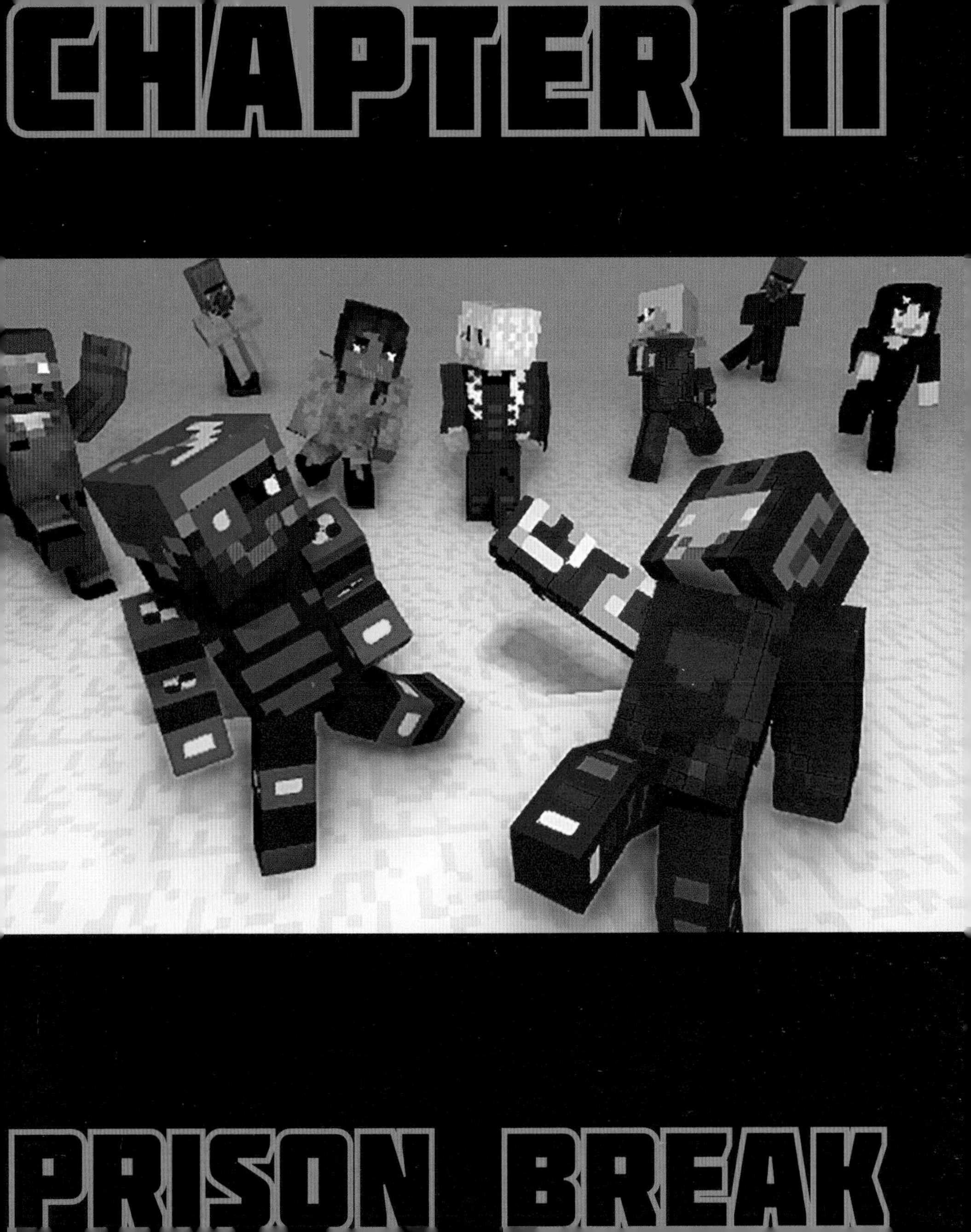

PRISON BREAK

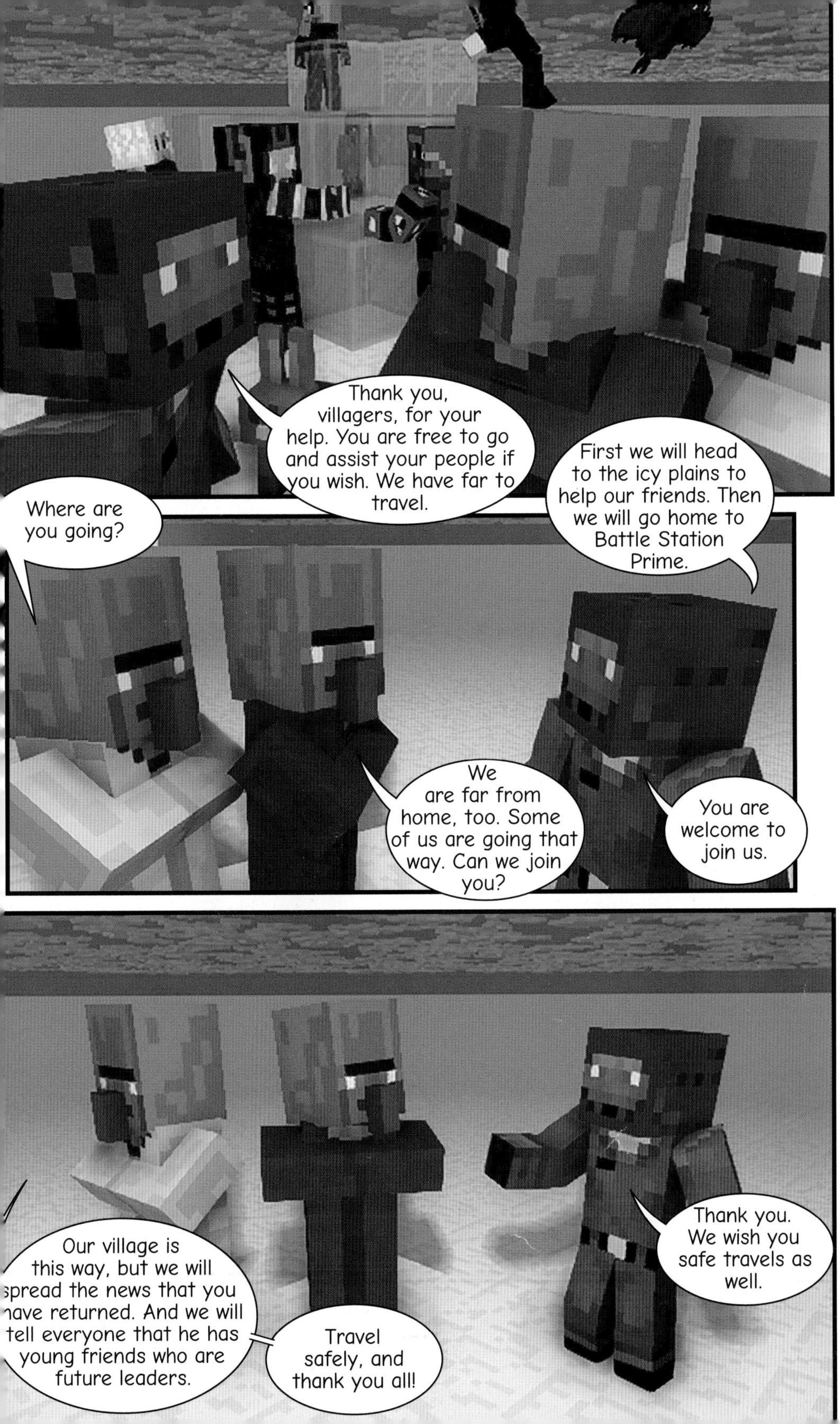
Thank you, villagers, for your help. You are free to go and assist your people if you wish. We have far to travel.
Where are you going?
First we will head to the icy plains to help our friends. Then we will go home to Battle Station Prime.
We are far from home, too. Some of us are going that way. Can we join you?
You are welcome to join us.
Our village is this way, but we will spread the news that you have returned. And we will tell everyone that he has young friends who are future leaders.
Travel safely, and thank you all!
Thank you. We wish you safe travels as well.

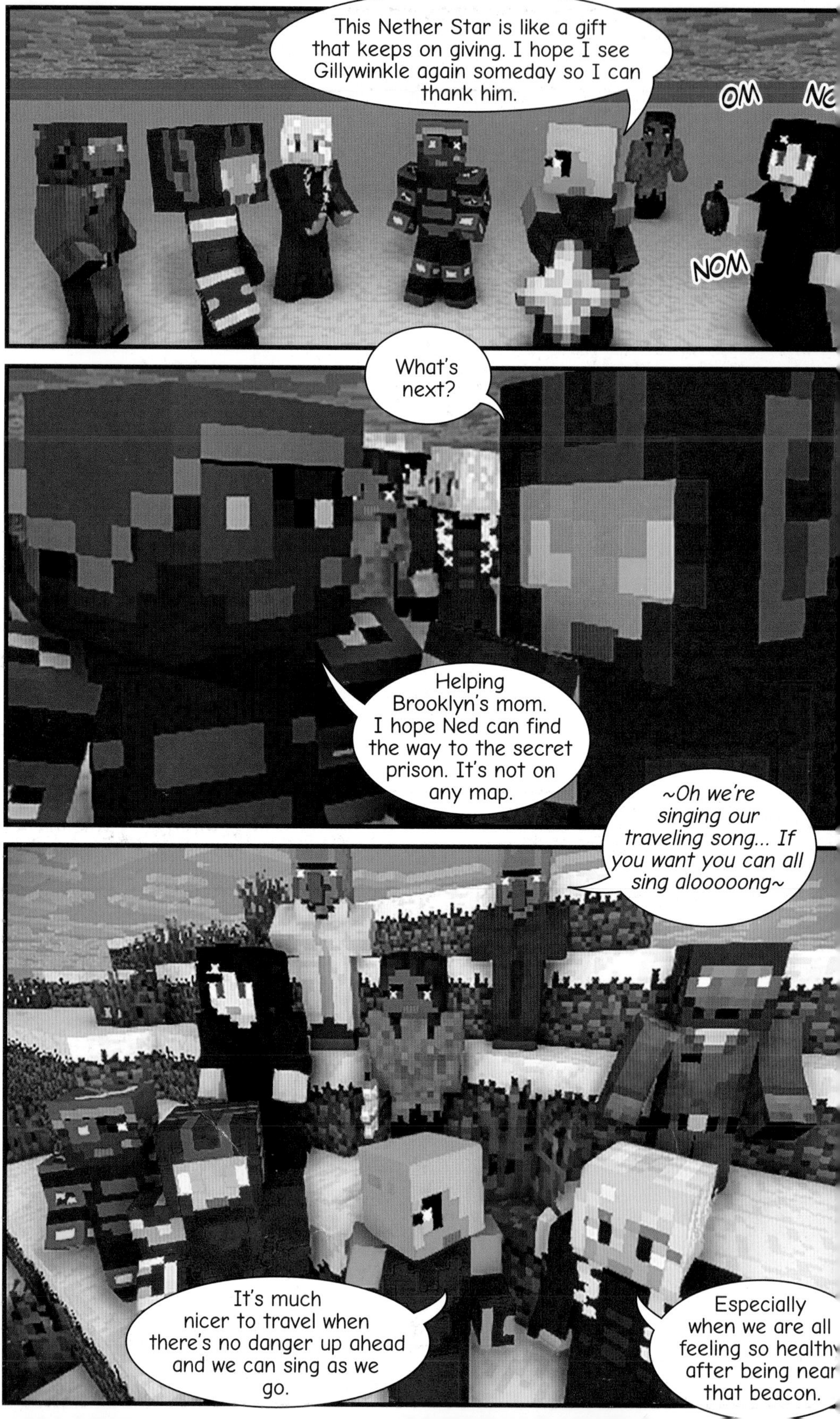
This Nether Star is like a gift that keeps on giving. I hope I see Gillywinkle again someday so I can thank him.
OM
NOM
What's next?
Helping Brooklyn's mom. I hope Ned can find the way to the secret prison. It's not on any map.
~Oh we're singing our traveling song... If you want you can all sing aloooong~
It's much nicer to travel when there's no danger up ahead and we can sing as we go.
Especially when we are all feeling so health after being near that beacon.

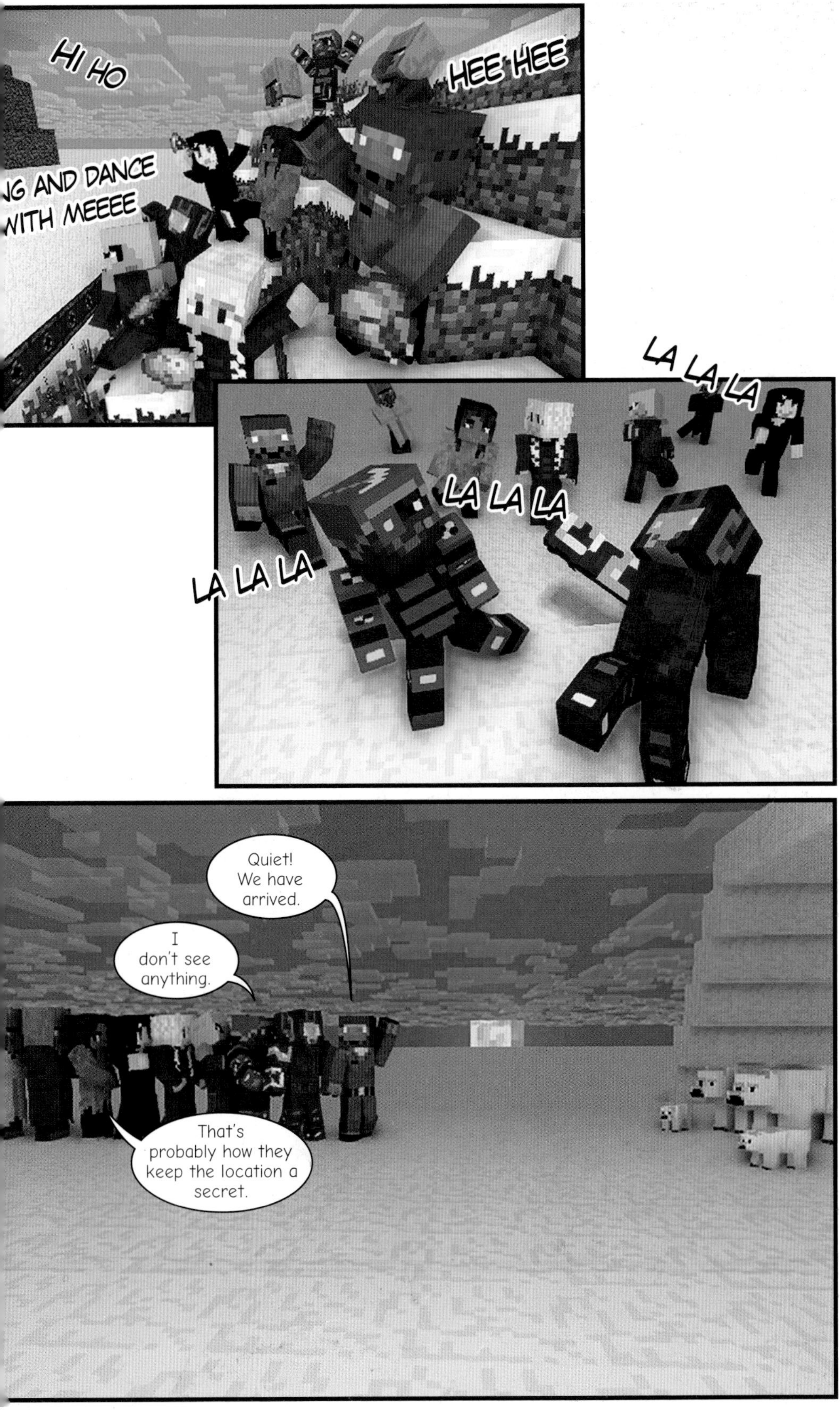
HI HO
G AND DANCE
WITH MEEEE
HEE HEE
LA LA LA
LA LA LA
LA LA LA
Quiet! We have arrived.
I don't see anything.
That's probably how they keep the location a secret.

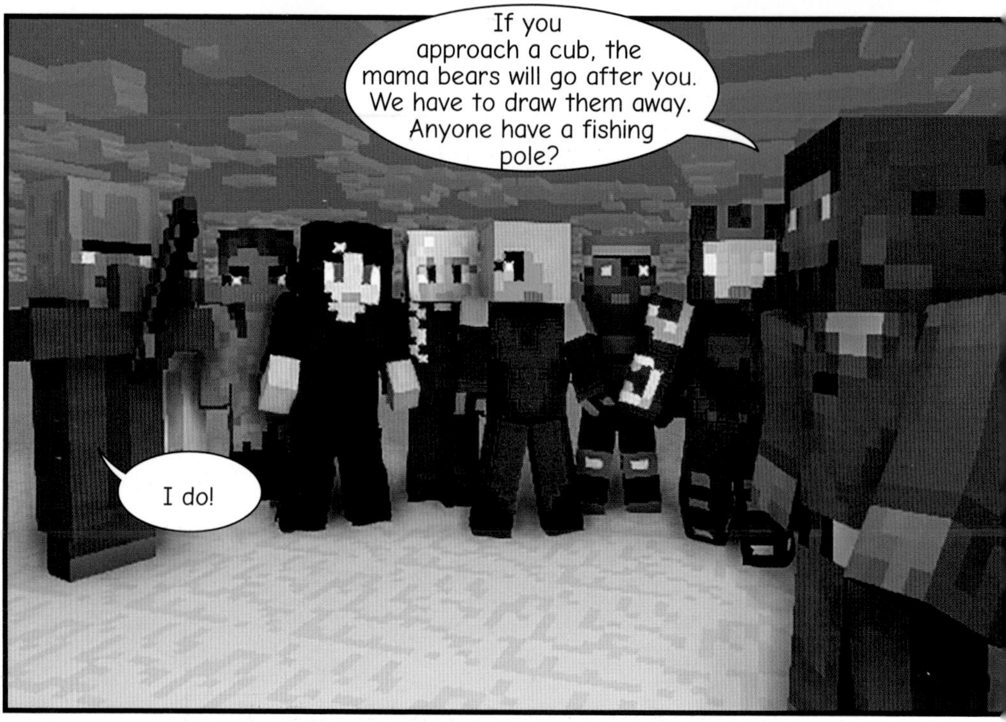
If you approach a cub, the mama bears will go after you. We have to draw them away. Anyone have a fishing pole?
I do!

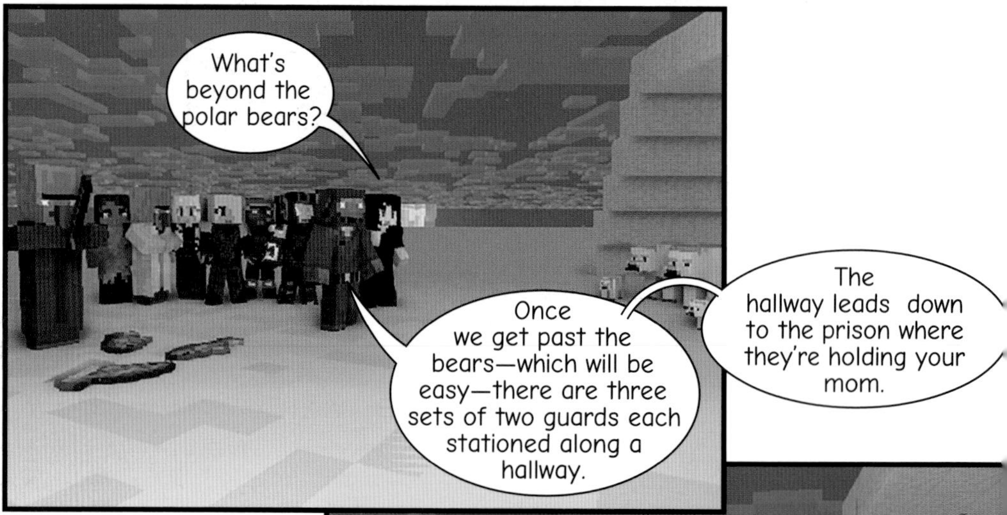
What's beyond the polar bears?
Once we get past the bears—which will be easy—there are three sets of two guards each stationed along a hallway.
The hallway leads down to the prison where they're holding your mom.

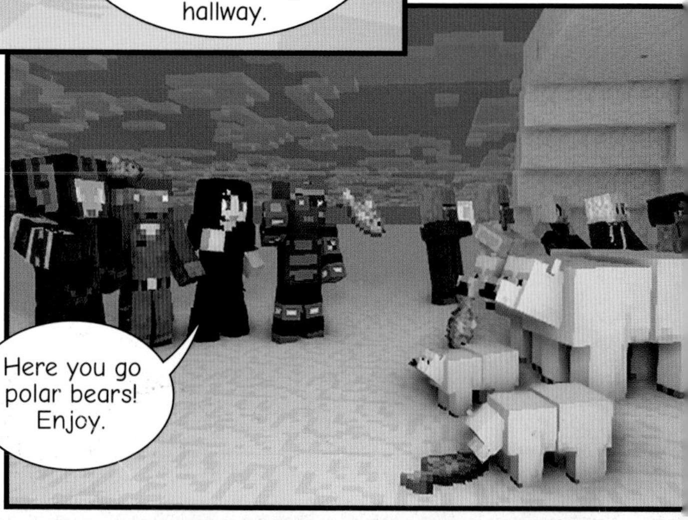
Here you go polar bears! Enjoy.

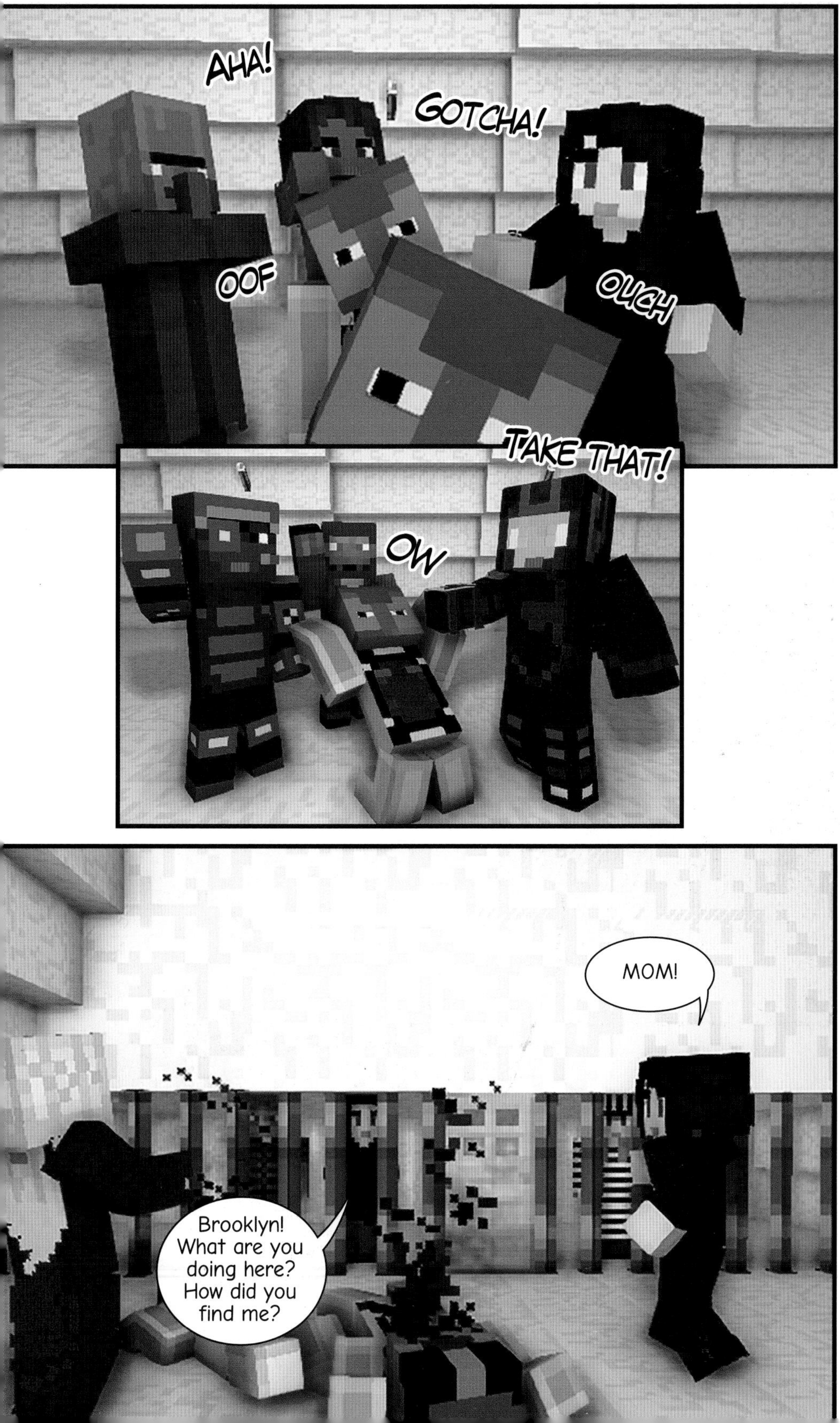
AHA!
GOTCHA!
OOF
OUCH
TAKE THAT!
OW
MOM!
Brooklyn! What are you doing here? How did you find me?

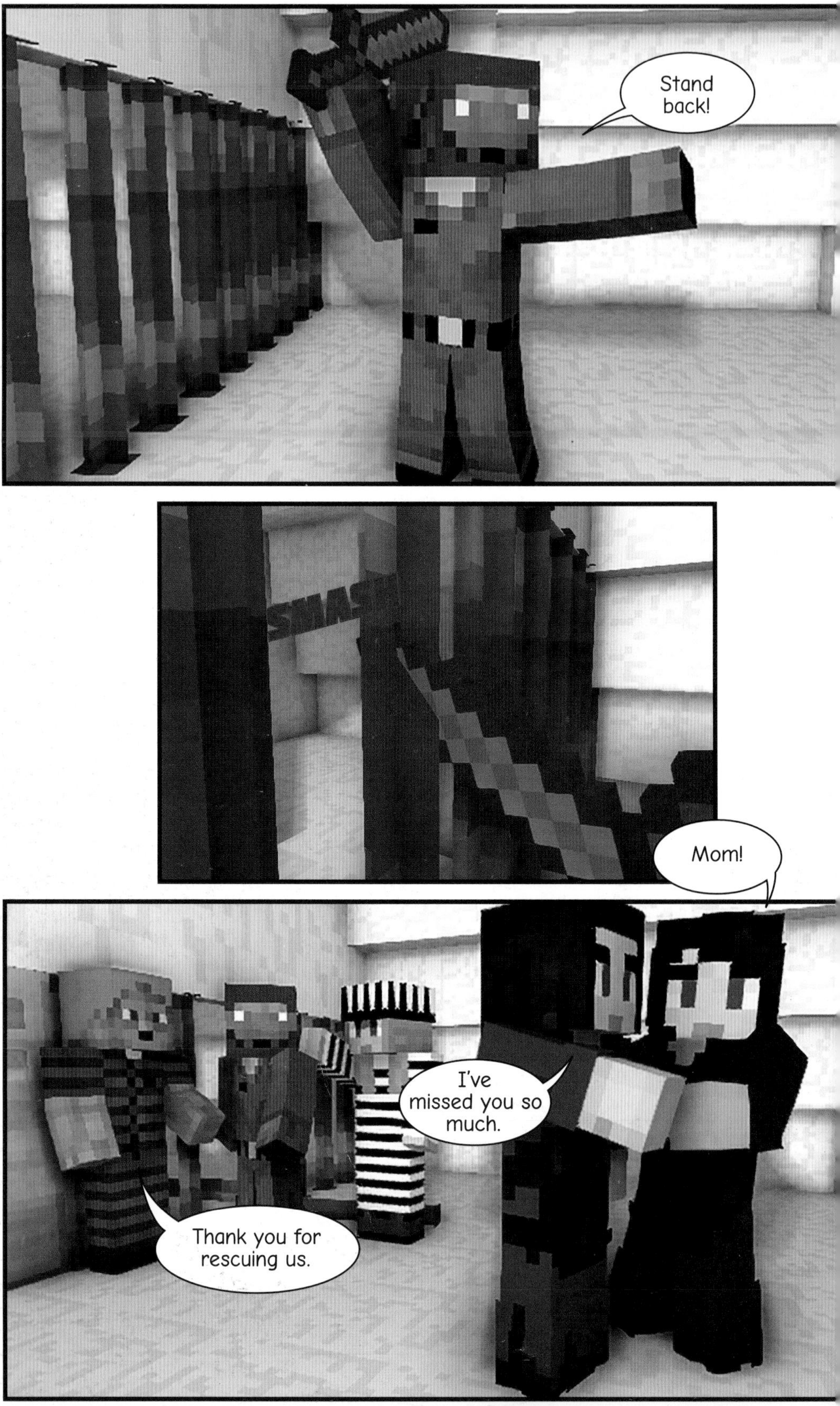
Stand back!
Mom!
I've missed you so much.
Thank you for rescuing us.

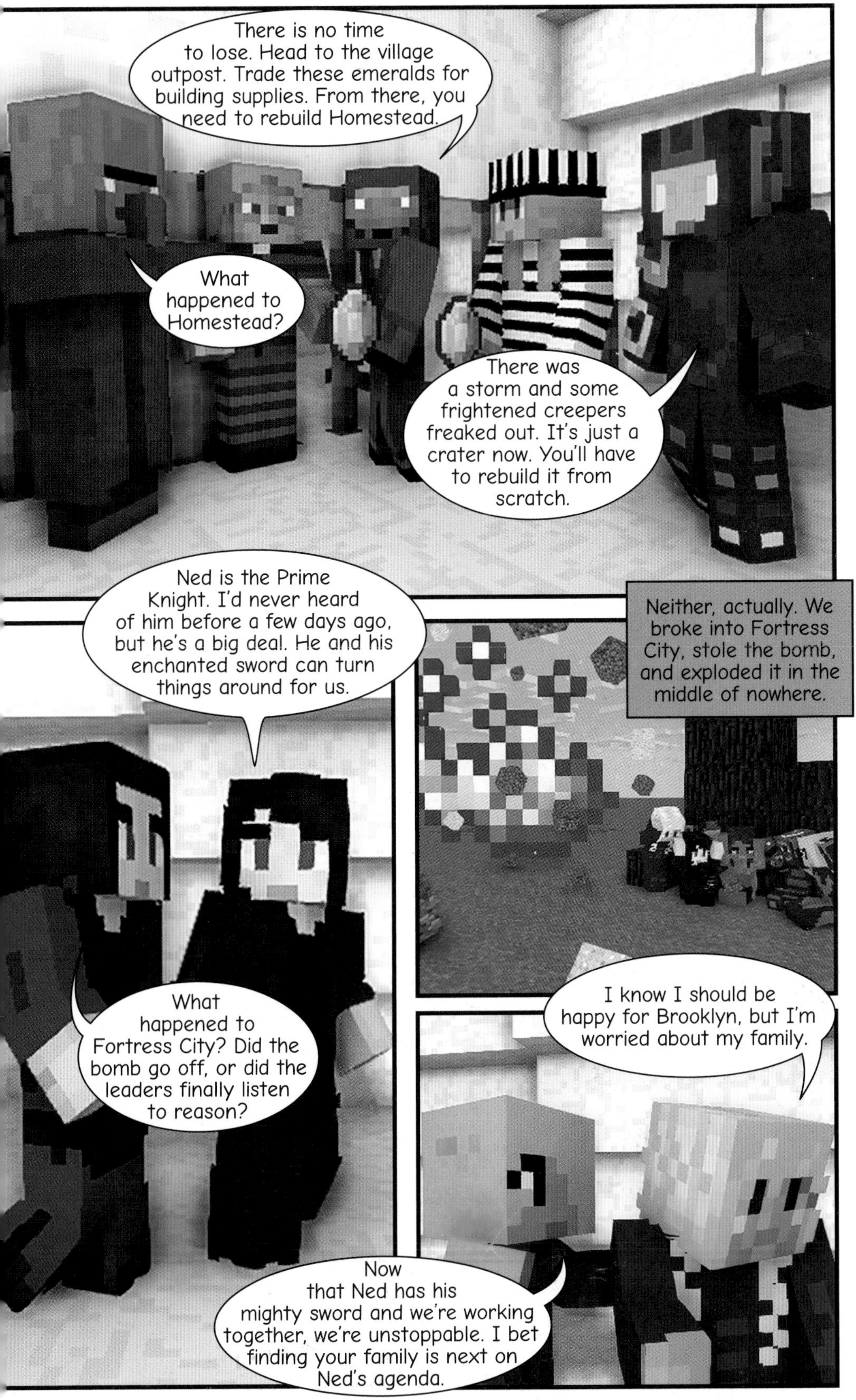
There is no time to lose. Head to the village outpost. Trade these emeralds for building supplies. From there, you need to rebuild Homestead.
What happened to Homestead?
There was a storm and some frightened creepers freaked out. It's just a crater now. You'll have to rebuild it from scratch.
Ned is the Prime Knight. I'd never heard of him before a few days ago, but he's a big deal. He and his enchanted sword can turn things around for us.
What happened to Fortress City? Did the bomb go off, or did the leaders finally listen to reason?
Neither, actually. We broke into Fortress City, stole the bomb, and exploded it in the middle of nowhere.
I know I should be happy for Brooklyn, but I'm worried about my family.
Now that Ned has his mighty sword and we're working together, we're unstoppable. I bet finding your family is next on Ned's agenda.

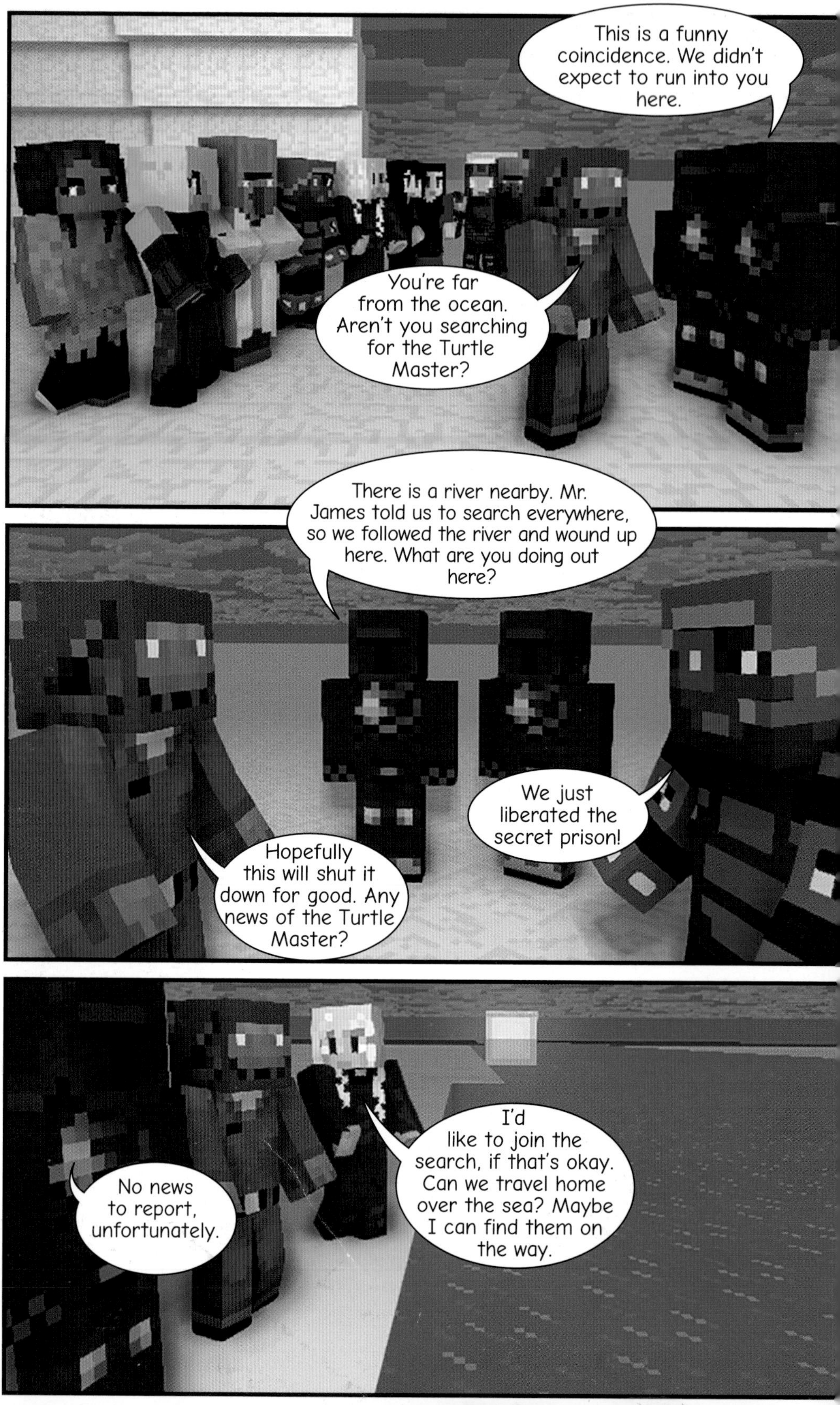
This is a funny coincidence. We didn't expect to run into you here.
You're far from the ocean. Aren't you searching for the Turtle Master?
There is a river nearby. Mr. James told us to search everywhere, so we followed the river and wound up here. What are you doing out here?
We just liberated the secret prison!
Hopefully this will shut it down for good. Any news of the Turtle Master?
No news to report, unfortunately.
I'd like to join the search, if that's okay. Can we travel home over the sea? Maybe I can find them on the way.

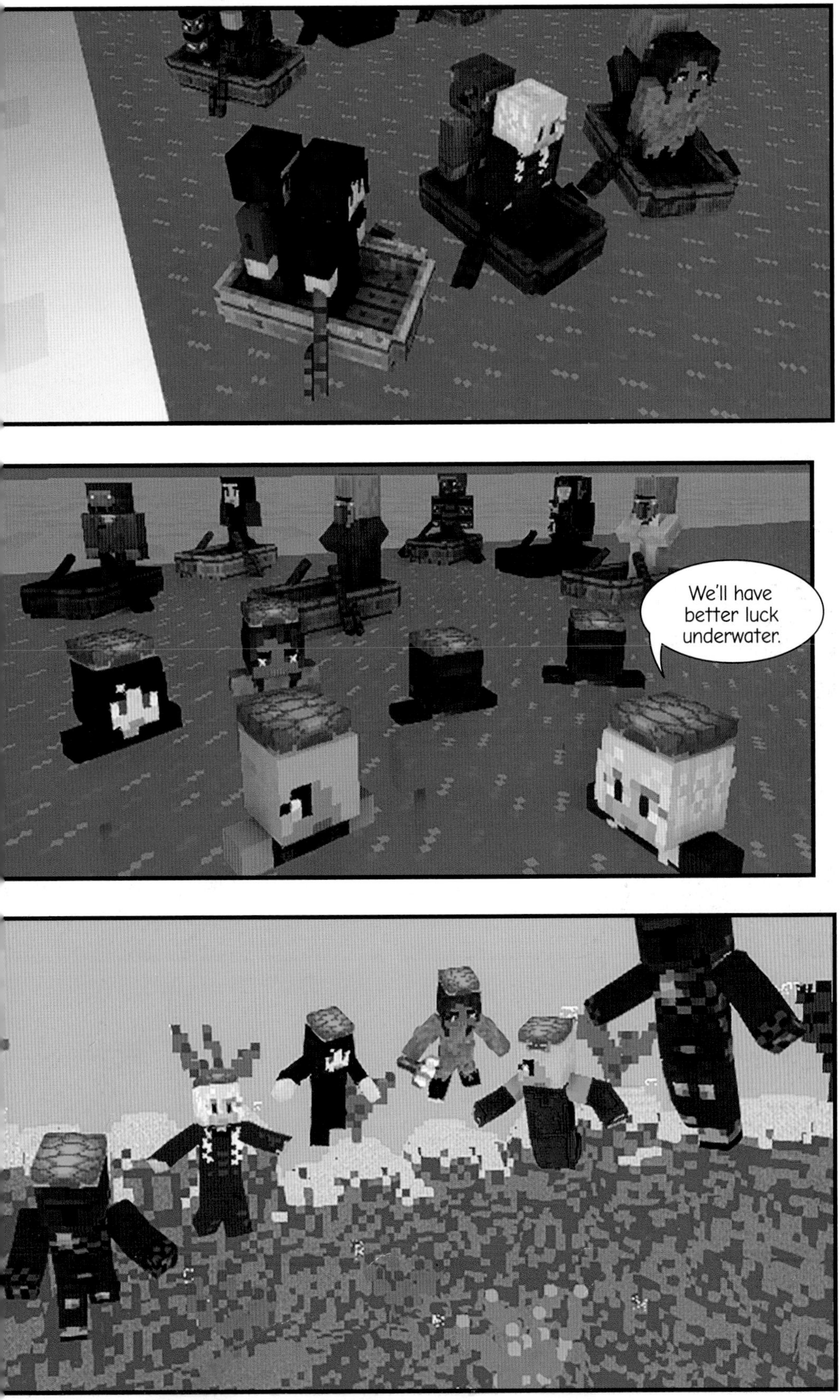
We'll have better luck underwater.

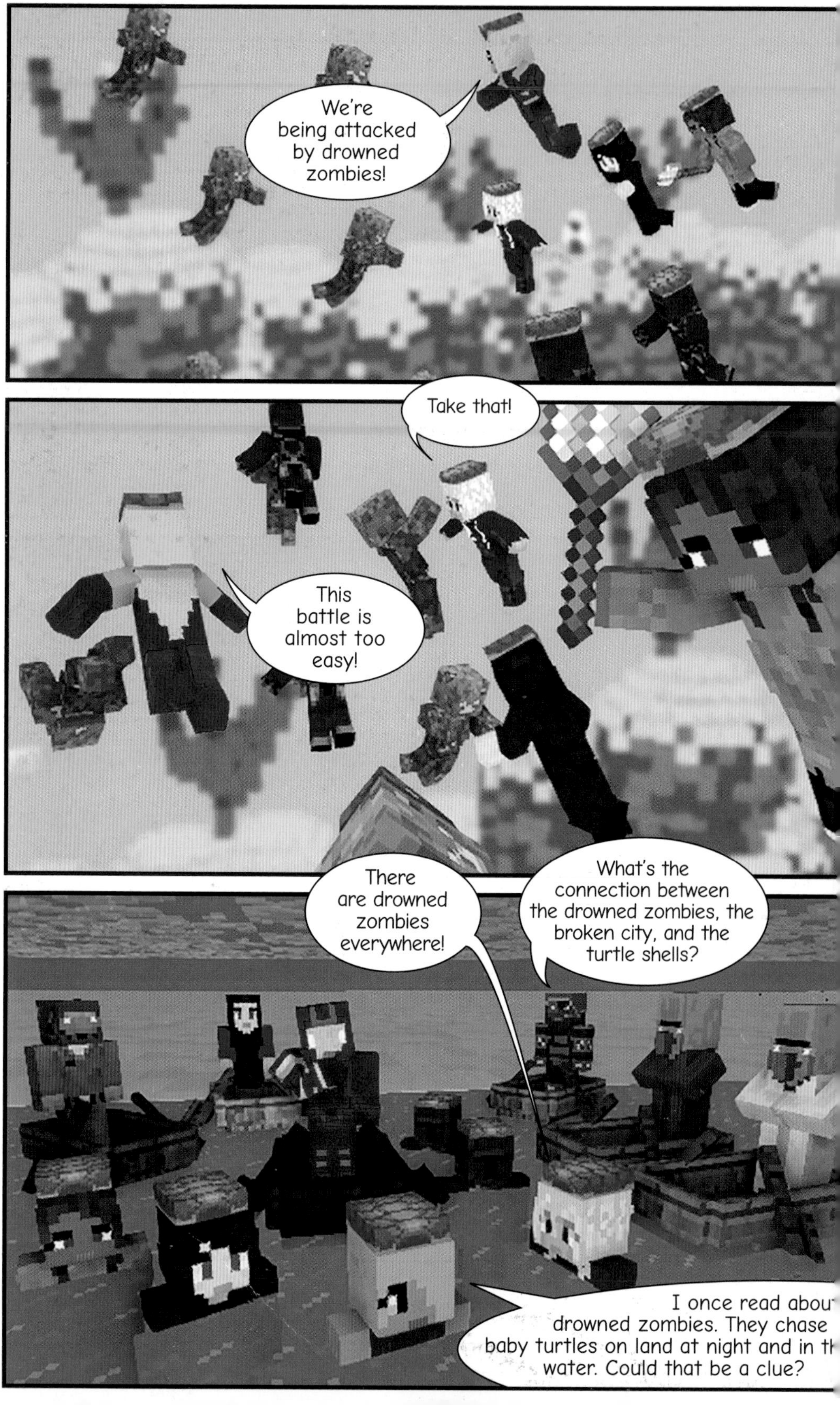
We're being attacked by drowned zombies!
Take that!
This battle is almost too easy!
There are drowned zombies everywhere!
What's the connection between the drowned zombies, the broken city, and the turtle shells?
I once read abou drowned zombies. They chase baby turtles on land at night and in t water. Could that be a clue?

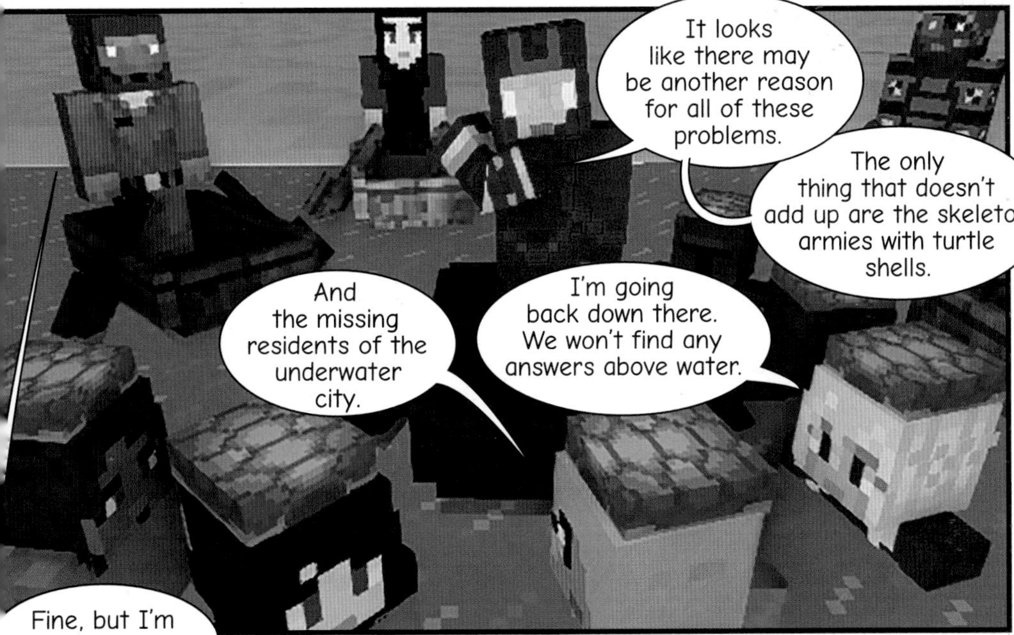
It looks like there may be another reason for all of these problems.
The only thing that doesn't add up are the skeleton armies with turtle shells.
And the missing residents of the underwater city.
I'm going back down there. We won't find any answers above water.
Fine, but I'm not sending you alone.

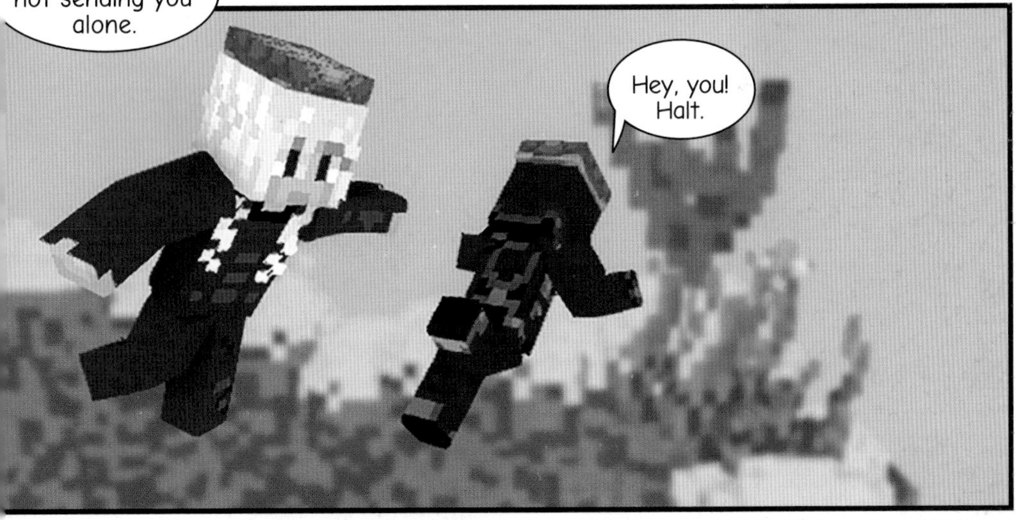
Hey, you! Halt.

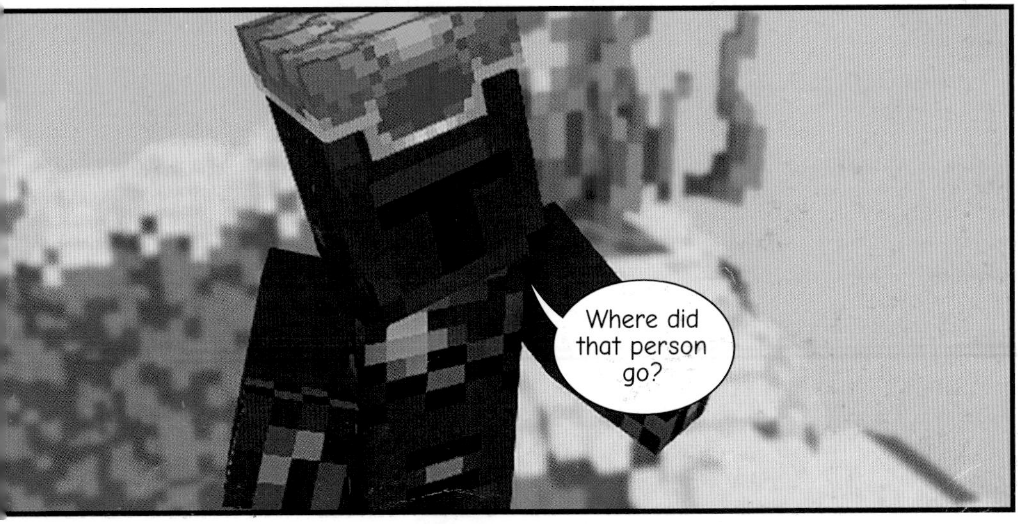
Where did that person go?

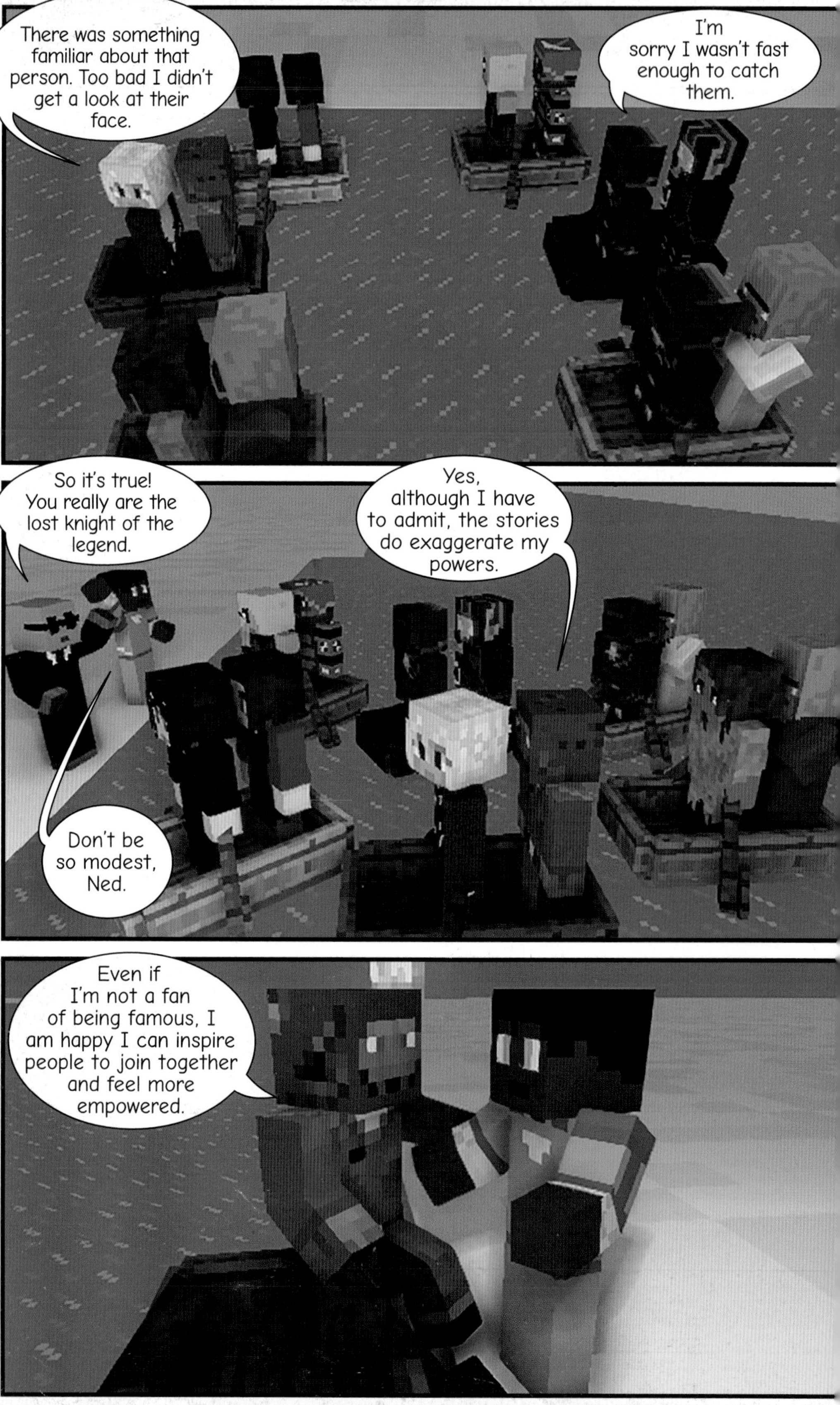
There was something familiar about that person. Too bad I didn't get a look at their face.
I'm sorry I wasn't fast enough to catch them.
So it's true! You really are the lost knight of the legend.
Yes, although I have to admit, the stories do exaggerate my powers.
Don't be so modest, Ned.
Even if I'm not a fan of being famous, I am happy I can inspire people to join together and feel more empowered.

CHAPTER 12

HOMECOMING
FOR A KNIGHT

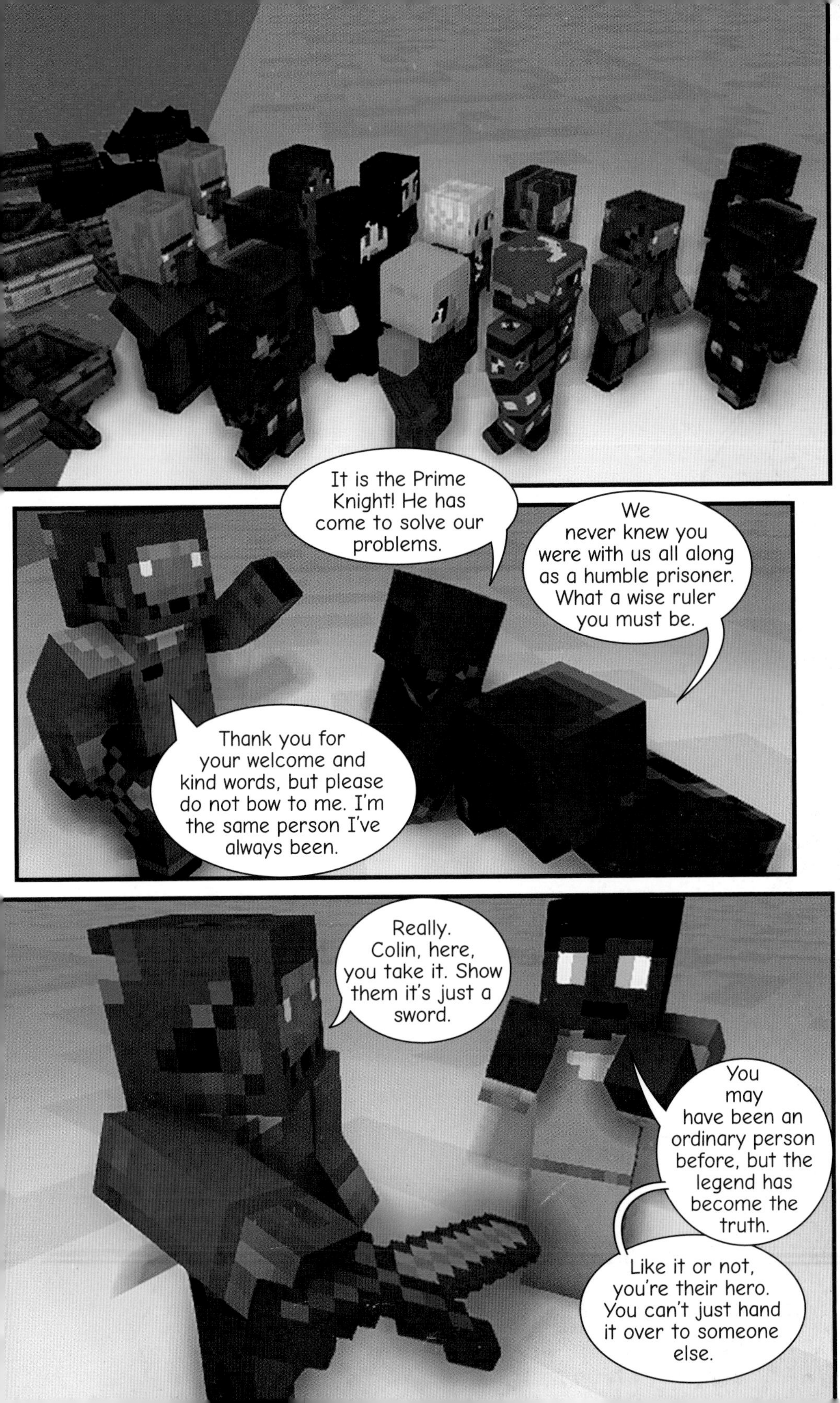

It is the Prime Knight! He has come to solve our problems.
We never knew you were with us all along as a humble prisoner. What a wise ruler you must be.
Thank you for your welcome and kind words, but please do not bow to me. I'm the same person I've always been.
Really. Colin, here, you take it. Show them it's just a sword.
You may have been an ordinary person before, but the legend has become the truth.
Like it or not, you're their hero. You can't just hand it over to someone else.

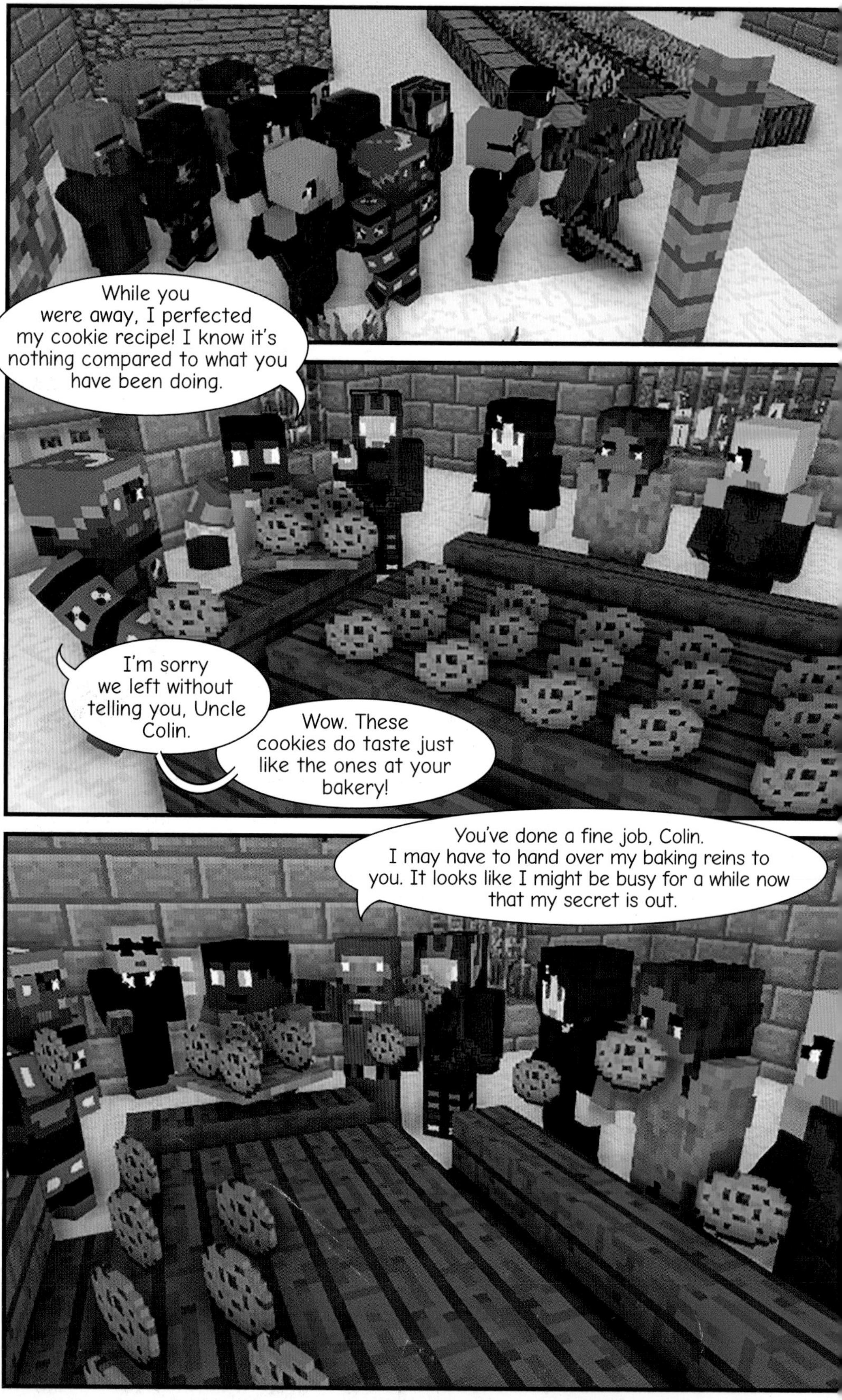
While you were away, I perfected my cookie recipe! I know it's nothing compared to what you have been doing.
I'm sorry we left without telling you, Uncle Colin.
Wow. These cookies do taste just like the ones at your bakery!
You've done a fine job, Colin. I may have to hand over my baking reins to you. It looks like I might be busy for a while now that my secret is out.

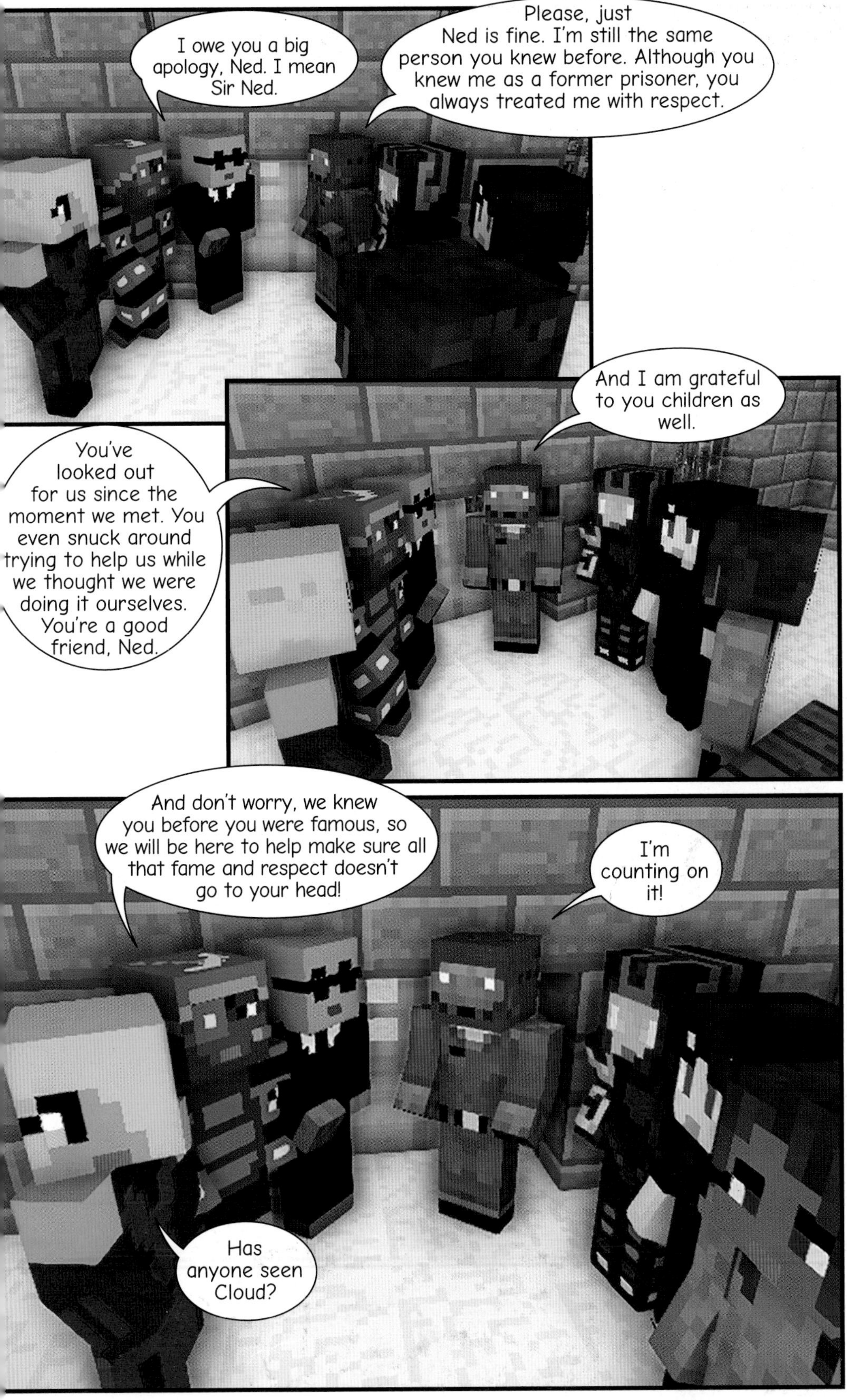
I owe you a big apology, Ned. I mean Sir Ned.
Please, just Ned is fine. I'm still the same person you knew before. Although you knew me as a former prisoner, you always treated me with respect.
And I am grateful to you children as well.
You've looked out for us since the moment we met. You even snuck around trying to help us while we thought we were doing it ourselves. You're a good friend, Ned.
And don't worry, we knew you before you were famous, so we will be here to help make sure all that fame and respect doesn't go to your head!
I'm counting on it!
Has anyone seen Cloud?

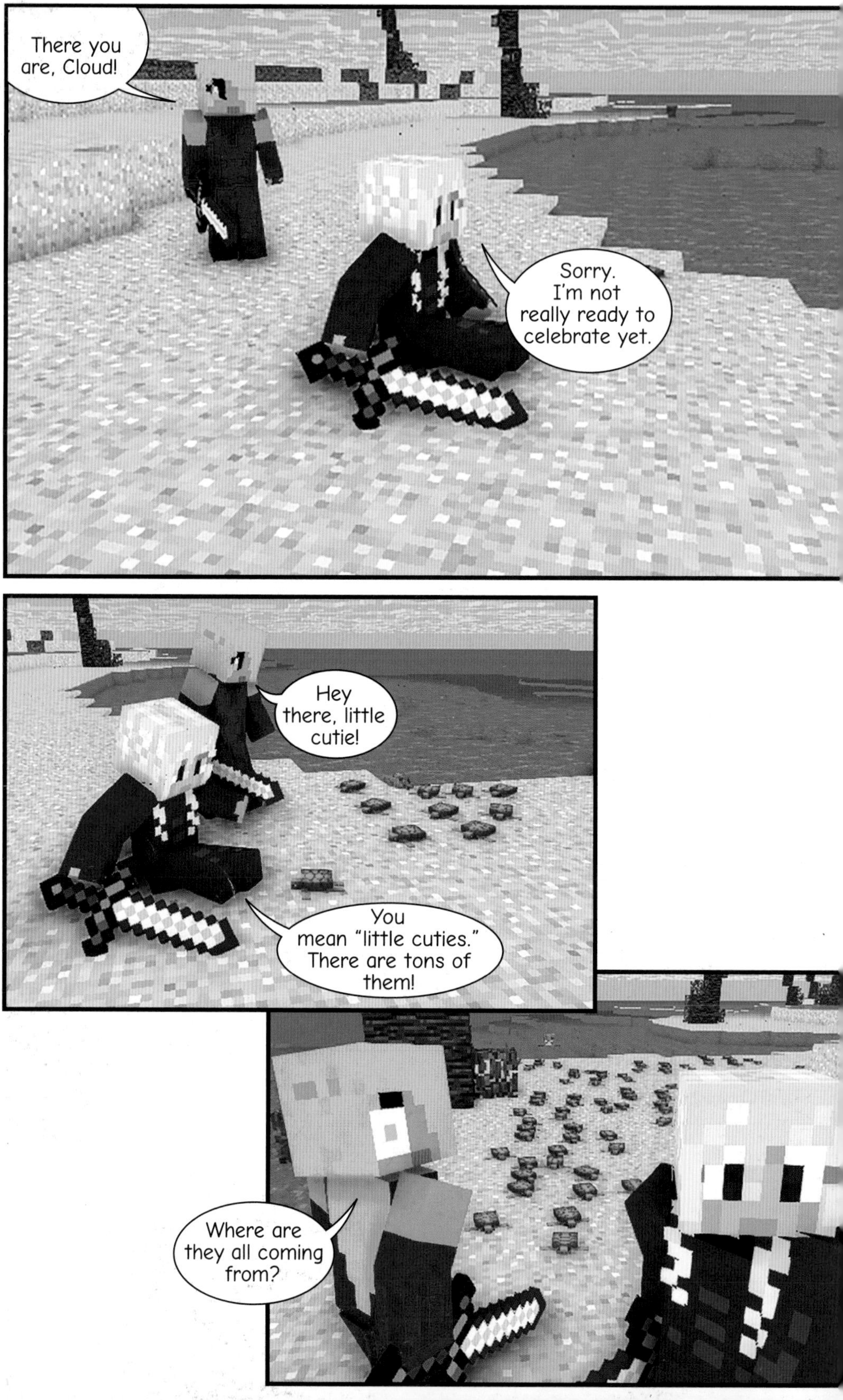
There you are, Cloud!
Sorry. I'm not really ready to celebrate yet.
Hey there, little cutie!
You mean "little cuties." There are tons of them!
Where are they all coming from?

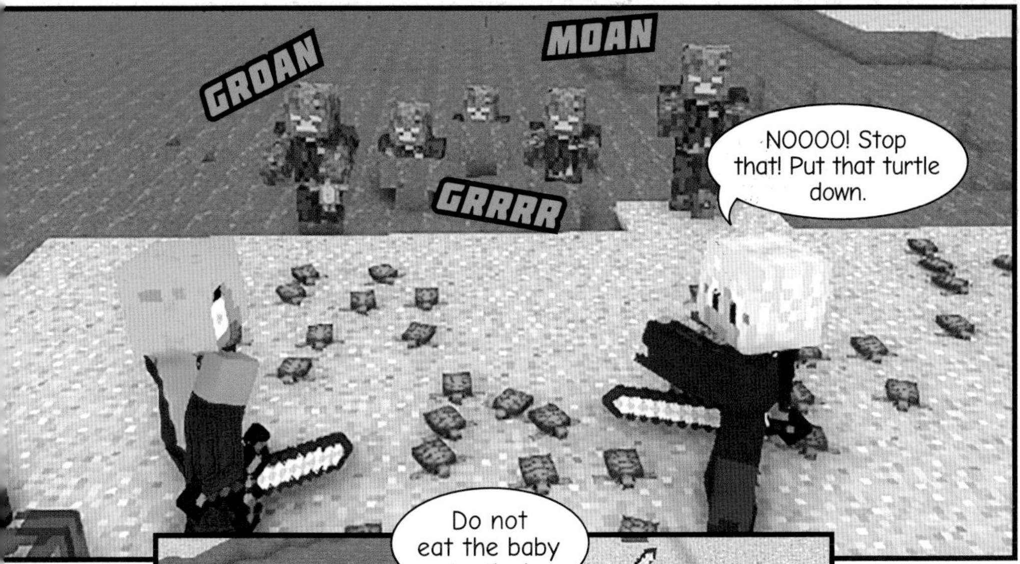
GROAN
MOAN
GRRRR
NOOOO! Stop that! Put that turtle down.

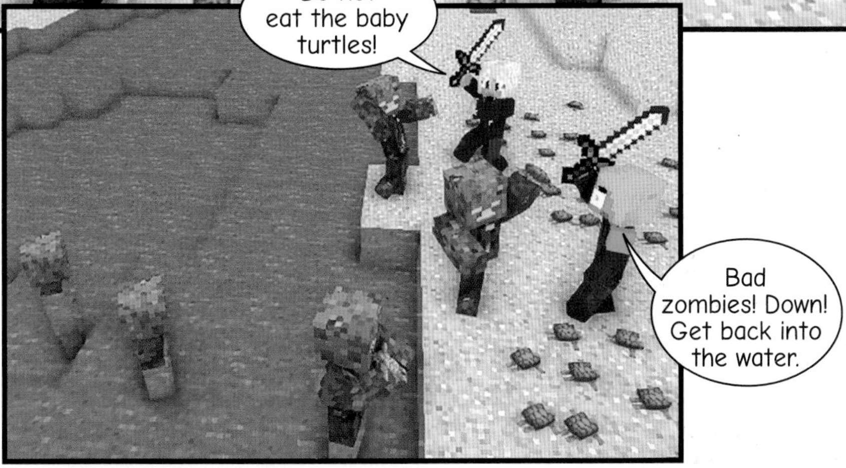
Do not eat the baby turtles!
Bad zombies! Down! Get back into the water.

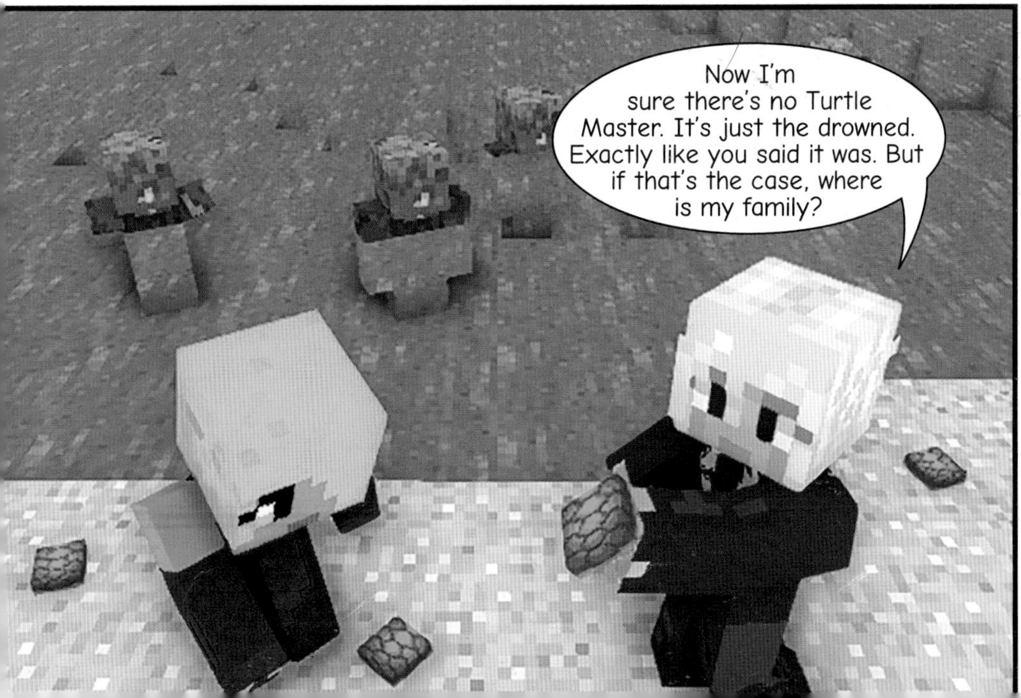
Now I'm sure there's no Turtle Master. It's just the drowned. Exactly like you said it was. But if that's the case, where is my family?

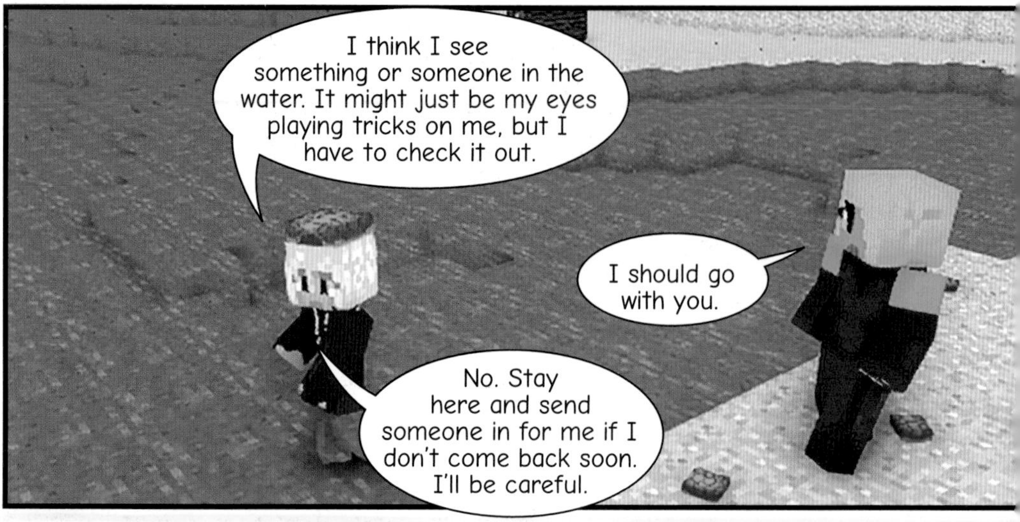
I think I see something or someone in the water. It might just be my eyes playing tricks on me, but I have to check it out.
I should go with you.
No. Stay here and send someone in for me if I don't come back soon. I'll be careful.

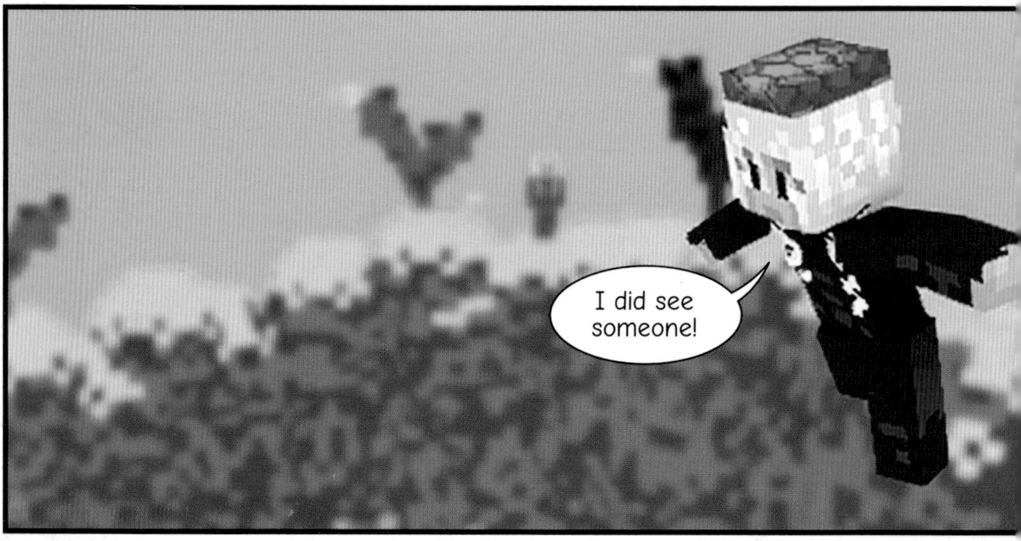
I did see someone!

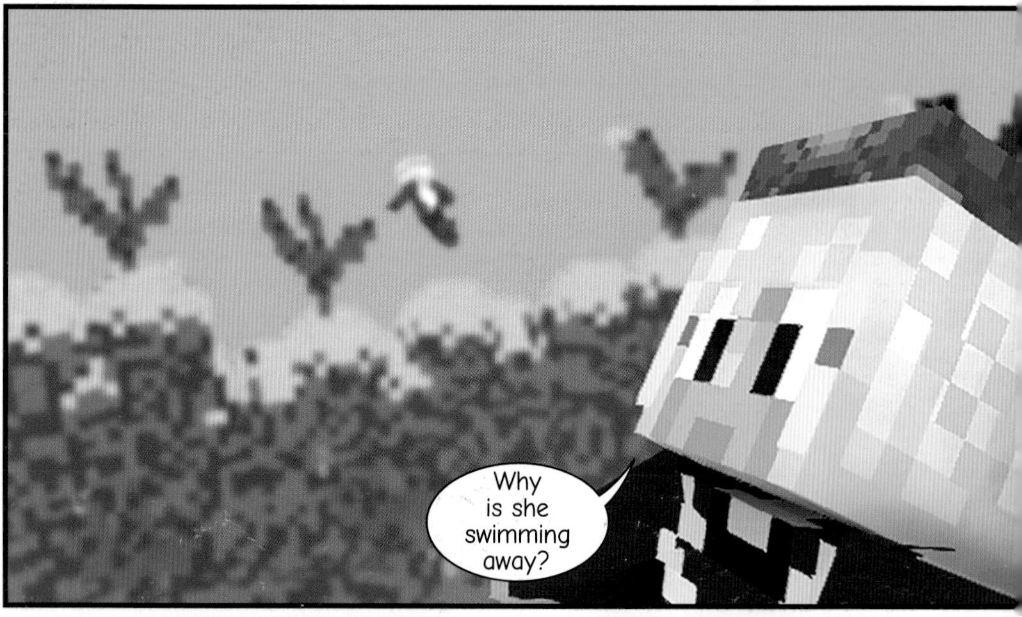
Why is she swimming away?

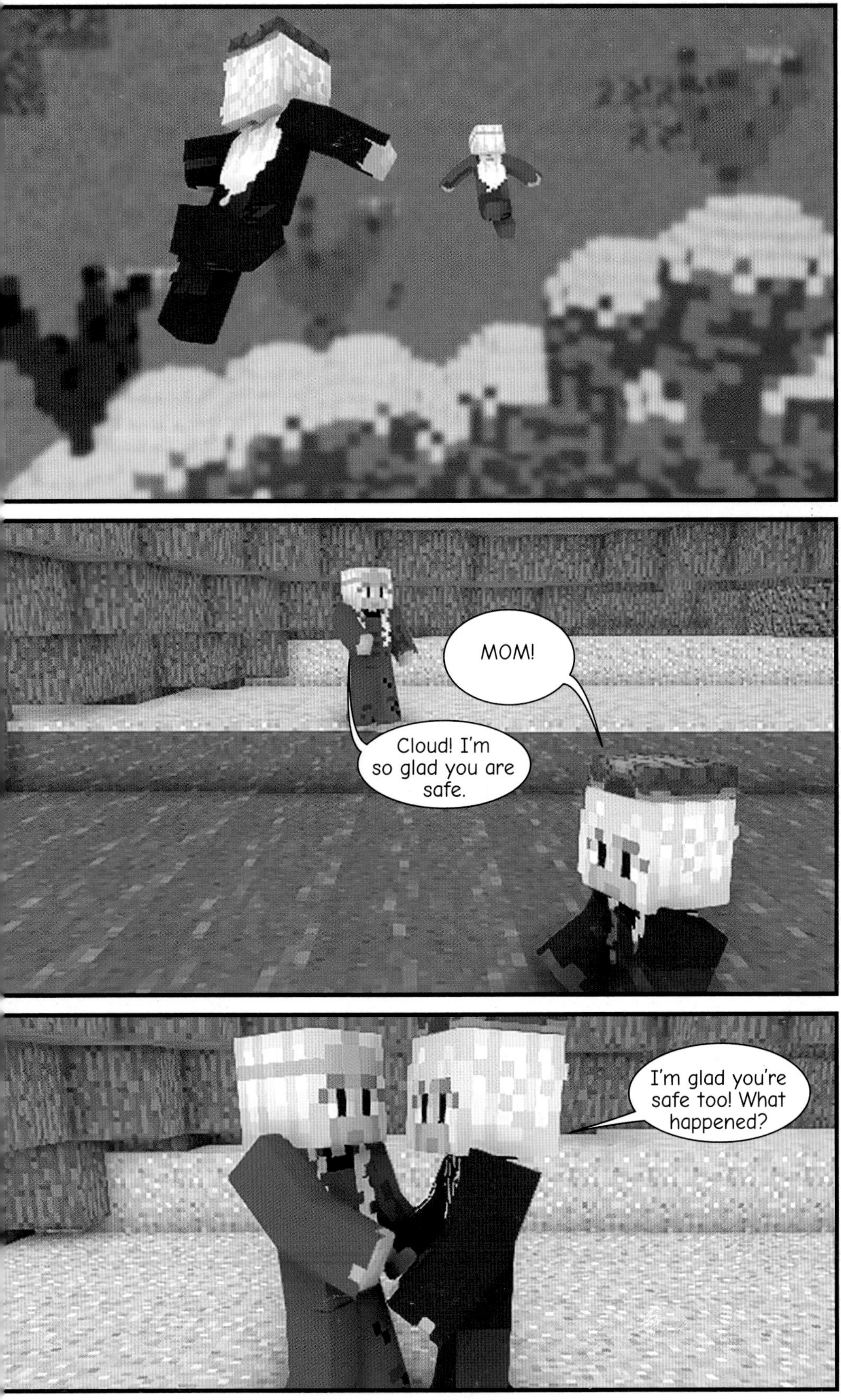
MOM!
Cloud! I'm so glad you are safe.
I'm glad you're safe too! What happened?

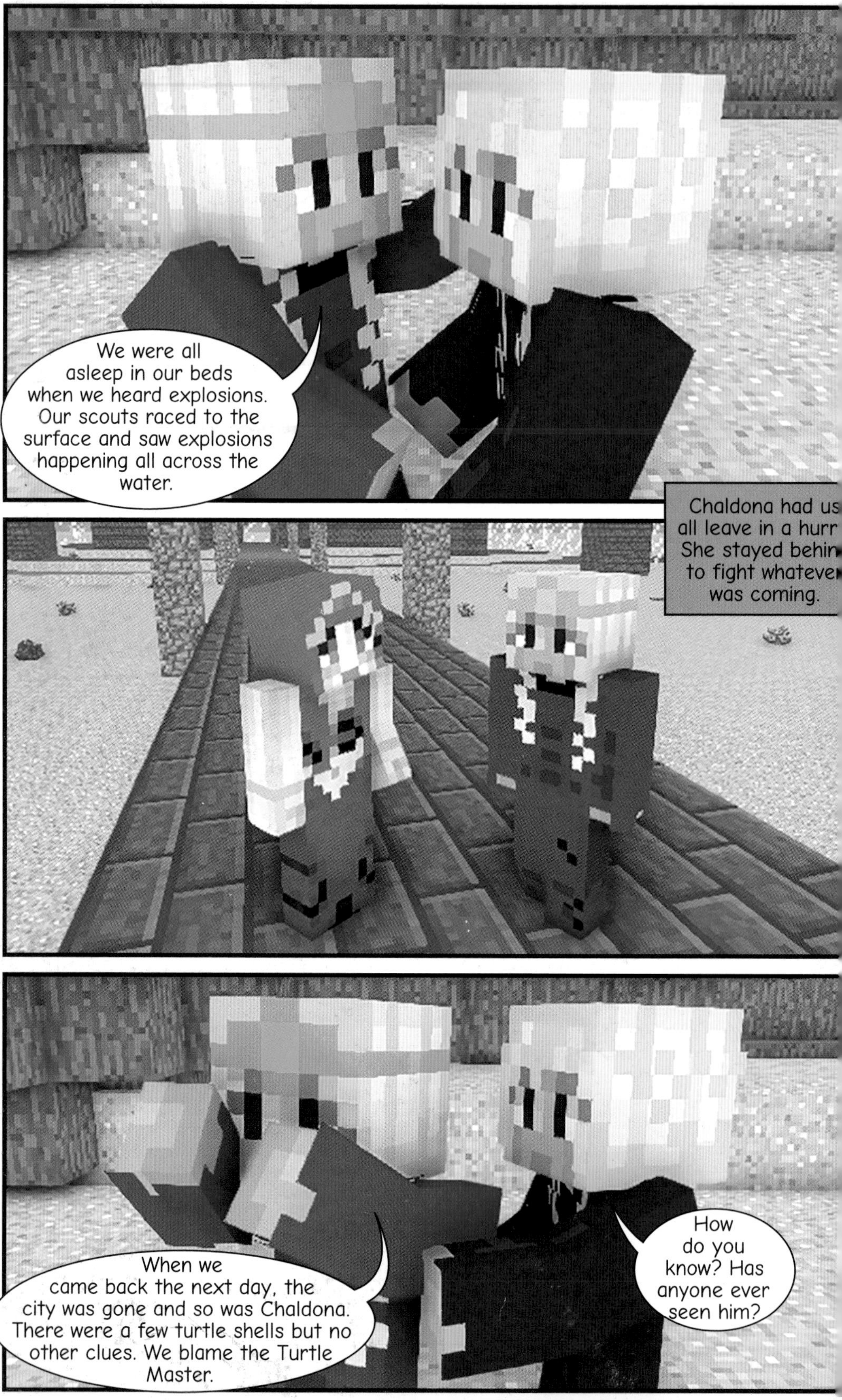
We were all asleep in our beds when we heard explosions. Our scouts raced to the surface and saw explosions happening all across the water.
Chaldona had us all leave in a hurr She stayed behin to fight whateve was coming.
When we came back the next day, the city was gone and so was Chaldona. There were a few turtle shells but no other clues. We blame the Turtle Master.
How do you know? Has anyone ever seen him?

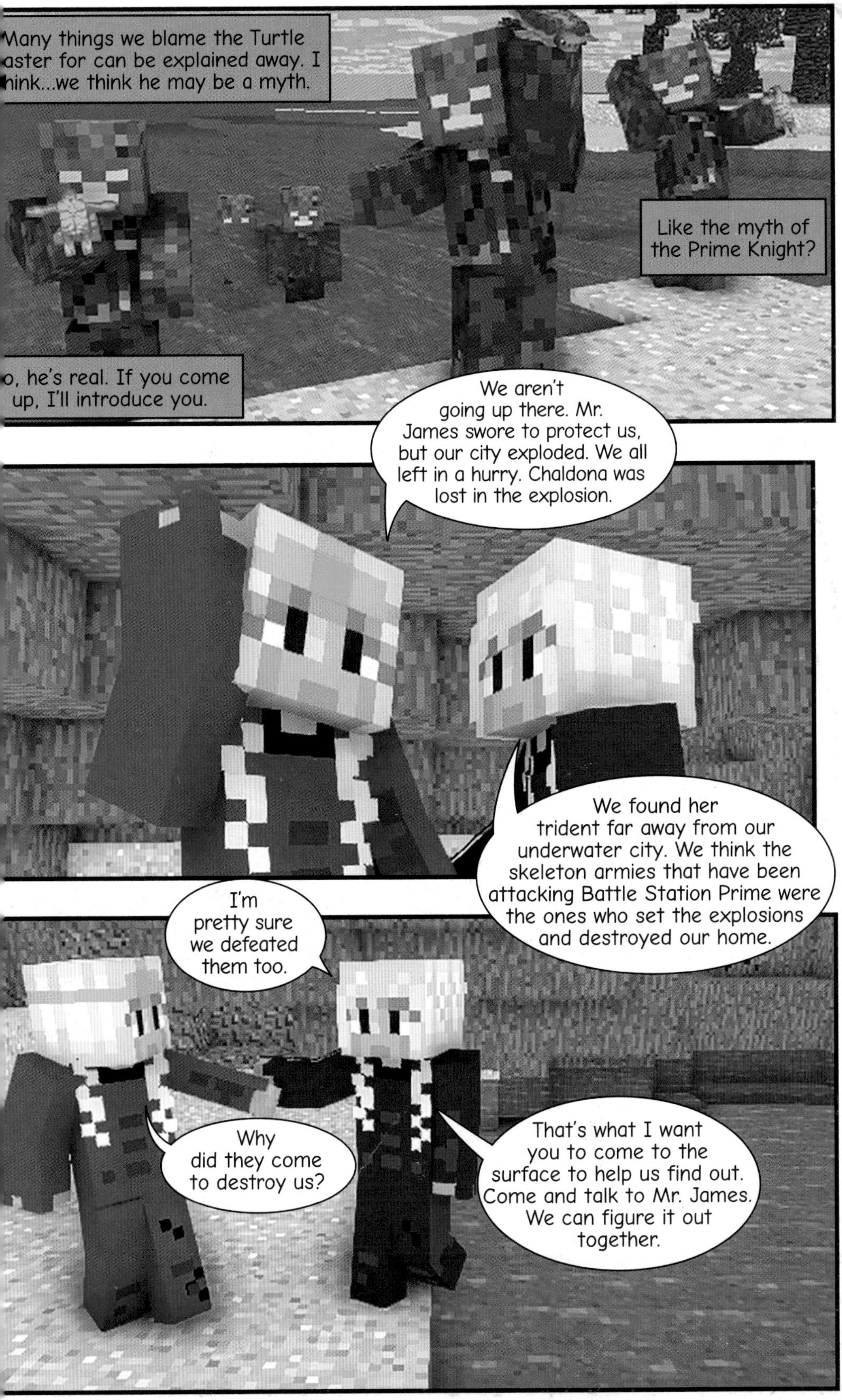

Many things we blame the Turtle aster for can be explained away. I hink...we think he may be a myth.
Like the myth of the Prime Knight?
o, he's real. If you come up, I'll introduce you.
We aren't going up there. Mr. James swore to protect us, but our city exploded. We all left in a hurry. Chaldona was lost in the explosion.
We found her trident far away from our underwater city. We think the skeleton armies that have been attacking Battle Station Prime were the ones who set the explosions and destroyed our home.
I'm pretty sure we defeated them too.
Why did they come to destroy us?
That's what I want you to come to the surface to help us find out. Come and talk to Mr. James. We can figure it out together.

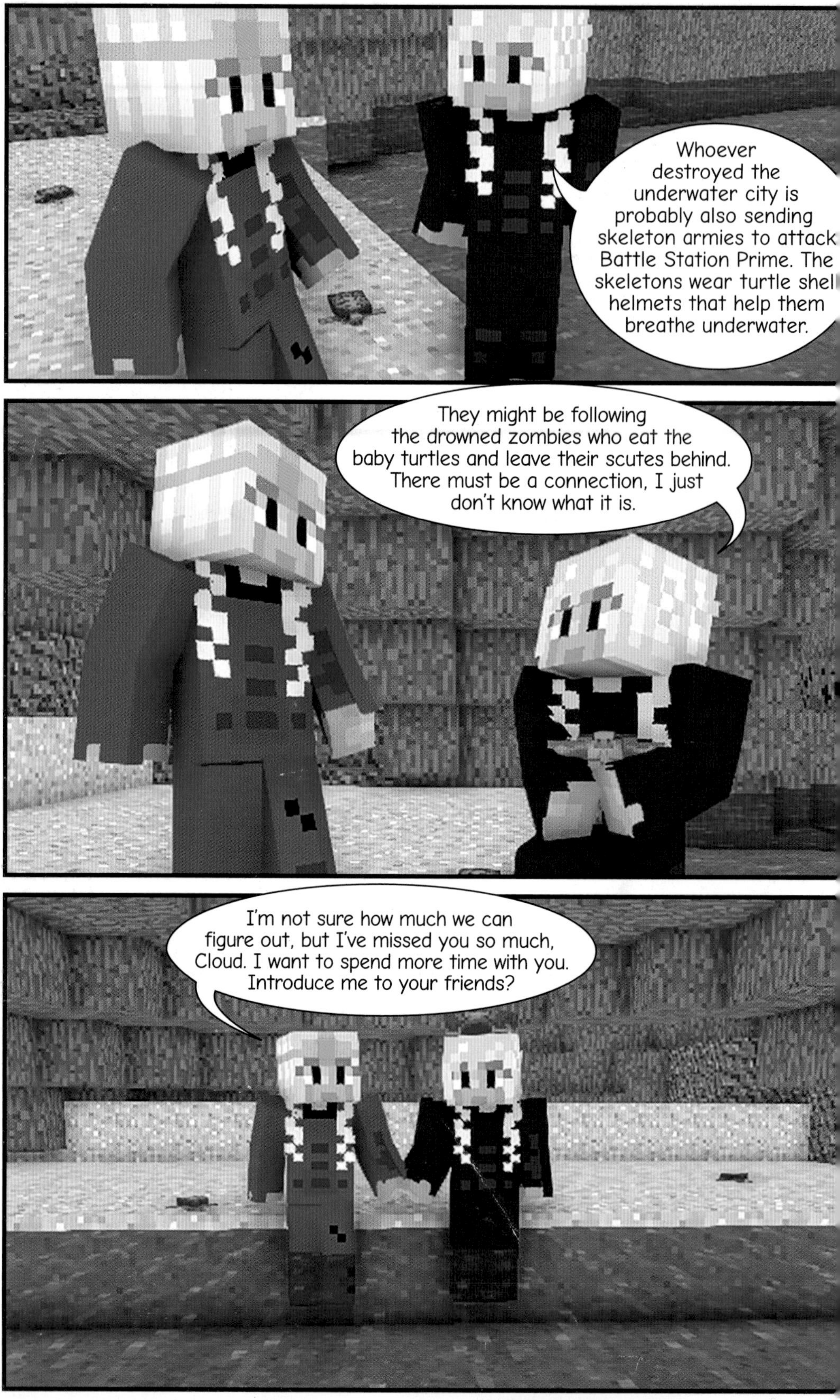
Whoever destroyed the underwater city is probably also sending skeleton armies to attack Battle Station Prime. The skeletons wear turtle shel helmets that help them breathe underwater.
They might be following the drowned zombies who eat the baby turtles and leave their scutes behind. There must be a connection, I just don't know what it is.
I'm not sure how much we can figure out, but I've missed you so much, Cloud. I want to spend more time with you. Introduce me to your friends?

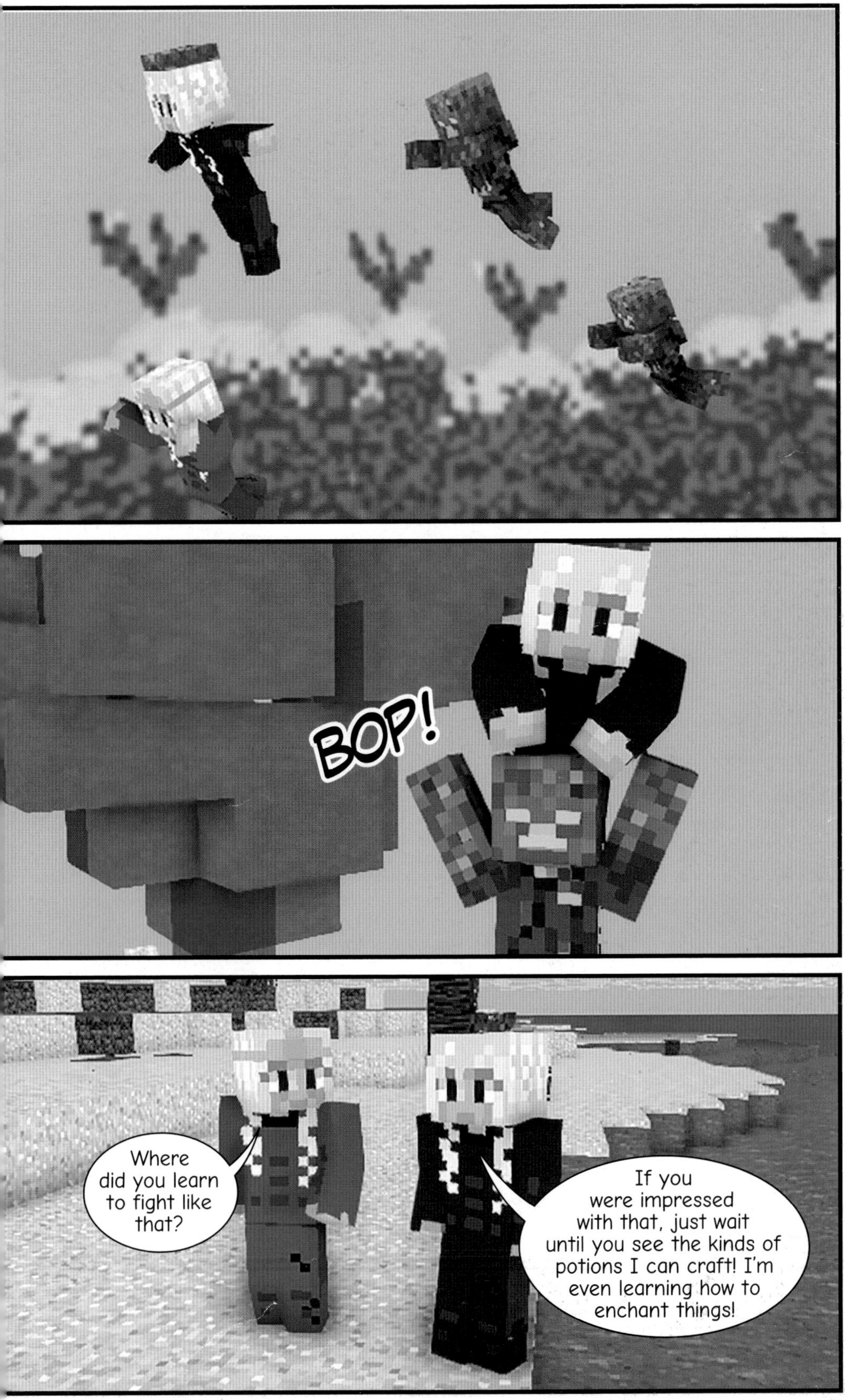
BOP!
Where did you learn to fight like that?
If you were impressed with that, just wait until you see the kinds of potions I can craft! I'm even learning how to enchant things!

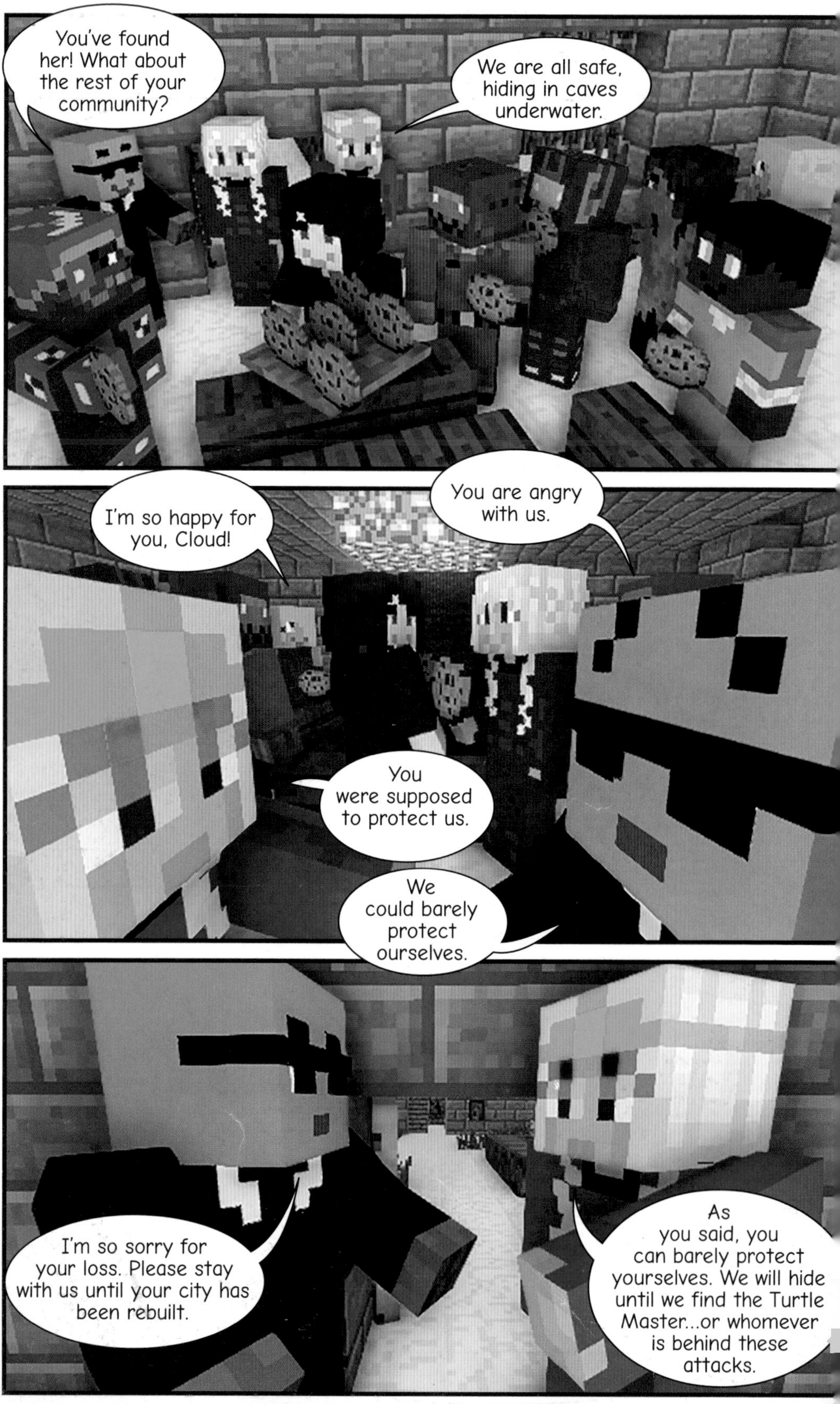
You've found her! What about the rest of your community?
We are all safe, hiding in caves underwater.
I'm so happy for you, Cloud!
You are angry with us.
You were supposed to protect us.
We could barely protect ourselves.
I'm so sorry for your loss. Please stay with us until your city has been rebuilt.
As you said, you can barely protect yourselves. We will hide until we find the Turtle Master...or whomever is behind these attacks.

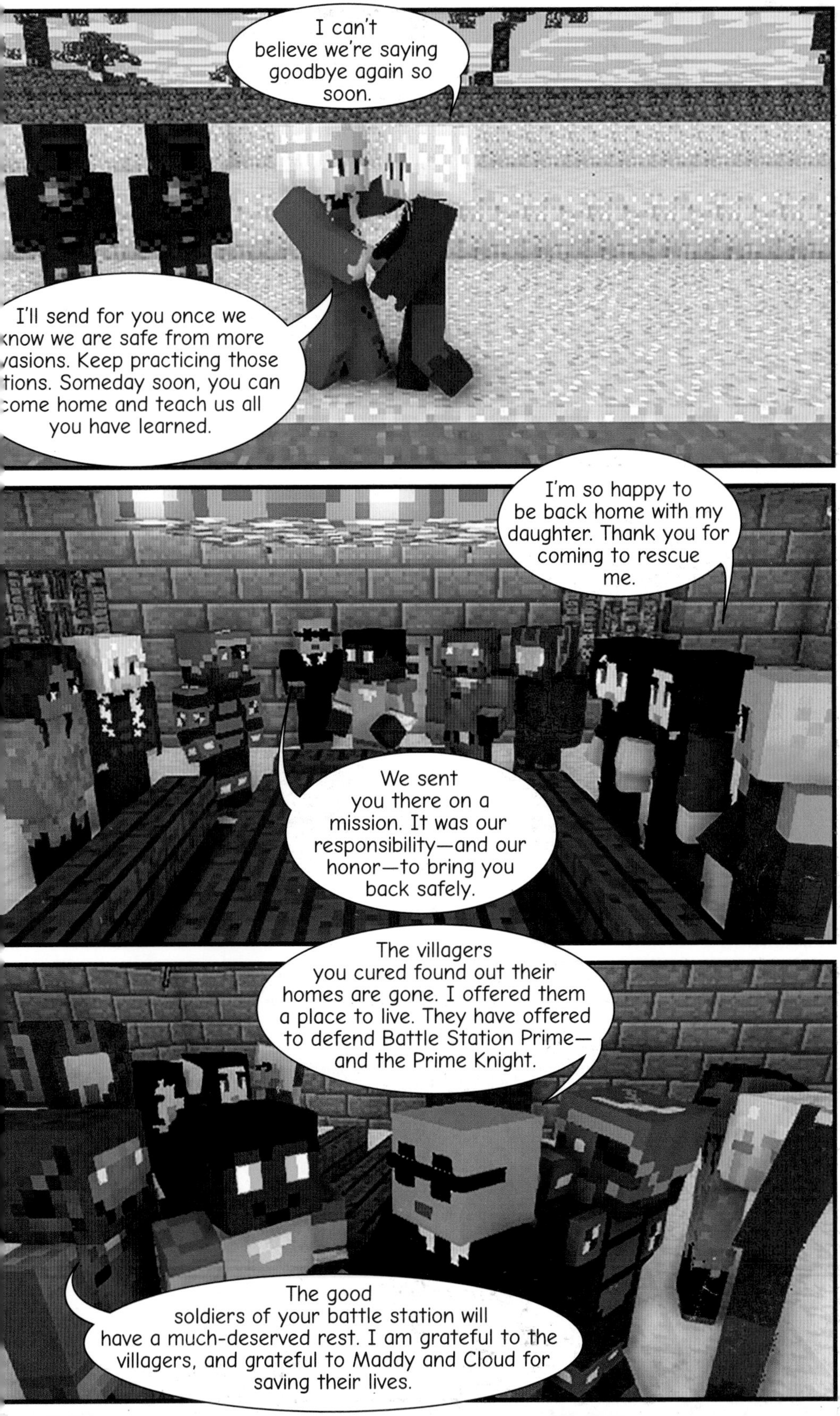
I can't believe we're saying goodbye again so soon.
I'll send for you once we now we are safe from more vasions. Keep practicing those tions. Someday soon, you can ome home and teach us all you have learned.
I'm so happy to be back home with my daughter. Thank you for coming to rescue me.
We sent you there on a mission. It was our responsibility—and our honor—to bring you back safely.
The villagers you cured found out their homes are gone. I offered them a place to live. They have offered to defend Battle Station Prime—and the Prime Knight.
The good soldiers of your battle station will have a much-deserved rest. I am grateful to the villagers, and grateful to Maddy and Cloud for saving their lives.

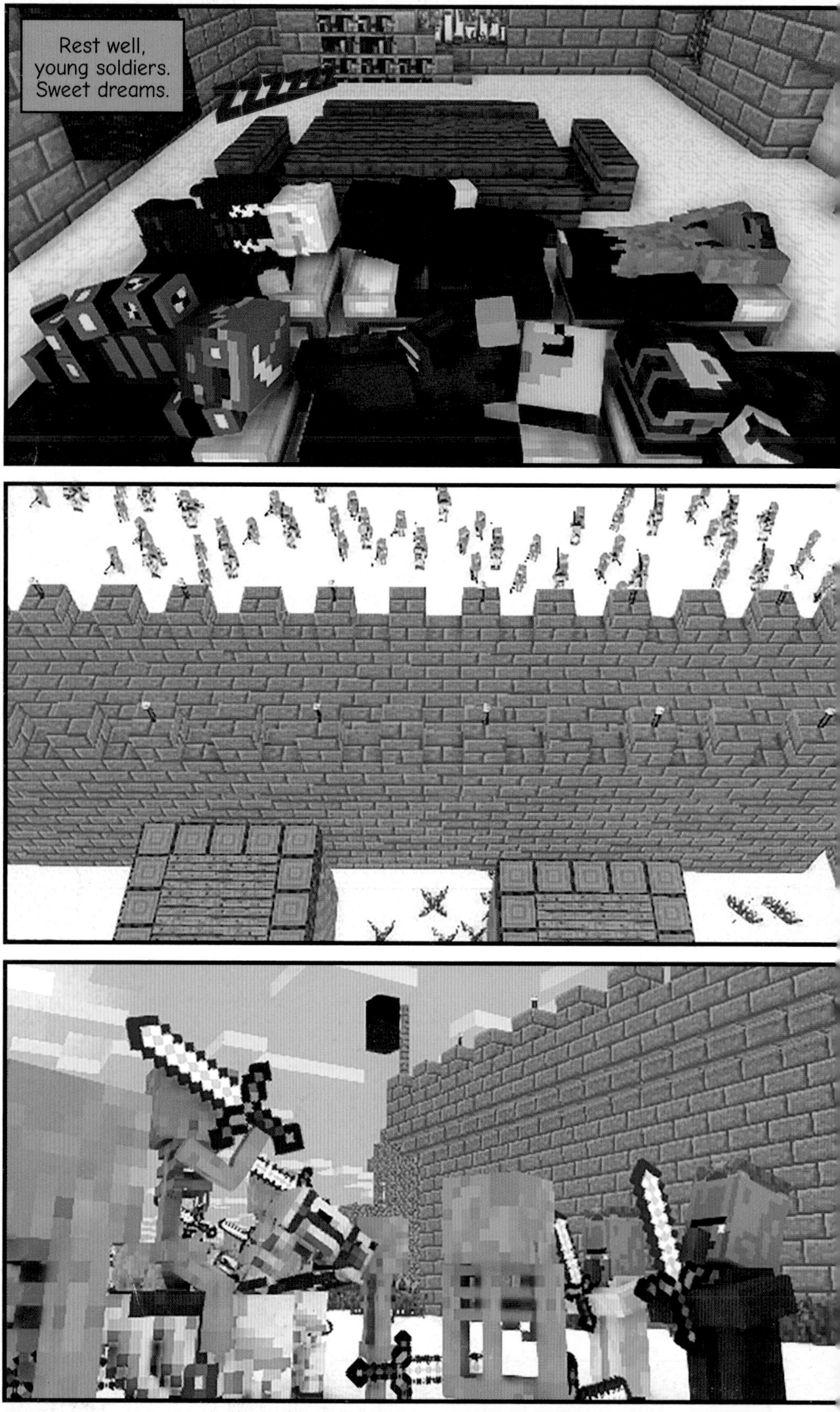
Rest well, young soldiers. Sweet dreams.